Most people don't know that deathmaidens exist. It is a silent profession, unmentionable, yet omnipresent as the quiet night. You are familiar with midwives who grab slippery armpits and pull babies screaming into this world. My job is not so different. Actually, it's the exact opposite.

I serve as midwife to the dying. Like the midwife, I help people pass into the next reality. Just as a baby is not expected to slide into this world of its own accord, so no one should have to die unassisted, to wither away alone in a hospital. Often I am called by a hospice to assist during the final hours of death labor. I don't kill people, nor do I help them pass on with drugs of any kind. I cannot minister someone to the next world before their time, no more than a midwife can slap life into a stillborn baby. Like a religious call, a career as a deathmaiden is not something you choose: It chooses you. . . .

CONFESSIONS OF A DEATHMAIDEN

RUTH FRANCISCO

WARNER BOOKS

NEW YORK   BOSTON

Copyright © 2003 by Ruth Francisco
Excerpt from *Good Morning, Darkness* copyright © 2003 by Ruth Francisco
All rights reserved. No part of this book may be reproduced in any form or by any electronic or mechanical means, including information storage and retrieval systems, without permission in writing from the publisher, except by a reviewer who may quote brief passages in a review.

Cover design by Mimi Bark
Cover photograph by Getty Images

Warner Books

Time Warner Book Group
1271 Avenue of the Americas, New York, NY 10020
Visit our Web site at www.twbookmark.com

Printed in the United States of America

Originally published in hardcover by The Mysterious Press
First Paperback Printing: September 2004

10 9 8 7 6 5 4 3 2 1

*There is a land of the living
and a land of the dead,
and the bridge is love.*

—THORNTON WILDER

Prologue

The room is ten by fifteen feet, with a double-paned glass window that looks into the hallway. The linoleum floor is worn and dirty. Several acoustic tiles are missing from the ceiling, exposing corroded pipes and puffs of pink insulation. There are two aluminum chairs and a table the size of a door. It looks like the set of every police movie I've ever seen. What movies don't tell you is how cold and lonely it is, the recycled air depleted of oxygen, smelling of sweat and fear, or how the smallest noise, a fingernail tapping, a shift in your seat, echoes against the cinder-block walls, or how the pea green paint reminds you of public toilets and the horrible things that happen there, or how the curious off-duty cops looking through the window fill you with helplessness and terror, or how the sense of persecution hatches in you a ferocious anger that digs its nails into your spine as it crawls up your back to scratch your face.

I am alone. I close my eyes and bow my head, trying to transport myself to a seashore or a field of wildflowers, but fear grounds me as fog grounds a plane.

Then I am not alone.

"You're quite a virago, Miss Oliver."

"Pardon me?" I say.

"A virago—a woman of great stature, strength, and courage. I'm working on my vocabulary." Detective Lieutenant Rexford Reid is a huge black man who looks about as interested in language skills as a rabid rottweiler. He yanks out one of the aluminum chairs and sits across from me.

I remind myself that American policemen do not torture people during interrogations, but that doesn't stop my hands from trembling. I put them in my lap, then say, "It must be reassuring to the citizens of your precinct to know their policemen have large vocabularies."

He forces a grin that exposes a row of white teeth as round and even as ninepins. "Am I going to have trouble with you, Miss Oliver?"

"Not anything you can't handle, I'm sure."

Instead of ninepins, I think maybe his teeth look like tombstones.

"How well did you know Elmer Afner?" he asks.

His questions fade into elusive vibrations, and I wonder, Who am I now? How did I get here?

PART ONE

Angel City

CHAPTER

1

There comes a time when a Santa Ana wind howls hot off the desert, gathering dust and toxic gases in her arms, when she slams into a cold north current over the Santa Ynez Mountains and spills her load against the horizon. At twilight, as the red sky darkens to vermilion, and as luminous white cicatrices streak across the heavens, you have, for a moment, the sense of being in a living, breathing organ.

This is what I see as I drive down Washington Boulevard and turn into the area of Venice called the Silver Triangle. Only a few blocks from the beach, the neighborhood has been left undeveloped to persist in its outdated and unremarkable appearance: white stucco boxes with neat rose gardens, hurricane fences squaring off dry patches of crabgrass, front yards featuring asphalt driveways as if they were a thing of beauty. The house next door to where I work has artificial flowers stuck in the ground along the front walk and in the window boxes. The old woman who lives there waters her plastic posies every day.

It is a neighborhood of retired civil servants and middle-class Mexican families. Yet this too is changing. Unlike most neighborhoods in Los Angeles, people seldom move from the Silver Triangle. When they do, some studio executive razes the stucco house and constructs a three-story mansion built out to the property line. Invariably these houses have no windows on the first floor, feature many skylights, and are landscaped with bamboo and cactus. Sterile, elegant, hostile. The inhabitants work long hours, their Mercedes disappearing into their garages late at night. I assume they enjoy thinking about their new homes, because they're so seldom there.

I park my racing green 1982 Jaguar at the curb by the stucco house where I'm employed. My heart is throbbing with excitement. I open the trunk and pull out two bags of toys. Some of the toys, like the kazoo and airplanes, I bought because I loved them when I was a child, others because they have bright colors or make noise: kites, balloons, a stuffed giraffe, a ukulele. I can't wait to see his eyes open and light up. I know they will. They have to.

As I walk up the paving stones to the house, I notice dead blossoms on the rosebushes, their branches bent and broken; dried purple petals litter the grass. I feel a sudden constriction, my ribs closing in around my heart. *No. It can't be.* I push the feeling away and quicken my pace.

Nervous, I swing open the screen door and place my packages on the oak writing desk by the door. It is warm and silent. Why would Mrs. Gomez go out and leave her son alone? I told her I would be back by four. I look at the clock on the wall: 3:58 P.M. I check her bedroom and the kitchen. I shout her name.

She's not here.

The house is small with low ceilings. Suddenly there's a heaviness in the air, and I feel as if I'm shrinking, as if the walls are squeezing in on me.

Tomás has the room in front facing the street. As I hurry down the thick mauve carpet to his bedroom, my head begins to throb. I brace myself in the doorway.

The blinds are drawn. Tomás lies on his back, his left cheek pressed against the pillow, lips parted. His skinny right arm angles over his head, palm out, as if he were pushing something away. His left hand hangs off the side of the bed, his fingers relaxed for the first time since I've known him. Balancing precariously on the curve of his first two fingers is a small green rock.

It's impossible to pinpoint the moment of death. It transpires through a blurring of boundaries: the heart's final beat, the last movement of blood, the brain's last impulse. Yet there is one moment, an extraordinary, barely perceptible moment, when, if you are trained, as I am, you see life expire.

I experience that moment now. As I walk into his bedroom and see the small green rock dangling on his fingers, then fall to the floor, Tomás dies.

I become aware of sirens turning up the block. Tires squeal in front of the house, doors slam, a gurney clatters onto the sidewalk, footsteps run up the walkway. I look out the window and see a white van with the words *Priority One Ambulance Service* painted in bright red letters. A second car, a white Mercedes, screeches to a stop. A tall man in a white lab coat leaps out and dashes past the paramedics. He slams open the front door and races in.

I hear his footsteps running through the living room into the hallway. "Nurse, step away!" he commands. He grabs my elbow and shoves me across the room into an oak bureau as the paramedics crash into the bedroom.

The edge of the bureau digs into my ribs. I spin around angrily and glare at the man in the white lab coat. "I am not a nurse."

He doesn't seem to hear me. "Get that heart going!" he yells to the paramedics. A defibrillator on Tomás's chest makes his small body jump a foot into the air. "Get him on a respirator! Check his nitrogen level! Let's keep the blood moving. Get the electrolyte solution going. Now!"

The doctor turns his attention to me. "Why wasn't I called immediately?" he demands. "I left explicit instructions to be called the instant the boy died."

I don't tell him there's been no time, that the boy just passed. "You left *instructions?* With whom? His mother?" Who is this bossy brute barking commands, violating this sacred moment? His arrogance burns my stomach.

He blinks at me as if I am a Polaroid photo developing before his eyes. Unflinching, I watch him watch me. He is tall, with thick gray hair and a long hooked nose. His white lab coat is wrinkled from sitting. A stethoscope hangs around his neck. He reminds me of an egret in the Ballona wetlands. "You may have ruined his heart," he says, his tone imperious and bitter, as if I had thoughtlessly run over his dog.

"Ruined his heart? What on earth do you mean?"

"The child is an organ donor. We must get him to the hospital as soon as possible."

Again the paramedics use the defibrillator. When Tomás's body jumps, the lights in the house dim as if reflecting his spirit caught between realities. The men cheer when his heart starts again.

I attempt to conceal how shocked I am. As I watch the three paramedics lift Tomás onto the gurney, their young, oversize muscles seizing upon his small body like scavengers, their white uniforms stretched tight over their hairy hyena bodies, I am filled with horror.

"Who must get him to the hospital?" I demand. "Why wasn't I told about this?" I block the doorway with my body. "The child is my responsibility."

The doctor suddenly stands straight, his lips stretched against his teeth in what he must imagine is a smile. He pulls me aside to let the paramedics by, but I stand firm. For a moment, I think we're going to wrestle, but he hesitates. All hospitals are terrified of lawsuits; it would not do to have a doctor sued for assault.

He tries a different tack. "I am Dr. Clyde Faust," he says. "I assume you are . . . ?"

"The hospice sent me," I say.

"Of course. I'm sorry to have sprung this on you. You should've been told, but sometimes it causes complications, you know."

"I'm sure I don't know," I snap. I feel my face getting as red as my hair. "I cannot let you take the body without Mrs. Gomez's permission."

"Mrs. Gomez already knows of the situation. If you're so concerned, Miss . . ."

"Oliver, Frances Oliver." One of the paramedics bangs

the gurney against my shin. I jump back in pain, ready to fight; then I relinquish. I have already lost. I cannot overcome four men. They push the gurney past me.

"Miss Oliver, if you're so concerned, why don't you ride to the hospital with us?"

The thought of being boxed inside a shrieking ambulance as the paramedics prod and poke at what is left of Tomás fills me with disgust. "Where are you taking him?"

"Abbot Kinney Medical Center in Culver City."

"I'll meet you there."

Dr. Faust turns and marches out of the house. I do something that I'll regret for the rest of my life: I let him.

I am not a woman who is easily intimidated. I stand close to six feet tall. In the course of my work, I have brushed aside gang members in South Central and backed up murderers in federal prisons. But something about Dr. Faust makes my flesh creep.

I watch as the paramedics roll Tomás away, his face obscured by an oxygen mask. A cold wind blows through my heart.

They are gone, the house is empty.

I am alone and still shaking. The toe of my shoe kicks something. I lean down to pick it up. It's the green rock that fell from Tomás's fingertips. I stare at it in the palm of my hand. It's a piece of carved jade.

As I look out the window into the rose garden, my skin tingles. I feel a profound sense of failure.

I let Tomás down.

CHAPTER

2

It was on a late October morning that I met Tomás for the first time.

I began the day at my house, a small bungalow that sits at the end of a windy road at the top of Paseo Miramar in the Pacific Palisades. Constructed in the thirties, the house has balconies on three sides, added by various owners over the years. One side looks out across the vast city, another out over the Pacific Ocean, another up into the Santa Monica Mountains. That morning, a cool northern wind brushed the smog out of the Los Angeles basin, and as the sun rose, the city glistened in the predawn light like stalagmites caught in a miner's lamp. The city was purple, the mountains Wedgwood blue, the sky a soft tangerine.

I always wake an hour before sunrise to enjoy the dark, moist air, to feel the excitement and anticipation of a new day, the trembling of the megalopolis before me. I sip my coffee on my balcony, watching the city, which, as the fog lifts, unfurls into the distance as far as the eye can see. Clusters of tall buildings look like several cities merging into one—Santa Monica, Westwood, Culver City, downtown—and from a distance they intimate the majesty one expects from a city, a grandeur of architecture and public space that Los Angeles oddly lacks.

It is in the mornings I feel most myself, perched high above the city in the dusty chaparral cliffs of the Santa Monica Mountains, witness to the city, yet apart. I love the solitude, the sound of birds, and the scuffling of rabbits and coyote in the sagebrush. I like to imagine people waking in their beds, already too warm, reaching out to naked lovers beneath damp and itchy sheets; dogs licking open the eyes of sleepy middle-aged women; drunks rolling out from under the lifeguard towers, shaking off the sand before the lifeguard truck patrol begins; young actors, home from their jobs as waiters, settling into a fitful sleep; children, exhausted from staring at computer screens, sleeping soundly, oblivious to it all, who despite their impatience with growing up are children still.

I watch over the city. My balcony rests precariously between civilization and eternity, vulnerable to fire, earthquakes, and mud slides. At night, I sometimes hear termites nibbling away at the beams, and on moist winter mornings, I smell rot and dust from the old redwood siding.

It seems the perfect place for someone of my profession.

I am a deathmaiden. That's my job. I help people die.

Most don't even know such a profession exists. It is a silent profession, unmentionable, yet omnipresent as the quiet of night.

You are familiar with midwives who grab slippery armpits and pull babies screaming into this world, a world no baby seems happy to enter. My job is not so different. Actually, it's the exact opposite.

I serve as midwife to the dying. Like the midwife, I help people pass into the next reality. Just as a baby is not expected to slide into this world of its own accord, so no one should have to die unassisted, to wither away alone in a hospital—or with tearful relatives, who as well intentioned as they are cannot be expected to understand what is required.

I am a professional. My services are usually called for by distraught relatives who can no longer bear to see their loved ones suffer in pain and fear. Often I am called on by a hospice to assist during the final hours of death labor.

With all the fuss about Dr. Kevorkian and doctor-assisted suicide, you may wonder at the legality of what I do. I don't kill people, nor do I help them pass on with drugs of any kind. I cannot minister someone to the next world before their time, no more than a midwife can slap life into a stillborn baby.

Some confuse my profession with that of hospice nurse. While deathmaidens are often called in by hospices, and many hospices include deathmaidens as part of their services, they are distinctly separate professions with different backgrounds.

The modern hospice movement was started in England in the late 1960s and has grown in popularity in the United States in the last twenty years as an alternative to dying in a hospital. Generally a hospice is not a place, although nursing home–type hospices do exist, but a team of people who assist with palliative care in the family home. Hospices accept patients with no more than six months to live. While the hospice's primary goal is pain management, different members of the team visit the family a few times a week to assist in the practical aspects of dying: the making of wills and funeral arrangements, and the settling of finances and unresolved issues within the family. The hospice team can include a coordinating nurse, a volunteer, a doctor, a nurse's aide, a pastor, a social worker, and a grief counselor.

A good hospice team can make the work of a deathmaiden much easier. The social worker and pastor prepare the patient emotionally and spiritually for passage, often working with the patient for months. But when the patient is ready, and asks to pass on, the hospice nurse will call a deathmaiden.

Whereas you might think of a deathmaiden as a midwife for the dying, a hospice is like the team of lactation consultants, social workers, grandmothers, and health consultants who assist a young mother with her baby during the first six months.

It took several years for the hospice movement to feel at ease with the use of deathmaidens. On the surface, it would appear they have conflicting objectives: A hospice team encourages a patient to live as long and fully as possible; a deathmaiden assists in proper passage. A hospice nurse would never be a deathmaiden. But with the success of the right to die bill in Oregon that decriminalizes assisted suicide for the terminally ill, hospices saw the need for a midwife to the dying. Now, most hospices offer the services of a deathmaiden for their terminal patients.

*   *   *

On my second cup of coffee, the telephone rang. My supervisor, Charlotte Wright, called with a new assignment, a child in what doctors call a "persistent vegetative state." Brain-dead, in other words. After the feeding tube is removed in such cases, it can take up to two weeks for a patient to pass on. His mother did not want to see her child starve to death. She brought him home from the hospital to die. She wanted him to pass quickly.

That same morning, I drove down to 1215 Clark Avenue in Venice. The house smelled frowsty and stale, as if the family had just returned from a trip abroad and not yet aired out the place. The windows were spattered with bird droppings. I was met at the door by the mother, a Mexican woman, round with no waist, short with skinny legs. She wore stretch pants and a sweatshirt, as if she were going to work out, something I doubted she'd ever done. Her name was Erlinda Gomez. She showed me into the child's room. I asked to be left alone.

Tomás was perhaps ten years old. He lay on his back covered with a white sheet. He had a long, pear-shaped nose that was slightly flared at the end, a prominent lower jaw with full lips, slanted almond eyes, and high cheekbones that dropped off like a shale cliff. His forehead sloped sharply away from his brow. At first, because of the shape of the head, I thought perhaps he was retarded, yet his features were symmetrical and perfect. His skin was flawless, the color of a dusty olive; his hair was shiny and straight, so black that it looked almost blue. His body was long limbed, with a slender neck and fine shoulders. He was at that age of sublime male beauty, a perfect man-child, all potential, strength without mass, ferocity without scars.

He looked nothing like his mother.

For a moment, I fell in love with him. I thought of the child I could have had, of what it must be like to watch such a beautiful creature mature. Then I settled down to business. I had a job to do.

His right hand was balled into a tight fist. I lifted his left hand and rested it in my palm. His fingers were long and fine, his nails smooth, pellucid as pearls. I pressed his palm to my forehead.

A sharp pain stabbed me behind the eyes, shooting down my spine. I dropped his hand and jumped back, my body shaking with violent emotions.

Once I stopped trembling, I took his hand and pinched on both sides of his fingertips, one finger at a time, the acupressure points for waking someone out of a coma. Again, bolts of pain ripped through my body, so excruciating that my eyes teared.

He didn't wake.

I called his mother into the bedroom. She waddled in holding a bag of tortilla chips, her hands covered in grease and salt; she wiped them on her ample hips and blinked.

"Mrs. Gomez, are you Tomás's natural mother?" I asked.

"Yes," she said. Her voice was soft. She looked away.

"May I speak to his father?"

"He's dead," she said quickly. She kept glancing out the window, which made me nervous.

"Was . . . is Tomás frightened of something?"

"No." She looked genuinely surprised. "Well, maybe as a young child he was afraid of the dark. He was a good boy. Brave. Not afraid of nothing."

"He's afraid of something now," I say.

*   *   *

On occasion, when I am called to midwife a comatose patient, it becomes clear to me that the patient does not want to die. If, when I hold his or her hand and close my eyes, I see a pastoral image, a field, a desert, a sea, or a light color, sky blue or yellow, then the patient is ready. But if images flicker beneath the eyelids, jamming on top of one another like an MTV video—faces, figures, gestures, voices, colors rich and deep—then the patient is not ready. The spirit is tangled, fighting, not for life, but for reason—*Why must I die?*—demanding explanation, as if death were a parking fine one could argue one's way out of paying. The body is willing, but the mind is not.

Such patients require much work. I must lead them out of the dark streets onto a plain of light. We work to overcome their fears: fear of death, fear of abandonment, fear of retribution, fear of nothingness.

Then there are patients who dream as a child dreams, reviewing scenes from the day, inventing stories for the future, startled and entertained by their own imaginations. These people, who appear to doctors and families alike to be "brain-dead," as they like to call it, are not at death's door. Nor are they tangled and bound in their fears of death. Rather, they find the state of "in-betweenness" pleasant and safe. They are like children lingering by the edge of a creek, hearing the dinner bell but not yet ready to leave their solitude, the warm summer day, the crickets and minnows and whispering marsh grasses. They wait for a reason to wake, and while they wait, their spirits bob on a pool of warm liquid, happy and undisturbed, relishing the feeling of suspended animation. They will come out of their coma, but they need time, time away from this reality, time to gain perspective on their purpose here, time to accept that they have responsibilities on this earth yet to complete.

Sometimes a person in a deep coma chooses to stay in a state of in-betweenness because he is afraid to live.

For all their machines and tests, doctors cannot measure the soul. They keep the body alive, suffering, while the spirit, in turmoil, is ready to move on. And so, families, unable to watch further suffering, and anxious to begin the process of mourning and healing, call a deathmaiden. But a deathmaiden knows and will refuse to proceed if she sees a patient is an in-betweener. She tells the family to have faith. The patient will wake.

As he lay in bed, I knew Tomás didn't need my professional skills. He needed me as a mother. He was not waiting to die. He was waiting for a reason to live. He was afraid to awaken. He felt happy and safe where he was.

I knew I needed to work fast. From years of experience with the medical world, I knew it would be impossible to convince the doctors to replace his feeding tube. Such decisions were final, as if reversing the course of treatment demonstrated incompetence on their part.

I needed Tomás to trust me. I had to find a way to rouse him.

I looked around the room. There were no toys, no posters, no drawings. It didn't look like a child's room at all.

I told Mrs. Gomez I was going shopping for a few hours. I would be back by four.

CHAPTER

3

When I wander airports—the wide hallways, cold and sterile, gleaming with stainless steel, the smells of disinfectant and fast food—I am struck by the dueling rhythms of exterior and interior: outside, a legato, painfully slow, of airplanes rolling to the gates like glaciers towed by tugboats; inside, a scherzo, travelers bustling in every direction, singularly focused on departure times, oblivious to all but the fleeting images of family and faraway places, excited yet filled with trepidation that what awaits at their destination—lover, job, vacation—will disappoint, a corrupted imprint of their expectation.

As I walk into Abbot Kinney Medical Center, I see a similar place: polished linoleum floors; long, echoing hallways overlit with fluorescent lights; the smell of canned green beans. The air vibrates with anxious anticipation, the torsion between hope and reality.

In an attempt to make the place more friendly, hospital administrators have hung pastel lithographs on the walls, the kind tourists from Kansas might buy in Santa Barbara: sailboats, sunsets, and palm trees. I wonder if anyone stops to look at them.

The nurse asks me to sit in the waiting room. Mostly women and children sit here, withdrawn into themselves, despair pushing down on them like a coffee press, anticipating the worst because that's the way life is. Their eyes are filled with fear and listless protest, like those of gang-bangers waiting to be arraigned in courthouse hallways, barely bothering to hope for clemency.

I wait close to an hour. I do not mind. I am used to waiting. I tell myself waiting will tame my temper, but it seems to be having the opposite effect, twisting tight a tourniquet of outrage.

A thought gnaws at me: Why was Tomás's mother munching chips during what she must've assumed would be his death? In my experience, it's not only the dying who lose their appetites, but those who love them as well. Yet there she was, cramming tortilla chips into her mouth, watching a *telenovela* on television with complete indifference. And where was she when I returned with the toys? Where was she now?

As I chew on this thought, a team of doctors and nurses charges down the hallway. One carries a red-and-white ice chest. A young woman in a white coat leads them, shuffling her feet rapidly, twisting to check if they're following. Her bleached hair is stiff as a paper hat, her face pinched as a mole in a compost heap. A red badge pinned to her lapel reads "Carol Nims, Transplant

Coordinator." They plunge through double doors at the end of the hall.

"What's going on?" I ask the nurse at the desk, a stout black woman who is penciling conjugations in a Spanish-language primer.

Her eyes suddenly sparkle as if she's about to tell me a particularly lurid piece of gossip. "That's the heart team from Raleigh. They're first."

"First?"

"The first surgical team. First the heart, then the liver. Then the kidneys. Then the rest . . . corneas, bones, ligaments, and cartilage. His body parts will be used in more than three dozen people," she says proudly.

"How nice," I say.

Visitors pass, all with the hesitation step, the stop-and-go you see at museums, their blurry eyes skimming over surfaces until they find the face they seek. I am invisible, as is the tangential suffering of those around me.

I watch a young black woman with three small children pulling at her skirt. Waiting on her husband's operation. She doesn't even hear her children. I can see, but will not tell her, that her husband will die, as will two of her boys before they reach twenty-five. It's her face that informs me, blank and exhausted, seeing nothing, numbed by poverty and fear. I think she knows, too.

Finally a doctor comes to speak with me. He introduces himself as Dr. Dan Prouty. He is tall with sandy hair; his handshake is flaccid, fingers cold, palms satin soft. He is balding, a feature that particularly pleases me in arrogant young doctors.

"I must speak with Dr. Faust," I demand.

"I'm sorry, he's not available. Dr. Faust is in surgery.

I would be glad to answer any of your questions." He wears an aura of courtesy and confidence. That's supposed to put me at ease. What could possibly make me feel more at ease than a six-foot blond doctor beaming at me in a hospital hallway?

As Dr. Prouty tries to talk me out of my mission, another team of doctors with a red-and-white ice chest charges by. There is an excited, festive air among them; I think of cannibals feasting on the flesh of their foes. The team of doctors from Raleigh passes them on the way out, rushing to their Lear jet. I overhear one of them say, "It's a great-looking heart."

I introduce myself and tell him I am a deathmaiden. He loses some of his bluster and begins to appear as if he has better things to do.

"Are you the one who examined Tomás when he came in?" I ask.

He nods.

"Have you spoken with Mrs. Gomez?"

"Who?"

"The boy's mother," I say.

"No. No one has shown up. Actually, I have never met the parents."

"Then who signed the release to harvest his organs?"

"Recovery."

"What?"

"We don't use the word *harvest*. It tends to put people off. Like the word *death*, you use *transpire*, *pass on*. . . ." He speaks like an ESL teacher instructing me on the amazing nuances of the English language.

"I use the word *death*," I say coldly.

"Well"—he blinks rapidly, as if afraid I might bite,

something I may consider—"we don't. Instead of *organ harvesting* or *organ procurement*, we say *organ recovery*."

"Like recovering a lost space probe. Or a polluted marshland."

He does his best to ignore my sarcasm. "Actually, once the body has been signed over, it becomes a national resource, the common property of the American people."

I am becoming impatient. Perhaps the doctor is not as dense as he seems but is trying to mollify me. This thought does nothing to help my mood. "Who signed off on the paperwork to have his organs donated?"

The doctor looks in the file, then snaps it shut, hugging it close to his chest; he laughs, embarrassed. "I don't know why I even looked. That information is strictly confidential. I couldn't possibly tell you."

I think of kicking him, grabbing the file, and running, then decide against it. "Did you sign the death certificate?"

"No. I won't be signing the death certificate until all of the organs have been recovered."

"Does that mean he's still alive?"

Prouty's eyes get big until he realizes I'm baiting him. He lets out a feeble laugh, pretending I've made a joke. When I don't smile, he says, "The boy was declared brain-dead when he was here at the hospital before."

"Then why didn't you harvest his organs then?"

He sighs loudly, as if this is not the first time today he's had to explain himself. "You see, Miss Oliver, although his cortex was dead, his brain stem was still functioning, the part of the brain that controls the respiratory and circulatory systems. There's a certain amount of controversy about how much of the brain has to be dead for someone to be declared brain-dead, but we like to play it safe. I assume that's why they hired you."

"So you figured as soon as I helped him die, you'd send over paramedics to hook him up to a respirator and heart machine, which is what you did."

"So we could save his organs."

"Why do I get the feeling I've been used?"

He snaps back his head in surprise. "What we did is all strictly in accordance to hospital policy, Miss Oliver."

I mull over this for a moment, thinking to myself that it's the second time he's used the word *strictly*. "What will you put on the death certificate as cause of death?"

"Massive head trauma."

"I'm curious, Dr. Prouty. When was Tomás first admitted to the hospital?"

He opens the file, which now is slightly warped from being hugged so hard. "On October tenth. That's fifteen days ago. We did a CAT scan . . . looks like there was a massive epidural hematoma—that's a blood clot between his skull and his brain. His skull was opened to relieve the pressure on his brain. He improved for a few days. We did a second CAT scan, which showed"—he refers to his file—"progressive cerebral edema."

"The accumulation of fluids inside the brain," I say. Part of our training as deathmaidens includes some medical instruction. Know thine enemy.

"Very good." I nearly gag when he winks at me. The thought occurs to me that if I tried real hard, I might be able to vomit on his clean white smock.

"The attending physician wrote that his pupils became fixed and dilated. He had no reflexes, could not breathe without a respirator. The line on his EEG was flat. In most respects, he was brain-dead."

I desperately want to look at the file. "Most respects? In what respect was he not dead?"

"Really, Miss Oliver, you're making quite a fuss about something that's quite . . ."

"Routine? The death of small children has become routine for you?"

I know it's a cheap jab, but I'm mad. He shakes his head slowly but doesn't answer. This is how he handles hysterical females.

I ask when I can see Tomás. The doctor tells me the entire "recovery" takes over six hours. I can see the body only after they are finished.

I can't think of any way to get my hands on that file. I decide to go home and wait.

My aversion to hospitals can be partly explained by the years of animosity between the American Medical Association and the Society of Deathmaidens.

The Society of Deathmaidens was founded in the late nineteenth century by a woman named Grace Parker, whom we call Sister Grace. When she was a child living in Lowell, Massachusetts, her mother had a terrible accident in a textile factory, dragged into a loom by her neck. Her mother was rushed off to a Catholic hospital, where she lay paralyzed and in pain for months. Grace watched at her mother's bedside as she screamed for someone to please help her die. The doctors gave her morphine, but nothing eased the pain. Finally, one day when she was alone, Grace took her mother's hand and pressed it against her forehead. In her writings, she describes what happened to her as "riding the rapids of light, through a deep canyon, into a wide, peaceful plain." When the nurses visited the room on their next rounds, they found Grace passed out on the floor, her mother dead.

Later, Grace formed a group of women, many of them midwives and ex-nuns. They developed a technique of seeing into the imaginations of the dying and of releasing their spirits. She eventually established a school in Boston, the Institute for Eternal Living.

During this time, the AMA was attempting to solidify its monopoly on medicine, squeezing out the homeopaths, chiropractors, faith healers, and practitioners of Native American and Asian medicine—the very same healers people are flocking to today. The AMA made virulent attacks against the Society of Deathmaidens, accusing them, among other things, of witchcraft. However, during World War I, deathmaidens gained wide acceptance when their services on the battlefield were desperately needed, and their use became firmly entrenched. It wasn't until the 1930s that the AMA had the political clout to bring charges of murder and conspiracy against Sister Grace. She fled the country with her followers and reestablished her school in an abandoned monastery in San Miguel de Allende, a small mountain town north of Mexico City.

The charges were dismissed, and deathmaidens were allowed to resume their practice in the United States, but Sister Grace, keenly aware of the ebb and flow of political conservatism, continued to operate her school out of Mexico.

Just as doctors see death as evidence of failure, they

see deathmaidens as a personal affront to their competency. In turn, deathmaidens feel doctors torment the dying, allocating mammoth resources only to prolong suffering.

Some doctors won't allow deathmaidens in their hospitals. Understandably, they are worried about their livelihoods. Over 80 percent of the money people spend on health care is spent in the last few months of their lives, usually to provide extraordinary treatments for incurable illnesses. Hospitals would stand to lose a great deal of money if people were allowed to pass on naturally. Or if they asked for a deathmaiden.

Ironically, it was the HMOs, ever conscious of rising health costs, that sanctioned the use of hospices and deathmaidens; the medical community, as they have in most circumstances, lay down before the dictates of the HMOs. No one, not even doctors, can stand up to big business.

The relationship between deathmaidens and the medical community remains a testy one. Doctors tolerate us but attempt to thwart our work whenever possible.

As my heels click down the hallway, trying to find a way out of the maze of corridors, I see a small office next to a kitchen that looks as if it were once a closet. The nameplate reads "Transplant Coordinator." The door is ajar. I knock lightly.

"Come in," says a weary voice.

Carol Nims has her head in her hands, elbows propped on her desk. Her hair has a dark stripe down its part and has seen so many dye jobs that it has the texture of charred bacon. When she glances up at me, she pushes back in her chair, alarmed; she doesn't expect a stranger to walk into her office. In her late twenties, she has deep bags under her eyes. She attempts to curl her hair behind her ears; it sticks out like scissors.

I must be wearing my sympathetic face, because once we exchange looks, she shrugs and slumps again in her chair.

"I'm sorry if I look disheveled," she says. "A family down the hall lost a son in a motorcycle accident. He's on a respirator . . . in a persistent vegetative state. I just asked them to consider donating his organs. I was afraid the father was going to kill me."

"He didn't find your request comforting?" She's too self-involved to hear the sarcasm in my voice.

"I tried! 'Think of the lives he'll be saving,' I said, but the father starts clenching his fists and asks me to leave. He acted like he was going to hit me—" Her voice breaks, incredulous, hurt.

I pull up a chair and take her hand. I notice a rash on her wrist. "You try so hard," I say.

Suddenly she bursts into tears. "I do!" she wails.

Like a caring colleague, I get up and shut the door. I pour her a glass of water from a bottle of Evian on the credenza.

"You have no idea what it's like . . . dealing with death day in and day out," she whimpers.

"I might have some idea."

"It's too much." She sips the water, blows her nose, then makes a feeble attempt to smile. "Thank you." She takes a comb from her desk drawer and pulls it through her much abused tresses. "Gosh," she says, "I've needed to do that for six months. Sometimes the pressure . . . it's horrible. You know, you try to convince people that they can do some good, but they're so pigheaded. Like a dead body would do *them* any good."

"People are funny about death," I say.

"Look," she says, rolling up her shirtsleeves, extending her forearms for me to inspect. "I'm allergic to perfusion fluid . . . that's what we use to transport kidneys. I have this horrible rash all over my arms and my chest, too. I itch all night. I can't sleep." She looks up as if only now realizing she doesn't know me. She drops her arms. "Are you a transplant coordinator, too?" she asks.

"No, I'm a schoolteacher." She nods. That seems to need no explanation. Or verification, for that matter. "We had a transplant coordinator come speak to our PTA meeting last week."

Her face suddenly brightens. "I do speaking engagements, too. It's simply ignorance that keeps people from donating their organs."

"That and those damn instincts of theirs." I feel my own rash of irritation spread over my body. She's oblivious, however. Evangelicals, convinced of the rightness of their cause, assume everyone agrees with them. It blinds her to my sarcasm. "After the lecture, some of our parents came to me with questions that I couldn't answer. I wondered if you could help me."

"Of course. I'd love to." Eager, fully recovered, she sits on the edge of her seat, ready to promote her faith.

"Could you tell me how doctors decide if someone is brain-dead?"

"Certainly. First, they must have a flat EEG, that's an electroencephalogram. That means there's no sign of brain activity. Then we make sure there is no response to painful stimuli and that his pupils remain dilated and fixed. Then a solution of ice water is poured into his ear to make sure there is no reflex action. The same test is done twenty-four hours later. Then, just to make sure, we do one last test. We take a special isotope scan of his head after a radioactive dye has been injected into the artery that carries blood to the brain. If there is no blood flow to any part of the brain, it's a certain sign of total and irreversible cessation of brain function."

"No one has ever woken after they've been declared brain-dead?"

"Well . . . a few times, but it's nearly impossible."

"Nearly impossible?"

"Oh, yes. We wouldn't want to be taking organs from someone who was still alive." She giggles, as if the notion is absurd, something out of a silly Hollywood horror flick. Something that could never happen.

In the hospital parking lot, I remember the toys I bought for Tomás still in the trunk of my car. I suppose I could return them, but it doesn't seem right. I feel like a young suitor who arrives with flowers at his girlfriend's house only to see her hop on a motorcycle behind a helmeted man in black leather. Like the wilting flowers, the toys are evidence of my failure.

I call a friend who just had a baby and drop them off on the way home. She looks at the toys and gives me a pitying look, as if I am totally clueless, her eyes expressing what she's too polite to say: *She's only a baby. But then, how would you know about such things.*

Sometimes silent accusations stab more deeply than public humiliations.

I return to the hospital at eleven P.M. and ask to see Tomás. An older nurse with short gray hair tells me the body has already been sent to the city morgue. "Usually we send recovered bodies directly to the funeral home, since the coroner has already signed off. But if nobody steps forward to claim the body, we send it to the morgue." She smiles at me and then adds, "It doesn't do any good to have dead bodies lying around a hospital."

CHAPTER

4

I wear a blue suit that I save for funerals and wind my long red hair into a bun. I find an old picture ID from a class I took at UCLA. I poke a hole in the plastic and string a chain through it. I loop it over my head. I think I look like a bureaucrat.

The Forensic Science Center is one block east of Interstate 5 on the corner of Mission and Marengo in an area called Lincoln Heights. Only a few blocks east of the modern, blue-glass skyscrapers of downtown Los Angeles, the area is shockingly barren: a vast and empty railyard, auto salvage lots, steep hills with decrepit houses that cling to eroding cliffs like favelas, the metastasizing slums of Rio de Janeiro. Everything is a dusty gray brown, as if the city suddenly ran out of water on this side of town. Most of the signs are in Spanish or a mixture of Spanish and English: "La Favorita Bakery," "Rosales Meat Distributor," and, hanging crooked over a one-story house with palm trees painted on it, its walls blighted with ghastly holes of flaking stucco, a sign of shot-out fluorescent tubes, "Las Palmas Inn." Just the place to get away from it all. I cruise by a lot with another sign: "Express Auto Dismantling." I drive the Jag a little faster.

It occurs to me that this is what the Hollywood Hills might look like after an earthquake.

The Forensic Science Center is two small, yellowish concrete buildings with odd little square windows; they look like flan cakes that have sat out too long. Gigantic blue letters spell out "Coroner" on the side. I wonder how such a small, innocuous building can handle all the deaths for Los Angeles County. Half a block away is a twenty-story hospital for women and children. So much attention given to birth, so little to death.

I park by a turn-of-the-century brick building undergoing restoration next door. The place seems deserted. I walk inside.

A Hispanic woman sits behind a bulletproof window in the lobby. I tell her that I am an INS agent investigating the death of Tomás Gomez. She calls back, and an eager-looking Asian man leads me back to the examination rooms.

His nametag reads "Dr. Webster." He tells me to call him Matty. It's hard to tell his age, but he talks like a surfer and babbles to me about his weekend trip snowboarding at Mammoth Lakes. He leads me through a maze of narrow white corridors, rapping his knuckles on each of the doors in the hallway. I wonder whom he's trying to wake. He pauses in front of a door of what looks like a large walk-in freezer: cold storage. He opens it and pulls out a body covered in a white plastic sheet. I assume it's Tomás.

He rolls the body down the hallway into a large room with six stainless-steel tables lined up in a row. Each table has its own sink, a cart for instruments, and what looks like a deli scale. The floors are white tile. One wall is floor-to-ceiling stainless-steel drawers and shelves. At the far end of the room, a pathologist and an assistant are weighing the heart of a black male whose corpse lies naked on a table. It's very cold, and I smell a mixture of blood, disinfectant, and Webster's cologne, Acqua di Giò. I find it odd that someone should waste expensive cologne in such a malodorous place. I'm sure he has his reasons; maybe he feels it protects him from something—evil spirits, death, vampires.

Webster rolls the gurney beside a table. Gently he pulls the sheet off Tomás's face.

Tomás's skin is pigeon gray, and his eyes are taped shut. I yank the plastic off his body. It's white and hairless. They shaved his entire body before they harvested his organs. A long neat seam extends from his chest down and across his abdomen; two others run down the fronts of his legs. "He looks so untouched," I say.

The coroner laughs. I've found someone who appreciates my humor. "He's twenty pounds lighter than he was before. The doctors replace the bones with wooden dowels and pack the cavities with something like bubble wrap in case the family wants to have an open casket."

"Have the parents been contacted?"

The coroner looks in his file. It's thinner than the hospital file, so I know it contains only part of Tomás's medical history. "The father, Fernandez Gomez, is listed here as deceased. It says the mother, Florencia, lives in Mexico. No address or telephone number. Doesn't even say what city."

"The mother's name is Florencia?"

"That's what it says. Why?"

I shrug and write in my notebook as if this were official business. "Was an autopsy performed?" I ask.

"No. You see, we process around twenty thousand bodies a year, but less than half receive autopsies, and only ten percent receive a complete autopsy."

"You have different kinds of autopsies?"

"Different strokes for different blokes. We have four on the menu. In case of possible homicide, we do a complete autopsy with photography, X-rays, full toxicology, et cetera. For traffic accidents we test the blood and urine for alcohol and drugs; for a suicide we might do a limited autopsy on the stomach with toxicology on the blood and urine. And for natural deaths we simply do an external examination and maybe a blood and urine test."

Webster appears to relish talking about his work. He smiles and looks in my eyes. Perhaps he enjoys talking to a live person.

"How do you decide to do an autopsy on a natural death?" I ask.

"Generally, we won't do one if they've seen a doctor twenty days prior to death. In this case, an autopsy would be highly unusual. We received a call at four-fifteen P.M. from the hospital transplant coordinator, asking for permission to harvest organs."

"And you gave permission?"

"If a person has been declared brain-dead, we always grant permission."

"Always?"

"Always."

"Who signed off for the organ donation?"

He looks into the file again. "In this case, the child was a ward of the state. From her notes here, it looks like the transplant coordinator called the state attorney general's office, then talked to a lawyer who gave her the number of the county director of human services. He gave his permission and, on the next day, signed off on the paperwork."

"Do you know how the boy died?"

"The death certificate says 'massive head trauma.'"

"You signed it?"

"No. Dr. Dan Prouty did."

"Did you do blood or urine tests?"

"No."

"Did you do a visual inspection of the body?"

"No."

"Do you know what drugs were in the body at the time of death?"

"No. We'd have to do an analysis of the blood and tissue."

"Could you do a toxicology analysis now . . . without performing an autopsy?"

"Why would we do that? It would be quite out of the ordinary."

I run my fingers through Tomás's limp black hair. Again I marvel at how his forehead slants back at a forty-five-degree angle from his brow. I feel Webster watching me. I turn and catch a look of longing in his eyes. As a professional, he can never indulge in sorrow. But he is young and human; I sense a vulnerability I can probe.

"Have you ever been uncomfortable with the definition of brain-dead?" I ask. "You might look at the EEG and it's flat, but you see that the person is breathing, his heart's pumping. He looks alive. Has it ever made you uncomfortable that these people were declared dead? Have you ever thought what it might be like to lie in a hospital bed, unconscious, helpless? The machines indicate that you're brain-dead, that you feel no pain, but then you are cut open and your organs are taken."

He blanches.

No one who deals with death as much as a coroner, or a deathmaiden, for that matter, can mistake the difference between a live body and a dead one. I am counting on the coroner's better instincts.

I give him my number. "Call me," I say, and walk out.

"The woman who takes care of insurance claims is at lunch. Who's calling?" asks a cold woman's voice.

I sigh into the receiver like an overworked bureaucrat, then try to sound officious. "This is Michele Price from the Claims Department at BlueCross BlueShield. There appears to be a problem with one of your claims." I seem to have unearthed a natural talent for lying.

"What's the patient's name, please?" There's something peevish about her, hostile and harassed. It makes me want to taunt her.

"Tomás Gomez. He was treated at your hospital for head trauma."

"Hold on. Let me pull up the file."

I hear the clicking of computer keys and the sound of voices echoing down a hallway.

"Here it is. It says here he's fully covered." Her voice rings, as though she's won an argument. "There's a note that the insurance agency was called and the policy was up-to-date."

"Perhaps he is covered under his parents' policy? I don't see any coverage under his name at all."

"Hold on. Let me grab the hard copy."

I'm put on hold and listen to a synthesized version of the Pachelbel Canon. Years ago, a public radio station used the tune as their fund-raising theme. Now when I hear it, I want to retch.

"Sorry that took so long. The boy died yesterday. I had to look in a different spot for his file." I hear her flipping through papers. "It says here that he was covered by a policy held with Silvanus Corporation."

"Did his father work there?"

"You should have that information," she says, her voice turning suspicious: I have asked one too many questions. "What did you say your name was?"

"I'm sure it's right here somewhere. I've got files piled up all over the place here, half in the computer, half in folders. You know how it is. Thank you for your help. Bye."

I hang up the phone, my heart beating wildly, as if I've been caught shoplifting. I let out a halfhearted giggle, then wipe my face; it's wet with tears.

At midnight I get a call from Matty Webster, the coroner. He tells me that he requested the complete medical file and read it through. He says he found something I might want to know. His voice is boyish and excited. I notice immediately that he refers to the body by name, Tomás. I think I've gotten to him.

"When the edema was found in his brain, Tomás was given a huge dose of phenobarbital that put him into a barbiturate coma, which has the same symptoms as brain death. Usually hospitals do a special isotope scan of the patient's brain after it's been injected with radioactive dye just to make sure a barbiturate coma is not mistaken for brain death. If the scan shows no blood flow in his brain, he passes the legal definition of brain-dead." He pauses to let this sink in.

A fierce tingling starts at the base of my neck. "You're telling me that this final isotope scan wasn't done?"

"It was not."

A silence pulses over the phone line. I realize it's my blood pumping in my ears. "So when Tomás was brought home to die, he could've been in a barbiturate coma?"

"It's unlikely, but yes, it is possible."

CHAPTER

5

The jade I hold in my palm is a squat little man with big earrings and an elaborate headdress. His features are incised with fine lines. His hands are in fists in front of him. His lips are pursed, his brow furrowed. The edges are worn smooth, and I think of Tomás passing it back and forth between his hands.

The carving looks old. I wonder where it came from.

Had I known Tomás for a few hours only? Could I include the hour I spent buying him toys?

I slip a lock of his soft black hair through my fingers. When Dr. Webster stepped out to answer a page, I snipped several inches of hair. I wanted something from his body, some kind of proof, something to reclaim him. This was the best I could do.

I look from my balcony across Santa Monica Bay. A low fog seeps ashore like smoke under a door. Near the horizon, I see pinpricks of light from sailboats caught in the fog.

An image of Tomás comes into my mind, lying in a barbiturate coma in a room that doesn't look like a child's room, on sheets with pink flowers, between pink blankets. Dying alone, crossing over without anyone to hold his hand. So brave. At least he was gone by the time they yanked out his organs, dead the moment I walked in. But how did he die? Not even his mother was there. Or was she his mother? Who was Florencia, the mother listed on his death certificate?

The telephone rings. It's my friend Pepper. Her real name is Margaret Dickie, but I've never known anyone to call her anything but Pepper.

"You sound bummed, kid. The death biz getting you down?"

"Death never bothers me. It's living I have trouble with."

"Aren't we chipper. Really, Fran, you don't sound good. What's up?"

"I don't want to talk about it."

I hear that peculiar echo on the line of someone trying to figure out your facial expression over the phone. "Why don't you come down to the studio for a beer."

"I don't drink beer."

"You can watch."

I try to make excuses, but she insists. I slip the jade into my pocket, get in my car, and drive down the coast to Venice.

Pepper is what you might call an eccentric. A Venice artist. She is the closest thing I have to a normal friendship, my best friend for fifteen years. I met her in Mexico during my training.

Pepper was never cut out to be a deathmaiden. She came to the society after a terrible accident in college. She was driving home from a party with three girlfriends, probably drunk, when they crashed. The other three girls were killed. I suppose she thought that if she was going to kill people she loved, she might as well get paid for it. She studied with me at the institute for about a year, then left to go to art school at Cal Arts.

Pepper is a petite woman with overdeveloped arm and back muscles from hauling around fifty-pound bags of clay, and she is the only woman I've ever known to have an abdominal six-pack. She has short fine hair, which she claims to cut with the kitchen shears. It looks it. Her eyes are big and brown, her mouth wide with oversize teeth. She speaks in a rapid-fire monotone, seldom pausing before she responds, as if she has heard your question before you asked it. She also has the annoying habit of remembering everything you've ever said to her.

I park in front of her house, a run-down craftsman cottage in the part of Venice that used to be canals, the kind of place with tacked-on garages that were never meant to be anything other than storage, but, like an unwelcome relative, slowly became part of the house—first a window, then some Sheetrock, then pictures on the walls.

I walk onto the sagging porch, stepping around a suspiciously rough spot. I open the screen door and walk in. A languorous young man with long dark hair reclines on a sofa by the door, his head falling back casually on top of the cushions. I think of the Marquis de Sade.

His name is Todd, Pepper's latest orphan, which is what she calls her boyfriends.

Pepper drives men crazy. Every time I go to her studio, I meet one or two young men hanging around like Mexican dogs, waiting patiently for her to be done with work, begging for a scrap of affection. She never tries to be attractive, always tells them exactly what she thinks of them, bosses them around, and, from what I've been told, is something of a contortionist in bed. She doesn't seem to need affection or reassurance or commitment. And men worship her. They don't dare be possessive, knowing that at the smallest hint of jealousy she will throw them out. So they gather at her place, and while they wait for her attention, they wash the dishes, cook, make the beds, clean the rabbit cages, and type her invoices.

Or lie on the couch looking like the Marquis de Sade.

As usual, Pepper is wearing clay-crusted jeans and a tight T-shirt without a bra. Her palms are callused from grog and are rough as barnacles. She passes the green stone from one hand to the other. "It looks Asian to me. See those etched lines on the headdress? It's real elaborate, like a dancer from Bali or something." She places the jade on a drafting board under the light. She gets down close to it, almost touching it with her nose.

"Jade is popular in Indonesia," I say, something I remember from a report on NPR.

"You said the boy was Mexican? Maybe it was something he found in Mexico. An Aztec amulet or something."

"Could be. I was thinking maybe Mayan or Olmec."

"Why don't you take it to the research center at the Getty?"

"Don't they have mostly Italian Renaissance art?"

"That's one of their specialties, but they just opened a show on Mayan art. Haven't you seen the banners all over town?"

"No."

"Well . . . they have all sorts of stuff now. Go check it out."

I suddenly feel heat on my shoulder. I turn around and see Todd lying on the couch unmoved, a hazy focus in our direction. "What does he do?" I whisper to Pepper.

"You mean like a job? Nothing, as far as I know." She slaps water on a huge mound of clay and covers it in plastic.

Pepper loves to work with large slabs that she molds and pinches together. Sometimes I think they look like body parts of obese women; other times they seem to have the heavy, twisted look of the underside of intersecting freeways. She uses dark-colored glazes, maroon, brown, navy. They sell fabulously well, and she always has a long list of commissions to fill.

The pieces she is working on now are large, curved tube shapes glazed in black with purple highlights. They remind me of the color of Tomás's hair.

"I think he was murdered," I say.

She scrapes clay off her workbench with a comb-shaped piece of wood, pressing the slugs of clay into a mound to be reused. "You know what I think? I think you're in love with him. That's what I think." Pepper thinks she's shocked me and smiles impishly, waiting for me to get angry. She gets no reaction, so she continues. "You've got all those unused maternal hormones rushing around in you without any place to go. Tell me, Fran, when was the last time you were spread supine on a divan, naked, with an erect penis bouncing on your belly? I swear, sometimes I think you know everything about death and nothing about life."

At another time, such jabs might hurt. "I saw his future," I say.

At the institute we learned to read the future. In one exercise, we sat in chairs lined up in two rows facing each other. We were to look into the other person's eyes. We were to tell them their past. Then their future. At first we giggled self-consciously; it seemed like such an invasion of privacy, like telling a stranger in line at a movie theater how you imagined him naked. It felt dangerous.

I sat across from a thin woman with mousy brown hair. I had never spoken to her before. When I began fabricating her history, she looked afraid, then offended, but then her eyes softened and pooled with tears. Her eyes turned dark blue, and as I looked into them, it was as if I were looking into a galaxy, traveling through space. I don't know if it was her reactions to what I said of her past that led me to understand her future, but it appeared clearly before me.

I realized this was the art of fortune-telling, and I was no different from the bad-smelling Gypsy who sits beneath a tattered tent at the carnival, her pendulous breasts resting on a card table, her brown fingers with crescents of dirt under the nails reaching toward your hand like a monstrous hairy spider. The Gypsy doesn't care about the lines on your hand, she's interested in what she sees in your eyes. Of course she can read you, her fingertips running over the millions of nerves on your palm, and as you open to her, she looks deep into your eyes and sees your future.

It is no more difficult to read someone's future than to love him. Perhaps it is easier. Perhaps it is the same thing.

Pepper stops teasing. Even though she didn't finish her training at the institute, she respects the art. "What did you see?"

I hesitate before speaking. I don't want to get emotional in front of Pepper. "A full life, school, soccer, college, job, marriage, children. Life to old age." I reach up to the top of one of Pepper's finished sculptures and slide my palm down a curvy slope to the base. The glaze is smooth, with the texture of ribs beneath it. "It wasn't his time to die. He wasn't even close."

"Who would want to kill a little Mexican boy?"

"I don't know."

"Maybe he was witness to a crime. Maybe he saw a murder, a gang shooting, got mixed up in a drug deal or something." Pepper's voice rises eagerly, as if fabricating the plot for a new TV movie. I give her a look. She shrugs.

"He was afraid of something," I say.

"Have you thought maybe his death was natural? Maybe when you were out, he had a stroke or something . . . something related to his head injury."

"He was fine. I know he was."

"I hate to point out the obvious, Fran, but you were hired to help the boy die. Does it really matter *how* he died? Someone did your work for you."

My head spins with rage. "He wasn't supposed to die. Don't you get it? He was a little boy with his whole life ahead of him. I was used as a cover for his murder! This compromises the integrity of our society. It could finish us."

I expect Pepper to scoff at me, to call me hysterical, but she doesn't. She thrusts out her lower jaw, sucking in her lower lip. "Then you have to find out who did it."

CHAPTER

6

Part of my job as a deathmaiden is to inform the relatives when their loved one has passed on. Seldom is that a problem; the family is in the parlor, nervously anticipating the last gasp, when they can finally relax, waiting as if for a tightrope walker to cross to the other side of a circus tent, for the moment when he grabs on to the steel pole and waves to the crowd, when they can breathe a collective sigh of relief, amazed, too, that they managed to survive the suspense.

The woman who said she was Tomás's mother disappeared just before his death. She did not show up at the hospital. She must have had her reasons, but I figure she will be home by now. I pull up to 1215 Clark Avenue and park. The house looks different. A purple plastic tricycle sits on the front lawn. Someone has recently watered the roses. I knock on the front door.

A slender woman with a head of brown corkscrew

curls opens the front door and peers around the edge, eyes suspicious. When she sees that I am a white woman, she relaxes a little and opens the door farther yet continues to block the entrance with her body. I hear the sounds of plastic wheels rolling over hardwood floors, a small child making siren sounds, a game show blaring from the television.

"I'm very sorry to disturb you," I say, "but I'm looking for Mrs. Gomez."

"You have the wrong address." Her tone is snippy, her face pinched like that of a petulant child whining for the bigger half of a candy bar.

"Did you move in recently?" I ask. "She was living here just a few days ago."

"We moved in yesterday. I don't know any woman named Mrs. Gomez."

"It's very important that I talk to her. Did she perhaps leave a forwarding address?"

"That's none of my concern. I'm very busy. I don't have time for your questions."

When I was a child, there was something about Barbie dolls that made me want to pull off their arms and legs. There's something about this woman that makes me feel the same way. "Please. It's regarding her child, a child about the age of your son."

She softens about as much as a week-old crepe. "I'm sorry, I really can't help you."

"All I need is your landlord's telephone number."

"Please, go away." She tries to close the door, but I block it with my foot.

Then I say something I know I'll feel ashamed of later.

"Does your little boy sleep in that front bedroom?" I point to the room with the raised blinds.

She looks alarmed, her big blue eyes popping. "What business is that of yours?"

"I thought so." I smile sweetly. "You might like to know a young boy was murdered in that room several days ago."

She lets out a gasp, then slams the door in my face. I chuckle to myself, but it already tastes bitter in my mouth.

As I open my car door, I glance up and see a Mexican gardener waving his pruning shears at me. I leave the door ajar and walk over to him. He straddles a rosebush and waits for me to come close.

"Are you looking for Señora Gomez?" he asks.

"Yes, I am."

"She's not here no more. She lived here only a short time . . . a few months. She comes out one day and has me trim the banana trees . . . over by the kitchen. *Muy simpática.*"

"Do you know how I might get in touch with her?"

"Maybe the management company. They rent out a lot of property around here. That house over there, too." He points to a stucco box across the street.

"What's their name?"

"Topsail Realty. They have an office on Washington. I do yardwork for them."

I look down at the gardener's hands. They're covered with scratches. "Don't the roses hurt your hands?" I ask.

He grins. "You get used to it."

I think that I should ask something more. My mind is blank. I'm not used to interrogating people.

"Señora Gomez goes to St. Clement's," he offers. "You might find her there. I saw her come back from morning service . . . every day. She must've been praying for her son."

I have my doubts.

I get myself a double espresso at Cow's End Café and wait for Topsail Realty to open. At nine-thirty A.M., the café is crowded. A half dozen dogs are tied up to parking meters in front. Everyone wears black sweatpants and fanny pouches. No one looks as though they're in a rush to go to work.

I find a public telephone that's working and make a call.

"Good morning. Priority One Ambulance Service. May I help you?"

"Yes, this is Sandy Silverstone from BlueCross BlueShield. I have a couple of questions regarding a claim here, and I need to talk to someone at your ambulance service. Is there a nonemergency number I should call?"

"You should probably talk to Carol Lohman. I'll connect you. Hold on."

I plug a few more quarters into the phone as I wait.

A clear, officious voice gets on the line. "This is Carol. How may I help you?"

I repeat my name and that I'm calling from the Claims Department at BlueCross. "I have a question about how long it took the ambulance to get to this patient."

"We have the shortest time between call and pickup on the west side." Her voice is defensive.

"I'm sure you do. I simply need something cleared up."

"What's the address of the patient and the date of pickup?"

I give it to her, and she tells me to hold.

"We got an emergency call at three forty-seven P.M. on the twenty-fifth for 1215 Clark Avenue. The ambulance arrived at three fifty-nine. We delivered the patient to Abbot Kinney at four-thirteen."

I ask her to fax the report to a number at a copy place in the Palisades where I get faxes when I need to, then get off the phone.

If I'm not mistaken, the ambulance was called before Tomás died.

At 10:08 I see a white BMW pull into the parking lot at Topsail Realty. A gray-haired woman in her late forties pokes a leg out of the car, twisting to collect something that has rolled under her seat. She staggers out of the car, her arms loaded with brochures and notebooks, her expensive power bob all askew. I amble over to the newsstand and buy a paper. I want to give her time to settle in. After ten minutes, I cross the street and enter the real estate office.

When I walk in, she quickly stashes her comb in her desk drawer. She's too surprised to give me her professional smile, her eyes big, her lips, bleached from constant use of lipstick, pressed into a pained smile as if receiving a compliment from someone she dislikes. I walk over brusquely and extend my hand over her desk.

"Good morning. My name is Sandy Silverstone. I'm

sorry to barge in on you so early, but I'm an agent for the Immigration and Naturalization Service. I'm trying to track down a Mrs. Gomez. I have reason to believe she is or was one of your tenants."

She looks me up and down. I don't know if she is suspicious or just doesn't want to be bothered. I begin to wonder if she even heard me. She puts her hand on the telephone, and I think she's going to call the police. I try the offensive. "You do check citizenship and legal status before you rent to someone, don't you?"

Suddenly she looks nervous. "Well, yes. Of course we do. What was her name? I'll look it up."

I tell her and she flips through a Rolodex. "We don't have anyone listed by that name," she says.

"The last address I have for her"—I run my finger down a blank page in my datebook—"is 1215 Clark Avenue in Venice."

"Oh, that house. We just rented that out to Mr. and Mrs. Weissman and their little boy. I don't think that's who you're looking for."

"Who rented it before them?"

"Let me look." She opens a cabinet, pulls out a file, and flips through it. "Looks like it was rented for corporate housing."

"What name is listed?"

"Silvanus Corporation. They're out in Simi Valley."

"Why would they rent corporate housing here?"

"It's close to the airport. It impresses visiting executives to be close to the marina. Or they might be building new headquarters at Ballona Creek. A lot of new companies are moving in."

"Who signed for the company?"

She flips to the end of the lease and studies the bottom line. "I can't read it. You want to try?"

She hands the file to me. The name might begin with an "M" or an "H," but it's impossible to say. The rest of the signature is a bunch of bumps. Before I hand back the lease, I notice the rent on the house is $2,800 a month. No wonder the management company didn't ask too many questions.

"There's no mention of Mrs. Gomez in that file?" I ask. "No note of who's staying there and when?"

"No. Once we rent a property, we don't check up on it much unless something goes wrong."

"So any number of people might stay in a house such as this, a house rented under a corporate name, and you wouldn't know about it?"

"Our tenants deserve their privacy." She slaps the folder together defensively. The interview is over.

An impish impulse squirms under my skin again. "If I were you, I'd just hope none of my tenants was involved in any criminal activity." Her face sickens, eyes stricken with fear. I walk out, oddly pleased.

It's Sunday morning. I park on Third Street on the border between Venice and Santa Monica, then cross the street to the church on the corner. The bulletin board at St. Clement's lists eight services beginning at six A.M. I kick myself. I should've waited until Monday, when there are only a morning and an evening service. Then I notice that half of the services are in English, the other half in Spanish. It's eleven A.M., and a service in Spanish is just ending.

I stand in the back of the sanctuary. I listen to the

mumbling of prayers in Spanish. The church is cold and damp. I pinch the end of my nose. The incense and mildew make me want to sneeze.

I look over the heads of the congregation, almost all women, all Latin American. I have a hollow feeling in my stomach. I'll never find her in this crowd. I'm not sure I even remember what she looks like. I plan to wait until the end of the service. Maybe I'll spot her when she comes out.

The organ plays, and people begin to file out of the pews. Many of the older women wear black, their heads covered in scarves. It's as if I'm suddenly in a rural hill town in Mexico. Walking slightly behind them, looking bored and petulant, come the teenage daughters, all wearing short skirts and bright red lipstick. They could be going to a disco. I imagine the mother-daughter fights that must've gone on while they were dressing for church.

The women look at me with hostility, as if I, a tall redhead, were lost, barging in at the wrong service.

Then I spot her. She's with an old woman in black and another woman about her age who cradles an infant in her arms.

"Mrs. Gomez," I call.

When she sees me, her body jerks and her eyes fill with terror. She turns abruptly and rushes back into the church, headed upstream, shoving women aside into the pews. I follow. She looks back and sees I'm following. She walks faster. She pushes open a door right of the altar. She runs through the baptistery into a long hallway. On one side, choirboys are running around, their robes falling in heaps at their feet. On the other side are administrative offices. Before she makes it to the emergency exit, I catch up to her.

"Mrs. Gomez, wait a moment, please. I need to talk to you."

She turns and hisses at me like a stray cat. "That's not my name. Leave me alone."

"Why are you running from me?"

She turns and pushes out the emergency door, setting off a fire alarm. She dashes across the parking lot.

Members of the congregation pause as they pile into their beat-up Toyota trucks and Datsuns, looking up, curious. They're not watching us; they're looking for fire. They gather in clusters and point at the church.

I grab her arm. "Mrs. Gomez, please, don't you care about your son?"

She turns angrily, twisting away. "I already told you that's not my name. I have no son."

She tugs and kicks, squirming like an eel; my fingers dig hard. I'm afraid she might scream, but I don't let go. "Your son is dead. I have to tell you. I'm sorry. Tomás is dead. Did you know that?"

"Leave me alone." She's pleading with me now, her voice a frightened whimper.

"Why didn't you come to the hospital? Is it an immigration problem?"

She stops struggling, pulls back, and straightens her posture. "I have my green card. I'm perfectly legal."

Over her head, I see the church custodian and the priest hurry people out of the church. Two deacons jog around the periphery, checking out the building.

"You have a job?" I ask.

"Of course, I work as a maid for Dr.—" She suddenly catches herself.

"You work for a doctor?"

"I don't know anything. Why don't you mind your own business." Her eyes dart back and forth, looking for an escape.

"Did someone do something bad to Tomás? Is that why you're afraid? He was only a little boy."

She lets out a whine like a coyote in a snare. I'm so surprised that I loosen my grip. She jerks away and runs back across the parking lot into the church.

Fire alarms rattle in pulsing rhythm until sirens sound in the distance.

CHAPTER

7

We tack out the channel in Marina del Rey, passing kayaks and sculls, dogs dashing along the low-tide sand, seals sunbathing on the rocky breakwater. As we sail out into the bay, a dozen dolphins leap in front of us as if escorting us toward the horizon. To the north, the Santa Monica Mountains, misty blue with a pink glow, jut far into the ocean like the tail of a slumbering iguana.

Pepper and I have spent many Sundays on this Santana. Her brother left it to her. He took his own life a few years ago, and when Pepper sails, she becomes a different person, quiet and soft. It's one of those sailboats that require too much work: Before setting off, we spent forty minutes at the dock stringing the sheets for the genoa, hanking on the sails, and rigging the spinnaker, which we'll raise once we get downwind. As we tack, Pepper holds the tiller while I scoot back and forth under the boom, yanking the jib from side to side. I think it amuses her to watch my big body crouch and lean. Pepper refuses to buy a motor, and more than once when the Santa Anas have blown over the basin like a furnace, we've been dead in the water.

As soon as we're out of the channel, Pepper handles the boat herself. I lean back and hang my neck over the side, letting the moist wind chill my face. I close my eyes and listen to the sound of the sail whopping, the light boat pulling and surging through the waves. It feels as if we're riding the back of a horse, and the motion lulls me into a sexual languor, both aroused and sated, like an epicure amid a ten-course feast.

I turn over on my belly and look toward shore. The placid bay, black as obsidian, glistens in the afternoon light. From a distance, the vast, polluted city suddenly seems like an ancient jeweled bracelet, its white buildings clustered like gems on a green copper band, open on one side to slip over your wrist. There's a magical quality to the sparkling megalopolis, appearing like a mirage, a heavenly city such as envisioned by Captain Fernando de Rivera y Moncada when he first sailed into Santa Monica Bay in 1769. The Gabrielino Indians called it the Bay of Smokes for the plumes rising from smoldering underground fires on the slopes of the Palisades. Now, when the city smog mixes with the ocean mist, a gray mink's tail wraps itself around the base of the mountains, and the city, obscured and mysterious, ascends as if from the smoke of a pipe, a hallucinogenic illusion.

If I didn't have these weekends out in the bay, in the absolute serenity of the water, I couldn't survive in Los Angeles. I reach out from the boat and place one hand on either side of the city. It seems manageable now.

I sit up and look west toward Catalina, a faded blue shadow looming flat on the horizon like the head of a crocodile. Pelicans swoop overhead, plunging into the surf. We pass a bell buoy clanking mournfully, its mechanical hammers hitting the cracked bell as it rocks in the waves.

I duck into the cabin to retrieve a brass urn. I cradle it on my lap for a moment. I feel the cold metal through my jeans. No one claimed Tomás's body, so I arranged to have it cremated. This is what's left.

Under the billowing sail, her left hand guiding the tiller, Pepper gives me a composite expression that I've become accustomed to: skepticism, fraying patience, wonder at why I make such a big deal over things, and worry that I'm losing my marbles. *Why do you care so much?*—I imagine her asking—*A little boy you hardly knew.* But Pepper and I have come to a point in our lives where we don't need to share our deepest thoughts; some things are too painful, too amorphous, too complex, to articulate.

Like the aching regret for leaving a child.

During my third year of training at the Institute for Eternal Living in San Miguel de Allende, I lived off campus on the second floor of an old pension at the top of a hill. The cobblestone street was so narrow that you could grasp the hand of someone in the window on the other side. Above the boxes of red geraniums, the windows stayed open; private dramas in the street were everyone's business. There was a little boy who roamed the town like a wild coyote. They called him Miguel after the patron saint of the city. A prankster and thief, he didn't go to school with the other children. He couldn't talk and didn't seem to have any parents. Shop owners gave him food scraps, mothers gave him clothes their own children had outgrown. I don't know where he slept, perhaps in the junkyard on the edge of town in one of the huge, ancient Cadillacs abandoned by American tourists.

He saw me one day on my way to school and followed me. When I stopped at the fruit market and bent to squeeze the mangoes in a basket, he stuck his head in my face and tapped his head. His eyes got real big. I pulled my red braid over my shoulder and held it out for him. He looked at it but was afraid to touch it. Suddenly he turned, excited, running in circles and making strangled cawing noises that I took to be laughing. He grabbed a piñata of red tissue paper from one of the vendors, held it on his head, and sauntered down the street like a knock-kneed woman trying to walk on cobblestones in heels. A perfect imitation of me. He came running back, shrieking like a porpoise. He stopped right in front of me, his nose almost touching mine, looking me straight in the eyes as if he were trying to steal my soul.

I have always had a weakness for American chocolate, particularly Reese's Peanut Butter Cups. I had a box shipped to me every month from the States. I reached into my pocket and gave him one that I was saving for my morning snack. From that morning on, he walked me to school every day, sometimes running ahead of me, sometimes striding beside me, waiting silently for his candy before I entered the institute.

I had to double my order from the States.

Several days after I told him I'd be leaving soon,

Miguel disappeared. I asked the neighbors about him, but they shrugged, unconcerned. I left my last box of Reese's Peanut Butter Cups for him with one of the shopkeepers, then got on the rickety bus that would take me to the airport in Mexico City. As I climbed over a woman with a chicken on her lap and settled into the seat by the window, I looked up out the glass; there he was, sitting on the hood of a battered Ford truck parked by the side of the road, watching me. He didn't take his eyes off me. Then he launched a wad of spit right at me. As the bus started its engine, and as his spit dripped down my window, he yelled, *"Pinche puta,"* and continued yelling, *"Pinche puta,"* as he chased the bus out of town, his legs kicking out, nearly tripping himself, tears streaking his dirty face.

The little squirt could talk after all. Considering his vocabulary, it's probably just fine he didn't talk more.

Yet I understood. I felt his anger grate at the bottom of my spine: I was not the first person to abandon him. I've thought many times over the years that I should've taken him with me. I regret the missed opportunity to make a real difference in someone's life, to give myself to a caring and nurturing that expand the soul. Young and single, I could've done it; I could've loved the unloved, nourished his body and spirit. I could've made the sacrifice.

But I didn't.

Late at night as I drop off to sleep, I try to picture him as he is now. Is he alive? Does he work? Is he married? Is he in prison?

As I sail with the ashes of another abandoned little boy in my lap, I think again of Miguel, who in his refusal to speak won the freedom to do as he pleased. I grieve for the thirty-five thousand children in foster care in Los Angeles County, unwanted, abandoned. And Tomás? Why do I feel this bond? Is it a case of transference, as Pepper would tease if I told her, of a ticking biological clock, of raging hormones? Does any allegiance of the human heart need explanation?

The ghostly mountains of Catalina appear on the horizon; I twist open the urn and pour Tomás's ashes into the wind.

After I drop off Pepper at her house in Venice, I drive down Pacific Avenue toward the Palisades. At Windward Circle, I see a gray mound of fluff and blood lying by the side of the road. Someone has hit a cat. I pull over and get a blanket out of the trunk. She's shaking and unconscious, but alive. I wrap her in the blanket and lay her in a cardboard box, which I wedge behind the driver's seat so she won't slide around.

I will take her home. I will help her die.

At my house, I place the box with the cat in the kitchen by the stove. I hold her paw and close my eyes. I see nothing. I've never tried to help an animal pass on before. I wipe the blood off her face with warm water. One leg is badly twisted. I'm sure she doesn't have a chance. I hold her paw again, close my eyes, and slip deep down within myself. Again, I see nothing. I hear only her labored breathing and the eucalyptus leaves scratching against the dining room window.

Maybe I've lost my knack.

I think I should take the cat to a veterinarian to be put down, but my recent encounter with the medical profession makes such an idea repugnant. I pray beside the cat until my knees hurt, wrap her in a blanket, then go to bed.

As I shut my eyes, questions swirl around my brain. Is it possible Tomás was murdered to harvest his organs? How is Silvanus Corporation involved? What is Dr. Faust's connection to Silvanus? How do I go about finding out?

Images of Tomás fill my head until I fall into a restless sleep.

My first experience with death was, as for most children, with my dog, Homer. He was old and blind and slept on my bed every night, his head on my pillow, his fetid breath blowing in my face. I didn't mind, and he didn't mind that I clung to him like a stuffed toy. One night we went to bed like that, my skinny arms wrapped around his neck; the next morning he was dead. Nothing traumatic in that. My grandmother passed on while she was shelling peas on our back porch. I was there beside her. "I think we're in for an early frost," she said. She dabbed her forehead with her handkerchief as if suddenly too warm, took my hand, and passed on. I discovered I had this peculiar talent only after three or four more passings, with a friend who overdosed in college, a boyfriend's mother with breast cancer, a friend with AIDS. Each time as I held their hands, a deep stillness settled over us; I felt a warm glow and sensed the vibrations of spinning electrons and protons; then they passed on. I didn't think I was cursed or anything like that, but I was feeling a little uneasy.

After I finished two years at Santa Monica College, I

drifted between jobs—a PA on film productions, clerking at a lingerie store, dog walking—with only a vague notion that I wanted to serve. I'm not cut out for martyrdom or physical discomfort, so the Peace Corps and refugee organizations were out. I don't fare well with constant humiliation, so social services were out. I wasn't religious, so I was saved from the nunnery. I finally took a job as assistant to a midwife. I worked several years at it; it suited me well. I seemed able to calm mothers, and that initial scream of protest from a newborn is a thrill beyond words.

During this time, a friend asked me to visit a woman in her thirties who was dying of cancer. When I walked into her room, I felt an incredible peace. The woman, named Clara, stood by the window, her belly swollen with cancer, looking pregnant, her hand on the small of her back, the sun catching in her hair. She asked me to help her pull a chair to the window so she could look out. I dragged over two chairs, and we both looked out the window, holding hands silently.

She began to go into what I now know as dying labor, her breathing erratic, groaning, sweating, laboring just like a woman giving birth. With a final push, she expired, and I felt again that awesome stillness I'd felt before. I realized this was the work I should be doing: a midwife to the dying.

Still I resisted. Why surround yourself with death when there are adorable babies to bring into the world? Then, my mother needed help passing. She was a proud woman who wanted to die at home; I flew back to Maine to care for her. One morning, she asked me to help dress her in a cream-colored suit she'd bought for Easter

Sunday; she wanted to sit in her sunroom, which was filled with blooming African violets and warmed as soon as the morning sun peeked over the mountains. I had errands to do, so I left her with a new day nurse who was briefed on my mother's wishes to have no medical intervention. When I returned home, I saw an ambulance in the driveway. I raced in: Mother was on the floor, naked, lying in a pool of her own urine and feces, a tracheal tube jammed into her mouth, white froth bubbling from her nose, her hands ballooning with intravenous infusions. A team of paramedics scrambled around her, trying to resuscitate her dead body, her pathetic gray shell jumping with the defibrillator.

It was horrible. Everything she didn't want in death.

No one, I decided, should die like this.

I began working as a hospice volunteer and one day witnessed the work of a deathmaiden. She put me in contact with the Institute for Eternal Living, where I trained for four years.

Like a religious call, a career as a deathmaiden is not something you choose: It chooses you.

The next morning I wake to the sound of mewing. I walk into the kitchen. The cat is awake and hungry. I give her a can of tuna, of which she eats half. She thanks me by scratching my calf.

She is very much alive.

CHAPTER

8

It should be an easy assignment: a woman in her eighties. I hold her hand yet see nothing. My vision is gone. I have no concentration. I hear a clock chime in the living room. My stomach rumbles with hunger. The relatives, two sons, their wives, and three granddaughters, are waiting impatiently in the living room as if for an oil change, wondering how it could possibly take so long. They all have things to do, lives to lead, wills to read. One son peeks in the doorway and asks if there's anything he can do for me. I shake my bowed head. I sit by her bed and fall into a deep slumber.

The technique of passage Sister Grace developed at the Institute for Eternal Living is based on Christian and Buddhist teachings, her work with a number of nineteenth-century faith healers, and rituals she observed from Native American shamans from a variety of tribes.

We lived a regimented life based on the Benedictine rule written in the fourth century. Rising at four, we divided the day among meditation, spiritual exercises, study, and manual labor for the sustenance of the community. We trained in the afternoons; most exercises were aimed at denying the material world, sublimating our egos, and strengthening our control over our innate spiritual and emotional powers.

Although structured, the institute was designed by Sister Grace to have the atmosphere of a small liberal arts college rather than a religious society. She studied religion-based colleges such as Swarthmore and Principia and designed a four-year curriculum that has been pretty consistent for over one hundred years.

In the first year, we studied comparative religion, political science, the history of medicine, nursing, and various meditation techniques. In the second year, we began exercises in the technique of passage (exercises to strengthen intuition, dream exercises, and astral projection) and learned techniques for dealing with pain such as massage and acupressure. In the third year, students achieved full knowledge of the technique of passage, which we perfected in the fourth year by spending six months with a shaman or spiritual healer and six months as an apprentice deathmaiden.

The third and fourth years of training also involved working in local hospitals. We observed patients suffering, in pain, nearing death. We sat by their beds and learned to enter their minds and imaginations, to offer a hand and lead them out of the material world.

Sister Grace insisted that deathmaidens receive full training as registered nurses. They need to know when a patient is ready for passage both medically and spiritually. She also wanted nursing to be a backup for her students in case the work of deathmaidens was outlawed, which even to this day has always seemed imminent.

In addition to this program, the curriculum included liberal arts electives in ethics, literature, history, and the arts. Sister Grace wanted to cultivate not only competent professionals, but women with ethical intelligence and social commitment.

It takes years to develop our skills, but it doesn't look like much: no machines, no dancing, no incantations, no shaking beads. If you were to watch me work, you might think I was praying or maybe even sleeping.

When I first meet a patient, I take a general reading of the energy force of the room, the vitality of the life force. This appears to me in a color: red, pink, and yellow for very vital energy; orange for great physical suffering; purple for emotional and spiritual distress; blue, gray, and green for sickness approaching death. I then go to the bed, take the patient's hand, and kiss the palm.

If they are conscious, I ask them if they are ready to make the journey. I don't really need to ask them, because I already know, but I do it anyhow. If they say yes, I ask them to close their eyes. I will then either place their palm over my forehead or hold their hand. To an observer, it looks as though I'm praying in silence. But I'm far from silent. I talk to them with my mind, and I open myself to all of their emotions and thoughts. I visit their memories and walk them through their fears. If they have an unresolved issue, or need to make peace with someone, we work through it. Sometimes I ask the attending relatives to call the person in question and have that person actually come to the patient's bedside.

There are four steps of preparation for dying. The first is attending to unfinished business. The second is that survivors must give the dying person permission to die. The third is to let go of the body and the ego. And the last is the visualization of an expansion beyond the self.

The first two steps are uncomplicated and often are taken care of before I arrive through the work of the hospice team. The third and fourth steps are where my skills come into play, to lead the dying to the next reality.

My work takes from a few minutes up to a week for those mired in fear. Old women are the easiest. They have had full lives and need only a little quiet assurance: *Yes, it's time to go; yes, we'll be all right here; yes, we'll remember you; yes, it's safe on the other side; yes, you'll be fine, it's time to go, time to go, time to go.* Smiling, they relax their gnarled fingers and slip away.

Children are also easy, full of adventure, fearless, trusting. They pass with excitement, with joy. The comatose pass easily as well, although it's a little harder to judge their passing. But I can see it. A light flutter of the eyelids. A twitch in the cheek. I need only to remind them that the "others" are waiting. Here, a little anger sometimes helps: *Get on with it. You're not doing any good here. Go!*

The most difficult cases are old men and young mothers. Old men are filled to their eyeballs with fear. Unlike women, who temper religious dogma with their own good judgment, men spend their lives committing adultery, stealing, killing, and lying, and only when they're dying do they remember their religious teaching. Suddenly they take it all very literally. Filled with fear of hell and retribution, they cling to life like a rock climber clinging to a precipice. Never do I feel more motherly than when I reassure them over and over again that they are good and lovable and that they won't go to hell. Slowly they pass, tentatively, furtively, usually at night, hoping, I suppose, to sneak away when no one is looking.

Then we come to young mothers. I nearly lose my patience with them. They drag on their dying for a week, sometimes longer. It's nearly impossible to convince them that their husbands and children will be okay without them. *Yes, they'll eat three times a day; yes, he'll marry again; yes, Jimmy will get over his preoccupation with video games; no, your dying won't make them all afraid to love again; no, your death won't drive them into years of therapy with sadistic doctors.* But even young mothers eventually let go, bored with their own anxiety, curious to move on.

When peace is made and all fears are resolved, we are ready. I kiss their forehead, then take their hand. I sit in a chair beside the bed and close my eyes.

We start what we call active death labor. Just as birth labor includes contractions and the dilation of the cervix, preparing the woman's body for release of the infant, so in death labor the body prepares for the release of the spirit. As in a birth, the intensity of pain and emotion escalates; body temperature fluctuates wildly. The skin cools and grays. The lungs fill with fluid; breathing is difficult. The person becomes hypersensitive to light, noise, and emotions. As in birth labor, just as the body is near exhaustion, it fills with a tremendous energy for the final push, in this case to push out the spirit.

Then, the moment of death. Like the final stage of birth—expelling the placenta—death releases fluids, the body relaxes. The heart and lungs stop. This may take several minutes to occur. The spirit hovers. If you were to watch, you would see small but active spasms in their face, as if something were running around underneath their skin. The room fills with a throbbing excitement, a golden glow. Then they relax and pass on.

We walk together through a dark tunnel toward the light. I stay with them until they are ready. Soon they are awash with a sense of well-being and become eager to move on. Sometimes they see deceased relatives or a spiritual guide come to assist them. We all walk toward the light. Then I let go of their hand.

Scientists dismiss stories of near death phenomena as hallucinations caused by cerebral anoxia, lack of oxygen to the brain. They deny the existence of the experience, as if the tunnel were a physical place, like a tunnel between England and France, and the light were the sun. It has nothing to do with a place; it's about the transference of energy.

Einstein wrote that energy never dies. It is simply transformed from one form of energy to another. So it is with our spirits.

Morning sun pours through the bedroom window and wakes me. I hear the sound of humming. It's the old woman. I am still holding her hand; my head rests against her atrophied thigh. I lift my head. Her eyes are wide open and she's smiling at me.

"My dear, lovely child," she says. She pulls me to her chest, holds me close, then pushes me away. "Help me up, dear."

I help her up to a sitting position and put pillows behind her back. I push the sheets aside and pull her nightgown down over her skinny, wrinkled thighs. She hoists herself off the side of the bed, gripping my hands like clothespins. Tentatively, we walk a couple of steps.

"What in hell are you doing?" One of the sons charges into the bedroom, his face creased, his clothes wrinkled from sleeping on the couch. He wants to push me away, but I can see he's afraid of touching the old woman. The old lady and I rock over to the other side of the room, where she clings to the bureau and brushes her hair. The son is aghast. "She hasn't walked in fifteen years!"

"Ralph, darling," she says, "would you please pour me some of that delicious coffee I smell?" The old woman doesn't even look at him. He glances at me with a look of exasperation and hatred. I don't know what kind of mother this old woman was, but it seems the son is none too pleased with her renewed vitality.

By the time I leave, she is bossing the entire family around. As the elder son hands me my coat, he scratches his head and shifts his weight from foot to foot. Our eyes meet. I raise my eyebrows. "I don't know if I'm supposed to pay you or not," he says. He expels air through his teeth in a weak attempt at a chuckle.

I feel I should apologize, but apologizing for healing

someone doesn't seem quite appropriate. "It's the first time it's happened to me," I say.

"Oh?"

"Well, once with a cat."

"A cat?"

"Don't worry about paying me," I say.

A flicker of relief in a face of consternation. "I feel bad about taking your time," he says. "I guess she wasn't ready to die."

I don't know what to say. I never did get a reading on her. "You can give me a call if she begins to fail again."

We both watch as she marches around the house rearranging knickknacks. With her cane, she knocks an oak picture frame off the mantel over the fireplace, shattering the glass. "What's his picture doing up here?" she demands.

He looks at me with an expression both apologetic and pained, like a parent with a three-year-old who's throwing a tantrum. "Will it last?" he asks. He's waited years for her to die, I can tell. Whatever love he had for his mother has dissipated in the years of waiting.

I want to say something encouraging, something to ease this distressed family. So many times by bringing death I've brought peace to a family. Now I've brought life and turmoil.

"She's an old woman," I say, then leave.

I whine at Pepper the way one can whine only at a longtime girlfriend. I see her patience wearing thin, but when she unleashes at me, I'm caught off guard, like a sudden gust of wind that hurls the rigging in my face.

"You are forgetting all your teaching. Of course you

can't do your work." Her voice is hoarse and angry. "You've let yourself get emotionally involved with one of your clients. These doctors . . . this boy's death . . . they're bringing you down to the material world. You better get it together, girl. What kind of job do you think you'll be able to get as an ex-deathmaiden? Nursing? Forget it. Who's going to hire a nurse who's been a deathmaiden? Look at me! I scrape by on the sidelines, an outsider. I see ghosts everywhere. If people didn't want to buy these twisted clay things I make, I'd be one of those crazy homeless ladies on Venice Beach."

The picture Pepper paints of herself is so different from the Pepper I know. I see her as dynamic, independent; she sees herself as suffering, alienated. It hurts deeply that I haven't picked up on it before. I wonder if my current blindness has been creeping up on me, like the cool obliviousness that grows in a dying marriage.

Her voice suddenly drops in pitch. She kneads grog into a new pile of clay. "Frannie, you can't make the compromises that everyone else makes every day without losing your powers. You cannot doubt. You cannot question. It'll turn you inside out."

"I'm not compromising," I say feebly.

"Yes, you are," she shouts, punching her thumbs deep into the clay. "Lying, sneaking around, digging into other people's business, asking personal questions. You're letting yourself sink into the quagmire of humanity."

"Quagmire! Oh, please . . . you're the one who said I should find out the truth about Tomás."

"Maybe I was wrong."

"Maybe you were right."

Pepper sighs, exasperated. "I'm serious, Fran. You better take some time off and get yourself straightened out."

What she doesn't know, and what I'm just realizing, is that I don't want to get straightened out.

As soon as I walk into my house, the cat attacks my feet, rubbing my legs, meowing.

Cat has made the house her own. I don't especially like cats and she knows it, but we are developing a bond, based primarily on her demands for food and attention. She refuses cat food and sits mewing in the middle of the kitchen until I give her tuna. In the evening as I settle down to read, I toss her off my bed; when I wake in the morning, she is sleeping on my pillow on top of my head.

I make myself a simple dinner of rice and vegetables. After I wash the dishes, I walk onto my deck and look out over the Los Angeles basin. Yellow and white lights blink on, and over on the freeway, the traffic dragon, red eyes flaming, snakes over Mulholland into the swamp. A thin tail of fog wraps around Santa Monica. I think of a comet trailing gases through the Milky Way.

I kneel on a pillow and practice a centering ritual. I relax, concentrating on my breathing. My body is a sack of sand sifting slowly out the base of my spine. I close my eyes and let the other senses take over.

The dampness of the evening brings out smells of eucalyptus and wild sage. I ride the vapor of my breath over the tops of the juniper and manzanita, over the rough cliffs of orange sand, over the streetlights on West Channel Road, over the traffic snake that hugs the coast all the way to Malibu, over the frothy waves lapping against the shore, over the Ferris wheel on Santa Monica Pier. I hover over the bay and feel the depth of the ocean beneath me. I absorb its purple black color, its moist, salty breath, like the kiss of a cave, a cave that beckons me.

I see Tomás's face rise up from the ocean. His oddly sloped forehead transforms into the side of a Mayan temple. I climb the temple stairs, and when I look down, I see a vast jungle. I hear the sounds of screeching parrots, the caterwaul of the jaguar. I sense I'm on the edge of something terrible and dangerous.

I place my palms over my face, resting them lightly on my skin. What does it mean? I wait for a sign, a voice.

Nothing comes.

I have long cherished the dying process, the unwanted child of God's creation. Perhaps I have regarded it too highly, forgetting to cherish life. I have been as unbalanced as the monk who prays too long, neglecting his garden and beehives.

My knees hurt. I hear Cat sharpening her claws on the redwood railing. She rubs against my thigh. I feel a powerful surge of energy followed immediately by lethargy. I lift up Cat and bury my face in her fur. The smell of asphalt and tuna brings tears to my eyes. I know I can't go back. I rock to my feet, walk into the living room, and pick up the phone.

I call Charlotte Wright and tell her I cannot take any more assignments for a while.

CHAPTER

9

An investigator believes that effects do not occur without causes. His method involves analysis, comparison, and evaluation of data that he has observed and collected. Confident in his belief that the world is real and knowable, he operates according to fixed rules. He uses his brain, not his heart.

I realize that I will have to change my whole way of thinking, of perceiving the world.

I drive to Sixth Avenue and Arizona in Santa Monica to the Santa Monica Library. I park beneath its exaggerated eaves that extend out over the building and give it the look of an enormous graduation cap. Very chic in the sixties, now a tad tawdry, like a disco dress pulled out for Halloween.

I wade through the debris left by street bums who park their carts of rags and go inside the library to stay warm. I like to imagine that in their fuzzy stupor they sometimes actually pick up a book to read. Once I found one passed out in the stacks right where I wanted to retrieve a book. Perhaps he'd collapsed in an inspired ecstasy.

I sign up for time on the Internet.

I do not own a computer. Or a television set. Or a CD player. Or a microwave oven. Pepper calls me a neo-Luddite, yet it's not technology I eschew, but its invasion of my thought, my time, my privacy. I don't want it in my home. So I use the library.

While I wait to use a computer, I flip through paper reference materials. In *Wards Business Directory,* a dozen massive green volumes that take up a whole shelf, I look for Silvanus Corporation. It's listed as a pharmaceuticals company, a private corporation with revenues of $55 million. That immediately cuts down on what I can find out about them. I try *Dun & Bradstreet* and get a better description: "Specializing in tissue replacement product," date of incorporation 1985, address Wild Oak Avenue in Simi Valley, and a list of officers: Dr. Bryant Hillary, chief executive officer; Dr. Leslie Folk, chief financial officer; Dr. Mike Rosenbaum, operations manager.

I find two articles listed in the *Los Angeles Times* index. I ask for microfilm for back issues. As I thread the film, it feels like such ancient technology, like a spinning wheel, and I wonder how much longer it will exist. I can't say I'll miss it.

The first article was written in August 1992. A former employee of Silvanus and founding partner, Ted Duncan, sued Silvanus for breach of contract. It appears that he was promised certain stock options as part of his terms of employment. When he decided to leave the company and wanted to cash in his shares, Silvanus diluted the stock, issuing one million more shares, in effect making his millions of dollars of stock worth no more than several thousand. "Who do they think got this company up and running?" he's quoted as saying. The case was settled out of court for an undisclosed amount of money.

The second article was written in 1998. Silvanus planned a merger with Biobreed, Inc., a biogenetic company involved in developing synthetic animal hormones and immunizations primarily for the swine industry. " 'We are very excited about the synergy of these two companies,' says Dr. Bryant Hillary. 'The way these two companies fit together, Biobreed's research, its wide network and expertise in animal husbandry, and our marketing provide infinite possibilities for growth and expansion.' "

My mind spins. It doesn't fit: a company that produces tissue replacement product and a drug company. I don't get it. And what exactly is "tissue replacement product"?

On the Internet, I find no references to Silvanus apart from their own Web site. It appears hospitals can order tissue right over the Web, but the catalog is not accessible without preregistration. For the fun of it, I make up the name of a hospital, St. Bertha's in Santa Monica. The second page of the registration form looks like an income tax return and requests federal ID numbers, doctors' names, institutional charge numbers, and so on.

I give up, then think to myself, If something were amiss in the company, who would be more likely to talk about it than a disgruntled former employee? I do an e-mail search for Ted Duncans in California and come up with about thirty-five names. I print them out and plan to whittle down the possibilities later.

*　　　*　　　*

I find Carol Nims in her office at the hospital. I hand her a bouquet of orange tiger lilies. "I thought you might need something to brighten your day," I say. She starts to blubber. The easiest way to ensnare the affections of those who feel underappreciated is to show small graces. I feel guilty for being manipulative . . . for a second.

"You know," she says, "after your last visit, I had to talk with another possible donor family, and when I started the sales pitch . . . well . . . I lost it. I started to cry and the mother cried. The father cried. It felt so good. All these years I thought I had to keep all these emotions hidden, but it helped me. The family donated their son's organs."

"I'm so pleased." The poor girl doesn't know how hard I'm trying to keep the sarcasm out of my voice.

"I feel so much better. Look!" She shows me her hands. "My rash is almost gone."

I think she's moving to hug me, so I turn to close the door. "I wondered if you might be able to help me with something," I say.

"Anything. Absolutely anything." Her face relaxes, her eyes sparkle, her cheeks glow.

"As you know, I'm doing research on organ donation for my students. I keep on running into the name Silvanus Corporation."

"Oh," she says, her face falling.

"But it's a private company, and I can't really find out much about them."

She is quiet for a moment. I see the wheels turning inside her head. She shifts in her seat; when she speaks, her voice becomes cool and pragmatic. "It's illegal to buy or sell human organs. Has been since 1984. But companies get around the law by charging what they call 'processing fees.' For instance, there is a company that takes donated hearts that aren't suitable for transplantation, preserves the valves by deep-freezing, then sells them back to cardiologists and heart surgeons. They get around $3,500 each for an aortic valve and a pulmonary valve. They reimburse $450 to the hospital that donated the organ, which makes their profit about $6,000 a heart."

My eyes become big as saucers. She nods in agreement, then continues. "Well, Silvanus is a company that processes bone, tendon, ligaments, cartilage, and connective tissue. When they hear of a potential tissue donor, they rush to the hospital or morgue and take their tissues, bone, skin, dura mater, whatever. Hospitals give it to them or charge a small administrative fee. Silvanus processes the tissue, sterilizes it, tests it for infection, packages and freezes it. Then they sell it back to doctors."

The image of vultures comes to mind.

She recites a menu of processing fees: ribs $150; bone dowels $200 an inch; thighbones $500; knee joints $2,600; three ear bones $750; powdered bone $200 a gram. "A body is never completely harvested, but a single cadaver easily generates $25,000 for a tissue bank." She adds that to avoid any appearance of impropriety, Silvanus procures the tissue and bone through a nonprofit subsidiary called Ossotech Foundation. The tissue is then processed and sold through Silvanus.

"So most of us are worth more dead than alive."

"That's right. Silvanus also gives generously to major hospitals and medical schools, which guarantees them a strong market as well as a certain amount of myopia when it comes to their business practices."

"This is legal?"

"Legal and unregulated."

"Did you know that Silvanus paid for the health insurance for one of your organ donors?"

She looks genuinely surprised. Why would she know about insurance? That's a different department. "No," she says softly, "I didn't know that."

"Do the families who donate their child's body know that companies are making a profit off them?"

"No." Again her voice is soft, childlike.

"Doesn't that make it hard for you to ask them to donate?"

She starts to cry again. "Yes, but we save lives."

Disgusted, I turn and leave.

The telephone rattles, waking me from a deep sleep.

"Frances, is that you?"

"Hello. Who's this?"

"Matty Webster, coroner's office. I did an analysis of the hair and tissue samples that you wanted."

I prop myself up on my elbow and try to shake myself awake. "What made you change your mind?"

"When I heard you were claiming his body and you were paying for his cremation, I took some tissue samples. I figured if you cared enough—" His voice cracks. He clears his throat, then pauses for a moment. When he speaks again, his voice is soft and tentative. "My father didn't claim me until I was five years old. I was living in a bamboo shack in the middle of a rice paddy. My mother had just died. Somehow he got word and took me out of Vietnam back to the States. I know what it feels like to be abandoned. You seemed to care about this boy. . . ." His voice drifts off, or else I am drifting back to sleep, deep into the black swamps of Vietnam.

My head slams against the headboard and I wake up. "What did you find out?" I ask.

"Well, there were extremely high levels of prednisone and cyclosporine in his tissue. Those are two drugs that are administered to patients with organ transplants."

"Are you telling me Tomás had an organ transplant?"

"No . . . let me finish. Sometimes, as a preventive measure against rejection, the organ donor is pumped up with cyclosporine before the transplant. They hope it will mitigate the rejection response of the recipient's immune system."

"You think they gave it to him before they took his organs?"

"Well, the thing is, traces of cyclosporine were all through his hair, from the roots to the ends. He was on the drug for at least four months."

"But he was only admitted for head trauma fifteen days before he died."

"That's what I'm saying."

"Oh . . . so either Tomás received a transplant that is not in any of his medical records, or someone was thinking of using him as an organ donor long before he ever hurt his head."

"That's what I'm thinking."

"Did you find out anything that might indicate how he died?"

"Like a poison or something? No."

"Should we inform the police?"

"They would dismiss it as irrelevant. The drugs prednisone and cyclosporine didn't cause his death, and the body has been cremated, so there's no chance for further investigation."

"I destroyed the only evidence."

There's something flirtatious in his voice. "That you did, Red. Don't feel so bad. I think cremation is the only civilized choice. It's how I'd want to go."

"I'll keep that in mind." I hang up without saying good-bye.

The Hall of Records for Los Angeles County sits at the end of a maze of dank underground passages in the basement of City Hall. The halls are dark and smell of rats and mildew. The passageway never ends, twisting and turning, the sloping floor descending farther and farther beneath the city. Like our private primordial perversities, the most important papers that document our lives are buried deep in the stinking earth. The only thing that keeps me from panicking is the handful of other people, unbelieving and confused, scattered throughout the hallways.

From the dark I step into a room white with fluorescent lights. I think of descriptions of near death experiences and wonder what I'm in for.

Messy shelves crammed with loose folders line the walls reaching from the floor to the twenty-foot ceiling. The public is barricaded from the files by a low wooden fence and a long counter. In front of the counter, impatient white people stand in a line, rocking, hopping from foot to foot, cursing under their breath. Periodically, like geysers, they sigh, then complain about how long they've waited. Behind the counter two obese black women and a young Hispanic man move in slow motion. Their day is eight hours long whether they help us or not. Half the time they come back to the counter and say they can't find the record and to go look through the card catalog. Nothing is computerized.

Finally it's my turn, and I ask for the death record of Tomás's father, Fernandez Gomez. I take the microfilm to an empty machine, and as I begin stringing in the film, a young man comes by and tells me it's broken. I wait ten minutes for another machine.

I page through the ghostly images until I find his records. The death certificate is signed by Vincent Bartholomew at the coroner's office. Death from two gunshot wounds to the head, .32-caliber police issue. The only other document on him is his green card. He was born in 1947 in Toluca, Mexico, and died in 1999 in Los Angeles. Never obtained U.S. citizenship. His occupation is listed as merchant. He's listed as married, but his wife's name isn't mentioned. No property deeds, no legal petitions, no indication he had a son named Tomás.

I call Matty Webster at home. When he picks up, I hear Roy Orbison crooning in the background and Webster munching something crunchy.

"Could you get me the autopsy report for Tomás's father? His name was Fernandez Gomez. Died March 1999, head gunshot wound, police issue."

"Are you kidding? Intense. Sure, I'll track it down." His voice is excited; he sounds like a kid with a new video game. "Hey, Frances, you wouldn't want to go out for lunch sometime, would you?"

"I'm allergic to tortilla chips," I say.

He laughs and hangs up.

CHAPTER

10

I do not have a lot of casual friends. I seldom go to parties, and wherever people go nowadays to meet people socially—health clubs, investment seminars, art classes—I do not go. Yet I have saved many people from the hell of watching someone they love suffer in terrible pain, helpless in the face of a market-driven health care system, and often they beg me to allow them to return the favor.

Several years ago, I helped a police officer with his wife, who was dying of breast cancer. I call him and ask him whom to talk to about a suspicious death in Venice. He gives me the name of Detective Lieutenant Paul Ortiz, Pacific Division. I call, and Ortiz agrees to meet with me tomorrow.

Los Angeles has the beauty of a scarred and cynical young woman who, in rare moments, when caught in a spontaneous laugh, radiates a transcendent perfection that takes your breath away.

Driving down Venice Boulevard to Culver City is not one of those moments.

I turn down Centinela Avenue, past the strip malls, a botanica, a *carnecería,* auto parts stores, pawnshops, signage in Spanish and English, bars on all the windows, trash cans overflowing, the word *Coffins* painted across the side of a garage, beat-up dusty Datsuns and fifteen-year-old Toyota trucks lining the streets, parked askew as if their owners arrived home at two in the morning, drunk. I drive past Culver Boulevard and on the first pass miss the one-story, brown brick building, despite the thirty-inch blue letters that spell out "Police." I glance over my shoulder and make an illegal U-turn. No police around.

I turn into the parking lot. The building is prosaic, apologetic, as if the city were embarrassed that it had to have police at all. It makes me sad, for in truth, police are an idea of peace and security, and what is more important to a community than that? But by an odd twist of history, the inherent violence of a city growing too quickly, the clash of many cultures, bad politics, and poor management, the LAPD is caught in the middle and blamed for our disharmony. So they slink around the edges, hoping to keep the lid on while not being noticed. In turn, ordinary citizens pretend the police don't exist and scurry by, heads down, minding their own business, acting guilty without cause or reason.

We do not love our police.

When I enter the station, I do not expect courtesy, but my request to speak with Detective Lieutenant Ortiz is met with a cool efficiency that, if it were not so wearily wary, might be considered politeness. I'm told to wait and that he'll be right with me. In a few minutes, a black female officer shows me back through a labyrinth of desks and blue uniforms.

He doesn't stand when I enter his office. He motions to a battered captain's chair in front of his desk. He presses a button on the telephone and asks the front desk to hold his calls.

I sit down. He has honey skin and black hair neatly cut and parted on the side, making him look like a kid just out of business school. He is stocky, with a square face and big sausage fingers. Meaty and solid. He holds a pen in his right hand, and he is staring down at the ink blotter on his desk. He seems transfixed for several moments, taps his pen three times as if undoing a spell, then looks up at me. His eyes are alert and observing.

"How can I help you, Miss Frances?" he says without smiling.

I haven't been called Miss Frances since the choir-mistress caught me switching organ pipes in the chapel. Although lovely and old-fashioned, it makes me feel as if I'm in trouble. I suspect that's what Ortiz intends.

I tell him about Tomás, how I left him for an hour when he was in a coma, really more like a deep sleep, and when I came back he was dead.

His listens quietly without moving, then lets several moments of silence pass before he speaks. "Miss Frances, weren't you hired to help the boy die?" He has no accent, and his voice resonates rich, golden tones. Like a cello in the woods.

"Yes. But he didn't die naturally. Somebody killed him."

"And how do you know this?"

"I just do. I'm a deathmaiden." I can tell this explanation doesn't carry much weight with him. I'm sure he thinks I'm a crackpot.

"Do you have any evidence that he died at the hands of another?" His way of speaking is oddly formal, like that of a funeral director.

I tell him about the presence of prednisone and cyclosporine in Tomás's hair and skin tissue, which apparently had been administered long before his head trauma, of how the dispatcher records indicate the ambulance was called before Tomás died, of how the woman who hired me was not his mother, but a maid to some doctor, of the house rented by Silvanus, a company that recycles body tissue from organ donors.

"So you think the hospital murdered him so they could harvest his organs?"

"I don't know."

Ortiz locks his hands together and rests his chin on his fists. He seems to find me tiresome. "I realize there is a shortage of people willing to donate their organs, but I can hardly believe the hospital would murder young children for their body parts. Not that I think they're above it, but it wouldn't make business sense for them to take such risks."

"But somebody did," I say.

He sits silently for nearly a half minute, staring down at his blotter, tapping the point of his pen. Then he looks at me as if he's deciding whether or not to tell me something. He slides a folder in front of him. "When you called, I pulled the file for the boy's father, Fernandez Gomez, from archives. He was arrested for drug trafficking, resisted arrest, and was shot. Anytime a police officer's gun goes off, there is a full internal investigation. There was no indication of wrongdoing on the part of the police officers."

"What quantity of drugs was confiscated?"

Ortiz opens the file and flips through several pages. Recently it seems I spend a lot of time looking at people riffling through files I want to see. "They found two and a half pounds of marijuana in some clay pots."

"I don't know much about drug enforcement, but that doesn't seem enough to involve a police sting, does it?"

"It wasn't a police sting. He was stopped near the border for a bad taillight. He must have panicked."

We sit in silence for a moment. Then something occurs to me. "You said the marijuana was in clay pots?"

"Yes." He looks through the file again and hands me a photo. It shows the rear of a truck, with several dozen crates stacked inside. Two open crates sit on the ground with splintered wood scattered over the shoulder of the road. At the point the photo was taken, the policemen must've opened the crates and found the drugs. Standing upright amid yellow straw, like gifts before the Christ child, are two clay cisterns. One is bell shaped, sitting on a tripod of breastlike legs, burnt orange with a stag dancing across the top, embellished with red, orange, and black designs. The other is squat, extremely textured with profiles, feathers, serpents, leaves. It looks as though the craftsman applied flat cutouts of clay to the surface of the jar, layer upon layer.

They are exquisite.

"It reminds me of a story I once heard," I say. "Before the Berlin Wall came down, East German police noticed a man who biked back and forth across the border every day. They suspected him of smuggling, but when they searched him, they found nothing but a heel of bread and some hard cheese for his lunch. One day, as the man biked west on his rusty old bike, a guard commented that he needed a new one. As it happens, the same guard stayed on for a double shift and saw the man bike back that evening. On an expensive, brand-new bike. Turns out the man was smuggling bikes."

Ortiz looks at me. "You think he was smuggling pots?"

"Aztec or Mayan artifacts. He probably brought in the marijuana as an afterthought, for friends."

Ortiz closes the file, sits back in his chair, and taps his pen. "What would you have the police do?"

"I don't know," I say feebly.

Ortiz watches me silently for a few moments. "The circumstances that you describe concerning the boy, while curious, are not illegal. I can document your complaint, but without evidence of illegal activity, I cannot open an investigation. As far as your speculation about his father . . ." He lets his voice trail off and shrugs.

"What happened to the truck of pots?"

He raises his eyebrows, surprised. "They would have been impounded along with the drugs. After the case was closed, the drugs would've been destroyed. The pots were probably auctioned."

"Who bought them?"

"There should be a note." He shuffles through the file again. "An antiques dealer on Melrose Avenue by the name of Elmer Afner."

"How much did he buy them for?"

"Two thousand dollars."

I suddenly feel overcome with anger but try to keep my voice steady. "Did it ever occur to the police that the only person who would know the police were auctioning off priceless Mexican pottery would be the person who hired Fernandez Gomez to smuggle them in the first place?"

"The pots really weren't a concern of ours. We thought they were a cover for drug trafficking."

"What's the address of this antiques dealer?"

Ortiz looks at me sternly. "Miss Frances, I highly recommend that you do not attempt amateur sleuthing. Although it appears you are on friendly terms with the coroner, I would not want to be the one to have to call him on your behalf."

"If you think that's a possibility, then you think there might be something to my story."

Ortiz sighs wearily. "You are a bright woman, Miss Frances. You were hired to help a young boy die, and he died. Please, let it alone."

I look deep into his murky brown eyes. "The problem is," I say, "that I can't."

I have heard other deathmaidens talk of how they can hypnotize people with their eyes. This, of course, is strictly forbidden. Any powers we develop for our art are to be used only to assist the dying. I cannot hypnotize with my eyes. I have never tried. But then, I have never wanted anything as much as I want Ortiz to believe me.

Before I leave, I slide my hand over his desk, take the photo of the pots, and slip it into my purse. He sees me do this and says nothing. I get up and walk briskly to the door.

"Miss Frances."

Slowly I turn, my face hot, tingling with embarrassment. I reach into my purse and finger the edge of the photo, ready to surrender it.

"Have a good day." Ortiz is smiling.

I nod my head, confused, annoyed that Ortiz seems to

have gotten the upper hand. A thought stabs me in the solar plexus, then a pain shoots up the back of my spine to behind my eyes. I turn and look at him. "That tumor they found in your colon? Don't worry about it. It'll be gone tomorrow."

He pales. I smile victoriously, then leave.

CHAPTER

11

I have taken leave, so I am surprised when I get a call from my supervisor, Charlotte Wright.

Charlotte is part dispatcher, part spiritual guide, part teacher. After a series of death threats in the 1980s and the bombing of the hospice unit in a New Jersey convalescent home, all gatherings of deathmaidens were discontinued outside of Mexico. The teachers at the institute realized our country was entering a period of intolerance, a period in which violent religious fundamentalism was considered, if not acceptable, certainly understandable. Crimes against abortion clinics, for instance, were seldom solved and never prosecuted. Gatherings made us vulnerable to attack. So our local supervisor remains our primary link to the society.

She sounds disturbed. "I hear you have been asking questions about one of your last assignments, Tomás Gomez."

I wonder how she's found out. Someone at the hospital? Detective Lieutenant Ortiz? I tell her about my doubts. I hear nothing but silence on the other end of the line. I know she is praying for direction. "Do you understand the seriousness of this situation, of the danger in which you are placing the society? Do you know what will happen if it were to come out that a child who was not terminal but merely comatose was helped to pass on by a deathmaiden?"

"But I didn't help him pass on," I protest.

"That's not how it looks and you know it. By raising questions like this, you are opening us up for attack."

"But we can't sit back and let ourselves be used as a cover for murder! We can't—"

"Frances, listen to me. The right-wing pro-life movement will tear us apart with a scandal like this. Vernon Keyes is waiting for something like this to destroy us." She's referring to a leader of the Christian Right, who during the Reagan administration nearly succeeded in getting a bill passed through Congress outlawing the Society of Deathmaidens. "This is the first time we have been used like this. We will watch vigilantly."

"But a child was murdered. I am sure of it." I try to keep my voice steady, respectful.

Again I hear silence. "You have no proof, Frances," she finally says. "We must watch and wait. Be wise as a serpent, harmless as a dove."

I hang up, furious. I think of Miguel's spit dripping down the bus window as I left Mexico and feel the pain of thwarted love.

I realize that I cannot remain passive in the face of murder, even if I do put my sisterhood in jeopardy.

*   *   *

I meet Matty Webster at Chinese Friends on North Broadway in Chinatown, a tiny, stark restaurant the size of a one-car garage with white Formica tile floors and cheap imitation-wood tables, a favorite among downtown bureaucrats, reporters for the *Los Angeles Times,* and Chinese locals. It has all the ambiance of a school cafeteria, but the food is good and cheap.

I have the unpleasant feeling that Matty might be getting a crush on me, but I dismiss the thought with a shiver. He couldn't possibly, could he? But there he is, face beaming, smelling faintly of formaldehyde, slopping down his shrimp fried rice, punctuating his sentences with a posed smirk as if to make sure I catch him at his wittiest.

"I can't let you look at the report," he says, his lips snagged between a taunt and a goofy grin. I imagine him teasing his little sister. Little sister I am not, considering I'm half a foot taller than him. "But I will tell you about it." He wipes his mouth, then places his fingertips on the edge of the report as if it were a Ouija board. "Are you really a redhead?"

"Yes." My annoyance seems only to encourage him.

"You don't mind if I call you Red, do you?"

I fight an urge to kick him and limit myself to a raised eyebrow. That seems to do the trick.

"Okay, okay. Fernandez Gomez was shot twice in the brain, both thirty-two-caliber bullets. He was rushed to the hospital and pronounced brain-dead. The doctors wanted to use him as an organ donor. He had no immediate family, so the transplant coordinator called downtown. The district attorney's office gave permission for the harvesting of his organs, but because Gomez was still part of a criminal investigation, the coroner went to the hospital to oversee the removal of his organs, then did the autopsy there in the operating room."

"Both father and son were organ donors?"

"Odd, isn't it. But just a coincidence, as far as I can see."

A thought then occurs to me. "Does it mention who the physicians were who removed his organs?"

"It should." He flips through the report. "Dr. Clyde Faust and Dr. Seth Cohen."

One of the same doctors who operated on Tomás. How odd indeed.

It is dark by the time I get back to the coast. It is late October, and the time has changed. Spring forward, fall back. Every year it shocks me. I take it as a personal offense. One hour stolen from me each spring. It shakes up my life. There are so few absolutes in life. Birth, death, taxes. Time is one of those things we rely on to be immutable. Then, twice a year, it changes.

I arrive home, expecting it also to be the same, not to have changed, but it has. As soon as I get out of my car, I know something is wrong.

Usually, at this time of the evening, the Palisades cool rapidly from onshore sea breezes. As warm air, trapped in the canyons, seeps up the hill to my house, crows and eagles ride the thermals, gliding in figure eights. When I walk up the redwood steps to my front door, a grocery bag hanging from each hand, I notice two changes. First, instead of a cool breeze, the air is stagnant. Second, there are no birds.

Many people fear death. Much of my job deals with allaying these fears: fear of pain and suffering; fear of punishment in the afterlife; fear of being separated from loved ones, of being alone, of being a burden, of losing dignity; fear of failure, of a life unrealized; fear of the unknown; fear of being trapped by life-support machines in the hospital.

Many people fear death. I fear invasion of my privacy. I do not want to be on mailing lists, I do not want to speak on the telephone to people I don't know, I do not want my supermarket to know my spending habits. Apart from the inevitable invasion from the IRS and the DMV, I try to limit my exposure to computer lists and marketers. I use my credit card only for emergencies, my phone number is unlisted, I don't register to vote, I give to charities anonymously, I belong to no clubs, I have no magazine subscriptions, I never enter sweepstakes.

Nothing makes me sink more quickly from the spiritual to the empirical than someone trying to sell me something.

As a deathmaiden, I've learned to take precautions. Every day when I lock the door, I stick a small piece of paper between the door and the doorjamb, then arrange a half dozen pinecones in a pattern on the landing in front of my door. I see from the driveway that the pinecones have been disturbed. On occasion, neighborhood cats or wild animals will move the pinecones. But it is my first line of defense. I approach with caution. I set down my groceries and climb the hill beside the steps, my heels snagging in the hard dirt. I slide my hands along the side of the house and peek into the living room window.

A chill pours over my body like a bucket of cold water.

I feel someone is watching me, that feeling you have as a child, alone in the dark, waiting for that monster who lives under your bed to grab your ankle. I withdraw slowly, then crawl to the front door. I see the paper in the doorjamb is missing. I've been invaded.

I decide to face the intruder head-on. I slide back down the hill, pick up my groceries, and walk up the front steps. I make a lot of noise. The front door is unlocked. I swing it open and switch on the lights.

No one is there. I set down my groceries in the kitchen. I notice the drawers have been opened and closed.

Cat mews at me from outside the sliding glass doors. She must've escaped when the intruder came in. I rush to slide open the doors, pluck her up, and bury my nose in her fur. Thank God, she's all right. I surprise myself at how much her presence relieves me, her spirit vanquishing the rage of violation.

The damn cat has made me love her.

There is a smell I can't put my finger on, perfume, sweat, and something reminiscent of a beef stock with garlic and onions.

In the bedroom, all the drawers are open, the contents shaken up. The pictures on the walls are askew. In the bathroom, they've squirted my perfume.

I can't imagine what they were looking for. Nothing seems to be missing, but everything is open, ajar, crooked. It's as if they simply want me to know they've been here.

Deathmaidens tend not to marry or have close ties to their family. A close family distracts them from their work and makes them vulnerable to threats. If their love and passions are tied too closely to the empirical world, to homes and family, they lose the emotional abandon they need to traverse the metaphysical. Some deathmaidens can handle a family. I cannot.

I do allow myself to love beautiful things. If someone slashes a painting, I may grieve, but the painting feels nothing. In my spare time, I buy modern paintings from artists I think may one day be famous, works that make me feel something new each time I look at them. I also love English farm animal portraits from the eighteenth and nineteenth centuries, cows and pigs with bizarre tumorous bellies and goofy grins.

The only pieces I have of any real value are my ceramics, faience from Italy, majolica, Greek vases. My prize piece is a Mexican bowl that sits in the center of my dining room table. Whimsical animals dance around the edge, and inside are delicately painted camellia blossoms.

I see the Mexican bowl has been moved a few inches. I look inside.

Someone has left me a human turd.

PART TWO

The Realm of Bewildered Spirits

CHAPTER

12

I turn off Sepulveda into the Getty parking structure, a dark and cavernous pit that winds deep into the earth. After locking the car, I ride an elevator up three floors, exiting onto an elegant plaza. I stand and admire the jacaranda and willow trees planted in neat rows, waiting with others like me, in a purgatorial hush, for the silent tram to descend the hill and take me aloft.

I step onto the tram, which then moves through the olive trees and up the hill with python stealth. I float, my body weightless, ascending slowly as the land of urban sprawl pulls away. Below, on the 405 freeway, the ribbon of bumper-to-bumper cars appears sublime and beautiful. Above, the museum comes into view, a sparkling jewel, beneficent and ethereal, white and imperious, drawing me toward it. The gleaming chariot carries me from the dark up through a tunnel to the sun. I step out into a city paved in light.

If I believed in such things as heaven and hell, heaven for me would look like the Getty Center.

I step out before a reflection pool, which, like the river Styx, washes away my earthly memory. I am prepared to be amazed.

Apart from the museum, half a dozen other buildings lie scattered over the top of the hill like temples of the Acropolis, jutting out at odd angles, creating a geometric play of light and shadow. I look up and see a long expanse of steps in glowing coffee-colored travertine rock striated like a scoop of cold ice cream. Climbing the steps, I find myself completely absorbed by the intersecting planes, the contrasting textures of steel, glass, and polished stone, shifting like a kaleidoscope as I walk. I seek signs for the Mayan exhibit.

I enter a gallery on the ground floor, dark and cool like the interior of a pyramid. Mayan artifacts are lit dramatically within glass cases. The first room has foot-high burial figurines of Mayan royalty. I pause before the head of Lord Pacal: a long triangular nose, high cheekbones, full lips, Asian eyes, and a forehead sloped away from his brow. The caption above the sculpture says that royal mothers wrapped the heads of their babies to force their skulls into high, sloped foreheads. It was the mark of royalty.

In his features, I see the face of Tomás.

I study a reproduction of a mural discovered in the Mayan city of Bonampak. In soft, seductive shades of turquoise and tangerine, it depicts Mayan royalty draped in jaguar skins and plumed headdresses topped with the heads of stags and jaguars. They stand on top of a dozen steps, looking proud and noble, I think, until I realize they are torturing prisoners by pulling out their finger-nails, then decapitating them.

Beside the mural is a figurine of a captive victim of sacrifice, his head twisted over his shoulder, howling in unimaginable pain, his body disemboweled, his hands and feet mangled. He wears a belt of wood bound to his back that his captors will set on fire. I am horrified. The artist dramatizes an excruciating moment of terror and suffering. I think of Picasso's *Guernica*.

I feel a presence behind me. I turn. A tall man stands looking over my shoulder. He has brown, shoulder-length hair and is wearing a stylish leather jacket, black jeans, and boots. Beneath his jacket, a finely spun Italian sweater. Over his shoulder hangs a bag of rainbow colors made from Guatemalan textiles. Holding a small black note-book, he sketches the twisted figurine in front of us. His fingers are long, and he wears a chunky gold ring on the pinkie of his left hand. There is something vaguely Byronic about him.

"Before they found this temple at Bonampak, archae-ologists thought the Maya were a peaceful civilization." He doesn't look at me as he speaks but continues to draw, his eyes glancing up and down at the page, his voice low and melodic with a Northern European accent. "The Aztecs were supposed to be the bad guys with all their wars and human sacrifices. Turns out the Maya were just as brutal."

Unlike many tall women, I love to wear heels. This puts me eye to eye with the man behind me. "Are you an artist?" I ask.

"No. I can't draw very well, but the museum doesn't

allow cameras, and I sure don't want to forget these images."

I step back and peek over his left arm. I've always had a soft spot for lefties. I expect him to snap shut his sketchbook, but he lets me look. His quick pencil drawings capture the suffering, the ecstasy, and the exotic drama of the art.

"Mayan cities were vast and sophisticated," he continues, "but within a few years, they dissolved back into the jungle. Nobody knows why. Maybe war, maybe drought and famine, maybe overpopulation, revolution. Nobody knows. A vanished civilization."

He smells like a gentlemen's hunting lodge, of woodsmoke, port, cinnamon, and deer stew. It makes me want to reach up under his leather jacket and root around the folds of his sweater.

"Maybe someday archaeologists will say that about Los Angeles."

"No, Los Angeles is like the Milky Way. It'll continue expanding until the end of time."

I laugh, surprised by the sound of it. Light and girlish. I realize it's the first time I've laughed out loud in weeks. Since my house was ransacked, my emotions have swung violently from guarded and suspicious to brazen and reckless. In surrendering my privacy, I shiver with a newfound freedom; sensing there is less to lose, I feel bold and slightly out of control. The anger of violation spurs me to daring.

And now I'm tittering.

The guard who stands at the doorway looks at me hard. Apparently he disapproves of levity.

"Come. You've got to see this." My new friend takes

my elbow and pulls me into the next room. In the display case is a sculpture, a grimacing figure, seated, legs crossed, a sharp wedge in his right hand pressing down on his testicles. "He's a priest, bleeding himself for sacrifice. It's part of their religious ceremony. Sacrificial bloodletting. They ran barbed ropes through their tongues and earlobes, too."

His enthusiasm seems a tad morbid, but I, too, am fascinated, drawn to the unrelenting tension of the figure's arms and neck. "What's the point?"

"It's hard for us to understand, but the concept is fundamental to all ancient religions. Sacrifice means 'to make holy,' from *sacer,* meaning 'holy,' and *facere,* 'to make.' In Mayan mythology, the gods offered their own blood to create the world, the sun, and the moon. They believed that maintaining life itself required them to mirror the self-sacrifice of the creator gods by offering their own blood."

I think of making some sarcastic comment about his expertise on sacrifice but am lulled into silence by his voice; I want to hear more.

"Maya priests engaged in autosacrifice nightly, piercing their earlobes or genitals and drawing through a rope with maguey thorns. They dripped their blood over offering plates filled with strips of paper, which were then set on fire. The sacred smoke carried their supplications to the gods." He points to a decorated pot in another case. "Like over here, you'll see images of the smoke turning into serpents, the symbol of ecstatic revelation. The whole purpose of bloodletting was to achieve ecstatic vision, oneness with God, through agony to divine rapture."

The face on the sculpture is a mixture of concentration and arousal, ecstasy and cruelty. I vaguely remember seeing that face before. It's the face of male orgasm.

The museum is cold. He stands close behind me. My skin tingles, my breath quickens; I feel his warmth like a thermal rising from a desert ravine. It's been a long time since I've let a healthy adult male in my territory.

He steps away as if pricked, as if he senses my arousal. "My name is Jack." He gives me his card. Jack Halmstad, photographer, white letters against a black-and-white photo of a Mexican boy playing soccer by himself on a rutted muddy road.

I can't resist touching him, and because I must, I turn his wrist to glance at his watch. I have an appointment. I don't want to go. I want to stay here in the dark with this man who smells like a hunting lodge.

"You have an interesting face," he says. "I'd like to take photos of you sometime." Again I laugh, immediately annoyed that I respond to such a clichéd come-on. He blushes. "I'm sorry. That didn't come out right, did it?" He feigns remorse, then gives me a crooked smile— the impish charm of a six-year-old who's learned how to get his way. I melt inside.

I shake my head and scurry to my appointment, feeling much too old for this kind of thing.

In the research building, one of the smaller temples below the museum, I meet Lloyd Overton, curator of the Mayan exhibit. He is a slight man, clean-shaven and balding, who speaks in a deliberate, overly articulated manner. As he fingers Tomás's jade in his palm, I gaze out the glass wall of his office; rising out of the haze, sparkling against the marine hills, the city is so beautiful, so silently awesome, my heart fills with guilt for the times I've cursed it.

"You can find these all around southern Mexico and Guatemala," Overton tells me. "Sometimes just sitting on top of the ground. Farmers are always picking them up."

"What were they used for?"

"Amulets. Jewelry. This one is of the jaguar sun god. A nice piece. Very good quality jade."

"Is it valuable?"

"To a certain extent, probably more from an archaeological point of view than as art. A piece like this at auction might be worth a hundred dollars. Jade was the Maya's most precious stone, you know. They believed it had secret powers. Mayan royalty wore it to assure themselves of their birthright."

I show him the photo of pots I took from Detective Lieutenant Ortiz. Overton's eyes get real big. "Where did you get this?" he barks.

I tell him, and he shakes his head. "Smuggling and grave robbing have always been a problem, but it's become epidemic in the last ten years. For a long time, the pyramids were somewhat protected. They contain little gold and were hidden deep in the jungles. The local Indians were superstitious and left them alone to disintegrate. The Mexican government didn't seem to have any interest. But then the art market for Mayan artifacts got hot—very hot—particularly in Europe and Japan. As you can imagine, many private collectors—Russian, American, Brazilian—have no qualms about buying stolen treasures."

"What can you tell me about these two pots?"

"Well . . . this tripod one with the breasts . . . I've seen similar pots from the Guatemalan highlands. It was probably ceremonial, used to catch blood. Human blood. See the slits on the legs? They inserted tiny clay balls inside so it rattled when the priests shook it. It's probably from the early classic period."

"When's that?"

"Oh . . . from, say, A.D. 250 to 600. This other piece you have is also probably a ceremonial vessel . . . from the late classic period, about A.D. 600 to 900. Probably used for the heart."

"The heart?"

"During a sacrifice, four men would pin down a captive to a sacrificial stone on top of a pyramid, each with an arm or leg. The priest slashed open the chest and ripped out the heart. Then they rolled the body down the steps of the pyramid, fertilizing the earth with blood."

I look away, out Overton's window across the Getty Acropolis, and imagine Maya priests standing high on their pyramids, tracking the shadows of sun and moon, attempting to discern the will of the gods. As the sun sinks below the horizon, setting office buildings ablaze, Catalina rises out of the purple mist like the lost island of Atlantis; I think about Tomás, sacrifice, and his human priests.

Overton interprets my stunned silence as fascination. "If you're interested in human sacrifice and Mayan ritual, you might talk to Chris Jensen." He circles a name at the bottom of a Getty brochure and hands it to me. "He teaches anthropology at UCLA and helped us put the show together. He's very into the whole human sacrifice thing."

I put the brochure in my purse. "How much are these pots worth?"

"They're priceless, of course . . . but on the open market, I'd say between fifty and one hundred thousand dollars each. Nowadays the Mexican government doesn't allow artifacts to be taken out of the country. Anything for sale is contraband."

"Where did the pieces in the exhibit come from?"

He suddenly looks upset. I've insulted him. His Adam's apple bobs up and down his neck like the strongman's gavel at the county fair. "The Getty would never procure something from the black market. All the pieces here are on loan from museums in Mexico and in the United States, brought back by archaeologists before Mexico's antiquities laws were enacted."

"I'm sorry. I didn't mean to imply anything. However, I need to know where, perhaps, this smuggler was planning to sell these pots."

"No need to apologize," he says, still offended. "We're . . . sensitive about it. Hell, all museums are sensitive about it. We all have pieces in our collections with dubious pasts. But to answer your question, I've heard of a fellow on Melrose Avenue, an antiques dealer who knows how to get Mayan and Aztec pieces for a price."

"Have you met him?"

"Of course not," he snaps. "You just hear about these things."

"What's his name?"

"I don't know his name. But his store is called the Golden Bough."

CHAPTER

13

Rain comes to Los Angeles like a distant recollection, jerking us back into a murky past we'd rather forget. Like suppressed memory, it comes upon us despite our denials. In some people it brings out dark, brooding emotions; in others, an awakening sensuality. Perhaps because of our balmy climate, an ever present sun that calls us outside, we are not a reflective people. But when the rains do come, it hits us all at once, and just as we are unprepared for the downpour—the sewers backing up, the streets flooding, the roofs leaking—we are never ready for the accompanying flood of emotions. We become ragged and vulnerable, we get sick, we have accidents, we crawl into our beds frightened, listening to the pounding rain, hoping we'll come out okay in the end.

Rain for us is a small death, a small preparation for the real thing.

It is raining the day I drive down Melrose Avenue

looking for the Golden Bough. Deep ponds form at intersections. The few cars that have ventured out charge through the puddles, splashing giant tsunamis across the street as if momentum is what will get them through. The strip malls and stucco chain stores, which in the sun have the appearance of shoddy convenience, sag like soaked milk cartons into the sidewalk. Unlike some cities that are made more beautiful without cars and pedestrians, unpeopled Los Angeles looks like roadside trash.

There is, however, plenty of parking. The Golden Bough sits between a store that sells art deco furniture and an S&M adult toy store that calls itself Pandora's Box.

A cowbell clanks when I walk in. It is dark. The moist air brings out smells of mildew, dust, and urine. A motheaten, three-legged pug hobbles toward me, yapping. Slowly, my eyes adjust to the darkness. It looks like a not particularly well-organized garage sale: Marilyn Monroe posters, top hats, leopard-print furniture, birdcages, Tiffany lamps, signed photos of Cary Grant, Jean Harlow, George Raft, a white feather boa draped over a photo of Mae West. Discarded trappings of glamour.

A man in his fifties shuffles out from the back. He is short and skinny, with a fringe of gray hair that circles his bald pate like fog at the base of Mount Fuji. "Pugsley, go to your bed," he commands. The dog sneezes at me, then waddles to the back room. The man looks at me over half-glasses that sit on the middle of a long hooked nose. "Elmer Afner, at your service."

I shouldn't have been surprised. Here was the antiques dealer Detective Lieutenant Ortiz said bought the police-auctioned Mayan pots.

"I'm looking for something a little unusual as a gift for

my sister," I say. An image suddenly pops into my mind of this fabricated sister, a widow, an eccentric collector who lives in Santa Barbara in a modern ranch house that looks out over the sea. "She has very exotic tastes." I want him to think I have a lot of money to spend. "It's a rather special occasion."

"Does she have an interest in history?"

"Oh yes. The longer the history, the better."

"Well, you've come to the right place." He flaps his hand at the photos and posters closest to the window. "This stuff's just for tourists, but I've got some real gems." He casts his eyes over the piles of junk like an eagle surveying a mountain range. "Let's see now." Like a twister, he whirls around the room picking up various items for me to see. "Mabel Normand's peignoir found at the bedside of the murdered Desmond Taylor. Or this, the bedside table where Marilyn Monroe left a half-used bottle of sleeping pills before she committed suicide. I got the coroner's photo to go with it. How about this . . . a set of dildos from the Garden of Allah? They don't make 'em like this anymore. Or the divan where Bugsy Siegel was shot. Those are real bloodstains. How about the purse found beside the chopped-up body of the Black Dahlia?"

"Is all your memorabilia so morbid?"

"Morbid sells."

"Where'd you get this stuff?"

"I have this friend at police evidence storage downtown. He was a friend of my father's and has been working there forever. Anyhow, they keep evidence . . . especially for unsolved murders . . . as long as they can. But this is Los Angeles, and eventually, after ten, twenty, thirty years, it's just too much. This guy lets me know what's going to be auctioned off. I get the stuff for a steal. You wouldn't believe what collectors will pay for this stuff. Museums too."

So maybe he didn't hire Fernandez. I walk around, touching things as if I'm fascinated. "I was thinking of something a little older, perhaps. Something pre-Hollywood, maybe something Native American."

"Oh . . ." A light snaps on behind his hooded eyes. "I've got just the thing." He turns, opens a drawer, and pulls out what looks like a blue velvet towel. He pushes aside post-cards and other knickknacks on the counter and unfolds the velvet. I see a dozen huge arrowheads. "I just got these in." He lets me admire them for a moment. The stones range from three to eight inches long, leaflike, gleaming, deadly. "These are Clovis spearheads. Clovis hunters used them to hunt mammoths about thirteen thousand years ago. These were found in Colorado. Here we have obsidian, red jasper, and smoky quartz crystal. No one knows how they made them, not even expert flint knappers."

I pick up one and run my thumb across the edge, so sharp that it makes a scraping sound against my skin. "I just read about this guy in Georgia who makes Clovis re-productions in his backyard and passes them off as real."

Afner raises an eyebrow. I see I've just earned points. He reevaluates me; perhaps I am a real collector. I make my move. "Do you have anything, perhaps, from Mexico?"

Both eyebrows inch up. His whole demeanor changes, relaxes; his high, wind-up voice deepens. It's as if I've said a password. "How much were you thinking of spending?"

"If I found something just right . . . four or five figures."

He tilts his head and nods. "If you'd like to step back

inside, I have a few things I could show you." He turns, then hesitates. "You aren't a cop, are you?"

"Goodness, no. Just a middle-aged lady on a shopping spree."

He laughs, crooking his finger for me to follow. "You're hardly middle-aged." His compliment jangles like tin. Flattery hardly concerns either of us.

I am nervous, hesitant, but it's too late to stop. I push through a bead curtain into a second room. Unlike the cluttered front room, this room is large and clean, with skylights and neat display cabinets. The floor is light gray cement, the walls white, the cabinets polished oak and glass. The first cabinet has jade beads and figurines. The others have Mayan and Aztec vases and sculptures. "I bet you shake in your boots every time we have an earthquake," I say.

He doesn't smile.

I notice a corner in the back, a minimalist office space, a computer on a modern mahogany desk with a printer, fax machine, and several telephones. Very organized, very modern.

I pull out the jade from my purse. "My sister has a collection of these. I thought I might find something to add to it."

"May I?" he asks as he takes the jade from me. He pulls off his glasses and sticks a jeweler's loupe in his eye. He looks at it silently for several moments. "Very nice," he says. "Very nice indeed . . . very high quality jade. I would say this piece is from the region around the Tikal Temple in Guatemala, perhaps from the time of Ah Cacaw, around A.D. 680." He looks at me with the confident expression of a *Jeopardy!* contestant.

"I wasn't testing you."

He smiles. "Of course not." There's something different about the way he moves now, like an actor making a transition to a new skit. He leans back on his heels. "Why don't you take a look around?"

I look at the monochrome vases, the stone figurines, eccentric flint carvings, and jade death masks. Bold, vigorous, alive. I suspect everything is museum quality. Elmer Afner pretends to be polishing a piece of obsidian, but his eyes follow me around the room. I hear the rain pounding on the skylight.

Then I see one of the Fernandez pots sitting in the corner. "What about this piece?" I ask.

"We have very good taste. Yes indeed."

I see he approves as he moves toward me. We have reached a new level. "Have you ever told a customer they had bad taste?" I tease.

"No," he says. "But I've certainly thought it." We are friends now. "This piece is extraordinary. It's from the volcanic region of Chiapas, Mexico. I had the hieroglyphs deciphered. The vase carried the heart of the high priest of Izapa. Apparently two cities were warring, and this was offered as a trophy. The layered technique is highly unusual, and the imagery is quite different from other Mayan work."

"It's exquisite," I say.

He sighs as if savoring a fine wine. "Yes, it is."

"How on earth did you come across this?"

Something like suspicion flashes in his eyes. "That's not a question I generally like to answer."

I backpedal fast. "I'm sorry. I'm not a professional art dealer, and I'm not from the FBI. I'm just looking for something special for my sister."

He looks at me hard, then shrugs. I think he believes me, but his voice is still arch. "Well . . . you will have to like your sister very much if you want this piece. I would sell it for a hundred and forty thousand dollars. That includes the cost of transcription and authentication."

"I see. Do you have something in a smaller size?"

He laughs. I think I'm out of the danger zone. I eye the computer. "I heard Sotheby's was having an auction this month of Mayan antiquities. Do you know anything about that?"

He looks surprised, nervous, as though maybe he's missed something. "No, I hadn't heard. Hold on. Let me find out. Step over here to my office." He does what I want him to do. He switches on the computer and types in his password. I watch. He brings up Sotheby's Web site and pages through their auction schedule. "Nothing like that for November. December eighteenth, Navajo art. January, Peruvian. Maybe you mean Christie's?"

"It's not that important," I say. He continues to click around, checking several auction houses. He eventually gives up.

I spend time looking at some smaller bowls, narrow it down to two, then tell him I'll have to think about it. He graciously shows me out, even lends me an umbrella.

"I suppose you'll tell me this was used by Gene Kelly in *Singin' in the Rain*?"

"Absolutely," he says, and laughs.

He wouldn't laugh if he knew I had his computer password. He wouldn't laugh if he knew I noticed his alarm system was relatively unsophisticated. He wouldn't laugh if he knew I saw water leaking through his skylight.

CHAPTER

14

The next morning, I take the San Diego Freeway north, then west on the 101 to the rolling hills of Simi Valley. As I head toward Thousand Oaks, the strip malls of Encino dissolve into dry desert knolls of prairie grass and eucalyptus trees, seemingly untouched by yesterday's cleansing rain. The air, trapped between the Santa Ynez and San Gabriel Mountains, bakes the foothills like tamales on a hot coal fire. I feel the moisture being sucked out of my skin; the membranes in my nose feel as fragile as snakeskin.

Since I met with Elmer Afner, I have begun to see a chain of links: Tomás to Dr. Faust, Tomás to Erlinda, Erlinda to Silvanus, Tomás to Fernandez Gomez, Fernandez Gomez to Mayan antiquities. How does it fit together? I haven't a clue. As recommended by popular movies, I follow the money.

Silvanus Corporation stands glistening on the top of

a hill like a spaceship alighting above a cow pasture. There's a surreal, bleached-out quality to the complex of white stucco buildings that make up the corporate offices: the landscaping, cactus and white gravel; the parking lot, freshly tarred; the hallways, white, unadorned, antiseptic.

I step into the silent corridor, my heels clicking on the shiny white Formica floor. My stockings make a swishing sound. I wear a tan suit, the one Pepper calls my flight attendant suit. The tight bun at the nape of my neck itches like a burr, but it makes me feel respectable. I've made myself a badge from my YMCA card: "Sandy Silverstone, Inspector, Hazardous Waste."

Every thirty feet there is a break in the white cinderblock walls: a thick window that looks into an empty lab. A steel door slams. A short man in a white lab coat waddles toward me, kicking his legs straight out as if he often accompanied men much taller than him. As he walks, his picture identification tag bounces on his chest. It reads "Dr. Paul DiFranco."

"This is quite a surprise," he says pleasantly. "We had an inspection just a few weeks ago. I didn't expect a visit for a few months."

"We find that we uncover more EPA violations if we make unannounced visits."

He nods, as if he's been told by his mechanic that his car needs new brake pads. "I guess that makes sense."

We turn and walk down the corridor. He is nearly a foot shorter than me. I see he is beginning to bald; his scalp gleams with sweat, sprinkled with large flakes of dandruff.

"Isn't Roberta Barrett still working with you?" he asks. "She's been our inspector for years."

"She's on maternity leave," I say.

He looks at me oddly. "I would've thought she was close to fifty," he says.

"Medical technology makes almost anything possible nowadays," I say.

He nods. This seems to be enough of an explanation for him; he doesn't want to hear more about female stuff. We continue down the corridor through a heavy steel door into a large warehouse area. It is very cold. In the bleached-out fluorescent light, I see several rows of shelves twenty feet high, stacked with storage drums, tools, lab equipment, and boxes of supplies. He shows me to a corner near an aluminum, roll-type garage door. There stand half a dozen silver canisters.

I look at them carefully, take out a white cotton glove, and run my finger around the tops. I scribble some notes in my address book. "You maintain a constant temperature here?"

"Oh yes," he says. "Between forty-five and forty-eight degrees."

"I see these canisters are sitting on the ground."

He suddenly looks flustered. "I didn't know . . ."

"I see no provision for earthquakes, no braces of any kind."

"But . . . I didn't think we needed . . ."

I have him on the defensive. "I need to see how your employees are handling hazardous waste. Could you show me now, please?" I try to sound like a schoolmistress asking to see a homework assignment.

"Yes, yes . . . of course. This way, please." His walk

is now clipped, his stride tight, nervous. I follow, scribbling in my book as though I've discovered shocking violations.

He uses his ID card to enter another corridor, this one narrower. People in white lab coats and ID badges hurry by, stopping occasionally to exchange a brief word. One side of the hallway is all glass and looks into laboratories where several dozen people clothed entirely in white scrubs with surgical masks, gloves, and goggles move decisively among microscopes, computers, and packing boxes. For some reason I think of the chocolate factory episode on *I Love Lucy.*

A red, three-petaled flower is painted on all of the doors—the international symbol for biohazard. Actually, the symbol is more menacing than that, more like the horns of three stag beetles locked in deadly battle.

"These labs are equipped for biosafety level three," explains DiFranco. "We really have no need for anything higher, but we do have one lab equipped for biosafety level four. That's the level where you need space suits. All of the labs are kept under negative air pressure so in case of some contamination, air will flow into the rooms instead of out. The labs were designed by a civilian army scientist from USAMRIID."

"Doesn't USAMRIID do research for biological weapons?"

"No, no. Not anymore. They develop vaccines for bacteria, such as anthrax and botulism . . . and viruses that might infect American troops. The point is, we have the latest technology."

"I see," I say, thinking that there is another, more ominous point, but I can't put my finger on it.

He shows me where they unpack recovered body tissue from various hospitals and morgues, where it is sorted, sterilized, tested, repackaged. Materials deemed hazardous waste, anything that has touched the tissue before it has been sterilized, waste by-products, tissue that fails tests for HIV and hepatitis, are dumped into red cylindrical cardboard boxes. They look like old-fashioned hatboxes.

"May I take a closer look?" I ask, tapping the window to the lab.

He glances at his watch as if worried about lunch, then looks back at me. "Yes, of course. But we'll have to go through decontamination."

"That's fine. I'm quite used to it," I say, wondering what in the world I'm getting myself into.

He leads me into a small room with stainless-steel lockers. He tells me he'll wait while I change, so I figure out what I'm supposed to do. I take off all my clothes and put on white scrubs, latex rubber surgical gloves, surgical cap and mask, and white slippers. I wait in an antechamber for DiFranco to change. When he enters, a deep blue ultraviolet light beams on us through a glass panel in the ceiling. As we open the door to the level two lab, the air pressure sucks us in.

In the first red biohazard container, I see blood and tissue that looks like chicken fat. I really don't want to know what it is. I scowl and shake my head. We go through several labs, entirely ignored by the staff. We come to a final lab. It doesn't appear that he intends to enter it. Through the window I see rows of extremely powerful microscopes and computers.

"What's this room used for?"

"Genetic research. No hazardous waste is produced

here. Most of the work is theoretical and analytical anyhow."

"I see," I say. "Didn't you say this lab was equipped for biosafety level four?"

"Yes, but we don't use it for that. It was more cost-effective to build out the lab like this when we constructed the building rather than later."

"So you anticipate needing a biosafety level four in the future?"

"Not at the moment."

"What kind of genetic research do you do?" I see him hesitating. "I'm not here to steal industrial secrets. My reports are maintained with extreme confidentiality."

"Well, I'm not exactly sure. It's all rather new. Staff from Biobreed, the company we merged with, is using this lab. It has to do with proteins that act as agents for viruses."

"You're handling viruses here? And you're not utilizing biosafety level four standards? That sounds like a code double C violation to me."

He looks stricken. "Is that bad?"

"Very bad," I say.

After we strip off the white scrubs and reenter the main hallway, I make some scribbles in my book.

"How'd we do?" DiFranco asks with a nervous titter.

"You'll get a written evaluation in the mail within ten days," I say sternly. His face falls, disappointed. Without speaking, he shows me out.

In the parking lot, I shiver with nervous exhaustion. I'm not used to pretending on this level. It's not the fear of being found out that exhausts me, although that's certainly part of it, but the energy it takes to assume another identity. I suppose most people assume different identities every day: The mother becomes an office executive, becomes an aerobic dancer, becomes a sexy wife. But I have never had to be anything but what I am, a deathmaiden. In the last week, I've changed identities a half dozen times and find myself exhilarated and depleted.

I am losing sense of who I am.

While I wait for my espresso pot to erupt, I sit at my kitchen table with the e-mail list of Ted Duncans, the name of the former employee who sued Silvanus. I find four in Los Angeles; later, I e-mail them from the Santa Monica Library, asking them to call me if they worked for Silvanus. By the time I get home, I have a message on my answering machine.

I call Ted Duncan back. I tell him I'm a reporter for the radio program *Living on Earth* and that I'm investigating biotechnology and its environmental impact.

"You gonna rip 'em a new asshole?"

"I'll try my best."

"Good." He agrees to meet me but says it has to be outside, in a park somewhere. Only when I see him on Venice Beach close to where he lives do I understand.

Short and thin, he has the ropy muscles of an Irish potato farmer. He wears a bushy mustache to cover badly decaying teeth and a bizarre costume consisting of two pairs of shorts over sweatpants, a ratty red flannel shirt, and sneakers with socks pulled halfway up his calves. He comes up on me fast, holding his forearms in front of his chest as if he's a doctor who has just scrubbed up for surgery. His hands are encased in plastic bags. He doesn't shake my hand.

He tells me that he suffers from OCD, obsessive-compulsive disorder, that he can't touch anything that's been touched by anyone else or he'll have to wash his hands for an hour. He's what clinicians call "a cleaner." We have to meet outside, because he can't touch door handles to restaurants, can't sit in chairs previously sat in by other people. He can't drive because cars are dirty, can't dry-clean his clothes because cleaners don't wash their hands between touching the clothes you bring in and the clothes you take home. "You never know the last place where someone has put his hands," he says.

It isn't hard for me to imagine that the sterile hallways of Silvanus could drive someone crazy. "Some things are better not to think about."

"Yeah, but what if you can't help it?"

We meet by the water west of Rose Avenue. The tide is out, and we walk on the hard sand toward Santa Monica. The mountains of Malibu wrap around the shimmering bay like a cool embrace. The white sand sparkles. I take off my shoes to sift the white powder between my toes, something my friend, unfortunately, cannot do.

Careful to walk so as not to brush my shoulder, Duncan begins in a staccato voice. "I was proud to work at Silvanus, proud to be at the forefront of this technology. Everyone says they work eighteen hours a day. It's like a status thing. But I really did. I didn't have OCD then. In the beginning, we all did at least two jobs. Half the day I worked in the lab, half the day I did the accounting. We all worked on marketing strategies. I fuckin' lived there. I had a cot in the lab. I burned out. I wanted to leave. I wanted to cash in my stock options. But they wanted to keep money in the company so they could merge with Biobreed."

"Who's 'they'?"

"Leslie Folk, Bryant Hillary. They acted like they owned majority stock, but they didn't. I understood where they were coming from, but I wanted my money. So what do they do? They dilute the stock. They issue like a million more shares so my stock is worth nothing. I wasn't going to stand for that. I gave them my life. So I took them to court. Sued them for twenty million dollars. We finally settled out of court."

A petite blonde jogs by us in black tights and a crop top. We must look odd to her. She makes a wide loop around us.

"Why did they want to merge with Biobreed? I mean . . . what does a company that develops drugs for animals have to do with tissue recovery?"

He utters an odd laugh, two bursts, "Ah, ah," followed by a machine-gun-firing monotone, "Ha-ha-ha-ha-ha-ha." He stops, blinks, then licks his lips. "Do you know what antigens are?"

"They're part of the body's immune system."

"Right. They're what make transplanting so difficult, why it's so hard to find a donor match. You see, tissue types are identified by specific proteins or antigens in the body. They are carried on the sixth chromosome on the DNA chain. The body has a very elaborate defense system. After a transplant, if the host's killer T cells detect the presence of foreign antigens or foreign proteins, they launch a swift and lethal attack. The helper T cells secrete a chemical that stimulates larger immune cells called macrophages, which in turn release a growth-factor protein called interleukin-two, which stimulates production of more T cells."

"How does that cause rejection?"

"Well, the killer T cells puncture the foreign cells and inject them with a toxin called perforin. The cells die. A kidney or heart that is rejected by the host can wither up into a lump of scar tissue in a matter of days."

"How often does that happen?"

"Well, in varying amounts, always."

"Always?"

"You see, it's very hard to find an antigen match between an organ donor and a transplant patient. Actually, it's impossible. Even after a successful transplant, every transplant recipient has to take antirejection drugs for the rest of his life to suppress his immune system. Even one day without these drugs, and the host's killer T cells start to attack the newly transplanted organ."

"What kinds of drugs?"

"Well, you got your basic antirejection drugs prednisone and cyclosporine. Then you got Prilosec, Demadex, digoxin, and bacitracin. We're talking fifty pills a day. The drugs all have side effects—depression, anxiety, impotence—and prednisone fucks up your liver, so even if you can keep your heart, you might end up needing a liver transplant."

I try not to sound as appalled as I feel. "Why would anyone put themselves through that?"

"Ha-ha-ha-ha-ha-ha . . ." He erupts into his odd laugh. "That's not the half of it. People think once you get a new heart or kidney, you'll be well. Hell, no. You just exchange one illness for another. Rejection episodes are inevitable, so back you go to the hospital. Maybe you have to get another transplant. Then you got bimonthly biopsies where they stick a catheter through a hole in your neck and work it down through the jugular to clip a small piece of your heart. You have these periodic heart biopsies for the rest of your life. Plus, you're not out running marathons. You're still fuckin' sick."

My heart aches for their suffering, all for an additional year or two of life spent in hospitals, in agony, preoccupied with pain and corporeal failure, draining the joy out of family and friends. "Sounds pretty lousy."

"And it's not guaranteed. Maybe fifty percent survive more than five years for heart transplants, only forty percent for liver transplants."

"Oh, dear."

"So you see, the big push is to try to find a way around our own complex immune systems. Scientists all over the world are trying to find a way to strip antigens off the surface of a transplant organ so the body's immune system doesn't recognize the organ as foreign tissue. Another way of attacking the same problem would be to suppress only those antibodies that attack a specific antigen, perhaps by altering the genetic structure of the organ after it's been taken from the donor but before it is transplanted."

"If a company could figure a way to suppress the antigen response, they could transplant any tissue into any body?"

"Yup. And they'd make a fuckin' fortune."

I remember my original question. "But what does this have to do with the merger of Silvanus and Biobreed?"

"Well, Biobreed was a small company out of North Carolina that worked on developing new synthetic hormones and vaccines for the swine industry. They assembled one of the finest genetic research teams in the country. One of the main questions they wanted to solve was how the immune system attacks a virus. Well, along the way, one of their scientists developed a synthetic tissue using cells from swine intestines. Turns out it was perfect to use as skin for burn victims. That's what got Silvanus interested in them. The two companies started talks about Silvanus buying their patent or establishing a spin-off company together. That's when Silvanus discovered their research team was close to figuring out the antigen response problem."

"So Silvanus bought them."

"Yes. They started doing research with fetal tissue."

"Fetal tissue?"

"Yeah, from abortions and encephalitic babies. The advantage of fetal tissue is that it is immunologically naive. Humans don't develop surface proteins on their cells that stimulate their immune system to reject organs until they're midsize children."

"Since Biobreed and Silvanus merged, is Silvanus doing genetic research on fetal tissue?"

"You mean at the Silvanus facility? I left before the merger . . . it's possible. They'd keep it quiet, of course. People make a tremendous fuss about such things."

"Indeed," I say. "If Biobreed developed other swine parts for human transplantation . . . I mean, if they could figure out the immune rejection thing . . . Silvanus already has a corner on the market for replacement tissue."

"Distribution is everything. The possibilities are enormous."

We are almost at Santa Monica Pier. Above, the Ferris

wheel, red and yellow, rotates slowly. The sand vibrates as the roller coaster thunders up the pier.

For a moment, I imagine Venice Beach in its past glory in the 1920s, when tens of thousands, dressed in their Sunday best, came by tram and Model T to scream in terror on enormous rickety roller coasters on Lick Pier and to dance in the Egyptian Ballroom on Ocean Park Pier, the beaches so crammed with umbrellas as to appear like a single polka-dotted blanket. For a moment, it is superimposed on this world, two realities, one world black and white, the other color.

A seagull cries. The waves slap against the shore.

Ted gazes at the water, mesmerized, perhaps sinking into memories of when he saw the world not as an interminable blight, a cesspool of contagion, but as a place for adventure and joy.

I turn and kiss him on the cheek. I'm surprised he doesn't recoil. "There's nothing to be afraid of," I say. "None of it is real. It's all a manifestation of your thought."

He blinks, his plastic-encased hands stretched out as if on a crucifix.

I turn and walk up the sand to the boardwalk.

CHAPTER

15

As I toss pasta for dinner, tuna tetrazzini in deference to Cat, and wonder how to find out if Elmer Afner knew Fernandez Gomez, Matty Webster calls and asks me to meet him at the Forensic Science Center. He tells me he has something interesting to show me. He sounds excited, like a kid who's discovered a stash of small jars filled with snakes and animal brains in formaldehyde beneath his brother's bed. I agree to meet him at ten P.M.

I drive to 1104 North Mission Road in Lincoln Heights and park in the lot beside the Forensic Science Center. As I wait for Webster in the hallway, I peek into the gift shop: Skeletons in the Closet. Through the window, I see toe-tag key chains; a coin bank of a 1938 Black Maria, the Chevy van once used to pick up corpses; bowling bags shaped like skulls; briefcases shaped like coffins. I really like the barbecue apron and the welcome mat designed with the chalk outline police draw around corpses. Make your guests feel at home. Good thing the shop is closed. I don't know if I could've restrained myself.

I don't wait long. Webster bursts into the hallway very animated, his eyes black as onyx, glistening. He pulls me into the toxicology lab and dashes around like the sorcerer's apprentice. He slips a slide under the lens of an overhead projector, which casts an abstract design on a white screen. Then he's back by my side.

"When I first came to work here in the early nineties, there was a sudden rash of deaths among narcotics users in Los Angeles. The police were hauling in bodies with classic signs of a heroin overdose. Dozens of them. You look awesome today, by the way."

"Thank you."

"You're welcome. But nothing showed up in the toxicology tests. So, we sent tissue to University of California, Davis. They had a new machine that did high-pressure liquid chromatography, which detects minuscule traces . . . less than a billionth of a gram per milliliter of blood. So, we get the results back and these kids have alpha-methylfentanyl in their blood. We're talking an incredibly potent narcotic, and these guys were shooting it like regular heroin . . . popped their gaskets. Would you like some coffee?"

"No thanks."

He pours himself another cup. "Now, of course, we have one of those machines, too. But when I began testing Tomás's tissue, ours was down. After I found the prednisone and cyclosporine with our gas chromatography . . . which I told you about . . . I get the feeling I'm still missing something. So I take a photomicrograph through a polarizing light microscope, and this is what I find." He points to the slide projected on the wall. It looks like dice floating on a purple background. "You know what that is?" Webster can barely contain himself.

"No."

"Those are starch grains."

"Starch? Like in cornstarch?"

"Yeah . . . starch is often used to cut drugs like heroin and cocaine. So, I ask myself, why would a kid have starch particles floating around in his blood? I figure there's something in Tomás's tissue that our gas chromatography didn't pick up, and I then remembered that case I just told you about. So I send a sample up to UC Davis. You know what they found?"

"What?" I think Webster might start jumping up and down.

"Alpha-methylfentanyl." He changes the slide that's projected on the wall. "There's a picture of it."

It isn't a picture at all, but a graph, a rainbow spectrum. It means nothing to me. "But wouldn't that interfere with harvesting his organs?"

"Not at all. It goes directly to the brain and fries it. The rest of the organs are fine."

"Can we take this to the police?"

"It's not really enough evidence. And someone cremated his body, so we can't do any more tests."

I gulp hard. "Is this drug hard to get?"

"Nearly impossible . . . that's the point. It's not a common street drug. There's hardly any market for it because it's so potent. You'd have to make it in the lab. Like LSD."

"So whoever made it has to be a chemist with access to a lab?"

"I would think so. Although, if you know what you're doing, it's probably not that complicated. You hear of people making amphetamines in their ranch homes in the San Fernando Valley all the time."

Webster seemed so excited before. Now he looks deflated in his lab coat. It's his big find, and I'm the only one he can tell about it.

Not everyone who has a near death experience tells of traveling through the tunnel to the great white light, of feeling overwhelmed with a sense of peace, of the joyous reunion with deceased relatives, of the splendiferous city of light. Not everyone. Some see the realm of bewildered spirits. Sucked down into a black vortex, they feel panic and confusion. They tumble onto a vast, barren landscape, where thousands upon thousands of people, wailing in desperation and misery, pitch their bodies about in anguish, prisoners of their own fears.

I have taken the wrong exit. I am lost. Against my will, I am turning around. I am being funneled into East Los Angeles.

The freeway becomes a knot of cement, a tangle of roads, twisting and turning in every direction. I panic. The signs say south to Santa Ana. How did I get on this freeway? My skin tingles. I break into a sweat; I take the first exit. Surely on the other side there will be an on-ramp going the opposite direction, back to civilization, back to the ocean. But no. There is no on-ramp.

I'm driving down First Street. I am suddenly in a different country. A barren, grimy landscape, streets filled with debris, crumbling stucco buildings that hug the streets like jettisoned trash. Smashed streetlights trail electrical wiring like exposed nerves. Words scrawled over billboards, buildings, and fences like a spider's web, menacing and black. Vacant lots filled with garbage and automobile parts. Discarded baby carriages every block. No trees, no plants. No color apart from the crude signs in Spanish: "El Tropico," "Yolanda's Flower Shop," "Los Tres Campadres," "Lavandería," "Carnicería." Squat buildings, squat people. It looks as if the whole place has been flattened by a tornado.

I pass the infamous Roosevelt High School, where children shoot one another, their barren playgrounds murder zones. On every block I pass liquor stores with barred windows and roofs covered in concertina. The faces, all Mexican, stare at me as I drive by. Teenagers hang out on street corners. Stray pit bulls, skinny with demented eyes, zigzag across the streets. Mexican women in long skirts and black braids, pregnant and fat, waddle down the sidewalks, dragging dirty-faced toddlers by their hands. Men, making benches out of beat-up cars, drink beer from cans in paper bags.

I continue south. I glance at my temperature gauge. The Jag is beginning to overheat. It knows I'm getting upset. I am sure I'll run into the freeway eventually. I see two gangs of kids throwing glass bottles at one another and low riders packed with young boys glaring out the windows, both hunting and hunted. Every block looks the same. It goes on forever.

I look in my rearview mirror. I spot two men in a navy blue Lexus several car lengths behind me. They are huge, the one driving a solid block of muscle. I've seen the car three times since I left the Forensic Science Center. A wobbly hysteria overwhelms me. My arms shake in panic. I've got to get out. The street is four lanes wide. I'm hemmed in by the low riders. Frantically, I speed up to try to get around them, but they stick with me.

I near a cemetery on Evergreen. Coming toward me, an elderly black man driving a fifteen-year-old Oldsmobile station wagon, all dents, painted in primer gray, slams into a white Volkswagen turning left. The cars skid sideways across the intersection in front of me, glass spewing like a fountain. I make my move. As the other cars slow to watch, I speed up and cut right, across traffic, up a narrow street.

The pavement suddenly disintegrates into potholes. I accelerate up the hill, past crumbling craftsman houses, chain-link fences, and salvaged cars. I turn again, more and more lost, swerving past surprised faces, driving irrationally, in panic, feeling as vulnerable as a nude bather chased by a horsefly. I've lost my sense of direction. I must turn west. West is my only salvation.

I run into De Soto Avenue and turn right, then left, onto First Street. I speed in the other direction. Now I'm sure I'll run into a freeway. I see it ahead. I swoop beneath the underpass, but still no on-ramp. I glance back. I don't see the Lexus; it gives me some comfort to know that they couldn't be any more comfortable driving around here than I am.

I stay on First Street, past Mission, and when I cross over the Los Angeles River and the railroad tracks, I see the glistening buildings of downtown burst out of the debris before me, as welcome as the Emerald City.

CHAPTER

16

"So, now . . . officially . . . you're in trouble." Pepper pauses on the steep, rutted fire road, wiping a T-shirt over her stomach. Flaunting her rock-hard thighs and abdominal muscles in a black sports bra and bike shorts, she gazes out at the glistening silver blue Pacific and waits for me to catch up. "Your house is ransacked, someone leaves you a pile of shit . . ."

"Literally."

". . . you're followed all over East L.A."

"I'm not absolutely positive I was being followed . . . maybe they were lost. Maybe they thought, since I was a white lady driving a Jag, if they followed, they'd find their way out."

"I've done that . . . follow someone when I was lost." She turns and continues up the Paseo Miramar trail, which hugs the cliffs seven miles to Malibu. Mostly up.

"You think that's what they were doing?"

"No."

"Neither do I."

"Not guys . . . they don't ask directions, they don't follow . . . they rely on their . . ."

"Hunting instincts."

That's the kind of comment that normally would make Pepper chuckle. She doesn't. They're hunting me.

"It's the way of the world," she says. "Women go on hikes, men watch TV. Women ask directions, men don't." She's bitter: Of her entire harem of hunky monkeys, not one will hike with her. She has to put up with me.

She turns and walks backward; this way we keep pace. "You're not going to drop it, are you."

"No."

"You're as stubborn as New Hampshire granite."

"I'm from Maine."

"Whatever. . . ." She rips a twig of sage off a bush and sniffs it—aromatherapy for dealing with me. "Right . . . so . . . what now?"

"I don't know." On the ocean I see two pinpricks: kayaks catching the winter current south. "The coroner says Tomás was killed with an obscure narcotic. Whoever used it knew it was barely traceable."

"I can't believe anyone, especially a transplant surgeon, would kill a boy for his organs. It doesn't make sense."

"Unless there was something special about him. Hey, look . . . a hawk." A dark shadow floats over the warm air thermals.

"You're thinking about his forehead . . . being Maya?"

"We don't know if he was Maya . . . but, yeah, that's what I was thinking."

My thighs are burning. I wore jeans because I think they'll protect me from rattlesnake bites, but they're hot and uncomfortable. I stop to catch my breath. "Elmer Afner has something to do with it. He's the key. I can feel it."

"No. Follow up on the Maya thing . . . that's what I think."

I recall the anthropologist at UCLA recommended by Lloyd Overton. A Maya specialist. He also might be more forthcoming than Overton about stolen artifacts. And there's a chance he knows something about Elmer Afner.

Later, I dig into my purse for the Getty brochure Overton gave me. I call Chris Jensen at UCLA but get voice mail. I hop in the Jag and head east on Sunset.

From Sunset, I turn right down Hilgard, then right again into Parking Structure Three. I never know where to park at UCLA and always end up having to walk across the entire campus. My legs hurt from the hike, but I want to park here so I can stroll through the Franklin Murphy Sculpture Garden.

Planted as a botanical garden with giant sycamore, magnolia, and California oak, the UCLA campus is one of the most beautiful places in Los Angeles. As I amble between the buildings, I say hi to my favorite bronze sculptures: Jean Arp's *Hybrid Fruit Called Pagoda,* which looks like two melting gumdrops; Deborah Butterfield's skeletal horse; Gaston Lachaise's porky woman with pomegranate breasts and a tiny head; Henry Moore's *Reclining Nude,* so heavy and disjointed that it makes me feel the danger of repose.

I look at a campus map and am not surprised that I need to walk south a quarter mile.

I take a wrong turn, walk through the Court of Sciences, then turn into Hershey Hall. I look for his name, Chris Jensen, then ride the elevator to the third floor.

I hear faint tapping echoing in the barren linoleum hallway. It grows louder as I walk to a room at the end. I step through the open door.

The large room has twenty folding tables, the kind used to feed movie crews, each covered with white paper; on top are piles of gray limestone. I look closer and realize bones are embedded in the rocks.

A man with a large belly in wrinkled khaki shorts gently sweeps the rocks with what looks like a makeup brush. His thick white hair stands erect like swamp grass. He wears a blue denim shirt, and his skinny calves stick out of work boots like Mickey Mouse legs. He picks up a small hammer and resumes tapping.

"Look what I found here," he says without turning around. "Another obsidian blade. Probably used to sacrifice these poor blokes." He reaches back and hands me a flat, curved stone with a very sharp edge. "Put it on the table, please, dear."

I lay it on the nearest table, which is piled with artifacts: skulls and bones on one side, tools and pottery on the other. "All these bones are from people who were sacrificed?" I ask.

"Oh?" He turns around, surprised. "You're not Connie. I thought you were one of my graduate students. So sorry."

"Please don't apologize. I snuck up on you. Are you Chris Jensen?"

"Hmmm." He regards me over the tops of his bifocals. "Lloyd Overton gave me your name up at the Getty."

"Lord Overton . . . that's what we call him around here."

"I noticed he was a tad . . . imperious."

"Hmmm . . ."

I sense the vibrations of academic bickering.

"How may I help you?" he asks.

"Well . . . I'm interested in knowing more about Mayan rituals. You said these bones were from people who were sacrificed?"

"Not only sacrificed, my dear. Let me show you something." He motions me over to the third table from the end. "I've been trying to sort these out. I got about twenty complete skeletons here, adult-size males." He hands me a bone broken in half and tugs me to a bright lamp. "Tell me what you see."

I place the two bones together. "It's from the forearm, a radius, I think. It seems short in comparison to a modern skeleton."

"Yes, most adult males stood under five feet. What else?"

I separate the pieces and look at the broken ends. "It looks like the marrow's been removed."

"Very good. But look here." He points with his pinkie finger to the end joints; his nail extends a half inch beyond the tip of his finger. I've seen such nails on coke dealers from South Central; I assume he has another use for it. "See the faint polishing on the ends? Look here where it's broken . . . the beveling on the sharp parts."

How quickly I slip into the student role, eager and amazed. "The bones were used as tools of some sort?"

"No." He smiles, playing with me, wanting me to guess. "Look." He points to scratches near the joints. "Those are sawing marks, probably made with flint tools."

"His arms were cut off?" I say in disbelief.

"Not only that, my dear." He leads me by the elbow to a fully assembled skeleton that lies on a far table. He hands me the skull. "What do you see?"

As I run my fingers over the back of the skull, the bone crumbles and flakes. "It looks burned . . . the cranial vault is crushed."

"Very good." He points to a ragged edge of broken skull where shattered pieces still cling to the edges. "These are perimortem breaks that occurred in fresh bone at the time of death." He points to the base of the skull. "You can tell they were decapitated because the heads have the top cervical vertebrae. You only get that when the head has been cut off at or soon after death."

"Someone cut off their heads, hacked apart the bodies, then put the heads in a fire? What for?"

"To roast them. Then they smashed the cranial vault and dug in. Yum."

"They ate human brains?"

"You betcha. And they hacked off the limbs to fit in ceramic cooking pots. That's what causes the polishing on the ends, from stirring the bones in pots."

I am too stunned to respond. Jensen seems amused at my shock. "Sharing blood is part of their resurrection. You have to think of it as communion."

I recall the little cups of grape juice I sipped at church as a child and suddenly feel sick to my stomach. I nearly forget why I'm here, flummoxed as to how to bring up the topic of stolen art. I finger the jade in my pocket. "Where are these bones from?"

"Caves in Mexico. The ground under the Yucatán is riddled with limestone caves that were used by the Maya for religious ritual."

"Are you saying the Maya were cannibals?"

"No, no . . . not *all* Maya. What we think of as Mayan civilization is actually dozens of different cultures occurring throughout Mesoamerica over fifteen hundred years. For most of their history, as far as we can tell, the Maya practiced ritualized human sacrifice, which includes some pretty gruesome torture but no cannibalism. You saw that represented pictorially at the Getty. What I'm discovering suggests cannibalism was pervasive in the Yucatán between A.D. 1100 and 1200."

"Why then?"

"Interesting question." He uses tweezers to piece together a jawbone. "Tell me, what do you know about the Toltec civilization?"

One of the prerequisite courses at the institute was comparative religion, much of which explored the influence of Native American and Mesoamerican Indian spirituality on Christian religious movements. It comes back clearly to me. "The Toltecs were ancestors of the Aztec in central Mexico."

"That's right. The height of their culture was between A.D. 450 and 650 in Teotihuacán. The Toltecs had a highly militaristic culture that used human sacrifice and cannibalism as state-sponsored ritual. Around A.D. 750, Teotihuacán was burned to the ground by its own people and abandoned . . . like they were trying to get rid of a terrible plague. Authority and order collapsed. War spread throughout the entire region. The Toltec aristocracy fled. Some north, some south. They brought with them Toltec culture as well as the practice of cannibalism."

"You're saying the Toltecs taught the Maya to incorporate cannibalism into their ceremonies?"

"Only in the Yucatán, only around A.D. 1100."

"How come?"

"The Toltecs had the greatest influence on the Chontal Maya of the Yucatán, who traded along the coast in seagoing canoes. They served as merchants for Mesoamerica much like the Dutch did for Europe during the seventeenth century. They spread their influence south to the Guatemalan highlands, over to the Pacific coast, and as far north as Tikal in central Mexico. It's my theory that it was the Chontal Maya who spread Toltec culture for several centuries before A.D. 1100."

"These bones are from Chontal Maya?"

"Yup. Several years ago, I began to notice a pattern. After about fifty years of contact with Chontal Maya, a city collapsed. We see that in Palenque, Piedras Negras, Tikal, Bonampak, Yaxchilán, Uaxactún, Copán, Uxmal. Cities of two hundred thousand disappeared within a few years. In Palenque, there's a half-finished stela where the scribe stopped in the middle of a sentence—like the whole city picked up and fled. We found evidence that shortly before their collapse, these cultures began to practice cannibalism."

"How would cannibalism cause the cities to collapse?"

"A state that rules by terrorism can't sustain itself for more than about fifty years. History supports that. Hitler, Stalin, Pinochet, Ivan the Terrible. Society implodes. The human spirit can't take the stress."

"Can you really prove their rituals included cannibalism?"

"Proof . . . pah! You sound like some of my colleagues. They argue that even if the Chontal Maya hacked up bodies and cooked them, there was no proof they actually ate them. Then I found something."

"Feces?"

"Precisely. I found a desiccated human turd, or coprolite, preserved in the hearth ashes. I nearly wet my shorts. If I could find evidence in that turd that human flesh was consumed, then I could prove my theories were correct."

"How did you do that?"

"We got it carbon-dated for around 1150. We had to find human cells in the coprolite that couldn't come from the blood or tissue of the intestinal tract."

"You mean you had to make sure the human cells in the feces didn't come from the cannibal himself?"

"Precisely. We tested the coprolite for human myoglobin, a protein that's found only in skeletal and heart muscle and can't get into the intestinal tract except through eating."

"You found human myoglobin?"

"Yup. But you know, people still don't want to believe the Maya ate people, especially all those new agers who run around burying crystals at Palenque." He laughs like a donkey. "This is what it looks like." He holds up a plastic bag of whitish clumps. "We also found traces of *balche,* peyote, toxic mushrooms, and morning glory seeds—hallucinogenic drugs they took during ritualized human sacrifices."

We stand in silence for a few moments, listening to students laugh and scuffle down the hall, the hum of fluorescent lights, a car alarm echoing in the nearest parking structure. "It's going to take me a while to digest your theories."

Jensen chuckles.

"Do modern Maya retain any of these rituals?"

"Cannibalism?"

"Or sacrifice. Or binding the heads of babies."

"I shouldn't think so. Catholics finished their culture like so many others." He glances at the stainless-steel clock over the chalkboard. "Oh dear, I really must send you off. I have a class in twenty minutes and haven't a clue where I put my lecture notes." He shakes my hand, then, as he searches under science tomes on his desk, adds, "Have you seen the new photography exhibit at the Thurston Art Gallery? I saw it going up on the way to work this morning. Photos of Mexico. Quite arresting. You might want to stop in."

As I take the elevator downstairs, I kick myself for not asking about the black market for Mayan antiquities, but what I've learned about sacrifice and cannibalism resonates deeply in me. I sense it has something to do with Tomás, but what?

I walk across the quadrangles and past the art center to the new Thurston Art Gallery, a one-story building of redwood beams and glass that looks like a large pagoda. A single black-and-white photo hangs in the window. Two figures move around inside. The door's unlocked. I walk in.

"We're not open yet," a woman says tartly. "Our opening is Friday."

"I was walking by and got fascinated. I'm afraid I won't have an opportunity to come back. Could I possibly take a look?"

"No, I'm sorry. You know . . . liability and all that."

"It's all right, Belinda. Please, please come in and look around."

I hear a voice behind a partition of white particleboard, a husky Northern European voice, soft as bog ferns, seductive as a midforest meadow, warm as a crackling fire in a gentlemen's hunting lodge.

He steps out and sees me. "Oh . . . it's you . . . come in, please." He extends his hand; he seems genuinely happy to see me. "Jack Halmstad . . . at the Getty . . . remember?"

"I remember." He wears black jeans, a black T-shirt, and a leather vest. "I'm astonished. Are these your photos?"

"Yes, yes . . . from my last trip to Mexico." He steps back toward a ringing phone while still talking to me. "Look around, please. Tell me what you think."

The black-and-white photos are bleak and brutal. An old man looks at his reflection in a shop window decorated with paper skeletons. A drunk lies passed out on the steps of a cathedral. A woman whose face is melting with leprosy lifts a knitted mask and looks into the distance as if at a vision of the Virgin Mary. A flooded, muddy street reflects a church edifice and storm clouds behind it. Children at play jump off a coffin as a young man with a rifle looks on. An Indian standing in a canoe poles through a marsh, smoke from an oil refinery spewing behind.

The photos are filled with despair, a culture and a land

being annihilated, a people whose faith is crushed, trying to exist, but not very hard. Faces of bewilderment and fear. The greed of others has damaged their land; their own greed and ignorance will finish it.

A coolness sweeps over me like a jellyfish over the surface of a wave.

Jack walks back into the front gallery, crosses his arms, and watches me study the photos.

"What made you take these pictures?" I ask.

He laughs, pleased that he's shocked me. "Some people say the people in my photos look anguished. But if you were to meet them in real life, you would find them good-humored and fun loving. It must be my Northern European brooding that makes them look so tortured."

"They look oblivious to the squalor around them."

"You see squalor. They don't. A man smiling with rotten teeth . . . we see poor dental hygiene, condemn his ignorance, his poverty. But the photo is about sharing."

I see he's right. The photo of a homeless man, pitifully dirty, barefoot, and deranged looking, sitting in a gutter talking to a young boy, is about companionship. The other photos are about hope, determination, bravery, endurance, joy. I am embarrassed I had to have it pointed out to me.

"Don't you want to take pictures of beauty?"

He laughs and pulls me into the next gallery. "If you want beauty, you've got to see the photos I took of the Tarascans."

"Tarascans?"

"They're a mountain tribe in Mexico."

He stands back and watches me circle the gallery.

Again, black-and-white photos, these of rural Indian peasants.

One photo is of a family at harvest. They look boldly into the camera. They are odd looking, small, proportioned like dwarves, big heads, long arms, short legs. Their eyes are vaguely Asian, with long, sloping foreheads, straight noses slightly flared at the end. Their jaws are prominent, both upper and lower mandibles, almost chimplike. Their bare feet are wide, with toes fanning out. The mother's skin is leathery and wrinkled like a turtle's. She wears a dark skirt and blouse, her head and shoulders wrapped in a shawl, like a clay sculpture in progress, covered for the night to stay moist. On her head sits a hat with a large circular brim.

The man wears a poncho and a cowboy hat. Strapped to his back is a huge straw basket that is nearly as big as him. The daughters, young teenagers, wear long dresses, their shoulders wrapped in striped shawls, their hair in two braids down their backs. Over her shawl, one girl wears a Nike sweat jacket.

They are beautiful and disturbing.

Other photos show muddy roads, crooked huts crowded together on a hill like hats in a crowd. Dormant pyramid-shaped volcanoes litter the background, surreal, like enormous children's blocks set in barren fields. Everything looks dirty; the children's faces are streaked with mud. Life looks achingly harsh.

In their native clothing they look noble, but in the Western clothes that the boys seem to prefer—jogging suits, tattered rayon shirts, pants held together with safety pins, sneakers untied and filthy—they simply look impoverished.

Even in Los Angeles, where half the population is Latino, I have never seen anyone like these people. Looking into their faces is like peering into a volcano, down through jagged lava rock into slow-moving rivers of liquid fire. The pictures make me feel exposed and vulnerable. "It hurts to look at them," I say. "They're so pensive."

"Nobody really knows where the Tarascans came from. Some experts think they migrated up from Peru."

"Do they bind the heads of their babies?"

"Looks like it . . . but I never saw it."

"They look into the camera like they have nothing to hide. Defiant, almost."

"At one time, their empire of several million people encompassed much of the state of Michoacán. When the Spanish came, they fled to these barren highlands and have lived there undisturbed ever since. Even the guerrillas don't bother them. They speak their own language, Purepecha, which is entirely different from Mayan or any other known language."

"Their lives look so colorless, like spirits," I say.

"That's why I used black-and-white film. It seems to suit them. Come, there's more back here." He takes me by the elbow and leads me around a partition.

Belinda is standing on the top of a ladder, adjusting the track lighting. She sighs, exasperated at getting no help.

I see a portrait of five boys dressed in dirty jeans and basketball clothes. The light glints off the glass, making it difficult to see. I step back. One of the boys holds a soccer ball under his arm. I catch my breath.

It's Tomás.

CHAPTER

17

I panic. I look at Jack; his face suddenly seems menacing to me. I clutch my purse to my side and run to the door.

"Where're you going? What did I say?" He reaches for my arm, his face genuinely perplexed.

"Let me go! I have to go." I stumble out of the gallery, blood pounding in my ears. I hear him call my name. I run to the parking structure, dash up the stairs to my car, and throw open the door. I dive onto the leather seat and slam the door. I am shaking all over, tears streaming down my face.

Furious, I race down Sunset Boulevard, driving dangerously fast around the curves to Pacific Coast Highway. By now it's dark. I speed up the coast, dodging cars, veering right and left, grinding my teeth, and I think that if I hear police sirens, I will not stop, destined to be the star of the next televised high-speed chase. But I hear no sirens.

I know I'm behaving irrationally, my muscles twitching with nervous energy—like a fox hearing a hunter's horn. I'm not sure it is a bad thing. Perhaps irrational behavior is your finer instincts coming to your rescue.

I drive until I come to a stretch of undeveloped beach in Malibu. I cut across headlights to park on the ocean side of the highway.

I slide down the sandy ledge to the beach, throw off my clothes, and run into the water.

The frigid surf jolts me awake; a strong riptide pulls at my calves. Seductive black waves reflecting lights from the highway look like ribbons of golden minnows. I dive beneath a swell and resurface twenty feet out. For a moment, I can't touch the bottom; then the wave recedes. I push off the sand, diving again, letting the current pull me out.

I surrender to the cold, blue-black deliciousness drawing me out, to the frisky waves flushing in my mouth, ears, and vagina, rocking me, luring me to sleep. I feel a terrible yearning to let go, to open my mouth and drink in this cool elixir, to dissolve and become one with the ocean.

A wave surprises me, breaking over my head. I am slammed to the bottom and somersault, scraping my shoulder against the sand. The pain charges me with energy. I dig into the sand with my toes and jump. My head bursts above the water. Indignant, I swim furiously, parallel to the shore.

The water warms, the current subsides; the tug that feels like terror releases me.

Resting, I bob in the waves to catch my breath. Above me, dark cliffs jut out. Car lights wind along the base like a moat of fire beneath castle walls. I feel my core begin to cool.

As my rage ebbs, I realize the possibility that Jack is part of a conspiracy against Tomás is absurd. He didn't know I knew Tomás; he doesn't know I am a death-maiden; he didn't know I would visit Chris Jensen at UCLA. I behaved atrociously; he deserves an apology.

I ride a wave ashore.

The air is warmer than the water. As I walk back to my clothes, I pass a couple strolling with two Dobermans dashing in and out of the waves. I say good evening. The man answers good evening, trying not to look at my breasts. The woman giggles.

I dry myself off with my sweater, then pull on my clothes. My skin is damp and covered with sand. I suddenly feel foolish walking up the hill to my car, more so because my major concern right now is not getting the leather seats wet and sandy. From my trunk, I get a blanket and cover the seat. I dig in my purse to find the card Jack gave me at the Getty, then drive back to Santa Monica.

I turn into an area of Santa Monica that's somehow escaped the encroachment of software developers and Web designers, half a dozen streets of warehouses, auto shops, and lumberyards. A lucky few have found loft spaces above a glass shop or a plumbing store. Jack's sits above a print shop on Seventeenth and Colorado.

My hair is still dripping when I show up at his door. He is surprised to see me. A table is set for two with wineglasses and candlesticks, as though he's expecting company.

"Am I interrupting something?" I ask, embarrassed.

"Oh, no. I had a cancellation of sorts." He wears a white pirate shirt open halfway down his chest, his hair back in a ponytail. He looks as if he might pirouette into grand jetés across the room. "Your skin is freezing." He ushers me in and hands me a towel. "You've got to get out of those clothes." He roots around in an armoire and finds sweatpants and a long jersey.

The loft is sparsely furnished, with polished hardwood floors. He gestures into his living room, an area marked off by a rug and a couch.

After I change and dry my hair, he brings me a large, steaming cup of tea topped with frothed milk. Yerba maté tea, he tells me. It smells of nutmeg, leather, and smoke; it smells like Jack. The tea is scalding.

I don't know why I'm here. I feel uncomfortable. I look out his bank of industrial windows. The Santa Monica Mountains, purple and sensual to the north; the San Gabriel Mountains, a ribbon of blue aloofness fifty miles to the east.

He picks up a hairbrush, sits beside me, and tells me to turn my back to him. He pulls the brush through my long hair, slowly, methodically. I feel myself relax, the tension flowing out of my shoulders.

I'm alarmed by my own reaction to his proximity, his touch. My nerves are alert, ready to bolt. Yet I sense the warmth of his body, his gravity, a weight I can sink into. He brushes under my hair, the bristles scratching the nape of my neck. My body tingles from the top of my skull to my toes. Slowly I relax. The rhythm of the brush, the whopping sound, the rhythm of harvest. I relax and let my neck spring back with each stroke.

I am ten years old, staring out my mother's bedroom window into the snow, my mother brushing and braiding my hair for school. I both resent and find comfort in the ritual.

That was the year my father died. After that, I had to braid my own hair.

"I've never had anyone throw themselves in the ocean after seeing my photos. I guess I should feel flattered."

"Where are you from?" I ask.

"Sweden," he says.

I think of a land of perpetual darkness, of snow, candles in the windows, and reindeer. The image doesn't quite fit Jack. "I suppose you know a hundred words for snow?"

"No. But I know a hundred words for vodka. We drink a lot there. An awful lot."

"We have something in common," I say. "I grew up in Maine." For some reason, I remember standing in the snow waiting for my father to pick me up, knowing he was at Freddy's, finally giving up and walking home, my breath making ice in the scarf wrapped around my face, my toes and fingers numb, my thighs and butt getting stiff, sure that I am going to freeze to death. "They drink a lot there, too."

I ask him what brings him to Los Angeles. He tells me that he worked as a photojournalist for *Der Spiegel* in Berlin for ten years and that he always had an interest in Latin America. He moved here three years ago and uses Los Angeles as a base between trips to Mexico and Central America.

"Americans don't understand why we Europeans are so attracted to the American West, to Los Angeles, to

Central America. There's a sense of wildness, of infinite possibilities, of remaking yourself from scratch. The freedom of anonymity."

After a while, he stops brushing and picks up a camera from his worktable, a door that sits on two sawhorses. He snaps off the lens cover and points it at me. I'm filled with panic.

"I want to take pictures of you," he says.

"No. I don't want to." I stand abruptly. I turn to go, I look for a place to set the wet towel. I spin around and he's in front of me. He lifts my chin and kisses me.

"I can't," I say.

"Isn't that why you came here?"

"No."

"Why did you, then?"

"Because of the death of a little boy."

This odd explanation doesn't seem to surprise him. He nods, puts down the camera, and sits on a stool. I do not know if I want to trust him. I distrust photographers on principle, masked thieves who cover their faces while sticking long lenses into people's privacy. It's these stolen moments of which they're most proud.

He stares into his palms for a few moments, then looks at me, waiting.

I tell him I'm a deathmaiden. He tells me doctor-assisted suicide is commonplace in Northern Europe. He is not put off. I ask him about the boy in the picture. He doesn't remember anything particular about him.

Then I tell him the story of Tomás.

*   *   *

I lie between his bedsheets. My conscience percolates with conflicting emotions, shaking with desire but filled with alarm at the prospect of sex.

He crawls in beside me, naked, and props himself up on his elbow. The streetlight shines over my shoulder, illuminating his face and body. His skin is very white. His hair falls over his shoulders. He looks at me, then pulls off the sheet. I feel embarrassed at my own shyness, confounded by my own opulence, like a peasant suddenly buried in riches. He draws his finger across my shoulder, over my breast, down the ridge between my ribs, over my hipbone, and down my thigh. Goose bumps shoot up my arms, my nipples contract. He places his palm on my soft, flat stomach and smiles. He slides his palms under my buttocks and pulls himself to me, pressing his nose into my pubic hair, inhaling deeply. He parts my thighs, his arms coiling around my buttocks and back, his nose burrowing in circles. I feel his tongue, cool and pointed, slip into me, probing in small circles. I feel myself falling backward. I grab on to his long hair and cry out. I pull him up urgently, hungrily, lifting him by his armpits, the dampness on my fingertips smelling oily and sweet, like burning chocolate. My mouth searches for his mouth, desperate, needing his air. I hear moaning, urgent yet tentative, like the sounds of a deaf child pointing to food. It's coming from me.

He slides his hands over my hips and cups my breasts. I gasp for air, and he leaves me to suck my nipples. I feel enraged, abandoned. I wrap my calves around his buttocks and slip my hand around his penis, moaning, guiding him into me. His head falls back and I run my lips up his neck, pressing the side of my face to his, stumbling like a drunk, searching blindly for his mouth. He slips inside, completely, and waits. My neck stiffens; I am focused entirely on the power, the trembling, inside me. A cold shiver races up my body and I cry out, lifting my insides, pulling and rocking with desperation as if clinging to a precipice, my body burning, tearing, the pain almost unbearable, made more excruciating by the sense that, riding above it all like seagulls drafting a ship, this ecstasy will be followed by betrayal.

Late at night, I watch Jack sleep. I think about something he told me, that the Tarascans don't have mirrors in their villages. When he showed them pictures he'd taken of them, they didn't recognize themselves until a friend pointed out their image. *Yes, that's you.* I thought how odd it would be to live a life not knowing what you looked like. Not knowing who you were.

Their faces haunt me, make me want to hold on to someone tight, someone warm and breathing, to bury my face in moist, sweaty arms. They make me feel so isolated, as if I stand on a lunar surface, cold, alone.

I suddenly understand why people fear death.

CHAPTER

18

"No way, nohow, not on your life! You are out of your mind, you know. Off the charts. Completely bonkers." Pepper sounds furious, but there's a slight lift to the corner of her mouth. I know she will help me. I need someone small enough to fit through the skylight. "Just what does this have to do with Tomás, anyhow?" she asks.

"I don't know. I'm following my instincts. There's a connection between Elmer Afner and Tomás's father."

"If he did know him, that's still not going to explain why police shot him. What do they care about art smuggling?"

"A rogue cop who's an art lover?"

"I don't think so." Pepper snorts through her nose and collapses onto a ratty old couch. She folds her legs under her and squints at me. "There's something different about you, something I can't put my finger on."

I want to tell her, but I don't. I'm afraid if I tell her, I will lose the experience; I don't want the memory cheapened by her teasing. It feels exciting to have a secret. "Will you help me?" I ask.

"You think you're Joan of Arc now or something?"

"No, I don't hear voices. I just have a feeling."

"Oh, you have a feeling. Tell me again, why is this your business?"

"You know why. It's something I must do. And I need your help."

Pepper jumps up and kicks the couch. "Dammit! You'll end up falling on some treasure, breaking your leg, getting arrested . . . fuck." She jogs a circle around her studio, falls to the floor, and does fifty push-ups. She rests flat for a moment, then cranes her neck to look at me. "When do we go?"

Researchers of near death experiences point to evidence of an afterlife from interviews with small children who speak of dead relatives they've never met and never heard mentioned, or who recognize pictures of ancestors they've never seen. Researchers say the "veil of forgetfulness" that accompanies us to earth is incomplete in these children, that they remember their preexistence.

That's what they say.

My mother told me that when I was around two years old, I talked about my great-uncle Dale. She was surprised because she'd never mentioned him. She asked me to describe him, which I did perfectly, with the addition that he had something that looked like a pet snake around his neck.

I don't remember any of this, but I wonder why I now find that breaking into things, lying, and wearing disguises come as naturally to me as if they were old habits revisited. Or ran in my family.

Then I recall what my mother told me about Great-Uncle Dale: He was hanged as a bank robber. Turns out the pet snake was a noose.

Three A.M. The air is cold and crisp after another day of rain. It smells fresh, but the scents of Hollywood—urine, gasoline, and onions—lie low and assault you at every corner. The only people out on Melrose this time of night are men wearing dresses, bums, and whores. I'm surprised at the number of people strolling casually as if on a Sunday afternoon promenade. A whole different set of people seems to use the city at night. I kind of like the idea. Like a time-share condominium.

I park the Jag around the corner. Pepper and I walk arm in arm like lesbian lovers. A police cruiser glides by. It flashes its brights at us.

In a plastic bag I carry a notebook, flashlight, tape, gloves, hammer, screwdrivers, and rope. I wear black sweatpants and a black turtleneck. My hair is braided and stuffed under a black knit cap. I am not nervous.

When we reach the Golden Bough, we cut into the alley. A bum is rooting through a Dumpster alongside the building. The alley smells of pee. I wonder if we should wait or hand the guy a twenty to scram. We decide to wait and walk around the block again. I figure we should probably do that anyhow. We come back five minutes later. The bum is gone.

I give Pepper a boost onto the Dumpster. I find I'm not strong enough to pull myself up. By the time I find a crate to use as a stepping stool, Pepper is already up on the flat roof. I tie one end of the rope to the Dumpster, then hand Pepper the rope and bag. She kneels and gives me a hand, pulling me up onto the roof.

There are shallow puddles on the roof that reflect the streetlights. We crawl around them over to the skylight.

I've brought both a Phillips and a flat-headed screwdriver. We try both, but the screws are rusted and worn. Through my gloves, I feel rainwater trapped between the plastic frame and the roof. I finally use the claw hammer to yank the screws out of the casing. No wonder it leaks.

We stop and listen. A car screeching around a corner a few blocks away. The low hum of a condenser from the Pakistani market across the street. We lift the plastic bubble and place it aside, waiting, anxious. No alarm. I throw the other end of the rope down through the skylight.

Pepper slips off her jacket, giving me a dirty look. She squats, her back to the hole, then probes with her left foot, wrapping it around the rope. Then her right leg. She props herself up on the edge with the heels of her hands. She grabs the rope with her left hand, then right, descending the rope slowly. I'm suddenly jealous of her agility.

I throw down her jacket, then a flashlight. "The alarm is by the back door," I whisper. I have already told her what I think the code is. In a minute she comes back.

"The red light is still blinking."

I press my gloved palms together and think. My mind's eye wanders through the souvenir shop in front, the gallery in back. "Try 'Marilyn,'" I whisper.

Twenty seconds later she says deep within, "The red light is off. I'll open the back door."

"Wait until I get off this roof," I say. I don't want to be caught up here if an alarm goes off. "When I knock, open the door."

I retrieve the rope and replace the skylight. The cruiser crawls by again, coasting to a stop. I freeze, thinking frantically, caught between the urge to duck and the instinct to remain motionless. I choose the latter. I don't think they can see the roof from inside their car. I listen to hear if they're getting out. I hold my breath and peer slowly over the roofline. I see only the nose of the cruiser.

I hear a car door slam, then young male voices: "I didn't do nuthin', motherfucker. Leave us the fuck alone." I hear the officer order them to put their hands on the cruiser. "Fuckin' police harassment. I didn't do nuthin'." I hear some low mumbling, then, "We're just giving you a ride home, sweetheart," then the sound of car doors opening, scuffling, doors slamming. The cruiser continues down the street.

My heart is racing. I back up to the side of the roof and reach down with my foot. It doesn't touch. I jump, bang onto the Dumpster, slide down the top, and fall to the ground. Terrified and bruised, I wait for voices, sirens, alarms. Nothing. I pick myself up and hobble to the back door. It's open.

I walk in. The gallery looks so different at night. The streetlights shining through the barred windows make diagonal stripes against the square display cabinets. The white walls have a ghostly gleam.

Pepper is transfixed in front of one of the Mayan figurines, her penlight roving over its contours. "Over here," I say, motioning to the desk.

I switch on the computer and sit Pepper in front of the screen. "Type in 'Lord Pacal.'" She taps away and we're in. Pepper seems to know what to do, browsing icons and directories. She finds what looks like a gallery inventory. I snap a disk into the hard drive. "Make a copy of that." Next she opens what looks like a client list—Japanese, European, Latin, and American names and addresses, along with lists of what they've previously bought from the gallery. I don't recognize any of the names. There's no reason I should. Then, in the middle, the name *Clyde Faust.* The doctor who showed up with the ambulance. I suddenly feel nervous. "Make a copy of that, then let's go."

Pepper shuts down the computer, then jumps back as if she's had a shock. She looks at me. "Now I know what it is."

"What?"

"What's different about you." She grins triumphantly, as if she's just finished a difficult crossword puzzle. "You've had sex."

I neither confirm nor deny. I push the computer chair to its original angle and look to see that everything is in order. We head toward the door.

Pepper pauses by one display case. "I'd love to take the jaguar mask."

"No," I say. I see her drawn to the object as if it has some power over her.

"You get sex. Don't I get anything?"

I give her a shove. "Let's go."

Pepper resets the alarm and we're out the door.

If we did it right, he'll never know we were there.

CHAPTER

19

People on the East Coast say Southern California has no weather. It's true. For most of the year, our weathermen have little to do but crack jokes to fill airtime. But when December comes, excitement pulses through their bodies and they ache to perform. While Los Angeles may not have weather, she does have moods, and in December, she is unpredictably petulant, like a woman caught between two choices, both of which grate against her better instincts. In a furious temper, she vacillates between hard rains and beautiful clear days, between cold, gusty winds and hot Santa Anas.

Tonight, the house shakes as a bitter gale blasts from the north, gathering speed over the Santa Ynez Mountains, blowing fifty miles an hour. The winds spiral up the canyons, hitting my house in violent gusts. I tremble under my quilts. Cat cries at the foot of my bed until I let her under the covers. She curls up under my arm, whiskers tickling my shoulder. I'm thankful for her warmth. I hear shutters bang, pots falling off neighbors' balconies, branches breaking, trash can lids clanking down the street.

The winds feel like tormented souls flinging themselves about in anguish. I fall into an uneasy sleep, thinking about Tomás.

The telephone blasts in my ear. I look at my alarm clock: 1:30 A.M. Cat digs her claws into my scalp as I reach for the phone.

"It's your favorite body bagger." His voice is soft and hoarse.

"Matty, if you are sitting next to a corpse and whacking off, I'm never going to speak to you again."

I hear a husky chuckle. "Can I help it if I find you irresistibly attractive?"

"I mean it, Matty."

"Don't get all festered."

"Now you're calling me a pustulant boil?"

"Cool it, Red. I thought I ought to tell you something."

"What?" I turn over on my other hip and scratch Cat's belly. She waves her front paws at me.

"I got a visit today from the district attorney's office. Two guys in suits . . . like something out of Kafka. Anyhow, they asked me questions about you, then told me I shouldn't have any more contact with you. You know how sexy that makes you?"

"What did you tell them?"

"Only that you wanted me to do forensic analysis of some kid's tissue."

"You didn't tell—"

"Of course not. I told them I thought you were nuts and I didn't have any tissue to analyze anyhow."

"Did they believe you?"

"It's hard to read those guys. They knew I'd checked out the autopsy report for Fernandez Gomez, which probably means they were looking for it."

"Did they ask you why you checked it out?"

"I said I was working on a longevity study of Los Angeles Latinos."

"They believed you?"

"Well, I may have stretched it a bit thin, even for those Cro-Magnon types."

"Thanks, Matty."

"Sure. Are you purring? You're getting me all excited."

I jerk Cat away from the receiver. " 'Night, Matty. Curl up on one of those morgue slabs and sleep tight."

"You sure you don't want to go out sometime?"

"Good-bye, Matty." I hang up.

The next day, I drive down Sunset Boulevard and turn left into the exclusive neighborhood of Bel Air. The streets, four lanes wide and empty, curve gently around thickly landscaped gardens. A late afternoon mist creeps in from the ocean like a manta ray, silently blocking the sun, sending shivers down the spines of gardeners. No cars sit parked on the sides of these streets. Cypress trees and Japanese maples stand like giant armed guards, and between fifteen-foot walls, one catches glimpses of swimming pools, tennis courts, fountains, and monstrous pastel mansions. Above the walls, private observatories peek out behind weeping willows. Smells of jasmine and roses hit me like the wake of expensive perfume that trails well-coiffed ladies on Rodeo Drive.

On the phone, Dr. Faust was most cordial. I told him I had some questions about Tomás, about the use of his organs for transplantation. He said he'd be glad to speak with me. His voice sounded neither defensive nor wary.

A Hispanic woman in her late twenties answers the door. That's typical; her reaction is not. Her eyes bug out in sheer terror. She acts as if she recognizes me, or as if I threaten her in some way. Has the neighborhood had a rash of home invasions? Or am I getting a reputation around town as the woman who brings death? She nearly slams the door in my face when Clyde Faust walks up behind.

"Miss Oliver, please come in," he says.

The woman bars the doorway, her left hand gripping the door handle, her right shoulder wedged against the doorjamb. Dr. Faust places his fingers gently on her neck. "It's all right, Marta. She's here to see me."

She glares at me, not moving. Faust squeezes his fingers; she backs up slowly. "Would you ask Pia to bring us tea in the solarium?"

"Yes, sir." She shuffles down the marble hallway, muttering to herself in Spanish. At the end, she turns to give me another dirty look.

"I'm sorry about that," Faust apologizes. "She's very protective of me. I don't encourage it, but you know how these Latin American women are. Sometimes I think she'd latch on to someone's ankle with her teeth before she'd let them bother me."

"Perhaps she needs obedience training," I say.

Faust chuckles and leads me down the hallway. Unlike

our first encounter, this time he appears relaxed and gracious. Tall, with thick gray hair, he leans back as he walks, kicking out his feet like a spoiled rich boy showing off his prep school to prospective students.

I stop at the end of the hallway. What looks like a ten-foot gravestone stands against the wall. I look closer at the figures carved in relief. A woman in an intricately embroidered robe kneels before a man in feather headdress. He holds a flaming torch above her as she pulls a thorn-barbed rope through her tongue.

"You're looking at a Mayan stela," he says, "made around A.D. 300 from Yaxchilán . . . that's on the border between Guatemala and Mexico. The king is Shield-Jaguar with his wife, Lady Xoc. It depicts a ritual bloodletting. She's making a sacrifice to the gods before he goes off to war."

The king's eyes are turned upward, the queen's face inches from his crotch with an expression of ecstatic adoration. "The king looks like he's getting oral sex," I say.

Faust jerks back, shocked; he turns his head to the stela, his eyes lingering over the king's erogenous zone; then he erupts in boisterous laughter. "He does indeed. I never thought of it in that way. The whole sexual aspect of it, I mean." He smiles at me. "You have a keen eye for art, Miss Oliver. Let me show you around. I do a bit of collecting here and there."

Faust takes me into a cavernous room with white walls twenty feet high. One side is a greenhouse built out into the gardens where another stela stands artfully posed beside a crab apple tree. The room is sparsely furnished with white upholstered Mission furniture. All along the wall are Plexiglas cases of Mayan and Aztec artifacts.

"What got you interested in Mayan treasures?" I ask, using a particular tone of flattery and admiration that sickens me.

"Well, I'm very proud to be a member of a group of physicians called Doctors International. Each one of us volunteers at least two weeks out of the year to work in a third world country. We train doctors there as well as administer medicine. The year I joined . . . I guess about fifteen years ago . . . I went down to Guatemala. The experience was quite exhilarating, but apart from the work, I had a chance to explore a few ruins and got interested in their art."

"Quite interested, I should say."

"Well, yes," he says. "I guess I've become something of a collector."

Hanging on one wall are several eight-by-ten photos of Dr. Faust surrounded by Maya children. "You look so happy," I say.

Faust laughs, a little embarrassed, perhaps, then regards the photo of himself for a moment. "No, you're right. It's very satisfying to work with these people. They're so grateful for what little we do. They come to me with faith that I'll heal them . . . with absolute trust. You know the Maya rulers were medicine men as well. The Indians still have respect for medicine men."

"And Americans don't?"

"God, no. They demand health care as if it were their legal right. They take no responsibility for their health. They bring us their broken, abused bodies and expect us to fix them like we're auto mechanics, and when we can't, they sue us."

"So you would like doctors to be thought of more as high priests?"

He laughs self-consciously. "Not as priests necessarily, but as healers."

In another photo, Dr. Faust stands on the steps of Mayan ruins. There's a second man in one of the photos, a tall Japanese man in Bermuda shorts.

"That's Dr. Kira Katsumi, a famous epidemiologist and immunologist. We visited the ruins at Bonampak together." He says this with obvious pride, as if I'm supposed to recognize the name. I try to look appropriately awestruck.

We seem to have run out of polite conversation. He sits back in a wooden chair that looks like a throne. "I assume, Miss Oliver, you didn't come here to talk about Mayan artifacts. What can I do for you?"

I hesitate. I stumble. I know I'm on to something. But I don't know where to start.

He helps me. "You said on the phone you had some questions about the sad case of that little boy Tomás Gomez."

"I guess I was somewhat shocked by how quickly the hospital responded to his death."

"Well, yes. As soon as the blood stops flowing, a process called warm ischemia begins to ruin the organs. Paramedics are trained to work fast to preserve them."

"Could you tell me who signed off for his body to be used as an organ donor?"

"In such circumstances, where the parents aren't available, in this case, the father dead, the mother someplace deep in Mexico, where the child becomes a ward of the courts, it's the county health commissioner who signs off."

"You say his mother lives in Mexico?"

"That was the information I received."

"Who was the woman who cared for him on Clark Avenue? She was introduced to me as his mother, Erlinda Gomez."

"She was his foster mother."

"Foster mother?"

"Yes. When the boy arrived at the hospital, he appeared homeless. In such cases, the hospital calls the Department of Child and Family Services. Within seventy-two hours, a social worker will petition the court for an emergency detention hearing. A foster parent is assigned while the social worker makes every attempt to locate a parent or relative."

"And if they can't find anyone?"

"The child becomes a ward of the courts and remains in the foster care system. Look, our tea is here. Thank you, Pia."

A petite woman dressed in black with a white apron pours our tea, then leaves.

"If he was comatose," I continue, "how did they know his name was Tomás Gomez?"

"Apparently the friend he was skateboarding with before the accident told the paramedics his name was Tomás, then disappeared. In the hospital, we referred to him as Tomás Gomez after his foster mother."

I find this very strange. The Erlinda I talked to denied her last name was Gomez. Nor did she appear particularly fond of Tomás. "Where does Erlinda Gomez live?"

"In Venice, of course."

"She still lives there?"

"I would assume so." Faust begins to look frayed

around the eyes. He jiggles his foot nervously. "Really, Miss Oliver, I fail to see how this has anything to do with Tomás's organ donation."

"I'm trying to establish who had legal authority to sign—"

"I told you . . . the county health commission. If you look at the paperwork, it was all done properly."

"You are implying that because the paperwork is in order everything was done properly?"

"Yes . . . what do you mean?"

"Aren't you worried that sometime you might make a mistake, that someone might simply be in a coma when you declare them brain-dead and rip out their organs?"

"You must be thinking of that case several years ago, where a brain-dead patient woke from a deep coma just as the doctors were rolling his body out to have his heart removed. That was a near tragedy. However, such things don't happen anymore."

"But it could."

"We have very elaborate safeguards. . . ."

"But it could happen."

Faust is suddenly angry. "Of course it could happen. Maybe one in a thousand. People expect doctors to be infallible. We aren't. Of course we aren't. But people sue us like we've broken a promise, broken a law. Medicine's not an exact science, for chrissake!"

I see I've hit a sore point. "Even if one in a thousand is mistakenly pronounced brain-dead, his organs subsequently harvested, don't you think the practice should be halted?"

"Absolutely not! I'll have you know, Miss Oliver, that there are at this very moment ninety thousand Americans on dialysis who need a new kidney. Fifteen thousand people die each year waiting for a new heart because there are only fifteen hundred viable donor hearts. Thousands more need livers, pancreases, corneas, skin, bone, and bone marrow. If one person dies mistakenly once in a while, so be it. We have a national health crisis on our hands."

"A health crisis?" I let my skepticism hang in the air for a moment. "How much does an average heart transplant cost?"

"I fail to see what—"

"About two hundred thousand, isn't that right?"

"Well, yes. . . ."

"You say fifteen thousand people died last year who didn't get the heart transplants they needed. That means the U.S. medical community lost close to three billion dollars in revenue. And that's just hearts."

"You make us sound like ruthless businessmen, Miss Oliver."

"You were the one to start quoting statistics, Dr. Faust."

"People are needlessly dying."

A sudden fury takes hold of me. "Nobody dies needlessly. Everyone dies. Everyone needs to die. You simply prolong it long enough to make tens of thousands of dollars off them. You can't give them health. You give them and their families false hope and months of suffering. Why don't you let them die?"

"As a doctor, it's my obligation to use whatever technology is available to help my patients live."

"Why?"

"Why?" he repeats, astounded.

"Why do you see death as a failure? You and your wars, war against cancer, war against lung disease, war against diabetes. War, war, war. What about compassion? What about the soul? What about God?"

Here I think I've lost him. Maybe I've lost myself. I'm invoking God, something I'm not sure I even believe in. "Why do you fear death so much?"

I coast out of Bel Air feeling like a champion asshole. I lost my temper and ruined the chance to find out anything more about Tomás. I don't think Faust killed Tomás. But he's somehow connected. He collects Mayan art. Tomás's father smuggled Mayan art. They both had a connection to Elmer Afner and the Golden Bough.

The business about Erlinda Gomez still bugs me. Apart from her hysteria at talking to me, denying her last name was Gomez, and disappearing from Clark Avenue after Tomás died, she said she worked for a doctor. Did she mean Faust? Was Faust that good a liar? Perhaps she works for another doctor at Abbot Kinney Medical Center? When I get home, I call the hot line for the Department of Child and Family Services. I ask to verify that Erlinda Gomez is a registered foster parent. I also ask about Tomás. I am told a social worker will get back to me within twenty-four hours.

Then I call Ted Duncan. He can't touch the receiver, so I have to put up with echoes from his speakerphone.

"Have you ever heard of Doctors International?" I ask.

"Yes, of course. In fact, Silvanus gives a large portion of their charity funds to them. Unless he's gotten too busy, Bryant Hillary used to volunteer every year."

My heart begins pounding wildly. "He didn't by any chance work in Mexico and Guatemala, did he?"

"Why, yes. How did you know?"

"Have you ever heard of Dr. Clyde Faust?"

"Sure. He's a heart specialist at Abbot Kinney Medical Center. Has an excellent reputation . . . world renowned, in fact. Why?"

My face prickles, embarrassed—I did have to choose a famous transplant surgeon to insult. Oh well. "He also volunteers in Latin America for Doctors International. Do you know if he knows Bryant Hillary?"

"It's possible, of course, but I don't know. It's quite the in thing now. But you wouldn't catch me down there for anything in the world."

"Germs?"

"Nothing but." He laughs.

CHAPTER

20

Melrose Avenue is clogged with cars until I reach Robertson. The stores are open late for holiday shoppers. The night is cool and crisp, the sidewalks buzzing with neon lights.

I find parking the next street over in a residential neighborhood. I walk north, then east on Melrose. The Golden Bough is dark, the shade on the front door pulled to the floor. When he called, Afner told me he'd leave the back door open.

As I head back between the stores, I see a dark figure slip between the two buildings into the alley. I fight the impulse to run back to my car, forcing my feet forward, sliding over the broken pavement past the Dumpster to the back door. It's ajar. I push it open.

Inside it's black. A foul stench, excrement and something metallic and bitter. I hear whimpering from the next room. "Mr. Afner?" I call stupidly. I push my feet across the floor, hands out, trying to remember where the display cases are.

The whimpering draws nearer. The skylight cuts a faint square of light in the middle of the gallery floor. My foot slides in something wet, then kicks a solid pile of clothes. The pug barks at me, his fat body trembling as he stamps the ground. He charges my legs, grabbing the cuff of my jeans with his teeth, growling, his head jerking back and twisting from side to side. I ignore him. At least he's stopped barking.

I take a penlight from my pocket and shine it on the floor. Afner's pants are pulled down to his knees. He wears boxer shorts, the crotch wet with blood. His torso is twisted, his arms tied behind his back, his mouth bleeding, his nose broken, his eyes open wide. I feel heat rising from his body. I press my fingers in his neck. There is no pulse.

I flash the penlight around the room. Several large vases lie shattered. Through the stench of body fluids, I smell turpentine.

I hear footsteps outside. A light step. Sneakers. The pug lets go of me and starts barking again, racing back and forth in front of the body. A champagne bottle smashes through the front window.

Flames burst beneath a wall of grimacing death masks. A line of fire shoots out around the perimeter of the room. I am transfixed. The figurines seem to dance in the fire, magically, tauntingly, like Indian shadow puppets. Flames engulf the walls. The heat is overwhelming. The glass cases pop and shatter like lightbulbs. I grab the pug and run toward the door. It wiggles, biting my hands. I don't let go.

Suddenly an explosion throws me back. I drop the dog and cover my head. It races back into the flames. Glass and plaster shower over me. My clothes are on fire. I roll on the floor, then scramble to my feet.

The fire sucks all the oxygen out of the room. I'm breathing hot plaster dust. My eyes sting as though they're shriveling up. I pull a piece of glass from my cheek, then crawl through a hole in the debris.

I hear sirens, footsteps running. My knees are wobbly, my hands and face bleeding. I run down the alley. I know I must look frightening. I slow my pace, trying to walk calmly. In my mind I pull a cloak of invisibility over me. People ignore me, running past me toward the fire. I turn the corner and walk quickly to my car.

I sit trembling. My eyes are tearing, smarting from the smoke, my body racked with coughing. At this moment I realize why I bought a Jaguar. The leather seat cradles me, the steel body comforts me. Outside, the burning building reflects against the gleaming hood like fireworks in a fountain. But I feel safe, as if hiding beneath cool water.

For a moment, I hold my breath. Another police car screeches past me to Melrose a block away. Coming west from La Brea, a fire truck clanks and toots. As I wrap my bleeding hands in my scarf, I watch the flames lick the sky. More police sirens, more voices yelling.

Only then do I realize that I never gave Elmer Afner my telephone number.

I start the car and pull away.

CHAPTER

21

I don't want to go home. I don't want to be alone. I pull into a 7-Eleven off the Santa Monica Freeway. The pay phone doesn't work, of course. My hands and face are killing me; I can't bear the thought of getting back in the car and driving around the city to search for a working phone.

Then I remember the cell phone Pepper bought me to carry in the Jag. I've refused ever to use it. Now I find it in the glove compartment and dial Pepper.

"Shit, girl. I'm glad you called. I went by your house to feed your cat . . . what's her name?"

"Cat."

"Short for Catalina?"

"No. Short for Cat."

"Well, anyhow, I went by your house to feed Cat . . ."

"Yes . . ."

"You know, Frannie, cats aren't dogs. You don't have

to get someone to feed them every time you're going to be home late."

"She's been traumatized. She needs a little extra attention. You were saying?"

"Well . . . I got there and two unmarked police cars were sitting out front. I pulled up and parked. I ignored them completely, like I didn't see them. When I walked up your front steps, they stopped me and asked me who I was, what I was doing. One of them was a massive block of flesh, Mexican, I think."

"Sounds like Paul Ortiz, Pacific Division."

"Yeah, could be. He didn't introduce himself. Anyhow, I told them that I was there to feed the cat. They grilled me about when I last saw you, where you might be, and I told them I didn't know. I asked what's going on, but they wouldn't tell me. They made me give my name and address, so you probably shouldn't crash here."

A skinny black guy and a fat white girl stumble out of the 7-Eleven arguing, grabbing at each other. She bops him on the forehead with her chubby palm. He starts slapping her shoulders, cursing. They both look drunk. They see me staring and stop. I have that effect on people.

"Did you feed Cat?" I ask.

"Dammit, you've got the LAPD camped out on your steps and you wanna know . . . Of course I fed Cat. She scratched me for thanks."

"That's Cat."

"I have the feeling there's stuff you're not telling me, girlfriend."

The cars on the freeway swish above me. Sometimes, if you close your eyes, traffic sounds like cataracts splashing down a mountain. I keep my eyes open. "Would you mind taking care of Cat for a few days?"

"You sure you know what you're doing, girl?"

"Haven't a clue."

"That's what I thought."

When, as teenagers, we leave home in search of adventure, in search of ourselves, we hope to meet someone who will find us interesting, unique, a creature like no other, hoping this person who finds us special will define us, give us purpose, direction, meaning to life. Everyone we encounter could be that person. We search their eyes. We listen to their stories. We fall in love.

Then we stop looking.

I don't want to analyze my feelings for Jack. Is it love or merely hysteria, a desperate, self-deluding need to simulate a love for which I'm incapable? Can I trust him?

He opens the door bare chested in black karate pants. I see alarm pass over his eyes, then he laughs as he pulls me into his loft. "I'm flattered you always make an effort to look your best when you come see me."

"I don't want you to think I'm trying too hard."

"I'm running out of clean towels." He pulls me under the kitchen light and lifts my chin. "Hold there." He dampens a washcloth with warm water and wipes my face. I jerk back. "Don't move. You have a piece of glass near your eye." He uses tweezers to pull a shard that's pierced my brow. He douses rubbing alcohol on the other glass cuts in my cheek until I howl. It feels like an ice pick through my face. When he unwraps the scarf around my hands, I hear a sudden intake of breath. I look. The muscle beneath the burned skin is raw, with pieces of glass and grit pressed in the flesh. "I don't suppose I could get you to go to a hospital?"

"No."

"Then you'd better sit." He switches on an architect's lamp, puts on a pair of wire-rimmed glasses, and begins to pick out the glass. Every time he places the tweezers on the raw skin, pain shoots up my arms like electric bolts. His body is coiled in concentration, and I watch his naked chest muscles flinch as he moves his fingertips. When he's done, he cleans the skin with hydrogen peroxide, then sprays on antiseptic. "It looks worse than it is," he says. "We'll wrap them later, but now I want air to get to the skin."

I sit like a supplicant, hands open, bloody. My clothes are singed and dirty.

"I guess I have to give you a bath, too," he says.

He draws bathwater in a claw tub that sits on a platform in the middle of the loft. He helps me out of my clothes, but every time they brush my palms I yelp. I sink into the warm water, my hands hanging out the sides of the tub. I see why he's put the tub on a platform. I have a perfect view of the full moon rising over the Santa Monica Mountains.

He scrubs me with a loofah in small, circular motions, my neck, back, underarms, legs, breasts. He then leaves me to make tea.

I'm not used to being fussed over. Slowly I give in— to the warm water, the view, the possibility that someone will comfort me.

When he comes back, I have nearly drifted off, imagining myself soaking in a natural hot spring at Joshua Tree, in the middle of the desert at night, looking up at the Milky Way. He dries me off and puts me into a heavy robe.

We sit in his living room, drinking tea. My hands feel numb. If I'm careful, I can use two unburned fingers to lift the teacup. The tea tastes of peppermint and chamomile. I look over the teacup. Jack is ready for an explanation.

I tell him everything, the hospital, the coroner, Silvanus, the police, Elmer Afner murdered, the explosion, the cops. He listens, sometimes cocking his head, then nodding. After I stop talking, we sit silently for a few minutes. Then he says, "What are you going to do?"

"I need to heal. I need to hide. I need to find out more about Doctors International. That's the only link I have between Faust and Silvanus."

"I remember running into them in Guatemala and Mexico. They set up for about six months at a time so word gets out among the Indians. Then they move on to another part of the country. One doctor told me that they've discovered that the Maya will walk three days for health care, but no more, so they set up camps in the middle of grids of about one hundred miles. They have an excellent reputation."

"An excellent reputation." As I repeat the words, twice, they take on a sinister tone. "I need to know where their camps are now."

"You're going there." He said this as a statement, not as a question.

"Yes. And I need your help."

The knock on the door comes at around two o'clock. Jack gets the door. A heavyset Mexican cop fills the doorway. He's dressed in tan slacks, a rumpled white shirt, and a leather jacket. His face is puffy and unshaven, and he has the grumpy look of a hungry infant.

"How did you find me?" I ask.

"You made a call from a cell phone."

"So . . ."

"It's still on."

Everyone is supposed to know that the police can track you down if your cell phone is on. It's in the news every time a serial killer is on the loose. I never paid attention.

I sit on the couch while Detective Lieutenant Ortiz glares at the bandages on my face and hands. "What did you do to your hands?" he asks.

"I was frying sausage in an iron skillet and forgot to use pot holders." Jack stands to one side, leaning against the wall, keeping his eyes on Ortiz.

"And your face?"

"Hot grease." I can tell he doesn't believe me.

Ortiz sighs heavily. "May I have a seat?"

I look at Jack, then nod. As Ortiz sits, his tight pants rise above his ankles. I notice he wears Docksiders with white socks.

He sinks deep into the couch. It's uncomfortable for him, so he slides up and perches on the edge. "There was a fire on Melrose Avenue tonight. It was arson. The owner of the Golden Bough, Elmer Afner, was found dead. The investigating criminologist suspects he was dead before the fire started. We'll know more once we get the coroner's report. A videocamera from a convenience store across the street puts you there at about nine-thirty P.M."

"Oh," I say.

"Hollywood Division is looking for you. They'll want to ask you a few questions."

"Are you going to arrest me?"

"No. I don't think it would be wise for you to speak with the Hollywood police. I think you are in great danger."

"Are you suggesting I should bolt?" It seems unfathomable.

"I cannot suggest anything remotely like that. But if I were you, and I knew what you know, I would make myself scarce."

"Why are you warning me?"

His face seems to darken; he squints his eyes, hesitating. "I had another MRI on Friday. The doctors couldn't find any sign of a tumor. Like you said." He's quiet for a moment, then presses his palms together. "It makes me feel . . ."

He's obviously struggling, but I don't help. The silence begins to throb. He looks up and I see a face drained, like that of a schoolboy unjustly accused of cheating. "I'd been having discomfort. The doctors found something, wanted to do a biopsy. I was scared to death. Then a woman I've never seen before tells me there's nothing wrong with me. The pain is gone and the doctors scratch their heads and say their tests must've been mistaken." He bites down on a smirk. "It makes me feel like a chump."

"I didn't do anything," I say.

"I didn't say you did," he snaps, not smiling, with all the charm of a velociraptor. If I were a waitress, I'd never want to serve Ortiz an overcooked burger.

He's quiet for a moment, then his voice suddenly bursts in angry staccato bullets. "Maybe you're crazy, maybe not, but I don't like the idea of doctors killing Mexican boys." He gets up and begins to pace around the room as if it helps him talk. Or maybe he's trying to stay awake. "I decided to track down more information on Fernandez Gomez. Files appeared altered, reports were missing. I got a call from some prick at the DA's office who told me to lay off." Ortiz rubs his chubby hand over his face, then smiles. "I didn't like that."

He turns and looks out the window. "You know, there are days when it doesn't matter what you have to lose, you just don't wanna listen to someone's attitude. So, I looked into the guy who bought the smuggled pots at police auction, Elmer Afner. It turns out he had a long string of arrests and false names, involving forgery, drugs, and art smuggling, but he was never convicted. Then I discovered that in 1984 he was arrested for practicing medicine without a license. That was in San Diego. He appears to have done some medical school in Grenada but was never licensed in California. The case was suspended for lack of evidence."

"You think he hired Fernandez Gomez to smuggle artifacts?"

"Perhaps. But there's more to it. Elmer Afner had an ex-wife, Teresa Gutierrez. She may have some involvement."

"Where is she now?"

"In Mexico. She's a medical researcher of some sort."

I think for a moment, then ask, "How hard will the Hollywood Division try to find me?"

"I wouldn't try commercial airports and I wouldn't try driving across the border."

Being a six-foot redhead has its disadvantages. "What are you going to do?" I ask.

"Me? Nothing. Maybe I'll answer the telephone if someone calls me from Mexico. I'm in the book. Culver City." He gets up and leaves.

CHAPTER

22

It seems odd to be in a hotel in one's hometown. I suppose plenty of people do it, office workers having affairs, writers who need to get away from their families, but to me it seems strange. As I look out the window of the Shangri-la, Santa Monica suddenly seems foreign, a city unknown and exotic. I think of Malta or Greece. The sunrise, pink and orange, paints the mountains an unearthly lavender, and the palm trees have a forced stillness, as if suddenly caught in a game of freeze tag.

After Ortiz left, I decided to check into a hotel; if he knew where I was, then he probably wasn't the only one. Jack drove me over, made sure I had what I needed, then left me to sleep. It's not half-bad being coddled and catered to; I could get used to it.

I try to relax, but I toss and turn. I've never been able to sleep during the day. I know I must; I need to heal. But something about the room makes my skin itch. Hotel rooms like this are filled not with happy thoughts, but with the anxious consciences of businessmen and adulterers.

Finally, I drag the pillows and blankets into the bathroom and make myself a nest in the tub. My long body doesn't fit, and the air smells of ammonia, but I feel safe for the first time in days. I fall into a half sleep.

I imagine Tomás playing soccer with his friends, then think of his mother, Florencia, perhaps one of the women in Jack's photographs. I cannot imagine how much she suffers for her son, fearing hunger and unhappiness, sensing, perhaps, something worse—despair or death. It must be a madness of sorts, praying, aching, worrying, dreading— part of her soul untethered and vulnerable. Why did Fernandez bring him to Los Angeles without having family here to care for him? Most Mexicans wait until a community is established, or at least an extended family, before they send for the children. Was the couple estranged? Did Fernandez kidnap his own son? It's hard to imagine custody battles between Maya Indians, but I suppose it happens.

The telephone rings, waking me. I wriggle out of the tub and stumble over to the phone; my body aches all over. It's Pepper calling me back.

"I got you a ride. Tonight. A private plane from Santa Monica Airport."

"How did you manage that?"

"An old friend, Bobby Crawford. Likes to be called Crawfish. He takes Cuba-bound U.S. tourists down to Cancún, then smuggles back Cuban cigars."

I vaguely recall when Pepper was going through a cigar phase. It suited her well, but she gave it up; slowed her down in her kickboxing classes, she'd explained. "One of your former beaux?"

"Maybe. I've gotta go. I'll pick you up tonight at twelve."

"I need to get some things from my house."

"Okay. Make it eleven." She hangs up without saying good-bye. That means she's mad. Or worried about me.

Jack wakes me about six P.M. His slim body is nervous, twitching; he's like a tennis player watching for a serve. He helps me change the bandages on my hands. The skin is healing quickly, but my fingers are weak and stiff. He smears on Silvadene, then wraps them lightly; he carefully inches on cotton gloves, the kind worn by people with pustulant eczema.

"I'm sorry they're white," he says.

"They'll be fine."

He shows me his purchases. He moves delicately, as if he's dealing with a very sick patient. I know it's because neither of us knows if we'll see each other again. He doesn't want to disturb the present, to precipitate the rapid course of events we both know is coming. "I bought you a knapsack so you don't have to carry anything with your hands. And this." He shows me a thin wallet on a string, the kind you wear under your clothes. I can see a thick wad of pesos sticking out the top.

"You don't need to give me money," I say.

"I know. But the last thing you'll want to be doing is fooling around exchanging currency. Banks have video-cameras."

"Thank you," I say.

He opens a manila envelope and lays copies of newspaper articles on the table. Several have to do with Doctors International. Others mention Clyde Faust. The Lions Club of Beverly Hills gave Faust a commendation for his work. One shows him in Mexico City after the earthquake of 1986, wrapping a splint around the leg of a small child. Other articles discuss his brilliant career as a transplant surgeon.

"Is there anything that links Silvanus and Dr. Faust?"

"No. I also called Doctors International to get their locations. I got some volunteer who didn't know anything, then asked for the Accounting Department. I figured they had to send checks somewhere. The woman I spoke to was very squirrelly about giving info until I said I was the purchasing agent for St. John's Hospital. I said that we'd overbought certain supplies and needed to place them. She gave me the name of their person who handles medical supply distribution. I called him and he said he didn't know where the current camp was, but that it was someplace in Chiapas. . . ."

"Isn't that near where you found the Tarascans?"

"Up in the mountains from there . . . the doctors use a small town called San Cristóbal de las Casas as base camp to get mail and supplies. Once you get there, it should be pretty easy to find them. Ask around."

Doubt overwhelms me. My recent failure at interviewing Dr. Faust makes me feel raw and foolish, like a beginner trying to bluff her way into an advanced class. "What am I doing? I'm not a journalist. I'm a terrible actress. How do I know what questions to ask?"

Something like relief passes over his face. "You don't

have to do any of this, Frances. You can simply go to Cancún and hang out until this all blows over."

I pull him close and lay my head on his stomach, seeking strength. "No, I can't."

I cling like a koala cub to its mother. If only I could stay like this forever. His jeans, warm, slightly damp, smell faintly of laundry detergent and the bittersweet musk of his genitals. A feeling of security diffuses through my body, as if his masculine essence could protect me.

I let out a soft moan, pulling him closer, pressing my lips against him. I want to sink into him as if into the bottomless black water of a spring-fed quarry.

I feel his stomach muscles tighten in alarm. I retreat. There is no time to know each other, time only to absorb an essential anonymous passion, the effect of our history, the mixture of loss, pain, and regret that makes up each of us.

I push myself up on my elbow and look into his bemused face, then kiss him, my entire experience, my soul, my past, present, and future, passing from my lips to his, all the while my heart aching, knowing he can't possibly understand.

At eleven o'clock, Pepper picks me up in her truck. We rattle up the coast to Sunset Boulevard, then turn right. The old truck makes so much noise that we don't have to worry about what to say to each other. We drive a quarter mile, then cut in left to the first canyon. After a mile or so, she drops me off at a Seventh-Day Adventist church.

This is the very bottom of the canyon. I have to hike a mile up through the chaparral to the back of my house.

"I'll be back in an hour," I say.

"Are you sure you don't want me to go with you?"

"I know these paths by night. I'll be quicker by myself."

"Don't trip on any rattlers," she says, attempting to be cheerful.

I don't bother to tell her that rattlers hide in warm crevices at night. My mind is on other things.

I'm not an athletic woman. I have never set foot in a gym. I don't like to exercise. The frenetic heartbeat, the sweat dripping down my body, the acrid taste in my mouth, the throbbing in my head, feel too much like fear. But every morning I hike the narrow dirt trails behind my house up into the Santa Monica Mountains, down into Topanga Canyon. On nights when the moon is full, I wake before the sun and hike to the top of the ridge to watch the moon set over the ocean, casting a wide, white path across the black water from the shore to the horizon.

There is no moon tonight, and there's just enough light to make out the trail. I rely on my other senses. I slide my feet over the hard dirt, up the steep path. Cool air rises from the dirt moistened from the recent rain. The air smells of sage, wild lilac, and something like nutmeg. The path, eight inches wide, switchbacks up a steep grade. Thorny bushes keep me on the path. I hear the rustling of an animal in the bushes. Up ahead, a deer steps onto the path and looks back, curious, then turns and trots up the hill. I see lights from the houses at the top of the ridge, and as I get closer, I hear the sounds of dishes scraping against each other and of running water. My neighbor cleaning up after dinner.

The back of my house is dark. The porch light, which is on a timer, glows softly in the moist night air. I'm tempted to take a peek to see if anyone is watching the front of the house, but I decide against it. It's better to assume they are there.

I let myself in the back door and crawl over the cool saltillo tiles. Cat mews loudly, winding her body in figure eights around my forearms. I can't use a can opener with my hands all bound up. I pull the plug on the refrigerator so the light won't turn on, then feel around inside. I find some leftover chicken and set it on the floor. She seems happy enough. I scrape around with the plug, trying to find the outlet, making too much noise. I realize how stupid it is to be worried about spoiled food. It slips into the socket, the refrigerator hums, Cat munches and licks, sliding the plastic bowl around the kitchen floor. The familiar sounds lull me into domestic reverie. I think of falling asleep on my couch.

A car door slams. I jump awake and crawl to the window, peeking through the shutters. There's a car in front next door. Could be guests or evening hikers. Could be someone else. I don't see anybody. I'm suddenly filled with urgency. I duck and walk quickly to the bedroom, yank the empty pack off my back, and begin stuffing in clothes. No time to be neat about it: jeans, blouses, skirts, a light jacket, underwear. I dump in some things from the bathroom and a survival kit I take on long hikes. I find my passport under a stack of bills. By my bed, I retrieve Tomás's jade and hold it in my palm for a moment. It feels warm. I sense I should get out of here.

I walk through the living room and am about to leave when I see a red light blinking on my message machine. I know I shouldn't listen to it, but maybe it's Jack, or Crawford, or Detective Lieutenant Ortiz. Maybe there's a change of plan. Doubt wins over my better judgment. I press the replay button.

It rewinds loudly. "Frances. This is Marion Godlove. Please give me a call." Why was the director of the institute calling me? *Beep!* "Hey, girl. Where are you? Call me." Pepper. *Beep!* "Dis is Montana Cleaners. Yo' dry cleanin' is ready t'pick up." *Beep, beep, beep.* I curse myself for bothering with the machine. Suddenly I hear footsteps running up the path to my house, up the redwood steps. Terror explodes up my spine. I'm paralyzed for a moment, then snap into action.

I throw on my pack and race to the back door. Glass smashes. The front light goes out. Fists pound on the front door. By the side of the house, a body crashes through the brush, elbows and fists knocking the siding. As my left hand yanks open the back door, my right sweeps over the counter to a butcher block, where I grab a chef's knife. I run out the door.

A large, stocky figure in a ski mask rounds the corner, almost knocking me down. He grabs me around the neck and waist. His weight and momentum propel me forward, stumbling over a bank of loose dirt. Surprised, he loses his footing, shoes slipping like a first-time ice-skater. I swing the knife over my head and jab at the back of his neck. He jumps back howling, releasing me. The other man crashes over a pile of firewood, then presses his shoulder against the corner of the house and aims. As I charge down the slope, bullets ricochet off the oak trees.

My terror is like stars of ice falling down on top of me, numbing my thinking, plunging me into a primal level of terror that floods me with ecstatic acuity. I scramble down the steep slope, jumping over a cactus. I hear both men skidding on the gravel behind me, then thudding on the ground. Bullets crack over my head. I charge blindly down the path, shadows deepening as I slide down the hill. I hear them yelling at each other, crashing, cursing. Birds and rabbits scramble away as if before a flood of volcanic ash, hideous and overpowering. I feel the men's footsteps fall heavy on the ground, violating the earth.

My pack bounces awkwardly, throwing me off balance. As I run, I reach back and tighten the straps, pulling it higher on my back. Gravel cascades above me as they slip down the ridge. They're trying to cut me off. They're closing in.

I dive off the trail onto a deer path. It follows a rocky ridge, then plunges me into a manzanita thicket. I'm stuck. I feel a wave of heat, their anger, spilling like lava down the mountain. They're crashing behind me, drawing closer. I smell onions.

I run back to the ridge, tiptoeing on the edge of shale. Cool, moist air seeps up from the black ravine. I don't hesitate. I jump into the arms of the black unknown.

I fall fifteen feet, branches snapping in my face, my heels scraping into the hard dirt, then snagging in a thick blanket of miner's lettuce. I roll, cold, wet muck soaking through my jeans. I must be close to a creek. Bullets ring out above me. I scramble to my feet. The silky mud is ankle deep. I push through it until I get to the water.

Several inches of water splash over the rocky creek bed. My ankle twists, pain jolting up my legs. I keep running. I hear them follow me up on the ridge, then skid to a stop at the edge of the sharp cliff. I hear them cursing, crashing back up the slope. I angle up to the trail and charge down into the canyon as fast as I can go. I know once they get back to their car they will try to cut me off at the bottom of the canyon. They'll have to fight their way through a thicket of laurel and thistle first.

I run as fast as I can. The last quarter mile, my mind is blank. My feet run themselves. Eyes all around me spur me forward.

I see Pepper's truck by the church.

When I throw myself into the cab, it's already moving.

We stop at a gas station on National and Bundy. I want to call Jack, to hear his voice once more, to tell him I'm close to the airport. It rings four times before he answers.

"Jack!" I'm shocked at the desperation in my voice.

"Mother, I'm so glad you called." His voice sounds relaxed, jovial. My mind races.

"Cops are there?"

"Yes indeed. A few friends from Hollywood. Did you make it back from the doctor's okay?"

"I'm fine. I've got to go." I hang up before I say what I want to say, something like thank you. Or good-bye. Or those three frightening words that men take both too seriously and not seriously enough.

As we coast down the hill into the small airport, I see cop cars parked at an angle by the first stop sign. There's only one road in and out of the airport, which has various administration buildings and warehouses they rent to digital designers and film production companies. The hangar where I'm supposed to meet Crawford is on the other side.

"What do we do now?" Pepper asks.

"Let me off here. When they stop you, I'll cut behind the warehouses. What does Crawfish look like?"

"He flies a Cessna . . . a skinny guy with a gray buzz cut and a walrus mustache." Pepper looks doubtful. "Are you sure you want to do this?"

"Of course not. Give Cat a kiss for me," I say, then swing out of the cab.

I crouch beside a low hedge and watch Pepper speed up through the stop sign. She races thirty feet, then slams on the brakes. The two cops run up to her, handguns drawn. I know I can count on Pepper to make a scene.

I sneak back behind the warehouses and jog parallel to the road. There's a sharp pain in my side. I must've bruised a rib during my tumble. I ignore it.

The hangars are empty and ominous. Nothing is marked. I dash between the shadows. I see no one. I walk half a mile to the western corner near the helicopter pad. The buildings have run out, and all I see is a string of olive trees that run beside the road. I crawl over a bank of ivy to the helicopter pad. Nothing. I look behind me. I barely see a Cessna a quarter of a mile away, rolling slowly out of a small hangar. I bolt toward it. I see a pilot in the cockpit in a hooded jacket and headset. I think I've made a mistake until I see something that looks like a sock hanging from his nose. It's got to be Crawford.

He sees me and stops.

"I almost gave up on you, kid," he says as he swings me aboard. Only after I stuff my pack under my seat and strap on a seat belt do I realize my clothes are soaking wet and covered with mud. I'm too exhausted to care.

The plane bumps down the tarmac. In the distance, I see Pepper arguing with the cops, hands gesticulating wildly. Even from here I can tell she's having a great time. She'll probably sweet-talk her way out of a ticket and into a dinner invitation.

As we lift off the ground, my stomach smacks against the base of my spine, bile and regret rising in my throat. Nervous exhaustion. Hot tears splash down my face, as indifferent and comforting as a hot shower. It's as if someone else is crying.

I reach into my pocket and clutch Tomás's jade in my bandaged hand, remembering how tightly he clasped it during his last few hours, as if it were a ticket to the next world, as if he knew he was about to die, to be sacrificed like a Toltec prisoner, his heart ripped from his body, offered to the lords of the underworld.

Looking out the airplane window, I remember a quote from Marcel Proust, "The voyage of discovery lies not in seeking new vistas, but in having new eyes," and think how the poor, mistaken man simply needed to get out a little more.

PART THREE

Xibalbá

CHAPTER

23

It never feels as though I'm leaving home when I take off from Los Angeles; it feels like escape.

The lights of the city pull away like a speeding galaxy. The higher we climb, the farther lights spread, until glittering specks fill the universe. Yet, as we head out over the ocean, sucked out into the mysterious dark void, I don't feel the relief I usually feel. Fear seeps into my bones as if it plans to stay; my skeleton, cold and fragile, rattles beneath my flesh.

It doesn't help that I'm afraid of flying. It's only my extreme fatigue that keeps me from panicking.

Nearly a quarter of an hour passes before I realize that Crawford and I aren't the only ones on board. A couple, middle-aged, deeply tanned, with matching safari outfits, ironed and starched, have a moneyed look that says they spend a lot of time worrying about how to entertain themselves. They hold hands and stare out the window, even though there's nothing to see now except blackness and occasional lights from a cargo ship. An obese man with a persistent cough and a big thatch of moldy gray hair, smelling of gin and cigars, sits in back, fanning himself with a puke bag. It's going to be a very long trip if he has to use it.

The plane is freezing, and the engine noise is too loud to carry on any kind of conversation. But no one looks inclined to talk anyhow. I begin to shiver, and once we level out, I realize I need to change clothes. I open my pack and strip out of my muddy garments. I figure this bunch has a lot more to worry about than a naked woman with bandaged hands stumbling and kicking her way into clean jeans. The couple glance at me once, then stare back out the window. The fat man watches me without real interest, the way you might watch pigeons eat bread crumbs in a park. I wrap my wet clothes in a towel and stash them back into my pack. Where I'm going, buying replacements is not an option. Once I settle down, Crawford throws me a blanket from behind his seat. It smells of cigars, but I gratefully wrap it around my entire body until only my braid and eyes poke out the top. I try to sleep like this.

Hours later, when we land, the tarmac is so rough that my head nearly bounces against the ceiling. The sun is beginning to come up, and I see the outline of a flat, dense jungle. The airport is nothing more than a few warehouses. We roll to a stop; Crawford cuts the engine and scrambles out of his seat.

"Stay here," he warns as he opens the door and climbs out. He meets three men dressed in camouflage uniforms. He talks for a few minutes, then hands each of them some money. They slap one another on the back. When Crawford returns, he delivers a speech in a sonorous voice as if to a 747 full of midwestern tourists. "Welcome to lovely Nautla. The gentlemen outside assure me that the next plane to Cancún leaves in two and a half hours. I would suggest that probably means four hours, so make yourselves comfortable in the small café in the airport. The coffee is poison, but a one-legged retarded boy sells tamales that aren't half-bad. Please watch your luggage carefully. Your passports will not be stamped, nor in Cuba, but please keep them handy. Please don't wander, and don't be alarmed if you hear gunfire or grenades. It's part of the local color. You'll see a young man in camouflage hanging around the waiting area. His name is Héctor. He'll make sure you get on the plane safely. You might want to express your gratitude to Héctor in a generous manner. Otherwise he might put you on the next plane to Colombia, and believe me, you don't want to go there. Thank you for your patronage, and I hope to see you flying soon again on the Crawford Express."

The couple and the fat man stagger to their feet and clank down the metal stairs to the runway. Crawford motions me to stay. "I wanted to get you closer. There's a private airstrip in Jalpan. Actually, it's a road that was built in the seventies that was never completed. Now it's used by drug runners and foreign archaeologists. Anyhow, those men I was talking to told me that guerrillas have taken it over."

"Where do I rent a car?" He gives me a pitying look. "Did I say something stupid?" I ask.

"You must have some notion that Mexico has entered

the twenty-first century. There's no place around here to rent a car. Besides, it leaves a paper trail, and you can't drive half of these roads anyhow." He pulls out a sketch pad from his pack. "I'll show you how to get to the bus station." He draws a rough map. It doesn't look too complicated. "Take a taxi or walk. If any authorities stop you, assume they're thugs. Tell them you're a tourist and give them some money. Same goes if you get stopped by guerrillas. Do not under any circumstances tell them that you are visiting Maya Indians."

I throw my pack onto my back and step onto the aluminum stairs. "Thanks, Crawfish."

The two sleepy guards at customs don't seem the slightest bit interested in my luggage or my passport. An immigration officer flashes a tourist card in front of me that has written on it in English that it costs three thousand pesos. He asks for ten thousand pesos. I pay him, but he forgets to give me the card until I ask for it. We both know the card is meaningless, but somehow it feels better that I get something for my pesos.

In front of the airport sits a single taxi, a 1968 Chevy. I look inside. The driver is fast asleep, his head crooked over the back of the seat, his snores rasping in the heavy, moist air like spoons against a washboard. I tap on the window with my gauzed knuckles. No response. I try a stick. No response. I open the door, grab his shoulders, and shake. He groans and, without opening his eyes, swats away my hand. A bit of drool forms at his mouth. I give up and hope it isn't too far to town.

The road appears to have been paved at one time but is now a muddy, rutted mess with shifting pieces of broken pavement the size of pies. As the sun rises, a heavy mist burns off over the flat jungle and dew drips on me from the coconut palms and mahogany above. Oropendola nests, like the testicles of old men, hang pendulously from the branches. I feel a cool dampness seep out from the jungle beside the road and smell skunk and the heavy organic odor of rotting leaves.

I walk past shacks built on stilts; hidden behind trees, dirty children stare at me from their porches, sucking their fists, their oily hair like spilled black paint, eyes wide with curiosity.

The town is a wretched place. A frontier town. Brothels, bars, one filling station, a flyblown market. Soldiers, young boys barely big enough to support their Galil rifles, slump against windows, asleep.

The bus station is a bench next to the gas station. The next bus will come at eight or nine o'clock depending on which schedule I read, but a Maya woman waiting with her two children tells me it will come at nine-thirty. I figure there's a better chance that the woman is right.

This gives me time to think of a plan. First I'll go to the institute in San Miguel de Allende. I'll rest, see what Marion Godlove wants, get some advice and contacts, then head down to Chiapas to look for the Tarascans and to find Doctors International. The plan seems simple, but I'd forgotten that simply getting around Mexico is a challenge.

The bus comes at ten o'clock, a cramped and foul-smelling school bus with a mound of luggage and chicken crates strapped on top that sways back and forth like the back end of an armadillo. A mass of humanity trundles off, mostly women and children on the way to market. I tower above the crowd, waiting to get on, and am swept aboard as if caught in a swift but shallow current. I wipe off the seat, which is smeared with chicken droppings and baby vomit. We wait. The driver wanders off with a prostitute, comes back, has coffee, then fills the tank with diesel fuel as he has a smoke. Half of the windows are jammed shut. The heat is insufferable, but no one dares leave the bus, knowing they'll forfeit their seat.

Finally the bus driver swaggers on board, kisses a pendant of the Virgin of Guadalupe that swings from his rearview mirror, farts loudly, and starts the engine.

I stagger off the bus at the base of the hill leading up to San Miguel de Allende, brushing chicken feathers off my sleeves. I feel as if I've been on it for a week. Twenty hours on three different buses, all disgusting, all late, one breakdown, a dozen near accidents—all considered, a successful journey.

As I trudge up the cobbled street, the sun peeks over the edge of the mountains, washing the white stucco homes with lavender. I smell roasting coffee beans and cinnamon. And gardenias. My shoes slip over the cobblestones, remembering. I am overcome with joy and excitement, yearning for the familiar, curious for the new.

Injured, the fox returns to her den. Divorced and laid-off, the middle-aged son moves back with his mother. The whooping crane, lost in the swamps of Louisiana, flies back to Michigan. Terrified and demented, the stallion gallops back into the burning barn. I, too, feel as though I'm coming home.

I pick up my pace, my heart beating hard. These are the stones I climbed for four years. These are the gardens and bodegas I passed as I transformed from adolescent to woman. These are the mountains that heard my thoughts and calmed my fears.

I peer through familiar open doors at cobbled courtyards, at gardens of bougainvillea and splashing fountains. I catch my breath in front of an ornate baroque church; women hurrying to market push around me, their babies wrapped in crimson rebozos, their plaid plastic *bolsas* already half-filled with mangoes, avocados, and tomatoes. An old man leads a burro piled high with cages of squawking green-and-blue parakeets. A flower vendor hums to herself, buckets of white tuberoses, yellow calla lilies, and orange gladioli at her feet. I pass the bilingual bookstore where I first learned to love the works of Octavio Paz and Carlos Fuentes. A familiar bakery draws me to its open doors. Starved, I buy *bolillos,* white rolls, and an *empanada de queso,* a cheese turnover. They melt in my mouth and warm my throat like cream liqueur.

Bells from La Concepción clang and echo against the walled streets. The dread and apprehension about returning I've held on to for so many years dissipates with each breath. Tears run down my face, warm and comforting. I am astonished by these feelings of sorrow and regret, sharp as broken hazelnut shells beneath my sternum.

I reach out with my arms with an incredible desire to embrace everything; my hands bob on the horizon like amputated and bandaged nubs; a guffaw erupts through my tears.

As I come to Calle Insurgentes and follow it to the main plaza, I notice changes: an Internet café, upscale Mayan pottery and jewelry shops, a French restaurant, an ATM, a Benetton store, and a branch office of Century 21

Realty. But I also see the same fruit stand, tile shop, plumber's shop. I recognize the village priest climbing the steps of the *parroquia*, the parish church. The town is cleaner and more touristy than I remember; with gratitude I realize these changes are what keep me from falling apart. I veer up a narrow street.

On the edge of town, I see the red volcanic rock walls of the old San Miguel monastery; immense agave cactus and eucalyptus trees stand like sentries beside the portal. Over the stone archway are letters in white: Institute for Eternal Living. I pull a rope on the side of the door; a gatekeeper lets me in.

I enter the main cloister and see women dressed in jeans scurrying under the arcades with books in their arms, chattering in every language of the world. It looks like the campus of any university.

In the center, a four-tiered terra-cotta fountain, rimmed with pots of geraniums and lilies, splashes boisterously. Roses climb the columns and arches and wind through the balustrades of the upstairs galleries; pink bougainvillea cascades over the roof. Red hibiscus trees, orange azaleas, and glossy lemon trees stand guard in massive terra-cotta pots. Rosemary and thyme, rebellious and wild, grow between the flagstones. The air smells of citrus and herbs.

First I check in with the admissions administrator, Alzorra Cerezo, whom we used to call *La Vieja*, the Old One; I am amazed she's still here. *"Qué milagro,"* she greets me, equally amazed. She is short, with copper-colored skin and gray hair, her face a mask of wrinkles going every direction; hundreds around her mouth give her an attractive catlike appearance. She wears a long blue wraparound skirt, a white *huipil* with delicate embroidery across the top, and leather sandals.

After I make an appointment to see Marion Godlove, Alzorra hands me a badge to wear around my neck, then runs a metal detector over my body. "I'm sorry," she says, "we've had to establish some security precautions. It's such a shame, but that's the way everything is nowadays."

"What happened?" I ask, but she simply shakes her head.

I walk through the quadrangle of the original monastery to a wide plaza of magnolia and weeping willows. I see several new buildings and can hardly wait to check them out. Later, I tell myself.

I hurry to the highest point in San Miguel de Allende, an ancient amphitheater carved out of the side of the mountain. Under majestic tulip poplars sit several hundred women, legs crossed on rising stone benches, open palms on their knees, eyes focused loosely on the sun rising over the plains of Guanajuato and the purple mountains beyond. The sky is a symphony of pink and orange, setting fire to the red tile roofs of haciendas across the valley. I quickly take a seat in back.

Morning meditation was always my favorite time at the institute, the night's dreams lingering at the edge of my mind, the women gathering close, still warm from their beds, their freshly washed faces smelling of lavender and chamomile.

I try to focus my thought on the present. I breathe deeply and quiet the blood in my body. The unfiltered air is sharp and clean. My eyes linger on the horizon touching the forms and colors. My senses work hard to bring me into the present—*What do you smell now? What do you hear now?*

My attempts are futile.

My mind spins and slips into error. I feel burned—not only my hands; my spirit is raw, violated, my good intentions punished harshly. Even as I begin to forget what he looked like, I see Tomás's face superimposed over the sloped hills, the citrus groves, the neatly terraced vegetable gardens.

I reach into the inside pocket of my Gore-Tex jacket and manage to fumble into my bandaged palm the green jade. I force my fingers to close around it: the pain of tight, healing skin, the hard stone like the anger in my chest.

I think about what I know and what I don't know: A child was killed, his organs transplanted; his father trafficked Mayan treasures; a famous surgeon performed the transplant; a biotech company paid for the child's housing and insurance. Somehow I have become a threat; someone breaks into my house. An assistant district attorney warns off the coroner and detective. Then an art dealer of dubious reputation who is somehow connected to both the child's father and the doctor is murdered. I realize Elmer Afner is the missing link in the chain. I have a sinking feeling that after the police investigate his murder, there will be no evidence linking him to Tomás.

I feel an impulse to turn around and go back to Los Angeles, but there are things here I must attend to. Florencia. I have her name, a tribe, a general locale. I will find her.

The sun breaks from behind a magenta cloud into my eyes, slamming me back into the present. The air warms me like the steam rising from a hot cup of coffee. I sense a restlessness among the women.

For a moment, I remember the young woman who once sat here, amazed and thrilled by her classes, her quotidian aperçus, her mind expanding to realities she never imagined, eager to explore her newfound powers and perceptions. A young woman of enthusiasm, joy, and expectation. She must be with me still, despite how I feel: burned, suspicious, and angry.

My synapses dance over an insight I can't quite grasp. Something about rediscovering that eager young woman, her joy and hope. How can that help me now?

The meditation slowly begins to break, not at the sound of a bell, but with the pangs of hunger. As I watch the women file to the refectory before their morning classes, I ignore my own gastric melodies until later. First, I want to see an old friend.

I walk into the kitchen and see a woman scrubbing pots in the sink. "Lilly!" I shout. She turns, spreads wide her soapy hands, and smiles, a smile that changes the brightness of the room as if shutters were swung open.

"Oh, Frances! I knew you would come." She embraces me, her head reaching my shoulders. I feel her fragile vertebrae under her garment, her matchstick arms around my waist, her hummingbird chest pressed against my heart. I kiss the top of her head, afraid I'll break her.

Lilly is the only truly kind person I've ever met. Even an avowed agnostic such as Pepper describes her as one of God's children. She never has a negative thought; she never has doubt; she loves everyone. Her face is radiant, and even though she must be in her fifties, her skin is soft, white, and unwrinkled, her hair jet black. Her goodness is alarming, her purity fragile and invincible; she is clearly not made for this world.

Sometimes I get the sense that she is staggering from God's loving kiss.

In learning to place one foot in two realities, there is always the danger of confusion, of losing one's sense of self entirely. As in most monastic orders, the institute emphasizes manual labor. Not only is it necessary for the functioning of the school—growing food, food preparation, laundry, caring for the sick, building maintenance— it also grounds the students' spirits in this reality. Yet instead of the austere environment of a monastery—to discourage attachment to the material world—the institute encourages students to engage the senses: The meals are fabulous; rooms are covered with artwork; students play music and sing; the gardens are exquisite; there is no dress code; sports are mandatory. These are all ways for deathmaidens to learn to root themselves solidly on this earth.

It is a matter of mental health.

In order to lure the soul back to earth after an encounter with eternity, an appetite for human delights and a love of people and earth are necessary. Otherwise, apart from a sense of duty, there would be little incentive to return.

Occasionally we lose someone. Sometimes students will pass through the careful screening process and begin the mastery of transcendence but will not want to return. They get caught between realities. Catholics used to call these people mystics and made a place for them in monasteries and convents; they were thought to be divinely inspired and holy. Nonbelievers would call them insane. Nowadays, even the Catholic Church has little tolerance for mystics and is more apt to send them to the doctor to check for brain tumors than to sanctify them.

The institute nearly lost Lilly Despres.

"Oh, Frances," she says, stepping back to see me, "you are so beautiful. I think about you every day."

An optometrist once surprised me by saying that it is the mind that sees, not the eyes. Lilly might see your face bloated, eyes puffy, hair a mess, but she will say, "Oh, you look beautiful today." I don't know what she sees, if the world has form or substance for her, but it is all beautiful. Apparently she doesn't see the burns on my hands, or my singed eyebrows, or the stress of urban living etched beneath my eyes, or the eczema of fear on my face.

Lilly came to the institute to become a deathmaiden and stayed. The institute takes care of her. She tethers herself to this world by taking on the most menial tasks—washing dishes, cleaning the chicken coop—but she floats between realities and at any moment will stop her chores and carry on a conversation with spirits or with God. She knows the name and history of every student who ever graced the grounds and has been at the institute as long as anyone remembers; only Alzorra remembers the day she came.

Lilly pets my hand as if it were a hamster. With anyone else I would feel annoyed. "You are here for First Collection?" she asks.

I had forgotten about the annual greeting ceremony for new deathmaidens that takes place in December. "No, not exactly. I came to see Marion Godlove."

"Oh, that's wonderful. She'll be so glad to see you."

I strongly doubt that; I haven't returned her telephone call. "How are you?" I ask.

"Wonderful, wonderful, wonderful. We have ninety-six candidates this year. Beautiful women from all over the world. I've made a rose arbor for them. Come with me. I'll show you."

She pulls me out of the kitchen, through the herb gardens of blossoming lavender and thyme, to a round lawn half the size of a basketball court encircled with blossoming rosebushes. It sits on top of a knoll that looks out over the valley, the blue mountains like gumdrops in the distance.

The air is clean and cool; I am quickly winded because of the altitude. She shows me what she's made in the center of the lawn—an amazing pagoda of manzanita branches and climbing roses.

"Welcome home, Frances."

I blink away tears and resist the impulse to fall to my knees and kiss the ground: I know this is no longer my home; I have moved on; I must go forward.

CHAPTER

24

I walk across the main cloister to the chapel. One of the first things Sister Grace did when she established her school in this monastery was to convert the chapel into a library. Under the east window where the altar would be is the periodicals room; I pass a number of students reading newspapers from their home countries. I'm surprised by a row of computers lined up in front of the rosette window. I spot a door on the left that leads to the old baptistery. I knock softly.

A Japanese woman opens the door. "Yes, may I help you?"

"I'm sorry. I was looking for Marion Godlove's office."

"She moved into the new Mind and Technology Building. I'm the new public relations director."

My, my . . . how we've grown. A marketing department at the institute. Something makes me feel uneasy about it. "Mind and Technology. Is that the building that looks like ice cubes?"

"Yes, her office is on the second floor."

"Thank you. How's it going with public relations?"

"Well . . . you know. A bit rough."

"They hired you to come up with a better name for deathmaiden?"

She looks astonished. "That and other things. How did you know?"

"I didn't know. It was a joke."

"Oh."

"What's it going to be, angel of mercy, terminal midwife, daughter of Charon, transition specialist?" She doesn't elucidate; perhaps she doesn't appreciate my suggestions. "I vote for transition specialist . . . sounds practical . . . down-to-earth . . . like a car mechanic."

I leave her and walk across campus to the ice cube building. It's much more attractive than that sounds; in a way it fits in with the Franciscan stucco cloisters and towers—how the chapel might look after an earthquake.

I walk upstairs to the second floor and pass classrooms with large glass windows into the hallway. I stop and watch a class in therapeutic touch, the use of energy fields to relax and ease pain. A dozen women pass their hands over their subjects' bodies. I notice the students all have their own massage tables and listen to new age music. My, my . . . how sophisticated we've grown.

I pass another classroom where women are playing glass harmonicas, an acupressure class, a yoga session, and a lecture hall where a slide of a Buddha is projected above the professor—probably a history of religion class.

I follow the hallway to an all-glass office that looks

out over an orangery. Something strikes me as odd about all this glass, as if it's trying too hard to be open and cheery.

A petite Irishwoman buzzes Marion Godlove to tell her I'm here. I look around and listen, expecting the sound of birds and the omnipresent splatter of the courtyard fountain. I realize none of the windows are open.

She's ready to see me.

A woman with short gray hair glances up as I walk in; she looks at my bandaged hands, then taps the edge of her desk, indicating I should sit. I obey.

Generally, I'm not the sort of person who has a problem with authority. I accept the necessity of rules, order, a chain of command. But that doesn't make me comfortable around Marion Godlove.

Marion Godlove is so smart, she knows what you're thinking a week before you think it. She looks at you in a way that makes you feel you're lying, even when you're telling the truth. A trim, energetic woman in her sixties with the body of a tennis player, she has a clipped English accent and is a perennial polyglot. She knows dozens of languages—"The first eight are a little hard," she says—and she's always learning a new one. She was going through African languages when I graduated, so delighting in the clucking and popping sounds that she peppered her commencement address with Fon, Mina, and Yoruba.

Marion Godlove was an orphan raised by missionaries in China before they were expelled by the Communists in 1950. As a young woman, she entered a monastic order and became active in the movement to allow women to become priests. I suspect she wanted to become pope. She would've been a good one.

"There's been a complaint filed against you, Frances."

I envision Mrs. Cleaver batting her cane around, and her children, mortified at the prospect of more years of catering to the witch, dashing to the phone to lodge a complaint. "I didn't mean to heal her. It was an accident."

"What? Who are you talking about?"

"Mrs. Cleaver . . . it wasn't her children who called?"

She gives me an annoyed look, as though I've given her something else she'll have to look into. "No." She makes a note to herself. "I've always felt you were a marginal case, Frances. If we were a music conservatory, you would be one of those pianists who end up playing for weddings and Christmas parties."

I am too stunned to be indignant. My head begins to throb, and I get a sick feeling in my stomach. "I have always tried to do my job well."

"Yes, you have. But you have a weakness I've never quite been able to pinpoint. No doubt that's why you've gotten yourself into trouble."

"A weakness?"

"Yes. A certain lack of compassion, perhaps. No, that's not it. An impatience? No. Self-righteousness? No. Lack of gratitude. Not exactly. You see, I'm at a bit of a loss with you."

"I try my hardest."

"No, darling, you don't. Perhaps that's the problem. Now, why don't you tell me why I'm getting calls from the L.A. chapter of deathmaidens. Tomás was the little boy's name, wasn't it?"

As I tell her the story of Tomás, Godlove looks me straight in the eye, blinking in ten-second intervals as if processing the information.

"You left the boy's bedside while you were on duty?"

"Yes. But the mother was there."

"You have already told me she wasn't the real mother."

"Well, yes . . ."

"So you left a child who was your charge with a strange woman."

"But I didn't know . . ."

"You should have known."

I feel my face blush, my forehead tingling with fury. She is right, of course. Many things didn't seem right on Clark Avenue—the mother didn't look like Tomás, there were no toys in the boy's room, the house smelled like it had been shut up, there were no other relatives around. My intuition picked up on these things, but in my excitement at discovering he was not brain-dead and in my self-congratulatory pride at this discovery, I ignored obvious signs of trouble.

"At your level of experience, we give you a great deal of freedom to use your own good judgment. I'm disappointed at your weak intuition. You should have immediately called your supervisor and the boy's medical doctor. You should never have left his side."

I want to defend myself. It's not that my intuition is weak, it's that my affections are strong. But I say nothing.

"Frankly, I find your behavior shockingly immature. I'm disappointed you didn't consult me. We are entering dangerous times, and a scandal of this magnitude puts the society in jeopardy. We have endured many cycles of conservatism; we have survived only because we are careful, politically astute, and, above all, silent."

"I wouldn't do anything to embarrass the society."

"No, I don't believe you would . . . intentionally. But

you allow yourself to be blindsided by your own sense of righteousness. We are servants, Frances, handmaidens to the dying; our allegiance is to their spiritual passage. It is not for you to make war with the medical world."

Suddenly angry, I erupt. "You would let them use us?"

"We will look into your story, Frances, but it is not your job to question your assignments. I shouldn't have to tell you how careful we must be. I am putting you on probation until this thing is cleared up." She stands and walks over to a window that looks out over the orange trees. She pauses, as if making up her mind about something, then turns to me. "As you sit here, I sense something has changed in you, Frances. I have my doubts as to whether you belong with us anymore."

Something catches in my throat. *You are my family,* a voice whimpers inside me; then a wave of anger smashes over me: I have proven myself. How dare she talk to me as if I were a child? I will not relinquish a profession I feel so passionately about—not without a fight. "Here I thought I was in line to be the next director of the institute."

"I've never liked your sarcasm, Frances. It's angry and defensive; it shows weakness."

Now I'm really pissed off, but I'll be damned if I'll show it. "I am proud to be a deathmaiden," I say calmly. "There is nothing else I want to be."

Marion Godlove studies me for a moment. "Frances, have you asked yourself why this has happened to you in particular?"

As I brace myself for a lecture on how we create our own realities, a wild heat rises in me: *I did nothing to deserve this,* a voice screams inside me. But Marion doesn't lecture me, nor does she seem to expect an answer. "Look around you, Frances. We have candidates from Brazil and Pakistan, from Japan and New Zealand. There are many women out there willing and able to be deathmaidens. Just because you have the talent and experience doesn't mean you are the only one for the job."

My insides tremble, and I feel a fissure crack open in the earth at my feet; I don't flinch. "I need to find Tomás's mother."

"Yes, you do." She lets her silence tell me how much I have disappointed her.

"I have reason to believe she lives with a tribe of Maya Indians in the mountains around Chiapas. Not Maya really . . . Tarascan."

"They speak Purepecha, a branch of the Inca languages. I haven't learned it yet."

I appreciate her emphasis on "yet." "I need help in finding them," I say.

She nods. "Travel is very dangerous in Chiapas right now. There's a great deal of guerrilla activity. Quite a number of kidnappings of both Americans and upper-class Mexicans. We'll find a contact for you." She gets up abruptly from her chair. "You'll have to excuse me. I have a finance meeting in a few minutes. We'll speak tomorrow. Get Alzorra to give you something for your hands." As I turn to leave, she says, "You'll join us for First Collection?"

Phrased as a question, but not a question. "Yes, of course," I say.

"Good. I sometimes think we give you deathmaidens too much independence. We need ceremonies to center ourselves."

What she means, I assume, is that I need to center myself. Unfortunately, she's right.

*   *   *

I expect Alzorra to wrap my hands in a poultice of rain forest herbs. When I was a student, we were wary of her concoctions; our second favorite nickname for her was *La Bruja*—"the Witch." But she gives me a shot of steroids, cleans my hands with antiseptic soap, and gently smears them with cortisone cream. "Don't you practice ancient healing anymore?" I ask.

"This works just as well," she says, shrugging. "It comes in a tube. It's a lot easier."

My hands are flaking; underneath, the skin is purple. I wonder if I'm molting.

"Your hands are healing well," she says as she wraps them in clean gauze.

Then I recall what I wanted to ask her. "Alzorra, you remember that little boy who used to follow me around . . . the street kid we called Miguel?"

She shakes her head. "That boy is no good. *Un ladrón.* He leaves the navy without permission to join the guerrillas. No good."

I ask her where he is, but she refuses to talk about him. As if he were some kind of curse.

After a midday meal of fish, black beans, and rice, followed by dishes of fried bananas and tropical fruit, I'm shown to a guest cell in the central courtyard of the old monastery. It looks out over the fountain of the main cloister. It has a telephone; I am surprised when I easily get through to the United States. I call Pepper. I need to hear a friendly voice.

"You got reamed, huh?"

"How'd you know?"

"You sound shaky . . . like you just totaled your car."

I catch my breath; I've never trusted Pepper behind the wheel. "How *is* my car?"

"Your car is fine. Look, I wouldn't take Godlove's lectures personally. She's got a lot of problems right now."

"She's never threatened to fire me before."

"She does it to others all the time. Don't worry about it."

I want to tell Pepper that things feel strange here, but something tells me not to talk about it over the phone. "Could you find out the academic backgrounds for the Silvanus principals and Clyde Faust? Those types often end up making careers with people they knew in school."

"I might know someone who could find that out."

"I thought you might." I give her the names: Leslie Folk, Bryant Hillary, Mike Rosenbaum. "And if you could find a contact down here for Doctors International. Maybe try their headquarters in Washington."

"Okay."

"And, Pepper, could you do me a favor?"

"Another?"

"I can't seem to get through to Jack's number." I had tried at the airport in Nautla and got a busy signal. I figured it was a crossed connection. "Would you give him a call?"

"You want me to tell him you love him?"

"God, no. Tell him I'm safe and where I am. That's all."

"Sure, Fran."

I give her his number.

After I hang up, I try Jack. Busy. I don't remember a computer in his apartment; could he be on the Internet?

Suddenly I feel woozy from the plane flight and bus ride. I lie down.

Marion Godlove's words lie heavy on my brain and keep me from sleeping: *Have you asked yourself why this has happened to you in particular?* Am I exercising my maternal ferocity because I need to feel these things and have no other outlet? Or is it pride, that after years of growing rage at medical technology, I want to wage war? Or am I driving myself for selfish reasons; am I searching for something else? Is Marion Godlove right? I no longer belong?

I get a nagging, unpleasant thought. Why doesn't Godlove want to know the truth about Tomás? Isn't she concerned that the society could be misused? Why does she want me to be quiet about it? Does she fear bad publicity, or is it something more?

There's something Godlove isn't telling me.

I give up trying to nap and hunt down Lilly. I find her in the herb garden, transplanting a flat of Saint-John's-wort. I kneel beside her and separate the roots of the seedlings while she digs holes for planting.

"Things have changed around here," I say.

She looks over her shoulder, a gesture that seems oddly guarded for Lilly. "Some of us are upset about it."

"What do you mean?"

"Godlove has been working with a senator from Oregon to introduce a bill to have Medicare cover the cost of deathmaidens. Our lobbyist in Washington—"

"Wait, we have a lobbyist?"

"Yes. That's what protected the hospice movement—when they got Medicare behind them." Lilly is referring to the Medicare Hospice Benefit Program of 1984, which pays for hospice for anyone eligible for Social Security.

"I remember."

"After that, hospices spread all over the country. Doctors recommended them. Private insurance began to cover it."

It began to make sense: the architecture of openness, the glass, the marketing department, Godlove's "finance meeting," the gift shop. "She wants that for the Society of Deathmaidens? She wants to go commercial?"

"It's either that or dissolve the fellowship. We'll still be nonprofit, but we'll have a much higher profile. We desperately need donations, and people need to know about us for donations."

"Wait . . . you're saying we're broke? But all the new buildings . . ."

"They were funded with project-specific donations . . . they can't be used for operating expenses. We're in a tough spot. We need money and we're politically vulnerable."

Then I think to ask, "What's with the new security? Alzorra wanded me when I came in."

"Well . . . a few years back . . . a man from West Virginia strapped a bomb to his chest and blew himself up in the main cloister. Several sisters were injured, and one side of the cloister was destroyed. He was killed."

I vaguely remember hearing about it. "Why? Who was he?"

"Factions of the Christian Coalition have taken the cue from Islamic fundamentalists . . . decided what they needed was a Christian jihad. He belonged to a group called the Christian Soldiers."

"Do we have to become part of all this? Marketing? Lobbying? Security clearance? Fund-raising? Next we'll have a football team."

Lilly looks at me balefully. "Tennis," she says.

"What in hell does this have to do with helping the dying pass with dignity?"

"Everything and nothing."

"And you're all right with this?"

"I'm too old to fight it. The younger women have never known anything else. I trust Marion Godlove. I have to believe it's necessary for our survival."

I feel shaken . . . raw. Perhaps it isn't wrong. Perhaps it's the way of the world. Perhaps I am the relic. Perhaps even the things we hold most sacred will feed into the marketing machine—capitalism exacting its pound of flesh by making everything a commodity. Even death.

Feeling faint, I go back to my cell and lie down on my cot. I roll to my side; my eyes rest on Tomás's jade, which lies on my bedstand. I think the little man is laughing at me.

I wake with a jolt. It is nearly dark, and for a moment, I'm not sure where I am. I look out the window and see pinpricks of light moving from every corner of the monastery toward the amphitheater. While I slept, someone set an eighteen-inch candle on my desk. Quickly I slip on my shoes, light the candle, and hurry out the cloister across campus.

It is not a requirement to attend First Collection, but every year, deathmaidens come from all over the world to welcome the new class; this is my first time since graduation.

Dusk turns to dark; five hundred candles glow in the amphitheater. A full moon, huge and white, rises up over the mountains as the last purple light fades to black.

Drumming thunders across the valley as a dozen women pound on massive drums with wooden bats. The drumming stops and the women begin to sing, four-part harmonic climbs, no words, only voices. The drums represent our bodies, our heartbeats; the singing represents our spirits, in community, ascending to the light.

Each woman stands facing her candle, a reflection of her inner light, of her personal and shared commitment to the search for truth.

Women's voices, clear as a glass harmonica, fill the valley. Then, overtones, unsung notes as clear as the voice of God, chime out like bells. Our bodies vibrate with song.

I feel tremendous admiration and love for these women. Yet an incipient rage grows inside me: Of all people, Marion Godlove has no right to dissuade me from seeking the truth.

The next morning, Marion Godlove waits for me in her office. She pulls down a detailed map of Latin America and points out where we are above Mexico City; she slides her finger down to the heel of Mexico. "San Cristóbal is about six hundred miles south from here up in the Sierra Madre de Chiapas. It may take you several days to get there by bus. I have a contact for you there, a young graduate student who spoke on Mayan culture this fall at the institute. He may be able to help you." She hands me a slip of paper with a name and telephone number. "After you inform Tomás's mother, I expect you to return to Los Angeles and wait for your review. You might use the time for reflection."

She looks at me hard; I suspect she knows I have no intention of obeying.

CHAPTER

25

The bus pitches from side to side as the driver swerves to miss potholes. My left shoulder slams into the window, the other into a soft, round Maya woman. She pretends not to notice.

I fall asleep; when my head bangs hard on the window, the shadows are long, the sun coloring the jungle a marine blue.

We arrive in a small town with an enormous cathedral and squat cement buildings around a square park. Everyone gets off the bus. I ask the driver if this is San Cristóbal. He says no. Today the bus doesn't go that far. The bridge is out. Tomorrow I can cross on a footbridge and catch a bus on the other side.

It's close to evening; I'm exhausted from a day and a half on the bus. There's no choice but to spend the night and walk to catch the Chiapas bus tomorrow.

As the sun sets, the light is muddy, the humidity oppressive. At the end of town, I find a rickety building that claims to be a motel. I walk into the lobby. Hanging from the wall are moth-eaten jaguar pelts and badly stuffed deer and ocelot heads with plastic eyeballs. A stuffed snake has fallen from the wall, and I kick it accidentally. It's like the junk shop of a taxidermist. It must be a big tourist draw.

The room is $5, the kind of place where the furniture is so filthy that you half expect it to get up and walk away while you sleep. It's damp and smells like dirt, sweat, and urine. The sheets are yellowed with cigarette holes and bloodstains. I lie down on the bedspread fully clothed and fall into a fitful sleep.

The jungle pulses, bursting with odd howls, caws, and rustling, setting my jangled nerves on edge. As the birds and insects begin their evening serenade, an oropendola sings like the sound of water dripping from a cliff into a deep pool. Spider monkeys screech and shake branches outside my window.

My own aching muscles throb to the jungle beat. The rhythm slowly lulls me into a fevered slumber, half-asleep, half-awake. I have the sense of falling backward into a bottomless pit.

I promised myself not to think of Jack. But as I close my eyes, my hands move up his spine, his skin soft as butter, his bulky shoulders embracing me like a cloak, his thighs sinuous and strong, his neck soft. My fingers trace the lines of his chin, sharp; his nose, slightly hooked; his hair, long and silky. His touch sends a mad convoy of impulses to the harp in my groin, striking a chord that reverberates back up my spine, through my bones, tingling my scalp and toes. I relish the tremendous power of his shoulders and buttocks when he enters me. I long for him inside me with such urgency, such despair, that I cry out.

My eyes blink open.

I am wildly hungry. I get up and look for food.

The only restaurant in town is three *palapas,* huge umbrellas of palm, with a cluster of tables underneath. The kitchen is an outside barbecue curtained off by a sheet. Eating at one table is a barefoot Huichol Indian couple in white-and-red costume on their way to San Cristóbal to sell their beaded masks. They too are stranded for the night.

I order *tostadas de ceviche,* a lime-marinated scallop salad on crisp fried tortilla, with a Coke. The young man who serves me wears jeans and an American T-shirt with a picture of the Hollywood sign and the words *I love L.A.* He tells me that he is going to Cancún to get a job and by summer he'll have enough money to buy a television. I guess he is trying to say that he's a fellow who's going places.

I drag myself back to the motel and fall into bed. Howler monkeys bellow nearby, cicadas wheeze rhythmically, and deep in the swamp, a jaguar makes his grunting call. I wonder how in the world I'm going to sleep when I'm suddenly awash with a happy sinking feeling that covers me like a warm quilt; I drift into the scented floor of the jungle.

The next day, I hike to the river where the bridge has washed out. Four men watch as a fifth clears wood out of the muddy stream; they help by telling him where to stack the wood. After a little, he sits down for a break. The men tell me there is a rope bridge above the stream.

I follow a muddy path parallel to the river until I get to

a sorry, twisted thing that looks like a railroad trestle after a tornado. A woman carrying an earthen pot on her head crosses without using her hands. She doesn't look down. I guess that's the key. I hold my breath and run across.

I cut back to the road. The landscape is flat second-growth jungle, thick with blue and red flowers. There are no houses, no shacks, no farmers. Occasionally I see a milpa, the mixed vegetable gardens of the Maya, or a banana grove. The heavy air buzzes with the drone of honeybees.

I walk for several miles until I come across a pile of rocks with two wooden crosses sticking out of it. When an old man passes carrying a basket with a tumpline around his forehead, I ask him if this is the bus stop. He nods and shuffles away quickly, as if I might be dangerous.

I wait an hour before I see a dust cloud with a yellow core coming slowly toward me. The bus to San Cristóbal.

The bus whines through the jungle, every pothole sending us all into the air like a chef sautéing scallions. As it begins to rain, the tires of the bus slide sideways in the mud. Twice the bus gets stuck. We all clamber out to help push. We get soaking wet and muddy, but no one complains. Back on the bus, one woman as wide as she is tall hands out tamales to everyone. Another cuts up mangoes and passes out slices. They taste nothing like American mangoes, but more like strawberries.

As the bus grinds toward higher ground, the dense jungle gives way to deep green valleys dotted with cornfields, feathery pines, and oaks. The road winds up and around sheer orange cliffs of loose scree, which threaten to avalanche at a sneeze. Rivers gush down ravines, only to disappear underground. Scattered on the hillsides, I see Indian women tending flocks and, in the distance, clusters of adobe huts with high-pitched thatched roofs that look like witches' hats.

Roadside shrines glitter as the sun hits them. The bus sways over the edge of the eroded highway, its bald tires skidding around the corners. I hear the luggage shift on the roof and feel the bus lurch. I wonder if we'll be carried over the side.

We climb seven thousand feet and arrive at San Cristóbal de las Casas, a colonial city of cobblestone streets and crumbling baroque churches. Whitewashed stucco walls line the streets, red roofs clustered behind. Flower boxes of pink geraniums spill into the streets.

The bus stops in front of a monstrous Roman Catholic church in the town plaza of jacaranda trees. Surrounding a bandstand is the marketplace, where Maya sell their produce and handicrafts: onions, potatoes, pepper, corn, handwoven belts and *huipiles*.

I ask a vendor where the tourist office is, and he points down the street to a small church. "It's there right beside it," he says.

I hitch my knapsack over my shoulder, dodge a dilapidated taxi, donkeys, and some runaway chickens, and walk to a small storefront that advertises cheap tickets to Los Angeles in the window. Apparently, for Mexicans the world is divided between Mexico and Los Angeles.

When I enter, a young blond woman in a neat blue suit welcomes me in German-accented English. I ask for a hotel recommendation, and she collects from various piles a city map, a detailed map of Chiapas, a bus schedule—"not to be trusted," she tells me—four postcards picturing Mayan festivals, and a brochure for balloon rides and hang gliding—her husband's business, she adds with a grin. Suddenly it makes sense—she and her husband have set themselves up for the European adventure tourism trade.

She notices that I look closely at the postcards. "You've just missed all the Christmas festivals, but there is a museum in town."

"I'm very interested in Mayan culture. I'll be sure to check it out. Do you know anything about the Tarascan Indians?"

"No . . . but there are many small tribes around. You could ask at the museum." She marks a hotel—"The only place I'd stay in," she says—and the museum on my map with a red marker and hands it back to me with an "Adios."

I find Hotel Imperial right off the main plaza, a three-story pension with orange saltillo tile floors, gigantic old-fashioned armoires, a balcony over the street, and, I'm delighted to discover, its own bathroom. The best in town. I prepare to take an hour-long shower, but there's no hot water. When I complain to the manager, he tells me hot water is provided only between ten A.M. and noon. "Luxury hotel" is a relative term.

I find a bar restaurant down the street where televisions hang in the corners blaring a barely visible soccer game. I order *sopa azteca:* a chile called *chipotle* served with fried tortilla strips, cheese, avocados, and chicken. While I wait for the food, I call the contact Marion Godlove gave me, the graduate student Javier Valero-Cuevas. He agrees to join me at the bar.

He enters as I finish my *sopa*. He orders *una cerveza* and sits beside me, eagerly telling me about his life. He is thin, with bad skin and straight hair to his collar, but his good teeth, expensive cologne, and nearly flawless English indicate he's from the Mexican upper middle class. He tells me his parents are both doctors in Mexico City and he's studying linguistics at the university. He just got back from the Yucatán, where he spent a month studying Mayan dialect groups.

"Do you know anything about the Tarascan Indians?"

"Why, are you studying them?" he asks enthusiastically.

I see no reason to lie. "No, it's a family matter. I need to find the mother of a boy I knew in Los Angeles."

"You could talk to my friend Manuel Guerrero. He's been staying in San Cristóbal for the last year studying Mayan religious rituals. If I remember right, he visited the Tarascans about a year ago."

I ask Javier where I can make a long-distance telephone call. He walks me outside and points to a *larga-distancia caseta* down the street. He also points out the café where I'll meet him and his friend tomorrow.

The shop I enter looks like a convenience store, with aisles of tortillas, toilet paper, and cigarettes. In the back, there are three old-fashioned wooden booths. A woman behind a desk negotiates lines with operators abroad.

When my turn comes, I give the clerk Jack's number. She tries for an hour before she can get through to an American operator; his line is busy. This is the third time I've tried; something's wrong. I complain to the operator about a crossed line; she only shrugs. I call Pepper.

"Are you all right?"

"Sure," I lie. "Why?"

"The papers are full of stories about guerrillas in

Chiapas. They're organizing the Maya to march to Mexico City."

"Haven't seen a thing. Have you found out anything about Doctors International?"

"When I called, they were all up in arms. Apparently, Mexican soldiers have been stalking the doctors' camps, waiting for the Maya to show up. Then they either kill them or arrest them. Headquarters in Washington didn't even know where the doctors were. They did give me a contact name in San Cristóbal. Padre Tom."

"At the main church?"

"I guess. By the way, I checked your answering machine when I went to pick up Cat. . . ."

"Any call from Jack?"

"No, but I never knew you had so many boyfriends in the police department."

"Who called? Ortiz?"

"Yeah, him and some other guy, Detective Lieutenant Rexford Reid, Hollywood Homicide and Robbery Division. There was also a call left by some lady from the Department of Child and Family Services."

"What did she say?"

"She said there was no registered foster parent by the name of Erlinda Gomez. She also said the only record she had of a Tomás Gomez was for a sixteen-year-old."

I'm not surprised. "Did you call Jack?"

"Jack, Jack, Jack. Yes, I called Jack. His number's been disconnected."

"You're kidding." I'm suddenly filled with panic. "See if you can find him."

Pepper sighs heavily as I give her his address. "For

crying out loud, Frances. I've got better things to do than run around delivering messages to—"

"Please, Pepper."

"Okay, okay . . . Oh, shit." I hear something thud on the other end like a fifty-pound bag of clay. "Frannie, I gotta go. Be safe."

I go back to the hotel and sleep badly on the sagging mattress. I finally get up and string a hammock on the balcony. I crawl into a cocoon of musty blankets. Ranchero music wafts down the street; noisy drunks stagger home; underpowered cars whine up steep side alleys.

My longing for Jack, which first tossed my body about as if I were a girl possessed, has abated to a dull hunger. I feel like Mr. Potato Head: Some part of me is missing, a small part that needs to be clicked into place. I try to remember what he looks like, the feel of his skin, the weight of his body, but it has bleached to a dim shadow. I can't remember the sound of his voice. I vainly rerun scenes in my head, but they become more and more faded, disjointed, like an old filmstrip that's been torn and left in the sun. I try to manufacture the urgent longing, the pain, the tears, but that, too, is a vague memory.

The mind protects itself from such mad wanting. It forgets.

I wake up early, hours before my meeting with the two students. I walk to the center square and watch the Maya farmers set up for *mercado de martes,* market day. I'm starved and munch a *churros,* a fried twist of dough covered in white powdered sugar, as I explore. Sellers arrive by truck, bike, and burro. They spread their wares over blankets and rickety tables, everything from fruits and vegetables to pirated CDs and electronics to the herbs and charms of the *curandera,* the medicine woman. I get stuck in front of a table of brightly colored chiles, mesmerized: *serrano, jalapeño, poblano, habanero, ancho,* and *chipotle* hanging in bunches and sold in jars of pesto. I notice a large, pleasant-looking Maya woman who has already set up her table of handicrafts. I admire them enthusiastically, then ask her in Spanish if she has any Tarascan textiles. Her eyes cloud over and she pretends not to understand. She ignores me and calls out to another customer, "*¡Barato! ¿Qué le doy, señora? ¡Escójale!*" I spend half an hour talking with other vendors, but as soon as I mention the Tarascans, they pretend not to understand.

Across the plaza, a young man sits at a café, watching me. Javier joins him with two coffees; he looks up and waves me over.

The other student's name is Manuel Guerrero. He is tall and thin, with slender fingers, lank hair, and glasses. He tells me he's writing a paper on the social dynamic between Maya and *Ladinos* in Chiapas.

I buy him another coffee and ask him about the Tarascans. He lights up a Gitane and twists his mouth to the side to blow out the smoke.

"I did a study on the Tarascans last year. They keep to themselves in the highest elevations in an area of live volcanoes. They were contemporaries of the Aztecs and had an empire of several million people in the state of Michoacán. That's north of us on the west coast. When the Spanish came and drove them out, a splinter group fled south to Chiapas. They've lived here pretty much undisturbed since the seventeenth century."

"Where can I find them?"

"The Tarascans are not easy to find. They do not like outsiders. The skirmishes between the Chiapas Maya and the army have driven them far up into the mountains. They have become nomadic, which is very destructive to their culture. Ancient people need to stick close to their places of worship, to their ancient ruins, which are mouths to the underworld. If you move too far, you lose your contact with the spirit world. You can no longer make sense of the world."

"Like being out of range on a cell phone."

"Something like that." He gives me a look, as though he's not sure if I'm being flip or not. "It's rumored they still practice their ancient religion, not the mixed-up, watered-down Christianized version these Maya practice, but the real stuff. That's why the Maya won't talk to you about them; they're afraid of them. They think the Tarascans are shape-shifters and will steal their souls at night."

"How can I meet them?" I ask.

He laughs, then, when he sees I'm serious, frowns and stubs out his cigarette. "Well . . . I took a bus to Tenejapa. That's a two-hour ride from here. Then it's a half day's walk after that." He tilts his head. "I have no idea if they're still there. Ask the villagers in Tenejapa. But I warn you, they're not very friendly up there to outsiders. And if they don't like you, they have a way of disappearing."

"Do they have weapons?"

"The Tarascans? No."

"Why do the Maya fear them? They don't still perform human sacrifices, do they?" I ask jokingly.

"There are stories. . . ." His voice drifts away. He seems embarrassed. It's one thing to admit to a foreigner that your country has an Indian population that's unique and irrepressible and quite another to suggest they practice human sacrifice.

At that moment Javier, who's been flirting with a young woman at another table, takes me by the elbow and pulls me up out of my chair. "I just saw a jeep of soldiers come in north of the plaza."

"So what?" I jerk my elbow away.

"Suit yourself. We're out of here."

Manuel stubs out his cigarette and shuffles his papers together into a bag. The two students dash down the street and around the corner.

CHAPTER

26

The next morning, I take the bus to Tenejapa. The view is breathtaking. Steep volcanoes jut out of wide plains like gigantic pyramids. In the distance, jagged mountain ranges soar and dip at vicious slants. It's as if the earth has been squeezed together like an accordion.

At ten thousand feet, we plunge downward into a deep valley. I see a tiny town of white stucco walls and red tile roofs nestled at the bottom. The bus hugs the side of an almost vertical cliff and coasts into a wide plaza with a massive white church surrounded by clusters of white stucco dwellings.

According to the bus driver, the Tarascans live in a village called Kakalak, accessible only by a footpath from Tenejapa. I see some men who look self-important wearing flat palm hats and knee-length brown woolen tunics tied with a sash over white shorts. They lean against the municipal building, doing nothing in particular. I ask one man in Spanish where Kakalak is. The man simply looks at me and blinks. I look around for someone else to ask, but everyone seems to have vanished.

A skinny white dog slinks across the square.

Strange chanting floats out of the church. I figure if anyone in the town knows Spanish, it will be the village priest. I climb the steps and creak open a heavy wooden door to an anteroom created by an ornately carved screen. On one side stands a wooden table stacked with leaflets and a metal box for donations. With the chanting, I hear something rattling. As I go around the partition to investigate, clouds of copal smoke sting my eyes. At first it is so dark, I can see nothing. Thin shafts of light streak down through broken roof tiles. As my eyes adjust, I see a shaman dancing in a circle, rolling eggs over the body of a young woman.

I see no sign of a priest. Then I realize a village of this size would be lucky to get a visit from a priest once a month. In the meantime, they use the church for their own purposes.

The walls are covered in grotesque fading frescoes of martyred saints; wooden statues are clothed like dolls in moldy red velvet. Bleeding naked Jesuses, glowing red votive candles: Everything seems to be covered in blood. It feels primitive, primeval, pagan.

I wonder how to gain their trust enough to give me directions. The woman screams again, obviously in terrible pain. The eggs don't seem to be having much effect. I have to do something; I can't take it. I approach and kneel in front of her. For some reason, the others let me.

Often in my work, I use therapeutic touch to relax a patient. This is what I intend. I pass my hands a few inches above the woman's body, my thumbs touching, palms facing down. I read her energy fields, sensations ranging from tingling, hot, cold, heaviness, and localize a blockage in her lower abdomen. I move my hands in a circular sweeping pattern over her body, balancing the energy by moving excess energy to areas of low flow, concentrating on the blockage. To modulate her pain, I hold my hands over her abdomen and concentrate on harmony. I manage to ease her suffering, but there is little more I can do. The roundness of her stomach is not, as the shaman believes, a pregnancy, but an enormous cyst.

When I leave the church, an old woman catches up to me and tugs at my sleeve. I give her a few pesos. She pockets the money but keeps on tugging. I follow her back through the plaza, up a rocky side street sprouting with weeds and littered with dried corncobs, behind a white stucco wall, then up a muddy path that rises steeply up the valley wall. She points and says, "Kakalak." I give her a few more pesos and begin climbing.

The air is thin, and my heart is pounding hard. I feel giddy, as if I am walking on a high scaffold with only the thinnest of tethers. I have to stop every ten minutes to quiet my pulse. Eventually the path levels off. I stop and look around at the undulating mountains and valleys. A waterfall plunges over the ridge beside me. The mountain peaks are marine blue, the shadows black green. Where exposed—the winding path, an eroded cliff—the earth is red orange. The sky is clear and luminous. I hear no planes, no trucks, no generators, no chain saws. It's so quiet that I hear the buzzing of my own ears.

My eyes spill over with tears. I am overcome by the beauty. I feel my mind ripping free from the walls of my brain, lifting, soaring, casting aside the sludge of despair I didn't even know I felt. I laugh out loud.

I think of other landscapes where I've felt my soul fill with such awe: the rolling hills of Tuscany covered with olive trees and vineyards; the tortuous, foggy coastline at Big Sur in California; Vermont apple orchards in October, hills bursting in red and orange, their exuberance tempered by the morning frost. Landscapes of aching beauty tinged with melancholy. A feeling of helplessness in the face of beauty washes over me, the feeling a father must have for his daughter verging on womanhood, knowing, despite her beauty and virtue, she will never find a man worthy of her.

I press onward.

I see one or two milpas, which must be why the path is here. Up ahead, I see a volcano wearing a ring of mist at its base like a grass skirt. Soon the path becomes faint, but considering the steep slopes and ragged cliffs, continuing up this ridge seems like the only possibility. By now I should be used to hiking without direction, but as I climb higher and higher, the landscape becoming more and more desolate, the temperature chilling, I wonder if I shouldn't turn back.

The path finally dumps out onto a surprisingly well-maintained road about eight feet across. A neat stone fence edges the road. Across the fields, shepherds' lean-tos dot the landscape, squat wedges of wood scraps and corrugated tin.

I walk half a mile into an empty dirt plaza that overlooks a valley of dried cornstalks and mountain pines. Scratchy ranchero music plays over a loudspeaker in the plaza. No people. Remarkably, no church. Burros bray behind some houses. Roosters crow. The place is bleak and desolate.

I knock on the door of one brown shack, then peek inside. No one. I sit in the plaza and wait.

Then I see them, a procession winding its way up from the valley, children dancing in front of the men, who carry something heavy between them. The women, holding hands, trail behind. They snake into the village, past me into a long, tin-roofed shack. I follow.

I enter a dark room thirty feet long, lit with hundreds of candles. There is no furniture except for benches that line the walls. The air is thick with the vanilla scent from sprays of cohune palm, which drop white petals on the dirt floor. Inside, they dance around a carved-wood figure. All around sit baskets of freshly harvested corn. Some of the women pass out food; others crouch to husk. The men sit on the benches, laughing and drinking *balche*, a fermented honey drink. A man without teeth hands me a jug and I take a swig. It tastes like rubbing alcohol mixed with sugar. It blows off the top of my head.

No one takes particular notice of me.

They all have odd, high sloped foreheads. Both the men and women wear their hair long, tied back in tassels, in imitation of cornsilk.

In a few minutes a band wanders in, six young men in black pants and white T-shirts carrying guitars, an accordion, a reed flute, and two drums made from hollowed-out logs. They begin singing even before they're fully set up, a chorus of high nasal voices.

The room warms up from body heat and the candles. Sweat pours down my body. I wonder why someone doesn't open a window. Bottles of *balche* are passed around, and I drink thirstily.

The music is hypnotic. Several men swing their heads from side to side. An old man stands on a bench and reaches up into the rafters, pulling down a jade mask with quetzal feathers attached like a fan on top. He puts it on his face and begins to twitch, spinning in a circle, chanting. As the music plays, men get up and dance with the mask, tears streaming down their cheeks. Finally the old man takes off the mask and lays it on a straw mat, then kneels and prays to each of the four sacred directions. Others light copal incense and make offerings of cigarettes, bananas, and batteries. Then everyone gets up and starts dancing, spinning in place, arms waving over their heads, chanting, crying. The music becomes more ethereal, spiraling upward. I'm carried with them, my mind soaring above the mountains.

During the dance, one of the men opens the carved figure and sticks his hand inside. He pulls out a heart. A sudden shiver shoots down my back. I try to convince myself that it's bigger than a human heart. He throws the heart in a pan on the fire, cooks it, slices it up, and passes it around to everyone in the room. They pass the plate in front of me. They expect me to take a piece.

When presented with a reality that cannot be endured, it helps to break down material reality into small, unthreatening elements. This is what I do. Whatever, whomever the heart came from, it is nothing more than cells, blood, muscles, veins, and corpuscles, and beneath the visible, atoms of spinning electrons and protons, composed of quanta, separated by space, nothingness. It is that or it doesn't exist at all, but is merely an idea of sacrifice, an act to recognize the sacredness of life.

All of the villagers watch me. I take a bite and swallow. It tastes like turkey gizzard.

After the men tire of dancing and everyone settles down to eat, I ask if anyone knows Spanish. A young woman with a three-year-old on her lap looks up. Her features are perfectly symmetrical: deep-set eyes, high cheekbones, her mouth a deep maroon. Her child's hand flutters at the base of her neck like a baby chick.

The only picture I have of Tomás is a facsimile of a Polaroid taken by Matty Webster, a photo of Tomás in the morgue. I unfold it and show it to her.

"*¿Conoce este muchacho?*" I ask. "I think he comes from your village. His name is Tomás Gomez. I am looking for his mother."

She looks at the picture. I see a shadow flicker over her features, as if someone were shaking a scarf over her face. Then she looks at me. "His last name is not Gomez, but Cherán. My name is Florencia Cherán. He is my son."

"I knew him in Los Angeles as Tomás Gomez."

She nods. "I sent him with a man named Fernandez Gomez to California."

"Why?"

"Our people are in very much danger from the army and the guerrillas. My husband was killed. My two brothers. We Tarascans know we live outside your world. We know that our time is ending. But we do not wish to give up the old ways. We need one of us to go and learn the ways of the outsiders, so we can negotiate with you. We know you outsiders have laws that will protect us. We need to know how to use this knowledge to save our way of life. We sent Tomás to be this man."

Across the room, the men now watch me with hard, suspicious expressions. I have to say what I've come to say. My voice trembles. "Your son is dead."

She does not blink. "I know. He came to me in a dream."

I think of the heart I just ate and glance at the machetes hanging on the wall. The villagers seem to penetrate my skin with their eyes. I feel my face flush, my head pound. "I am responsible for his death. I could have prevented it if I had used better judgment."

A certain sangfroid can wash over you when you stand before a firing squad, a feeling of liberation. The tension melts from my body, and I'm left shaking, depleted.

She looks at me for several moments, her face implacable, her eyes narrowing, reading me like an electronic scanner. "When the farmer brings home corn that is dry and tasteless, he faces his hungry family and feels at fault. But the farmer does not bring drought. You are not responsible. Otherwise, you would not be here."

I suddenly feel embarrassed and angry, furious at myself for thinking I could find some relief. Had I thought this would be enough? To be forgiven by his mother? A heat passes over me. I feel more driven than before. I must understand. "Was Fernandez Gomez a member of your tribe?"

"No."

"Was he Maya?"

"No. He was Tarascan, but from up north, from Toluca."

"How did you meet him?"

"Once a year, doctors come from outside to give us medicine and take care of our teeth. One doctor asked me if I knew of anyone from our tribe who wanted to go to the United States to become a doctor. He would make sure they learned English and got an education. I said yes, and he told me to talk to Fernandez Gomez."

"Where did you find him?"

"He was with the doctors. He came to talk to me."

"Do you remember the doctor's name who recommended you talk to him?"

"No."

"What did he look like?"

"White, tall, very big hands."

I sigh. That could describe almost any American male. "Have others left your village to go to the United States?"

"Other men have left to find work."

"How many?"

"Eight."

I realize that the myth of the Indians' isolation is just that, a myth. They allow doctors to see them, they leave to find work. They are acutely aware of the world outside. "Have any of your men come back?"

"No."

"Have you heard from them?"

"No. No letters. No money."

"So you don't know if they are alive or dead?"

"Oh, we know that," she says. "Most are dead. They come to us in our dreams."

"Have they all gone through this Fernandez Gomez?"

"No. They used other coyotes."

Coyotes, I remember, is a term used for men who help

smuggle Mexicans across the border illegally. "Were these other coyotes recommended by these doctors?"

"I don't know."

"Are you afraid that if you say yes, the doctors won't come to your village anymore?"

She nods.

"Do you know where these doctors are now?"

"Not here. They left many moons ago."

"Your village isn't sending any more people to the United States, are you."

"No. Our women need husbands."

It occurs to me to ask, "How did you pay for the coyote to take your son?"

"I didn't pay. He paid me."

"He *paid* you?"

"A thousand pesos."

Fifty dollars for a little boy. It hurts like a knife in my gut. A culture slipping below the horizon like an island at sea sells part of its soul.

I need air. I shoulder my way outside, stumbling, where I puke against the building. I hear someone laughing.

Later, Florencia shows me pictures of the men who have left to go to the United States. The men are young, all in their late teens or twenties, wearing an expression of competence and belligerence. They are the same pictures Jack showed me. It's as if he is suddenly here with me, looking at the same images that he saw through his camera lens.

There is a group photo of the eight who left, leaning

against a stucco wall, eyes sleepy as if woken from their siesta. "May I have this photo?" I ask.

At first I think she's going to turn me down. But then she says yes. "Take it back up north where you come from and burn it. You will release their spirits to return to us."

Also among the photos is a shaky Polaroid of a much taller man dressed in a fisherman's vest and khaki pants. He sits with a child on each knee, a stethoscope around his neck. It's Kira Katsumi, the doctor who climbed pyramids with Clyde Faust.

Before I leave, Florencia brings me to her house, a one-room shack divided by a handwoven blanket. It is very neat, the dirt floor swept clean. Foot-high chairs hang from the wall. A low bed is shoved up against the wall; everything is built low, as if they wanted to stay close to the ground. She pulls aside the blanket. Behind is a weaver's studio with several looms. Handwoven textiles cover the walls.

The beauty of the textiles is astounding. Shawls, tablecloths, belts in muted magenta, orange, and brown. Florencia presents me with a beautifully embroidered *huipil*. Across the bodice, the sun's passage through the thirteen layers of heaven. On the arms, toads, servants of the earthlord, driving rain clouds out of caves. Crosses on the sleeves and on either side of the neck show the four sacred directions, and the wearer, her head in the middle of embroidered leaves, the fifth direction, the center, the tree of life, the entrance to Xibalbá, to the underworld.

I have nothing to give her in return. All I have is in my pack, a change of clothes, a few papers. I give her a satin bra, Victoria's Secret, maroon with old-fashioned red roses. Her eyes sparkle with astonishment and pleasure.

I leave the village the way I came. I see the land, humble, desolate, beautiful in its austerity, in the sweep of monochromatic plains, the golden brown cornfields, the faded blue sky. It is a landscape of feeling, not of earth.

I feel dangerously opened, sentimental, sensitive to the point of being out of control. I don't know where this feeling will take me.

As I descend into the valley, the orange sun slips below the jagged purple peaks. Like a far-off galaxy, it feels abstract and elusive, filled with the spirits of formidable warrior-priests, a reality we can never know.

I sense an aching emptiness in the landscape, something like disappointment, something like unfulfilled potential, something like a beautiful woman, aging, alone, living half in this world, half in her mind, not deranged, but managing to survive despite excruciating loneliness.

I see something of myself.

CHAPTER

27

The young priest looks at me with amusement, as if I am a teenage girl with grandiose ambitions. Padre Tom is Irish. Short and wiry, he is dressed in olive army trousers with floppy pockets on the thighs, a black T-shirt, and a fisherman's vest. His curly brown hair falls over his ears, and he wears wire-framed glasses.

"Doctors International in Washington gave me your name. They said you worked as liaison for the organization down here."

"Yes, of course, please come in."

The priest invites me to the parish house office that stands next to the church off the main plaza. The room is large and dark, overwhelmed by a massive desk and an ornate mahogany armoire. A bookshelf completely covers one wall. A shortwave radio sits in the corner next to an old-fashioned twin sleigh bed. It doesn't seem to occur to him that it might be improper to have a woman in the room where he sleeps.

I sit in a leather chair and am overcome by its luxury. I fight my lethargy and slide to the edge of the chair to stay awake.

He tells me he was recruited to work at St. Francis in San Cristóbal four years ago, after a Ladino priest was murdered. He seems to have a deep affection for the Indians as well as cynicism about any good he can do for them. I ask him if he knows where Doctors International has their camp.

"Doctors International always tells us village priests where they're going to set up camp so we can tell the Indians. Whatever can be said about the Catholic Church down here, we do have an effective network. They make use of us. The last I knew, they were in a town called Yaxchilán near the Guatemalan border on the Rio Usumacinta."

"Do buses go there?"

"Yes, but it's very, very dangerous. They chose the town because it is right across the river from a Guatemalan cooperative, Centro Campesino, so they can be close to the Indians, but it acts like a magnet for the army. I told the doctors not to go there, but they think somehow since they're doctors they won't get shot . . . like they're invincible or something. They shoot priests, they shoot doctors, they shoot mysterious American women with long red hair."

He smiles like an indulgent uncle, which looks odd on such a young man. I wonder if he practices that smile in the mirror at night after a glass or two of sherry. He continues.

"The Guatemalan army makes frequent attacks across the border. They want to discourage any refugees from attempting to return to the Guatemalan highlands. The Mexican army in turn rounds up the refugees and ships them to camps in Quintana Roo. That's on the east coast near Belize. The doctors are caught between two undisciplined armies, between the devil and the deep blue sea."

"Or the deep green sea."

"To be more precise. Then you've got the guerrillas."

"The guerrillas?"

"They say they're fighting for the rights of the Indians, but it's almost like they use them as bait. They know the army will show up wherever there are displaced Indians, so they hang around them, waiting for a chance to strike, which puts the Indians in the middle of gunfire."

"Would you give me a letter of introduction?"

He laughs wildly. "You mean like to the hostess of a French salon?"

"Have I just said something terribly stupid?"

"No," he says kindly. "I didn't mean to be condescending. It is customary to have an introduction when going to a new town in Mexico. It simply isn't quite the same right now. We're in the middle of an undeclared war."

"Oh." I feel my face reddening.

He crosses the room and pours himself a glass of whiskey from a crystal decanter. When he doesn't offer me a glass, I realize I've made him uncomfortable. "You may use my name, of course. They probably will talk to you. But why, may I ask, do you want to go there?"

I look at him silently. I don't have the energy to lie, I

don't have the patience to tell my story. "I'm looking for a little boy who has disappeared," I say.

He shakes his head. His cockiness vanishes, and he retreats into himself. I don't need to explain further. He has heard this story before. Women looking for men who have disappeared: fathers, husbands, sons.

When I was in college, I volunteered at a methadone clinic. Addicts stumbled in begging for a fix, promising to clean up, to get help, to straighten out. Just one more fix. The counselors looked at them with a mixture of resignation and amused pity, but behind their eyes, you could see how they absorbed the addicts' pain. This is how the priest looks at me now.

As I turn to leave, he says, "May God be with you." He does not disguise the grief in his voice.

The benediction sends chills up my spine. But I thank him for the blessing. I can use any help I can get.

I walk down to the bus station; the bus schedule says a bus leaves to Yaxchilán twice a week on Tuesdays and Thursdays. I kick myself for just missing it, then recall that the schedules are unreliable. When I ask the ticket seller, she looks at the same schedule, so I try asking several people waiting at the station. They tell me it leaves once a week on Wednesday. I have to wait only a day.

I wander around the old town, trying to kill time. I go back to the *larga-distancia caseta*. Again I try calling Jack, knowing his line will be disconnected. I'm beginning to get an odd, panicky feeling. I call Pepper.

"I checked your messages. You got a call from Marion

Godlove. She requested you return to the institute immediately."

"Again? I was just there."

"Then *I* get a call from your supervisor, Charlotte Wright, and she asks me if I hear from you to tell you the same thing. You'd better make a detour back to San Miguel before you're out of a job."

That world seems a lifetime away. "She's going to have to wait."

"I'm glad it's you and not me. By the way, my friend at the admissions office at UCLA got me transcripts for those four guys?"

"Yeah?"

"Clyde Faust and Bryant Hillary—he's your CEO at Silvanus—both went to Johns Hopkins Medical School. Hillary dropped out before he graduated. Actually, he was thrown out. The reason for the disciplinary action wasn't in his academic records, but my friend made some calls and found that he'd got caught manufacturing LSD in the science lab at night."

I immediately think of the alpha-methylfentanyl found in Tomás's body tissue. "Anything else that ties them together?"

"A small thing. This Hillary guy is pretty interesting. He must've stashed away some of his college drug profits, because he started a business of building medical testing labs, and later MRI labs. He got doctors to invest, and then, because the doctors had a vested interest in their success, they ordered tons of tests and MRI scans for their patients, even when it wasn't necessary. He made a fortune before consumer advocacy groups got on the AMA to crack down."

"I remember that. You said there was some connection to Faust?"

"Yeah, Faust was a big investor in the MRI labs. I found an article in the *L.A. Times* how he made a big deal about selling his stock."

They could know each other well. It could be just an investment. "Biobreed was a public company before Silvanus took it private. We should be able to get a list of major investors."

"I'll look into it. Oh, by the way, I drove by that address you gave me for Jack?"

"Yeah . . ."

"He's gone."

"What?"

"The place was empty."

My mind whirs desperately, making excuses. "Well, that's the style . . . you know, the loft look."

"Empty, Fran. We're talking not a stick of furniture. *Nada. Bupkis.* Zip."

"Are you sure you got the right—"

"I got the right address. Face it, Frannie. You've been dumped, jilted, bamboozled."

At this moment, her chuckle does not endear her to me. "You have an annoying habit of pointing out the unpleasant and obvious."

"Just the truth, girlfriend. Just the truth."

I stagger out of the phone booth as a Mexican woman and her five children try to cram themselves in to call Los Angeles, shouting loudly over a bad line. I pay for my call and, to wake myself, drink a *liquado* of orange juice with bananas.

I step into the street; the sun is bright and harsh.

*   *   *

I need to hear his voice the way I need oxygen.

I feel dizzy, numb, as though I can't move, a satellite spun out of orbit, drifting toward a distant galaxy. I feel as if my head is expanding, its molecules moving farther and farther apart, turning into vapor. One moment I am charged with powerful resolve, the next I can't even remember why I'm down here. All the events that have led to this point, to my sitting on a sagging mattress in a pension that smells of mildew and sausage, and a ceiling fan thwacking the still air, feel like they never happened.

Jack . . . gone without a word? His phone disconnected? If something happened to him, his phone would still be working, his furniture still in his loft. Didn't we connect? Didn't we mean something to each other? Was Pepper right? Was I dumped or, worse, duped? Is it possible Jack was working with Silvanus? No. He wouldn't have helped me escape if that were the case. He had an exhibit space at UCLA. Surely that gave him some credibility.

But where did he go? How could he not know I'd worry about him? He could've at least left a message on my machine. It didn't make sense.

A pressure close to hysteria pushes against my diaphragm. The taste of bile lies thick on my tongue. He must be in danger. But that's not the feeling I'm getting.

The feeling I'm getting—nauseated, empty, numb— is betrayal.

I wake in late afternoon. I remember that Manuel Guerrero agreed to meet me at the museum, which reopens around four. I push myself out of bed, splash water on my face, and join the paseo, the afternoon promenade.

Young women in tight jeans and white blouses sashay down the street arm in arm, balancing on heels, giggling too hard, looking around, hoping to be noticed as they walk by cafés full of young men drinking coffee and smoking cigarettes. The girls stop at a table and flirt for a moment, then move on, hoping to catch the eye of someone special, someone with ambition, someone to take them away from this town.

I flow with the tide, enjoying the sexual energy until I get to the museum. When I don't see Manuel, I describe him to the woman who sells me a ticket and ask her to tell him I'm already inside when he shows.

I look for anything specifically Tarascan. Textiles, masks, pottery. One artifact strikes me in particular, a human femur incised with Mayan calligraphy, the lines rubbed with vermilion dye. It reminds me of scrimshaw.

The bone depicts death as a canoe trip. The king sits in the middle; a jaguar paddles in front, an iguana in back. The canoe is bearing him to the cosmic turtle shell to be reborn; the same moment his soul is struck down and the canoe plunges into the underworld, Xibalbá, into the mouth of the Cauac monster, his spirit transcends. For the Maya, death and rebirth are one and the same.

The caption says the bone was from a human sacrifice and that before their rituals, the Maya used it as an enema tube to take hallucinogenic drugs. The drugs were absorbed directly into the bloodstream in the colon.

In case American tourists aren't completely grossed out, the curators add that the etching was done when the bone was still fresh. Otherwise the bone gets too brittle.

I head back to the pension wondering why Manuel never showed up. I am about to shrug it off—this is Mexico, after all—when I see Javier walking toward me. I wave and he looks around before motioning me into a bodega. He looks jittery.

"Your friend Manuel stood me up at the museum."

Javier lowers his head and whispers, "He didn't stand you up; he's gone. *Un desaparecido.*"

"Disappeared? You mean kidnapped? Who? The army?"

"I don't know. I went to the apartment he rents over by the *supermercado,* and his neighbor said two guys came and took him away."

"You think because he talked to me?"

"No. Why? He is a student from Guatemala. Soldiers do not need excuses to arrest students, especially foreigners."

Shaken, I hurry back to my pension.

"You just missed them, *señora,*" the tunnel-eyed *velador* tells me as I enter the pension. He sleeps on a couch behind the front counter, waking only when someone enters the door.

For a moment, my heart jumps with excitement. Maybe Jack has come to help me. "Who?"

"Your two cousins."

I have no cousins. A chill breaks out on my forearms, and I get a sick feeling in my stomach. "What did my cousins look like?"

"Two big Mexican men with American accents. I

didn't like the looks of them, so I told them you were at the museum."

"I *was* at the museum. Did they leave a message?"

"They said they'll come back."

"I'm sure. Do you have a back way out of here?"

"Yes, of course." I grab my pack from my room and run downstairs. I tuck my braid inside my blouse and yank a black mantilla off the couch. I see it was there to disguise a bloodstain; I don't have time to ask. I throw it over my head; it's not much of a disguise, but it'll have to do. I follow the *velador* through the courtyard, through a storage area into an alley.

"If they come again, I'll say that you are napping."

I jog to the bus station, ears pounding, breath wheezing, my spine tingling with adrenaline. I have little doubt my two cousins are the same cousins who visited my house in Los Angeles. I stop as soon as I see the corrugated tin roof of the bus station and the dozen or so Maya women waiting with bundles and babies. There is no cover for me here. They'll know it's the only way out of town; they'll be here next. Too many people will see me. I spin around. I run back to the market, where the farmers are packing up their unsold produce.

The sun sinks quickly over the horizon, leaving a violet haze; the market is emptying quickly. A gibbous moon rises beside the church tower as big as a pomelo. I round my back like an old woman and crouch near a statue of an illustrious revolutionary. The fountain splashes; weary farmers chatter; chickens and pigs protest being caged for the trip home; rickety old trucks grind out of the square.

Then I see them, two men working as a team: As one scans the square, the other talks briefly with locals, probably asking if they've seen me. Methodically, they move around the square.

A street lamp flickers on the one who's keeping watch: His face is deeply pockmarked, his chest thick and deep, his shoulders and arms massive. He has an improbable cleft chin, and his nose has been fixed more than once. He sweeps his eyes over the square without moving his head. Intensely still. A predator. He reminds me of Minotaur, head of a bull, body of a man.

The younger one comes out of a botanica; he is thinner, with a strangely narrow, dented head, as though he'd been delivered with forceps. He looks in my direction; Minotaur follows his gaze. Their bodies lunge forward simultaneously: Forceps-Boy walks toward me slowly, twenty yards away; Minotaur takes three steps and pauses to see what direction I run. Then they charge.

I stumble backward, turn, and dart down an alley around the church. I hear one of them shout, their shoes smacking against the cobblestones; a kicked crate skitters against a wall. I plunge around the corner to an even darker alley, my legs moving on their own, my eyes seeking out dark corners, doors, passages. Any way out. *What do they want from me?* I don't wait to ask.

I follow my nose—peppers, pork, and fried chicken— to the back of a restaurant. I slip through the kitchen, past bubbling pots of mole and chicken stock, surprised that it is empty until I get to the dining room, where the tables are pushed together, a big birthday cake, the cooks and waiters gathered around to toast someone. They hardly pay attention as I walk to the front door, unlock it, and slip out.

I find myself back in the farmers' market. I dash behind the open trucks, runaway pigs, and skulking dogs.

On the other side, I see a farmer loading the last of his goats, about to close the gate to his truck. I run over to him and beg him to hide me: My husband just caught me with my lover, I say. "He's after me with a machete." The farmer sees the Mexican Americans charge out of the restaurant into the square. Quickly he packs me in back with the goats and onions.

The farmer backs up the truck, sending chickens squawking. I peek through the slats: A man in a white smock charges out of the restaurant and argues with Minotaur; Forceps-Boy stands in the middle of the empty market, spinning in a circle. He grabs the elbow of a widow with a black mantilla; she kicks his shin.

When we get to the next town, the farmer stops his truck and points out where the bus stop is. Fortunately, it's on the route to Yaxchilán. He invites me to spend the night with his goats, but I spot a pile of corn husks that looks more inviting. I will hide myself there until the bus comes through town at dawn.

CHAPTER

28

Whether because of the heat and humidity or the sense that no amount of effort can really change things, small villages in Mexico are invariably sleepy.

This is not what I see when I arrive at Yaxchilán.

As I get off the bus, people squeeze by me, scrambling up the steps; I notice I'm the only one getting off. I step into chaos. A massive exodus. Mothers shout at their children. Men, edgy as mongooses, display their rifles, slung across their front or carried by their side. Everyone lugs large bundles, which they hug to their chests like life vests. Their eyes are pools of terror.

Shopkeepers board up their windows with plywood. Weary donkeys drag carts piled high with chairs, tables, suitcases, pots, tools. Rusty Datsuns filled with entire families grind over the muddy ditches, their suitcases on top swaying dangerously. Mothers dash across the plaza, clinging to their children as if someone were about to grab them. The one gas station has a sign, in English, hanging from its gas pump: "No Gas."

I see three Americans, two men, one woman, throwing their packs into a black Ford Bronco. They drive off before I can run up to talk to them.

I ask several of the Indians where the doctors are. They don't answer, either because they don't speak Spanish or because they're in too big a hurry.

One saloon appears to be open. I push open the ripped screen door and walk in. Behind the bar, a man is busy packing bottles of liquor back in the boxes they came in.

"Could you tell me if Doctors International is around here?" I ask.

He doesn't look at me. "Down the road about a half mile. Turn right where there's some crosses and a photo of a boy. But everyone's leaving, you know."

"Why?"

"See for yourself."

As I walk down the muddy road, more wagons and beat-up trucks rattle past. I turn right at the roadside shrine and see a compound of a dozen U.S. Army surplus tents beside the road. Several Americans are yanking down the tents as others pack provisions into a Volkswagen van.

Indian women carrying screaming children scurry away. A young man with a gauze stump for one of his legs hobbles off on crutches. They look terrified.

I stop a short, muscular white woman who is stacking boxes of provisions in the back of the van. Her methodical efficiency speaks of a panic barely in control. I ask her what's going on.

"Who are you?" she snaps. She has an Australian accent.

"I'm a reporter from the *L.A. Weekly* in Los Angeles."

"More reporters . . . Christ . . . that's all we fucking need," she says.

"What do you mean?"

"Look around you. Can't you see what's going on? We're running for our lives." She hands me a box to hold while she juggles other boxes to make room in the van.

"What happened?"

"Fucking guerrillas is what happened. We're out of here." She calls to a young man who's talking to a man in green scrubs outside a tent. He waves farewell to the man, swings a heavy bag over his shoulder, then hops into the van with the girl. The tires spin in the mud for a few moments before the van grinds its way up the rutted road.

The man by the tent watches the van drive off, lingering until it disappears. He glances at me, then shuffles inside the tent. I follow.

When I enter the tent, I see his back. He's moving medicines from a shelf and packing them in a box. He's short, with the lean muscles of a tennis player. He has wispy brown hair that shows he'll bald before he's thirty. He does not turn around.

"What do you want?" he asks.

Second time around, the lie seems more plausible. "My name is Frances Oliver. I'm a reporter for the *L.A. Weekly.* I'm doing a story on the refugees."

"For that pinko rag?" Without looking at me, he says, "You don't look like a reporter."

"How do reporters look?"

"Like hungry hyenas."

"And what do I look like?"

He snaps around. His face surprises me. It's so angry. "You look like a sunflower."

I remember I've wound my braid around the top of my head to keep cool and wear a yellow cotton dress. "Could you tell me what's going on?"

He turns his back on me and continues to pack. "I suppose you're going to write that these guerrillas are great guys fighting for a noble cause, for the return of the land to the Indians, for social and economic justice. A merry band of fucking Robin Hoods. That's fucking horseshit."

"Why? What happened?"

"Two nights ago, a couple dozen guerrillas raided our camp, took food, medicine, scared the Indians in the hospital half to death. They were nice enough not to tear up the place and to leave us with some supplies. Then the Mexican army comes in to run them out. They march right through, interrogating our patients. They load the ones that don't look like they're going to die into a truck and take them away. The guerrillas stole our stuff, so the army figures that makes us collaborators. Then we got shelling from the Guatemalan army across the border. They don't want any of the refugees to come back. Last week they were shooting howitzers fifteen feet from our supply tent. So don't go telling those bleeding heart liberals in their fucking Malibu mansions that the guerrillas are great guys."

If I were a reporter, I suppose I would know what to say. Bitterness is something I've never known how to respond to, when a young wife watches her husband die, leaving her alone, in debt, with children to raise, or when a son execrates his dying father who never loved him. Such bitterness burns hotter when doused with water. "I have no polemical agenda," I say. "I'm concerned about the welfare of the refugees."

"Oh, great. Concern is good, concern is just fine. How about some fucking supplies?"

His sarcasm cuts me to the quick. But I am an actor now. My role sheathes my feelings and protects me. "People have to know about a situation before they can respond to it. I'm a reporter. I report. Will you answer some questions?"

"Fucking reporters." He carries the full box to a stack of other boxes at the front of the tent. "Sure, go ahead. Just don't get in my way."

"Are you moving camp?"

"No. Everyone's off to spend the day on a picnic. Of course we're moving camp. Even if it weren't so dangerous, the Indians won't come to us here. They're as scared of the guerrillas as the army."

"Why?"

"Are you dense? 'Cause if they're seen with a guerrilla, or the army thinks they've helped them, they'll be shot."

"Where are you moving?"

"The army has set up a temporary refugee camp farther west in Chiapas. We'll set up there for a while."

"Does the medical staff here ever assist in placing refugees in the United States?"

He looks at me with genuine surprise. "Not that I've heard." He hesitates. "Wait, that's not true. When someone has a medical condition that can't be treated in Mexico, like complicated skin grafting, sometimes we'll take them to Los Angeles or Miami."

"Have you ever known doctors to offer to help healthy patients emigrate?"

"Hell, no. We give the Indians medical care so they can live reasonably healthy lives down here. The answer to Mexico's problems is not to bring everyone to the States."

"Have you ever heard of Dr. Clyde Faust or Dr. Kira Katsumi?"

He pauses a moment to think. "Yes, I've met Dr. Katsumi. He's a famous epidemiologist. For the last few years he's been working on a study of the immune system of Maya Indians. He's visited our camp quite a few times."

"Is their immune system different from ours?"

"Everyone's immune system is different. But that's not my area of expertise. I don't think he's published his research yet. If he has, I haven't had time to read it."

"Was he studying a particular epidemic or something?"

"No. I think it was more general than that."

"Is Dr. Katsumi a member of Doctors International?"

"No. He's affiliated with the medical school at National University in Mexico City."

Suddenly a flash of light, followed by an earth-shattering explosion. The doctor looks up for a moment, as if trying to catch a scent. "Over the river. They're starting early today."

"Guerrillas?"

"No. Army." He seems nonchalant, but I detect an acceleration in his packing speed.

"Do the Indians ever talk about people going to the United States and disappearing?"

"Sure. All the time. It's only natural. Once they get to the States, it's hard to stay connected. It's expensive.

Communications are poor. And they get selfish. They see everyone else with all this great stuff, cars and clothes, but they're supposed to send money home. They get to feeling that they've made all the sacrifices, that they're doing all the work, so why should they try so hard to stay connected to a way of life they'd rather forget? So they stop writing. They lose contact."

"Do the Maya that you've talked to say their relatives who left are dead?"

"Sure. It's their way of speaking. You're gone from the tribe, you're lost to the tribe, you're dead to the tribe."

"Do you have a telephone number or address for Dr. Katsumi?"

He gives me a look like this is the last thing he wants to do, but maybe it'll make me go away. "Let me take a look." He walks to his desk, a plank resting on two boxes marked "Plasma" in big red letters. He unearths an address book beneath the piles of medicine bottles and papers. He flips through the pages. "Amazing. I found it: 511-22-47. That's in Mexico City."

Then it occurs to me to ask, "Do you ever perform organ transplants?"

"Down here? Are you out of your mind? We don't have the facilities for anything as complicated as that. Jesus Christ! What made you ask that?"

"Just wondering."

"Anyhow, the Maya are generally very healthy. Heart disease, kidney failure, liver failure. Those are rich men's diseases."

*   *   *

Padre Tom told me there was a pyramid close to Yaxchilán. I feel compelled to see it despite the pop of gunfire in the distance. I ask the doctor where it is before I leave. "Great time to play tourist. Why don't you climb a pyramid and wave your arms? I'll take a picture and send it back to the *L.A. Weekly* along with your coffin." He continues ranting as I turn and follow a muddy path into the jungle.

I emerge in a clearing by the river, scattering a dozen wild turkeys. Looming in front of me is a temple two hundred feet high, covered in moss and lianas. Enormous stone serpents guard the base. Shallow ditches dot the grounds, evidence of recent grave robbing. I see one of the pyramids has been recently shelled, the limestone rock white and raw like broken concrete.

I climb the steep, lichen-covered stairs, pulling myself up by the vines that grow between the stones. The steps are wet and slippery. My foot slips, and my knee slams on the stone. The moss I cling to peels off, and I slip another two steps. My foot catches in a crack, and I grab on to a vine. I hug the steps for a moment, panting, then continue the ascent.

My heart is pounding loudly by the time I reach the top. The forest stretches to the horizon on all sides. A light blue mist undulates over the top of the dark canopy like cheesecloth.

I feel wonderfully alone, a tranquillity that belies the activity all around me, like looking down on a busy town from a cathedral tower. A bright red macaw darts out across the Usumacinta River.

I close my eyes and try to imagine the world of the ancient Maya, the irrigation canals, the elevated roads, the grid of raised farm plots that once made up this land-scape. It seems incredible that the jungle has returned with such impenetrable ferocity.

What will Los Angeles look like after it's been abandoned for a thousand years? Pulverized cement dust, a mess of thorns and cactus as inviting as concertina. What from our culture will archaeologists put in museums or sell on the black market for thousands of dollars: a refrigerator, a toaster, an automobile? What is our equivalent of a carefully painted bloodletting bowl that depicts an entire cosmology? My mind draws a blank.

At the top of the pyramid are two chambers. I duck into a corbel-vaulted room, dark and close, the walls covered with guano and running water. I think of the people sacrificed where I stand, the moment the flint sliced through their necks, their heads yanked aloft, their eyes still seeing images of the jungle, the upturned faces of the crowd, the fading horizon. I tremble, sensing a powerful pull down into the crypt deep within the pyramid, of the nobles buried there who traverse the membrane between light and darkness, their souls plunging into the black waters of Xibalbá, their spirits vaulting into the heavens beyond the Thirteenth Sky.

I climb down the pyramid and walk to the river's edge. Something is floating downstream, something white. It snags on a branch, then frees itself to float toward me. I know what it is even before I see it clearly.

The body looks serene as it floats past, on its back, arms outstretched, its white shirt bloated like a water balloon. It causes no disturbance gliding by. No one notices.

I hear a rustling behind me. Not much. Barely detectable amid the birds and insects.

Suddenly, black fabric cascades over my head. I scream, but the musty wool muffles the sound. Someone grabs my shoulders from behind and binds my hands.

I sense two people, one on each side. They don't say a word. I don't struggle. My pack hangs low on my back. I wiggle my fingers into the outer pocket and grasp my knife. I jump as high as I can and tuck forward. The men lose their balance and collide into each other. I scramble to my feet and run, tripping over branches, slipping in mud. If only I can get back to the doctors' camp.

They grab me from behind. My hands still bound behind me, I slash blindly, slicing something solid, unyielding. Flesh. I plunge the knife hard. I hear a yowl. Then a foot kicks the knife from my hand, another lands in my side. I collapse on the ground.

"¡Pinche puta!"

The boot keeps coming, slamming against my side. I taste blood in my mouth. I can't catch my breath between the kicks. Then there's scuffling, and the kicking stops. They pick me up and march me through the woods.

The pain in my ribs is excruciating. Dizziness engulfs me. I gag, vomit rising in my throat. I can't breathe.

I vaguely hear a car door open.

I feel myself falling, slamming onto something hard. Then there's blackness.

CHAPTER

29

I lie on my left side in the backseat of a car. My knees are close to my chest, so I know it's a small car. The black hood over my head smells of blood and damp wool. It's hard to breathe. I feel groggy and nauseated, and my side throbs with a steady, deep pain. I don't know how long we've been driving. I think I must have passed out. The car rocks on a rutted road, sending bolts of excruciating pain up my spine. I'll do anything, say anything. Just stop the car.

I hear two voices up front speaking Spanish with a lot of slang. I catch only a few words. They speak in bursts, then fall silent.

One or both of them are smoking. That makes it even harder to breathe.

The car stops. The jolting pain subsides. Relief washes over me, quickly replaced by fear of what comes next. The men get out. The one from the passenger side, the one who smells of pork and sweet peppers, opens the rear door.

"*Levántate,*" he says. Get up.

I try, but as I contract my stomach muscles to sit, a rib stabs my gut. I cry out. The man grabs the fabric on my shoulder and gently pulls me upright and to the edge of the seat.

"Get out," he says. "Careful with your feet. The ground is muddy."

His voice, midrange with a Mayan accent, soft as rustling cattails, pauses in the air like a poem in a dark, smoky coffeehouse. Two thoughts flash through my mind: that his mother must think he's a lovely boy, and that soon I will be tortured horribly.

I have no choice. I step out of the car.

At once I feel an openness, the smell of a wheat field, of cow manure. It must be a farm.

He leads me by the elbow as though he's leading his blind grandmother to church. I try to see something through the black hood but can't make out anything. It seems as if we walk for hours, but it's probably no more than fifty yards to the stairs. We walk up five steps into a building.

Inside there's a deep chill in the air, and it smells like a butcher's shop. I guess the building is stone or concrete, which surprises me. I've seen mostly thatched stucco buildings in the area.

He takes me down what feels like a corridor and opens a door that sounds like the door to a commercial refrigerator.

Smells of old meat and blood make me gag. He pushes me into the room and tells me not to turn around. He takes off my hood and unties my hands. I hear him walk back, then the clank of the heavy door.

I inhale deeply and wipe the vomit from my lips. My eyes adjust to the darkness. Two small windows ten feet above me let in moonlight. The room is twenty-five feet by fifteen feet, with footwide gutters running down the room like tire tracks. The walls are cinder block, the floor cement. Hay lies scattered on the floor with clumps of cow manure.

I realize I'm in a slaughterhouse. The gutters must be for blood or animal waste.

My jaw vibrates from the cold. Or fear. I know I have to get warm. I make a nest, using my foot to sweep the cleaner piles of hay into a corner. I climb into it and cover my body. Only my head pokes out. As my body warms, I relax, my eyes resting on the squares of moonlight reflected on the wall opposite. I close my eyes and listen.

I hear voices, a few doors slamming. Then nothing for a long time.

I drift in and out of sleep.

Suddenly screaming, a horrible rasping, guttural sound. I think they're butchering a pig until I hear words: *"No. No. Por favor. Ah Dio,"* then a long, soaring screech.

It is a woman. The screaming stops for several minutes, then starts again.

My body tenses, filled with panic, my breathing rapid, my forehead breaking out in sweat. When she screams, I hear myself whine like a frightened terrier. We must be very deep in the jungle; they don't even attempt to cover the screaming with recorded music. The screaming seems to go on for hours, intermittently, like a malfunctioning car alarm.

Finally silence. Minutes later footsteps, two sets falling evenly, another pair stumbling and dragging.

The door slams open. Two men, one a heavyset Mexican, the other smaller, darker, shove a naked woman inside. She stumbles and falls into my nest of hay. She is crying, and her body vibrates as if electricity is coursing through her.

I reach out to comfort her. She cries out, shrinking into a fetal position.

"It's only me," I say.

She looks up, her eyes huge, frightened, surprised, I suspect, at hearing English. I touch her hair. She starts to whimper, then crawls into my lap like a frightened child, her face flat against my stomach, gripping me hard around my waist, crushing my bruised ribs.

Blood leaks from her body where they've put electrodes: ears, neck, fingers, toes. Her nose is broken, purple and bloody. Her thighs are sticky with blood. Her body shakes all over.

I take off my sweater and wrap it around her shoulders.

She is light skinned and fine featured, her hair light brown and curly. She is probably about eighteen years old. She could be my daughter.

Suddenly she screams and convulses, her hands struggling, clawing at the air. A thick clot of blood and membrane oozes between her legs. A fetus several months old. We are both covered in blood.

"Let me die," she wails over and over.

I've heard that plea many times over, and I know when the desire is real and when it's a cry for help. I can't imagine the torture she's endured to make such a young woman want to die. But she does.

It is clear the girl is dying. I can ease her suffering. I press the palm of her hand to my lips.

I suddenly feel an overwhelming peace. My pain is gone. I feel light and joyful. I am engulfed by warmth and comfort. From above, a light shines down on me. The girl sleeps quietly beside my body. For a moment the role reversal confuses me. Am I dying? I let go of her hand, and as the light draws me upward, I am filled with happiness.

My mother greets me, as does my father, Great-Uncle Dale, and Grandma. My roommate from college and many other people welcome me. I enter a land of indescribable beauty, flowers and rolling hills all made up of light. In the distance sits a golden city.

I am filled with such joy. My fingertips dance over the faces of those I love, over the flowers, over the turrets and bridges of the city.

A figure comes toward me. It is Tomás, smiling, but it is Tomás as a youth, not as a child. He speaks with the voice of a man. "It's not your time," he says.

"Can't I stay? It's so beautiful here."

"You have much to do. It's not your time, Frances."

As soon as he says my name, I find myself falling backward. Disappointment washes over me. I slam back into my body, my wounds throbbing with a vengeance. I catch my breath. My head bangs against the cinder-block wall.

I look down into my lap, half expecting a corpse. But the young woman is sleeping peacefully, her broken nose blowing a bubble of blood.

Frightened, yet filled with something approaching awe, I cover her body with straw and hold her tight.

*   *   *

"Who do you work for?"

As soon as I hear his English, I realize these are not the same men who grabbed me. They aren't guerrillas; they are Americans.

Someone yanks off the black hood they jammed on my head when they dragged me to this room. A chill bolts down my spine: Minotaur sits at a table across from me. On top of the table sits my pack, dumped and picked through: my clothes, Tomás's autopsy report, my passport, the photo of the Tarascans.

"Who sent you here?" His voice is midrange but lilts— second-generation Mexican with a Texan inflection.

"I don't work for anybody."

"Bullshit," he yells. "You lie. Who hired you? Biopork? PETA? The FBI?"

He reminds me I could lie: Whom would they think twice about killing? An FBI agent? No. A nun? No. A movie star? Dream on. No lie will save me. Nor will the truth. "Who's Biopork?"

Forceps-Boy slaps me across the face. Apparently, I'm not supposed to ask questions.

Apart from my two cousins, there are three guerrillas; I sense they are different from the ones who kidnapped me, older, more authoritative, which means there are others in the building. Two of them stand on either side of the table, looking away, almost embarrassed. The third, who sits by the door, stares at me hard; he is short, with straight dark hair cut like a bowl. He is around twenty-five years old, with a round Maya face and deep-set eyes, black, intense. A tattoo of an anchor covers the inside of his forearm, left over from a former life, perhaps the Mexican navy. He doesn't look happy that Minotaur is controlling the situation. I wonder. . . .

The guerrillas cut my hair, the first step in taking my identity, my dignity, then strip me naked. They allow me to keep my underpants; I suppose that comes later.

I try to figure out the dynamic between the guerrillas and the Americans; I assume Minotaur offered them money for me. Use of the torture equipment is probably part of a package deal.

I see no chance of escape. The room is fifteen feet square, with no windows. Around the edges of the room are apparatuses. An iron bar between two tables where I suppose I'll be trussed upside down like poultry. A chair of corrugated aluminum with straps covered with foam. A small generator with wires and electrodes. One of the guerrillas gives me the names: parrot's perch, dragon's chair, the telephone.

For the moment they are content to let me stand in my underwear and to ask me questions. A vain hope passes over me: Perhaps they only want to scare me.

"Where are you from?" demands Minotaur.

"Los Angeles."

"Who do you work for?"

"Nobody. I am alone."

"You lie. Why are you here? You told the doctors that you work for a newspaper, but we find no press credentials on you."

None of these men are professional torturers. Real torturers torture first, interrogate later. Better to instill terror. Nor have they drugged me with sodium thiopental. The youngest guerrilla is pale and looks a little shaken. I sense an opportunity. "Why did you torture that young woman?" I ask.

All five men look at me in disbelief. To my surprise, the guerrilla with the tattoo answers. "The ranchers who built this slaughterhouse stole Indian land for their cattle. They used this room to torture Indians, to terrorize them off their land. That young woman's father owned this ranch. He built these machines you see."

"She has nothing to do with it."

"She has everything to do with it!" he shouts. One of the other guerrillas cautions him with a hand on his shoulder. "We have asked for a hundred thousand U.S. dollars for her return."

Minotaur stands uneasily: The interrogation has slipped out of his control.

"Do you think you'll get it?" I ask the guerrilla.

He jumps to his feet and kicks a chair across the room. In rapid-fire slang, he yells at the other two. They rush at me, grab my arms, and shove me down in the dragon's chair. They pull tight the foam-covered straps and bind my hands and feet with rope. They cut off my underwear and throw it in the corner.

"I was particularly fond of that pair," I say.

They aren't amused. They attach cold electrodes to my ears, fingers, breasts, groin, and ankles, taping them down with strips of silver duct tape. The wires run to a shoebox-shaped machine on the table. I'm already shaking with fear.

Minotaur turns a knob on the machine.

Bolts of current rip into my flesh, sharp as acid, my limbs convulsing, the straps and ropes tearing into my flesh. I smell burning flesh and hear a piercing shriek. The screaming is from me.

He lets go of the knob. He waits for me to catch my breath, for my eyes to open, then repeats, "Why are you here?"

My lips are numb; drool drips down my chin as I try to form words. "A little boy was murdered in Los Angeles. I am here to find out why."

They don't believe me. Of course they don't. I see his hand move toward the knob. My heart throbs in my ears. I feel it flutter like a wounded, frightened bird. Sweat pours down my face. I know I will die.

His hand touches the knob.

My vision blurs, but I see movement out of the corner of my eye; the guerrilla with the tattoo signals the other two. They spring behind Minotaur and Forceps-Boy, grab them by the hair, and slit their throats. Blood spurts into the room. Their bodies fall over the table.

I cry out. Suddenly the room flashes white. A loud, earth-shattering explosion outside. The guerrillas forget about me and run out the door. Machine guns rattle, followed by sputtering yelps.

Then silence.

A second round of gunfire. My fear of torture is pushed aside by a greater terror of the unknown. For a moment, I am alone. I have no reason to think I'll fare any better with the Mexican army. I struggle against the bindings, heave my body back and forth, trying to tip over the chair. It's no use.

Footsteps run along the outside of the building. A door bangs open. More footsteps. A boot kicks open the door.

My eyes land on a machete covered with blood, then move up the tattooed arm. I look at the face; he grins.

At that moment, I recognize the snot-nosed boy who used to tag beside me in San Miguel waiting for his Reese's Peanut Butter Cups. "I knew it was you when they dragged you in," he says.

"Miguel?"

"They call me *Gerente*."

"Why did you let them . . . ?" I rasp. My throat hurts from screaming.

"I wanted to see what you were made of."

He rips off the tape that holds the electrodes. I groan in protest. My body is drenched in sweat. Blood oozes from where the electrodes burned my flesh. My skin is red from the voltage and tingles as if ants are crawling on it. My lips feel like sticks of wood, and I'm drooling.

He regards my body, trying to assess the damage. I feel like a used car. He sees my pack on the table. He walks over and pulls out a clean pair of jeans, underwear, and a jersey. He places the clothes on my lap. "We must move quickly. There are more army soldiers a mile north. After that grenade, they will be here soon."

I command my fingers to pick up my clothes, but they don't move.

Miguel glances at me and sighs. "Here. Let me." He thrusts his arms into the sleeves of the jersey and pulls my arms through as if I were a child. *Does he have children? Why is he helping me?* He lifts my foot and pulls up my underwear, then my jeans and boots. "Can you stand?"

My muscles ache and burn, yet I shiver as if chilled; I have no strength; gradually I regain control over my voluntary muscles. I look at my feet on the floor and think of pushing away with my thighs. "Yes. I can stand."

"Good. We must go." He hooks my elbow and pulls me toward the door.

As we pass the table, I grab my pack with one hand. I pause outside the door. "Wait," I say. "There's someone else."

"Fuck that *puta*. . . ."

I'm already down the hallway. Suddenly I have strength again. When I get to the slaughter room, I heave my shoulder against the heavy door and wedge it open.

Moonlight angles across her face. She lies in the hay, dead, a bullet hole in her forehead. I feel my heart stop.

Miguel rushes in beside me. "You must leave," he says, pulling my elbow. He can't budge me. "Do you not understand? The Mexican and Guatemalan armies come at us from both sides. The Yucatán is a mess. The Maya have run Ladinos out of their towns and burned their houses. The last devaluation has the country crazy. The government is panicking."

I don't hear him. I try to make sense of it—the boy I knew, this man who tortures young women, who wants to help me. "Did you shoot her?" I demand, furious.

He spits in the straw. "No. Whoever did saved her a shitload of suffering."

I don't know whether to believe him. My fury fizzles out; I let him guide me out to a jeep.

"I will take you to the next town. There you can catch a bus to Mexico City. You must get on a plane out of Mexico."

No doubt good advice. Which I won't follow.

Miguel pulls off the road outside a small town. He

helps me out of the jeep, hands me my pack, and says, "You know, Red, when I was a kid . . . I did not hate you for leaving me. It let me know there was a world out there."

Speechless, I nod. He climbs back into the jeep and starts the engine. I watch it rock down the road over potholes the size of fishponds. A logging truck barrels past me, covering the grass and trees with a cloud of white dust.

I turn and walk toward the village.

The brief encounter with the past chills me to the core, turning my assumptions of morality upside down. I am relieved to know Miguel is alive, appalled at what he's become. He murders and tortures, yet he slit the throats of men who planned to kill me. He showed me compassion; he forgave me for a crime that no law would prosecute but lay heavy on my heart. I stop trying to make sense of it, what I should have done years ago, whether he is a murderer or a hero to his cause.

I ask two boys where to catch a bus. I must look as bad as I feel because they make no rude comments. They point to a bench.

I feel dizzy, a sense of vertigo, a desire to sleep forever. My forehead is wet with sweat. I worry I'm getting a fever. I can't get sick. I have to get to Mexico City; there is someone I must talk to.

CHAPTER

30

I need a new suit. From my pension on Calle San Jerónimo, I walk down Avenida Reforma into the Zona Rosa, an area of pink pedestrian malls and slick towers where the high-heel crowd of Mexico City do their shopping. I follow a group of German tourists, stop when they stop to point at a window display. After two blocks, they enter a mustard-colored building with a sign that reads "Buffoni." If the store caters to European tourists, they might have something in my size.

I enter the golden-framed glass doors to a salon of white marble, art deco floor-to-ceiling mirrors, and brown velvet couches shaped like kidney beans. I choose a simple greenish gray suit with slim pants, gray boots, and a white silk blouse. The clerk asks me if I am a model, twice, which means she thinks I'm too skinny.

Only when I look in the mirror do I realize how much weight I've lost.

I risk paying with plastic. I have no choice. I need my cash for a plane ticket. If someone wants to find me, they'll find me. At least I'll be well dressed.

I collapse back in my hotel. I have newfound respect for the criminal, the woman who wears disguises, who slinks around the edges of society trying to avoid detection. It occurs to me that most of us are law-abiding citizens because constant subterfuge takes too much energy.

Shopping took everything out of me. A fever comes in waves about once every three hours. I've had malaria before; I hope that's not what I have. I refuse to let it be any more serious than the flu. I look for the antibiotics Pepper slipped in my pack before I left Los Angeles; I stuff a handful in my mouth and drink a liter of bottled water. I ride another wave of dizziness and stretch out on the threadbare bedspread.

I will allow myself two hours.

I close my eyes and find myself floating down Rio Usumacinta, red macaws flapping over my head.

According to quantum mechanics, the heavy particles that make up atoms behave in peculiar, unpredictable ways. Sometimes they orbit, sometimes they act like waves. Sometimes two particles a million miles apart will interact with each other with no obvious connection between them.

I feel Jack is out there, circling in a parallel orbit, pulling me, his spinning creating a greater and greater gravitational force that will yank me out of my orbit and draw me toward him.

I cannot accept that you can touch someone's core, tumble with him down into the pyramid, into the mouth of the Cauac monster, into the blue waters of Xibalbá, and not see him again.

It's inevitable that we will orbit once more.

From a café, I make a call to Dr. Kira Katsumi at the university. I tell him that I am writing a paper to present to FUNAI, Brazil's Department of Indian Affairs, on the tolerance of native Indian populations to outside pathogens and the best way to protect them. I flatter him, telling him that his work is widely respected in Brazil and that I would like his input from his work in Mexico for comparative purposes.

Katsumi graciously invites me to his office at four P.M. He hands the phone to his secretary, who gives me exact directions.

If he presses me about my work, I'll bluff him with my knowledge of the Yanomami, maybe sing some chants for him.

I have several hours to kill. Before I head back to my pension, I find a place to call Pepper.

"You don't sound so good. Where are you?"

"I'm in Mexico City."

"Marion Godlove called me again. She's sounding real pissed off. She wants you back at the institute."

"I have someone to talk to here. Then I'm going back to Los Angeles."

"I can barely hear you, Frances. Are you all right?"

"I'll be back in a few days."

"Where are you staying?"

I give her the name of my pension. "There's no telephone there. I'll call you."

"Wait . . . Frances—"

I hang up before I lose my resolve.

I take a bus down Avenida Insurgentes to the National University. Several thousand students with scraggly goatees gather at the entrance to the campus, standing around wearing ponchos, warming their hands over a few barrels of burning oil, protesting something or other. I don't stop to ask. I walk past the murals of Juan O'Gorman, Siqueiros, and Diego Rivera, past the botanical gardens to the modern medical center.

When I stop students to ask directions, they respond with the typical diffidence of Mexican students, preoccupied and listless. They tell me the Research Department is on the third floor. I wander around peeking into several classrooms until I find him in the teachers' lounge drinking a *café con leche*.

From a distance, Kira Katsumi looks like an upper-class Mexican. He is tall, with straight black hair that hangs in his eyes. He has broad shoulders and narrow hips, with the slight stoop of those accustomed to bending over a microscope. His skin is almond brown, and only when you get close do you see Asian eyes behind his thick glasses. Although he's in his late forties, he acts excited and boyish. He takes me by the hand to his lab, and there shows me cages of rats, different experiments, his new equipment, like a child showing off his Christmas toys.

He treats his mostly Mexican researchers with pride and affection, a kind word to each as he peers over their shoulders, speaking a clipped, oddly accented Spanish that sounds kind of German.

He tells me that he's Japanese American and that he's been working in Mexico for about two years.

"How did you get started in this work?" I ask.

"Several years ago, while I was working at Cornell, I got a MacArthur Fellowship to study the Fore tribe in New Guinea." He says this in a way that I know I'm supposed to look impressed. I tilt my head and raise my eyebrows with what I hope is the right expression. He gives an almost imperceptible nod, then continues. "As an epidemiologist, I wanted to see if there wasn't a way to boost the immune system of highly isolated indigenous tribes so when they have contact with the outside world, which eventually happens to all of them, their health will recover more quickly from exposure to Western contagious diseases. What I discovered was fascinating."

"What was that?"

"Well, many in the Fore tribe, particularly women and children, were stricken with a disease they called kuru, a chronic wasting disease."

"Like AIDS?"

"No, no. Very different from AIDS. I discovered it was a virus related to Creutzfeldt-Jakob disease, a class of diseases called 'transmissible spongiform encephalopathies,' or TSE. It causes microscopic sponge-like holes in the brains of victims, leading to fatal dementia. It eats away the neuron connections. There's no cure, and it's one hundred percent fatal. Like AIDS, it has a long incubation period of about six to eight years.

"But what's amazing about kuru is that it's very hard to diagnose, because unlike any other virus, the body's immune system doesn't respond to it."

"How is that possible?"

"No one knows. You see, usually a virus causes the immune system to create inflammation and fevers, and we identify the infectious agent by testing antibodies in the blood. But kuru provokes no response from the body's immune system, no changes in white blood cells or in cerebrospinal fluid. We weren't even sure it was a virus."

"Was it a sexually transmitted disease?"

"No, no. The Fore tribe still practices cannibalism."

That word *cannibalism,* like a sledgehammer on my head, keeps cropping up when I start asking questions. I don't want to hear more, but I must, so I say with surprise, "Cannibalism? You must be kidding."

"No, really. As a sign of devotion, or respect, the women eat portions of a dead relative when they prepare the body for burial. The women give some of the meat to their children. It was the women and children who got kuru.

"I published my findings in the *New England Journal of Medicine.* That was about the time of the so-called mad cow disease epidemic in England. When I read that one of the theories behind the epidemic was that mad cow disease was caused by giving livestock 'rendered animal protein,' my head exploded. Rendered animal protein is feed derived from carcasses of cows and other dead animals. They were feeding their cows cow meat."

"Making them cannibals."

"Precisely. I flew over there immediately and began working with their epidemiologists and immunologists at Leeds University. Turns out the cows had the same sponge-like holes in their brains as the cannibals in New Guinea. They called it 'bovine spongiform encephalopathy.'"

"Didn't they find that mad cow disease could be passed on to humans?"

"That's right. There were several dozen cases. The British government had to exterminate millions of cattle, which caused the collapse of the British meat market."

"Did you find a cure or a vaccine?"

"No. Researchers were at each other's throats trying to find the virus agent. No one could find it.

"Around this time I got a call from the University of Mexico to work on an immunology study on Maya Indians. The money they offered was great, so I took it. We have a fabulous team of researchers, American, Mexican, Cuban, and whatever we want—new equipment, extra assistants—it's here tomorrow. I can't tell you what a relief it is after squeaking by on academic scholarships for so long.

"Anyhow, these Maya tribes are very skittish about giving blood, so we worked through Doctors International, which has established a level of trust with these people. What we're discovering is fascinating. Their antigen system is very different from ours. Some viruses are attacked violently, others are ignored. What's even more fascinating is that in some very isolated Indian groups, their antigen response is almost entirely suppressed."

"The Tarascans."

"Yes, how did you know?"

"A guess."

"In fact, their immune system is much like that of the Fore Indians in New Guinea. We managed to do an autopsy on the brain of a Tarascan, and what we saw was something similar to kuru, but not the same. I thought maybe their livestock was infected, but then I heard a rumor that some Tarascans have reintroduced rituals of human sacrifice and cannibalism."

"Did you find any evidence of that?"

"No. Everyone denied it. All the Westerners said it was a rumor the Tarascans spread themselves to keep people away. But there it was. They had some kind of TSE."

"Were they sick?"

"No, not at all. Viruses can be very shifty and change, sometimes rapidly, into other viruses. This virus . . . if it is a virus . . . didn't seem to harm them."

"They didn't get it from their animals?"

"No. None of their animals exhibited any sign of mad cow disease; they don't feed them animal protein. But here, let me show you something." He turns on a light box and clips three X-ray–like images of cell tissue. "These are the brain cells of a Fore Indian with kuru, a cow with mad cow disease, and a Tarascan Indian. See these gaping holes? Look at these strange plaques." He points out star-shaped cells. "These are astrocytes with a waxy buildup of a protein called amyloid. Look here, we have holes where neurons should be."

"How did they get it?"

"The Tarascans? I don't know. But I began to think that from a historical point of view, this was beginning to make sense. You see, by the 1200s the cannibalistic culture of the Aztecs had spread to most of Mesoamerica."

"Through trading routes set up by the Chontal Maya," I add, recalling Jensen's lecture.

"Well, yes, that's one theory. It's actually a theory I agree with. In my opinion, the Chontal Maya spread a virus, a virus passed on through cannibalizing, a virus like . . ."

"A virus like kuru?"

"Yes . . . which affected their immune systems, inhibiting their antigen response to outside pathogens. What I'm discovering is that there is something in these viruses that actually prevents the immune system from seeing it."

"You're saying the end of the great Indian empires, the Olmec, the Toltec, the Maya, was caused by this virus?"

"Yes. The rapidity of their collapse, often within a few years, defies traditional explanations of drought, famine, and war. These viruses tend to have a life cycle of about fifty years. Fifty years after contact with the Chontal Maya, the cultures collapsed."

I think of the people of Teotihuacán, terrified, burning their glorious city to the ground.

"This may also explain why when Europeans first began to have contact with Mesoamerica, the region suffered so terribly. Between 1520 and 1600, the populations were decimated by ninety percent because of pathogens brought over from the Old World: smallpox, malaria, influenza. It was the greatest demographic catastrophe in human history. At least forty million people died."

"And you think it's because their immune system was

crippled by a virus caused by cannibalism and lingering in their bodies?"

"Maybe. But listen to this other piece of the puzzle. The first appearance of mad cow disease actually occurred in prized merino sheep in seventeenth-century Spain. This is the disease the English call scrapie. I think the virus was brought from Mexico to Spain. The merino sheep were highly inbred, which may have caused a predisposition to scrapie. Anyhow, there have been periodic outbreaks of scrapie throughout Europe during the last three centuries."

"How did the sheep get it?"

"Well, one theory of the origin of syphilis is that it arose from shepherds sodomizing their sheep. I think it's possible that sailors from Spanish expeditions returned from the New World carrying the virus from Mayan and Aztec women, then infected their sheep."

"Why didn't they infect their wives?"

"Probably they did. Scrapie and syphilis may actually come from the same virus. Both appeared in Europe about the same time. Remember, viruses are tricky things. They can mutate and change when they jump across species. For instance, the Ebola virus changes dramatically when passed from monkeys to humans."

A cynical thought comes to me. "Why is the National University putting up so many resources to help a handful of Indians?"

"Because there are wider applications."

"What do you mean?"

"You see, whereas the HIV virus infects T cells in the immune system, the TSE virus seems to turn off the immune system so it can hide. This is what I'm studying now, something that may help us enormously in finding a cure for various immune-deficiency syndromes, such as AIDS, and autoimmune diseases where the immune system turns on the body and attacks itself."

"Like lupus."

"Or something as common as allergies."

"Would it be useful in curbing the rejection response in transplant patients?"

"Well, yes, I suppose it could."

"Have you ever heard of Dr. Bryant Hillary or Dr. Clyde Faust?"

"No. No, I don't think so. Are they virologists? Wait. I think I may have met Faust at Doctors International. He's a surgeon of some kind. Great guy. He was crazy about anything that had to do with Mayan culture. We visited one of the ruins together. I think it was Bonampak."

"Have you had any further contact with him?"

"No."

"Tell me something. Would the antigen system that the Tarascans have, for example, make them good candidates for organ transplants?"

He looks alarmed, his eyebrows arched, frozen for several moments, as if trying to overhear a conversation in the next room. "Well, the problem of organ transplanting is the host's antigen response to foreign antigens. But if there's a virus that is turning off the immune system, then yes, I guess that would make them good candidates for transplants. But, of course, you might be transmitting a form of the CJD virus."

"What if you killed the virus?"

"That's very interesting. I don't know how you'd do it. It's impervious to heat and disinfectants. That's actually caused a problem with CJD patients where sterilized instruments have passed on the virus."

"Have you ever heard of Tarascans or other Maya Indians being used as organ donors?"

"No. Most live in locations too isolated to be transported to a hospital in time to be donors."

"What if they lived in Mexico City or Los Angeles?"

"It's possible, I suppose."

"Has your program brought Tarascans or other Maya into the city for you to study?"

"No. That's why we go into the field. It only harms those cultures to expose them to Western ways."

"This research grant you have with the university . . . are you working with an outside sponsor?"

"How do you mean?"

"You know, like drug companies often give grants to the research departments at universities in exchange for patents on new drugs. Something like that."

"Oh? I'm sure it's possible. I haven't bothered to ask."

He didn't need to ask. Nor did I. I look at a beaker that sits empty on the counter. Running around the bottom, in raised glass, are letters that spell "Silvanus."

As I go back across campus to Avenida Insurgentes, I begin to feel woozy and faint; the world seems to wobble as I plod forward with wooden feet. A pathetic whine escapes every time I falter.

I lean against a wall for a moment. It's fatigue, I tell myself, that's all. I only need to get to the bus stop. The fever crashes down on me like a bucket from a scaffold: My face is hot, my breasts clammy and wet. My blouse becomes soaked and my ears hum. Determined, I push off and stumble forward; my knees buckle.

I hear cars honk furiously. One slams on its brakes, its fender tapping my knees lightly, sending me flying onto the pavement. More shouting, more honking.

I feel myself falling into a dark tunnel, deep into Xibalbá, down into the mouth of the Cauac monster.

I wake briefly. I'm lying on my back on my bed in the pension. I have no idea how I got there. Blankets smother me, but I shiver from the cold. My mouth is dry; I can't lift my head. My arms and legs throb with a dull pain. I can't move. When I try to call out, a dry caw rasps out of my mouth.

I sense someone beside me. A woman. I feel her kindness. I trust her completely. She takes my hand, opens my palm, and presses it to her forehead.

With all my strength I fling away her arm. "I'm not dead yet," I shout furiously.

"Shhhhh . . . it's all right, Frances. It's Lilly. Pepper called me. You collapsed in the street. Someone brought you here; you must've been able to tell them where you were staying. I came last night. You've been in a coma."

Sweat is streaming down my face; every muscle and bone in my body aches as if someone is feeding it through a meat grinder. I collapse back in the pillow. "You're not trying to cross me over?"

"You're sick, not dying." Lilly shuffles over to me, a cup of broth in her hands. She ladles a tablespoonful between my lips. "Now be still and sleep."

It's then I realize I'm naked under the blankets.

She sees the alarm in my eyes and understands. "I had to get you out of your wet clothes," she says nonchalantly. "You fell in a puddle."

Across the room, I see my suit, cleaned and hanging on the open door of the wardrobe. Everything is blurry until I focus on it hard. Then it's too sharp, like an image on a 3-D screen.

"You saw . . ." I can't seem to remember the words. I can only see the room, feel the aluminum chair beneath my thighs, the clips on my nipples and clitoris.

"Yes, I saw the marks from the electrodes. We'll talk about it later."

An acrid stench, a mix of ammonia, shit, and sweat, burns the membranes inside my nose. "I have malaria?"

"No. I don't think so. Go back to sleep."

I feel each of my vertebrae grating against one another. My heart hurts.

I want to die.

Slipping in and out of consciousness, I lose all sense of time. Have I been here hours, days, weeks? The sheets are wet beneath me. Chills shake my body, and my head pounds as if it is rolling down an endless flight of stairs. I will my legs to move to a dry spot, but they don't respond. I'm trapped in melting ice, the cold seeping slowly to my core.

My eyes flicker open. I see Lilly watching me, her thin, pale face, her small, amber eyes. She's rolling me over, tucking a towel beneath me, covering me with dry blankets. Before I fade back into oblivion, I notice short hairs sticking out of her chin, straggly tufts poking out like marsh grass. For some reason this gives me comfort.

Jack lies beside me, his long hard thighs tangled around mine, his fingers tracing the curve of my hipbone, up the ridge of muscles on either side of my spine to my shoulder bones. "You've lost weight," he says, then kisses me deeply so I feel as though I'm falling and flowing into him at the same time, into his heart—not his heart of blood and flesh, but a heart of dark mists and music—down into a place of pure eros.

My mother sits by my bed, dressed in a crisp lime suit and pillbox hat, off to pour coffee at a charity function, but not before she pulls off the glove on her right hand to lay her cool, soft palm on my forehead. She smiles at me like this only when I'm sick. When I cough weakly, she takes off her other glove and rubs Vicks VapoRub on my chest and on the bottoms of my feet, smiling at me the entire time. I want her to stay with me, but she kisses my forehead and leaves, hesitating by the doorjamb, then clomping down the narrow wooden stairs in her heels.

I sit at the foot of an enormous sleigh bed made from cherrywood. I've been called to help someone pass on. She lies on her back, beneath cream-colored sheets with yellow forsythia blossoms, her face turned away. Her bones poke up through the sheets like mountain peaks. When I take her hand and press it to my lips, she turns toward me. Her face is mine.

I wake with a start, my heart fluttering. Lilly jumps in

her seat. "How do I get to Orchard Beach?" I shout, then collapse back into unconsciousness.

My fever broke yesterday. I am weak, but I can sit up. My joints ache, and my muscles feel worn out like old rubber.

Lilly is mixing a brew of cheap black hair dye. She pulls a small table up to the back of the chair and tells me to lean back. She pours the foul mixture on my hair, massaging my scalp in circles. Later she cuts it in a smart bob.

When she hands me a mirror, I'm shocked. I don't recognize myself. My weight loss shows in my face; it looks like a skull with skin stretched over it. The short dark hair makes my eyes look like huge blue saucers. My exposed neck looks vulnerable, unnaturally long and white. My mouth is chapped, without color. It's the face of a marathon runner, sexless and frail. It speaks of an underlying fury I haven't the energy to feel.

"You did a nice job on the hair," I say.

"There's not much we can do to disguise your height."

"I'll be fine," I say without conviction.

"You talked a lot in your fever," she says. "That torture stuff is nasty business. Almost makes human sacrifice look civilized."

I think of the girl in my arms, blood and tissue oozing from her groin. I send a silent prayer.

"You need to get out of Mexico as soon as possible." She hands me a passport.

I look at the picture. "That's you?" With my new haircut and hair color, we look remarkably alike.

"Yes. I'm not going to need it again. The institute is

my life. I will never leave it no matter what happens. Here, take this, too." She hands me a piece of plastic. It's her driver's license. "It's expired, but if you need a second ID, it'll get you through. Airport security will be tight with all of this guerrilla activity going on."

"You lived in San Diego?"

"I was married once. We had a house there. He died." Her face is suddenly wistful, her eyes browner, her lips parted, trembling. I've evoked memories I shouldn't have; her pain stabs me deep in the gut. I see a woman who invested her entire emotional life in one man, the kind of woman who never recovers from the death of a spouse, living the rest of her life in a divided reality. A piece of her history slips into place; my heart floods with compassion for her.

Embarrassed for myself and for her, I press my fingers to my lips. The moment passes.

"I'm sorry," she says, bustling over to the hot plate. When she brings me a cup of tea, she says, "I made a reservation for you under my name. I'll put you on a plane tomorrow morning."

Something that has been bothering me suddenly percolates into my consciousness. "How did you make it down from the institute?"

"I took a bus."

"You? You haven't left the institute in thirty years."

"That's true." She smiles what can only be described as an angelic smile. "I came for you."

I am speechless with gratitude, sensing there is so much I don't understand.

*   *   *

From Benito Juárez Airport, I call Katsumi with another question I want to ask him.

"Oh . . . I'm terribly sorry . . . you haven't heard?"

"No, what?"

"It's terrible . . . just terrible. He was driving home from a dinner party with his wife. A car accident. They were both killed."

I'm shocked. How could this happen so fast? I realize how many days I lost being sick—a week or more. "What will happen to his work?"

"We're moving the research team to the United States . . . to North Carolina College of Agriculture and Life Sciences."

I hang up shaken; it can't be a coincidence that Katsumi's research is being moved to the same state where Biobreed has its research lab. I can't help thinking Katsumi was killed to keep him from answering questions from me . . . or whoever follows me.

"Your license has expired, *Señora* Despres." The stewardess behind the counter is not smiling.

I wear my new suit. I bought makeup at an overpriced gift shop when I first entered Benito Juárez Airport and put it on in the bathroom. I try to look respectable, but I can't prevent sweat from breaking out on my forehead. "Yes, I realize that. I've been out of the country for some time. It's one of those things I look forward to taking care of on my return." I use the voice of a woman juggling family and career, harassed by too many obligations, too many details. Perhaps I should mention my small children.

"Do you still live at this address in San Diego?"

"Yes, I do."

"Where's your luggage?"

"This bag is all I have. I'll carry it on."

She frowns and calls a steward over to her. "May I look in your bag, please?"

I hand her my muddy knapsack, realizing I should have bought something else, something without bloodstains on it. They rummage through my few things, inspecting my bottle of antibiotics.

"For such a long trip, you pack very light, *señora*."

"My company is paying for my moving expenses, so I decided to have them move everything."

"That must be nice." She looks at my passport one more time, then whispers to the man beside her. The two of them now look at the pictures on the license and passport, then at me.

Then she hands me my ticket tucked into my passport. "Have a nice flight, *señora*."

PART FOUR

Skull Rock

CHAPTER

31

Pepper has an old-fashioned couch, the kind they don't make anymore, seven feet long, reupholstered in dark green velvet. I sleep on it for fourteen hours. It's the middle of the afternoon when I wake. Cat is sleeping on my stomach. As I rock to a sitting position, Cat kneads her scalpel claws into my stomach, then darts across the room.

I'm wearing a blue silk Japanese robe that covers me to midthigh. I don't remember undressing. Every muscle in my body hurts, and my bones feel weightless, as if I'm a marionette made of balsa wood. I toddle into the kitchen, where Pepper is making chili. I collapse at a turquoise Formica table she picked up years ago from a fifties diner that went out of business.

Pepper stirs a cast-iron pot with a big wooden spoon. She is dressed in cutoffs and a man's oxford shirt with the shirttail tied up under her breasts. She's barefoot, and her naked legs are speckled with clay. She turns and inspects me head to toe the way her father, General Dickie, did when she came home late from dates. "I hope that hair color washes out."

When I twist to look at her, my insides lag behind like an olive in a martini glass. "It came off on your pillowcase, so probably."

With a jerk of her head, she tosses her bangs off her forehead. "A woman's work is never done." She dumps several tablespoons of chili powder into the pot and stirs vigorously.

"How did I get here?"

"A cab pulled up around ten o'clock last night. You must've passed out after you gave him my address. He was nice enough to help me lug you in."

"Thanks."

"De nada."

Out the window I see the neighbor's eaves dripping with dusty Christmas lights, in daytime as attractive as toilet paper. The holidays have passed and I'm just now noticing. I feel cheated, as if I've experienced a hiccup in time or have awakened from a coma. I notice my Jaguar parked in front; it needs a bath. Pepper catches my glance. "Have you been driving it?" I ask.

"Yes." A tone of petulance rides on her words like a surfer on the waves. "At least twice a week, twenty minutes on the freeway. I swear it's more work than your cat."

As if on cue, Cat stalks into the kitchen and scratches Pepper's leg. Pepper kicks her across the room, then glances at me to see if I'm going to get all protective. "They both love you for it," I say.

"Yeah? Well, she has an odd way of showing it."

"We have to make allowances. She had a difficult kittenhood."

Pepper serves me a big bowl of steaming kidney beans, ground beef, onions, tomatoes, and peppers. I eat silently, incredibly hungry, incredibly grateful.

She hops up on the edge of the sink, watching me eat, waiting for me to talk.

I must look terrible, because I see an expression on Pepper's face I've never seen before, an expression that seems to be trying to break out like lava under a crust of earth, an expression that is oddly maternal. "That's why you're pissed off—you're worried about me."

She shrugs. "You owe me twenty dollars for the cab." She finds a piece of loose grout on the edge of the sink and tugs at it.

I don't think I'm strong enough to see Pepper get emotional; I save us both by talking. I tell her everything. She hardly moves for the hour it takes to tell my story. "What are you going to do now?" she asks.

"I'm not sure," I say honestly.

She slides off the sink and sits at the table beside me. I've never seen her look so serious. As she pours herself a cup of cranberry tea, she presses her lips together. "There are some things I have to tell you. A lot has happened since you left, Fran."

"I've only been gone a month."

"A lot can happen in a month. You remember how in the seventies a Podunk senator named Joseph Battenfield gave a speech to a Rotary Club in Utah, which started a whole wave of protests against the society?"

"How could I forget? Two deathmaidens were murdered. One on the steps of a post office in Atlanta."

"Well, it's happening again."

"What's happening?"

"Vernon Keyes. He's been attacking the Society of Deathmaidens on his talk show. Two weeks ago, the Right to Life people filed a class-action lawsuit against the society up in Sacramento. A wrongful death lawsuit. Marion Godlove called me, trying to get in contact with you. You are one of the deathmaidens named in the lawsuit."

"Me? Why? Who are they saying I killed?"

"Tomás Gomez."

"What?"

"They're saying you used drugs to kill him."

My mind reels. Matty Webster wouldn't have told anyone about his autopsy findings. Not unless someone threatened him. I don't imagine that he would withhold information under pressure. But who? How did they find out? Who was behind this?

Pepper continues. "Vernon Keyes seems to be in cahoots with Republican senator Harry Orwell from North Carolina, who's calling on Attorney General Gillian Russell for a full investigation of the Society of Deathmaidens. It looks like Orwell plans to use the issue for his reelection campaign."

"It can't be that serious. We've been through this before. It's like the abortion issue. Every few years someone tries to repeal the right to choose, and every few years someone tries to outlaw the right to die with dignity. It's no big deal."

"Well, Godlove wants you to talk to the lawyer she's hired. She wants you to call her as soon as possible."

"Not yet. I don't want anyone to know I'm back. Not until I find some answers."

Pepper looks at me as if I've told her I plan to take up skydiving. "You don't think it's a coincidence, do you?"

"That the society is under attack? Of course not. I think someone is very scared of what I might find out and is going to use any tactic they can to force me to surface."

"Who?"

"Somebody with political clout. Somebody with money. Somebody who can work through a powerful lobby group in Washington and stir up trouble fast."

"You mean someone working through AMPAC?"

"Yes, the lobby group for the American Medical Association. Harry Orwell has been their patsy for thirty years. AMPAC doesn't care about any of these issues on philosophical grounds. All they care about is protecting the incomes of doctors. They'll even enlist a nut like Vernon Keyes if they have to."

"What in hell are you up to that threatens the livelihood of doctors?"

"If Silvanus develops a drug or a gene therapy that suppresses antigen rejection, they can transplant any human tissue from one human to another. That's a huge market . . . we're talking about billions of dollars' worth of transplant surgery, billions of dollars' worth of recycled body parts. . . ."

"They're afraid you might dig up something that will stop them?"

"You betcha."

*   *   *

After I shower, I call Matty Webster's home phone. It's been disconnected. I call the coroner's office, and they say that he no longer works there. "Where'd he go?" I ask.

"He got a job offer out of this hellhole."

"Where?"

"Washington, D.C." Somehow, I'm not surprised.

By the time I dress and hobble downstairs, Pepper has been on the Internet and printed out ten pages. She sits on her bed, cross-legged, a computer notebook glowing in front of her with Cat purring in her lap. I ignore a twinge of jealousy. "What are you finding?"

"I'm looking up campaign contributions to Harry Orwell . . . it's really disgusting. We might as well send representatives from big business to run Congress."

"Where does his money come from?"

"Well . . . AMPAC . . . we knew that. The U.S. hog industry . . . but that makes sense 'cause North Carolina is a huge pork-producing state. Guess who else?" She doesn't wait for me to answer. "Silvanus."

"Why would they support Harry Orwell?"

"Don't know."

"Biobreed was located in North Carolina before they merged with Silvanus. Maybe they still have facilities there."

Pepper hands me the phone. "You'd better call Marion Godlove. Please."

I look at the phone, swallow my pride, and call the institute.

The connection to Mexico is amazingly clear. "Ms. Godlove is in Washington for a few days. Would you like me to have her call you back?"

"No thanks. I'll be in touch."

After a moment of relief that I don't have to handle that one right now, I feel weak and overwhelmed. I stuff a handful of antibiotics into my mouth and drink a glass of water. I ride another wave of dizziness and stretch out on the bedspread beside Pepper. Lilly said the fever might come back, and that when it did, to take it seriously, to stay in bed for two or three days.

I don't have two or three days.

As I lie there listening to Pepper tap on her keyboard, I figure Marion Godlove is in Washington working with our lobbyist on her Medicare bill. Then something shoots to the surface of my thought, something that's been simmering deep inside of me. "Pepper, did you tell Marion Godlove I was in Yaxchilán?"

She opens her eyes wide and blinks at me. "I don't remember. Godlove called me soon after I got your first call from San Cristóbal. I suppose I did."

"Nobody else knew I was going there."

"She couldn't . . . wait . . . those guys could've followed you."

"Nobody followed me."

"There was a contract out on you. Anybody . . . anybody could've noticed you and called them."

"Do you know about our lobby group in Washington? Did you know Marion Godlove is trying to get passed a bill that would get deathmaiden services paid by Medicare? She has a tremendous amount at stake right now."

"You think she's being pressured?"

I can barely say the words. "I think she's fighting back with everything she has. I think she's using the information I gave her to make a deal. Vernon Keyes will lay off, Harry Orwell will lay off, they won't obstruct her Medicare package—"

"Frances, no . . . she couldn't know they would try to kill—"

"—if she'll shut me up."

The shock of betrayal is stunning. It hollows out my chest, leaving a shell of dry corn husks.

No doubt Godlove is doing what she feels she has to do to save the institute. Yet to discover that the woman who melted my soul with her eloquence, who taught me to think critically, who expanded my mind with her brilliance and insight, has used me strips me bare.

I tremble with a horrible truth—that I am expendable; my greatest worth to my profession, to the women I love, to the work I passionately believe in, is as a bargaining chip.

If I thought it would help, I might make the sacrifice. But Marion Godlove is wrong this time. I will not let it go. Tomás will not let me.

I stand alone with a handful of suppositions and theories. I need evidence.

I call Pacific Division and ask for Detective Lieutenant Paul Ortiz. I don't need to tell him my name. He recognizes my voice. "Where are you?" he asks.

"I'm in Los Angeles."

"There's a warrant out for your arrest. You need to come to the station immediately."

"Am I a suspect? For murder?"

"No. For material witness. We have reason to believe

that you may have been at the scene of the murder at the Golden Bough. We have found evidence that points to a possible suspect."

"A suspect? What evidence?"

"I can't tell you that."

"I need to talk to you, Ortiz."

"Come into the station. We'll talk plenty."

"Not yet. Someplace else."

"That's out of the question."

"I'll be at the end of Santa Monica Pier at eleven o'clock."

"Frances, I will have to arrest you."

I notice he's used my first name without the "Miss." I take that as a sign I might have some wiggle room. "Fine. Arrest me. But please hear me out first." I hang up before he can say he won't come.

The night is cold and clear, yet the earth expires a heavy blanket of moisture from the recent rains. Santa Monica Pier smells of damp creosote, buttered popcorn, and hot dogs. I listen to the clack of Skee-Ball in the arcades, bells and whistles, electronic whizzing noises, the voices of bored teenagers jostling one another. I walk to the end, where I can hear the pounding of the surf and the melancholy clank of the buoy bell. The waves, ink black, slap against the pilings. Wisps of fog whisper in on the gentle sea breeze like the curling vapor from a solitary smoker exiled to a fire escape on a cold winter's night.

Paul Ortiz walks toward me, not looking too happy, his solid body rocking back and forth. He doesn't walk, exactly. He stomps.

"Am I keeping you out past your bedtime?" I ask.

He glares at me like he might slug me, looks over his shoulder, then jerks his chin in the general direction of a bench.

Twenty feet away, a lone Mexican leans on his elbows, staring into the black night, standing in silent harmony with his fishing pole that flexes with the tug of the surf.

"I have a wife and two children," says Ortiz, "and three years before I can retire with a full pension. You can understand if I don't want it all to go to waste, can't you?"

"When you waste something valuable, it's called a sacrifice."

He lets out an uncomfortable laugh. "Sacrifice is exactly what I'm afraid of."

I tell him everything. He listens without blinking.

"Tell me if I got this right," he says. "This company Silvanus, a tissue recovery company, sponsors a research program in Mexico City under a world-renowned epidemiologist. They are studying these Indians who have an unusual immune system, which evolved from their bodies fighting a virus that's spread through cannibalism. Silvanus hopes to find whatever turns off their immune system so they can develop a drug for transplant donors that will make them a match for any recipient. You think Silvanus has been smuggling these special Indians into the U.S., and that they've been experimenting on them, then killing them and using them as organ donors."

"That's about it."

"You don't have any proof, do you?"

"No."

"Only conjecture and speculation."

"That's why you need to give me a few days."

Ortiz sits in silence for a few moments. "Sacrifice," he says, snorting through his nose. "Okay. I'll give you two days. Then you must hand yourself over to the police."

Then it occurs to me to ask, "You said you have a murder suspect . . . can you tell me who?"

Ortiz looks at me hard, then shrugs. "The Hollywood Division found evidence that Elmer Afner was blackmailing someone."

"Who?"

"One of his clients, I think. They're contacting people on his client list. Although no one appears to be willing to talk, the detectives suspect that this might not be the first time Afner has tried blackmail."

"What are they basing it on?"

"Some cryptic notes on his computer. Large deposits made to his bank that don't correlate to sales. Papers in his security box. He also appears to have been having serious financial problems."

"Someone wanted to get rid of Afner and pin the murder on me at the same time?"

"That's a possibility. You need to come into the station if only for your own protection."

"Why is the district attorney so interested in this case?"

"You're not the only one who's noticed that Afner trafficked in stolen Mexican artifacts. Also, if they are aware of even half of what you told me, then I suspect there are people in our local government who want very badly to keep it secret."

"Are you saying the DA's office is involved in a cover-up?"

"Cover-up." He rolls the word around in his mouth. "I

think they're trying to find out how deep this goes, how much has to be revealed for public safety, how much political damage will occur if it is as bad as they think. Maybe someone is being paid not to look too closely. I don't know. I do know there are a lot of loose ends that are not being followed up, and a lot of people who are not answering telephone calls."

A half mile out, a sailboat motors back to the marina, its lights pinpricks in the dark. A thought comes to me. "You remember telling me that Elmer Afner had an ex-wife who was a medical researcher in Mexico City?"

"Yeah. What about it?"

"You might look in Raleigh, North Carolina . . . where Katsumi's research is moving. Look at the North Carolina College of Agriculture and Life Sciences."

CHAPTER

32

Carol Nims glances up as I walk into her office. Her cardboard blond hair sits on her head like a tepee, her face is drawn, her mouth a hard line. Empty boxes litter the floor. She grabs a handful of books from the shelf by the window and stacks them in a carton on her desk.

"I think I'm losing my mind." She's not talking to me so much as ranting aloud. "All I do is cry. My boyfriend can't stand it anymore. I cry at work, I cry at the gym, I cry at the supermarket. Any little thing sets me off. I get so emotional when I meet with the prospective donor families that I can't even talk. The crazy thing is I don't even know what I'm crying about."

"You're quitting?"

"Yes, I'm quitting. Dr. Prouty said I could take a long vacation . . . said he'd hold the job for me . . . but I can't come back. It all feels so . . ." She stands motionless, a handful of books suspended in midair, gazing at her poster of the Austrian Alps. "It's like the movies they make now. All these special effects and fast edits, trying to cover up the fact that they can't come up with an interesting story. It's all fake. I used to think organ transplants were such a good thing, helping people to live longer. Now it seems like a special effect, a cover-up, like pretending that we don't die. I can't ask people to donate the organs of their husband or daughter. It's like I'm stealing or something. I can't do it. I can't stand being in a hospital anymore. I find myself talking people out of organ donation."

I look where she has taken down the picture of her dog, the nail, the outline of dust, the square of less faded paint. I suddenly have a bad headache. I ask myself if there would be all these empty boxes on the floor if I had never met Carol.

Once when a girlfriend was complaining about her husband, I asked her if she loved him. She looked at me blankly, then changed the subject. That night, she asked her husband for a divorce. If you spend too much time worrying about the influence you have on people, you'll end up taking a vow of silence. I have time for neither regrets nor silence. "I need your help, Carol."

She stops and sits down. She looks into her palms for a moment, then up at me as if she knows what I'm going to ask. "I'm listening," she says.

"I need a list of your donors who are Hispanic."

She stares at me for almost a full minute. "You're not a schoolteacher, are you."

"No, I'm not."

"And you're not going to tell me why you need those names, are you."

"No."

She packs two more books, then gets up and walks to the window. "It's funny. You admire someone, maybe model yourself after them, maybe change your life based on that person, and then you find out they aren't who you thought they were, but somehow it doesn't make any difference, because you'd still be packing boxes, moving on to something else."

I think of Jack. I think of Marion Godlove. I think of that moment of disappointment when you recognize the mutability of your perceptions, how the image you have of someone may change in a nanosecond. If our perceptions cannot be trusted, what can? "You don't mean me, do you?"

She laughs. "Of course not." She comes back from wherever she drifted. "You want a list of Hispanic donors? Sure, why not? Why should I care? I'm leaving. Someone tells you, 'These are the rules,' and you think you have to obey. But then you see it doesn't matter. Not one bit." She jiggles her computer mouse, and the field of flying toasters dissolves into a blue screen dotted with icons. "How far back do you want me to go?"

"Four years."

"A lot of Hispanics come in as possible donors . . . shots to the brain from gang fights, drunk driving . . . but their families almost never agree to organ donation. It's not a Catholic thing, necessarily. I don't know what it is." Her finger clicks a number of times before she gets to the right screen. "Here we go."

"Can you print out their corresponding antigen maps?"

"Sure."

"And the names of the performing surgeons?"

She looks at me as though she's trying to piece it all together, then says, "I don't want to know, do I."

"Probably not."

Within a half hour, I have a list of twelve Hispanic organ donors, all of them male. I flip through them quickly. "No females?"

"As I said, most organ donors are victims of gunshots or traffic accidents. In the Hispanic community, that means male. They're also very sentimental. The husbands and fathers can't imagine someone dissecting their daughters and wives."

"They don't sacrifice women."

"What?"

"The Aztec and Maya seldom sacrificed women."

She gives me an odd look.

"Dr. Faust performed all of these surgeries?"

"Oh, no. He's the head of the department, so his name appears on all of the reports. The surgeon who performed the organ removal is on the second page."

"Can you find out where the parts of one of your donors went?"

"Who?"

"Tomás Gomez."

As she types on her computer to bring up his file, she says, "I can tell you what hospital, but I can't tell you the patients' names. That's kept confidential by the receiving hospital . . . they don't even tell me."

"I'll take what I can get."

"This is surprising. . . ."

"What?"

"Well, usually body parts go all over the country. Sometimes all over the world. Everything from Tomás went to only two places."

"Where?"

"Raleigh, North Carolina, and here at Abbot Kinney. That's unusual . . . to have a donor and recipient in the same hospital."

It doesn't surprise me.

Before I leave, I look at Carol Nims and suddenly glimpse a five-year-old child, towheaded, blue eyed, giggling, running down the driveway into her father's arms. "Carol, do you remember your first years of high school? Before you got interested in boys?"

She looks up, bewildered. "Yes."

"Did you wonder what you might be as a grown-up?"

She doesn't hesitate. "I wanted to be a veterinarian like my dad."

"She's sitting right beside you."

"Who?"

"The girl who wants to be a veterinarian. It's not too late."

"I know," she says.

The familiar voice stops me cold. There in the hospital corridor, his voice nasal, strident, the cadences of a Southern Baptist preacher. I peek into the hospital room. An elderly black man sits up in bed, remote in hand, watching a television that's suspended from the ceiling.

"Is that too loud?" he asks me.

I shake my head no, my eyes drawn to the handsome, gray-haired man on the screen. "These deathmaidens are murderers, and they need to be prosecuted as murderers. God gives life to every creature on this earth. Anyone who ends a life, whether it's an unborn child or a dying grandmother, is a murderer. Some say deathmaidens end suffering. But who's to say that God does not want the dying to suffer? Who's to say that in these final hours of suffering, the spirit doesn't blossom and reach out to God? God would not allow suffering if there were no purpose. Who is to say that God will not perform a miracle and grant life to the dying? It is a travesty that we as a society sanction these murders. Why do we allow it? Because we're greedy, that's why."

Vernon Keyes wipes tears from his eyes. "Permitting abortions and deathmaidens has caused the collapse of morality in America. Where's our respect for human life? Where are our family values? We cannot allow this to continue. We cannot stand by and watch the murder of our babies and our parents."

Without blinking, the old man lifts the remote, aims it at the television, and turns the station to a basketball game. He smiles and leans back in his pillow.

I haven't been in my house for a month. I am struck with the same sensation that always hits me when I return home after a trip. It feels like the house of a stranger. The rooms seem smaller than I remember. The doorways have shrunk, the ceiling is lower. Furniture and shadows cut alarming angles. There's an odd stillness, the moist, dusty feel of a wine cellar. Objects that I'd chosen with care hold no particular importance to me. They seem smaller, as though they're contracting into themselves.

Is it memory that can't hold an image accurately? Or have I changed?

A small red light blinks frenetically on my answering machine. Three new messages from Marion Godlove, two messages from Detective Lieutenant Rexford Reid, Hollywood Division, messages from my stockbroker, picture framer, an artist Pepper's been trying to set me up with for months. The tape runs into the old messages. I know I should turn it off now, but I let it play. There's a message from Jack. I play it three times. As soon as I realize that I'm tempted to listen to it a fourth time, that my heart is beating faster, that I'm listening to every word for a hesitation, a nervous articulation, a sigh, something to tell me his emotional state, his feelings for me, I erase the tape.

I cannot face the thought of another betrayal right now.

CHAPTER

33

Ted Duncan opens the door to his apartment with rubber gloves on his hands. "Don't touch anything," he says. I enter a room along a narrow pathway, chest-high piles of debris on either side. "If you think this is bad, you should've seen it last week." He turns and grins at me, his gums so infected that the tops of his teeth are streaked with blood. "I have you to thank for that."

"Me? What did I do?"

"Well, you started me thinking. About a year ago, a doctor prescribed Prozac for me, but I've never been able to fill the prescription. When I saw the pharmacist count out the pills, he used a dish that he'd just used for someone else's pills. I realized they were contaminated. I threw them into the trash as soon as I walked out of the pharmacy. But after I talked to you, I thought maybe it wasn't such a big risk. So I got a new prescription and I've been taking the pills. And look now." He gestures at a row of white trash bags. "This stuff has been piling up for years. You see, I couldn't put stuff in garbage bags without contaminating my clothes, and if I carried them downstairs and brushed the walls, I'd contaminate the walls, and then I'd have to spend hours washing the walls. Then I'd touch the Dumpster and forget about it. But I figured out that if I do it all at one time, I only have to decontaminate once."

I count twenty bags of garbage neatly lined up in the hallway.

"I've already filled a hundred bags. Oh, and look at this." He points to a wall covered with a schedule. He's very excited. "I keep track of my cleaning rituals, like an hour to wash my hands, two hours for a shower. Each day I try to take five minutes off the time. It's like a contest with myself. Pretty good, huh?"

I see on his chart that it took him only twenty minutes to wash the phone after I called him.

"Yesterday, I even went to a coffee shop and had coffee. The waitress wiped off the table with a filthy sponge. My skin was crawling, but I drank the coffee. It's like there's a whole new world out there."

When I start to sit on a kitchen chair, he says, "Wait! Don't sit down." He puts a white towel on the seat, then looks at me bashfully. "I'm not cured yet." He washes his gloves, then hands me a bottle of water. "Sorry I can't open it for you. You said you wanted to ask me something?"

I have to shake the most obvious questions from my head and focus. On the table, I spread out the twelve antigen maps Carol Nims gave me. "What can you tell me about these men?"

He leans over the table and studies them. "Well, I can tell you one thing. You only have six donors here."

"What do you mean?"

"Seven are the same. No two people have the exact same antigen map. It's how the immune system keeps a virus from wiping out an entire population. Seven of yours are the same, so they must've come from one person . . . not the same, exactly, but too close to be from different people."

"No. These are twelve different men."

"That's impossible."

"What if their immune system has been altered?" I tell him Kira Katsumi's theory that the TSE virus genetically alters the immune system.

"Well, I suppose it's possible."

"I need to break into Silvanus. Can you help me?"

"Okay."

He says this so quickly that I'm momentarily confused. "What?"

"I said, 'Okay.' I'm the one who set up their security system. I'm sure they've changed the codes, but I can override them. They have two night watchmen. You'll want to break into their lab computers as well as their accounting records. That's two different parts of the building."

"You'll help me break in?"

"I can't touch anything."

"Oh, for chrissake."

"If you hurt my feelings, I won't help you."

"I'm sorry. I need your help, but I'm no good with computers. They know when I'm coming, freeze up, and crash."

"Now who's giving irrational power to the external world?"

"Please. You won't have to touch anything. Just tell me what to do."

"You'll drive?"

"Yes, I'll drive. I'll even get the car detailed."

"You won't hurt my feelings?"

I'm at the end of my rope. "If it puts you at too much of a risk, I'll manage alone."

"No, no. I'll help. It's not like I might lose my pension or anything."

"When?"

"Tonight is Friday. Nobody stays late, and the guards are the same ones who've been on all week, so they're lazy and anxious for their shift to end."

"Okay. We'll go tonight."

I park my car half a mile away in a residential neighborhood of new single-story ranch homes. We walk through the parking lots of adjacent buildings. The industrial park looks as if it's been there awhile. Boxwood hedges and bottlebrush trees give us some cover.

We pause at the corner of a branch of Wells Fargo Bank. Probably not the best place to avoid surveillance. We dash behind the hedges to another office building and look up the hill at Silvanus.

The building is U shaped. Duncan points out the arm closest to us. "That's the warehouse," he says.

Two guards stand together, talking. One of them gets in a car and drives off as the other walks to the opposite side of the building.

"He's probably making a coffee run," I speculate.

That leaves one car in the parking lot.

"The other car must belong to the other guard."

"Maybe. But why did he park so far away from his buddy? That's not the way people park."

"What makes you think so?"

"If you're meeting someone, you park next to them, or maybe one or two spaces away from them. It's socialized behavior. You hang your coat where everyone else does. If two strangers go into an empty Laundromat, they won't use machines on opposite sides, but a few machines apart.

"It's also a Mercedes," adds Duncan.

"Not the car of choice for a security guard."

"Maybe they came in one car, which would mean someone else is in the building."

"Maybe. We'll have to take that chance. Is there a security guard inside?"

"No. There are two main entrances, three fire exits. The warehouse air filtration system is in back. It's big enough for a man to crawl through."

I remember who I'm talking to. "You're going to crawl through a cooling duct?"

He shrugs like it's no big deal.

We sneak to the back of the building. An aluminum box the size of two refrigerators on top of each other hums loudly. At the base, a large fan spins intermittently. "That fan cools the whole building?" I ask.

"No. The fan is to cool the cooling unit. It has a second generator. You can't take the chance of the power going out and have a bunch of corpses thawing."

I use a screwdriver to undo ten screws. I yank away

the panel. Between the blades of the fan and a mass of hot pipes is a space of about ten inches. I suck in my breath and squeeze past the hot pipes. A sharp right turn leads back four feet to a grate. The air is hot and dusty. I imagine what it must be like working underneath a car with its engine on. I try not to panic. One of us on the edge of sheer terror is enough. I take off another ten screws and try to push in the grate. It doesn't budge. I wiggle it. Still doesn't budge. I kick it lightly in the corner. Then hard.

"Jesus! What the fuck are you doing?" Duncan hisses from outside.

Then the grate pops open. I slide it to the inside of the wall. I listen for an alarm, running footsteps, cocking guns. Nothing. I turn around and whisper loudly to Duncan, "Come on through. It's all right."

"I'm claustrophobic."

"Why am I not surprised?"

"I'm sorry, I can't."

He's lowered me to begging. "Please, Ted. All the cooties came off on me. There's none left."

Whining like a kicked dog, he inches through the space, hesitantly, his hands pulling both sides of his shirt so it lies tight against his torso, trying to prevent it from brushing against anything. When I see him step into the warehouse, he looks like a frightened mole.

I go back into the duct and refasten the outside panel with two screws.

When I step back into the warehouse, Duncan is brushing off imaginary tarantulas from his shoulders and arms. Whimpering like a frightened chimp, he stands on one leg, shaking the other vigorously like an electric current. It's too late to wonder if I made a mistake in bringing him.

The warehouse is dark, with a pale glimmer of light coming through the skylights thirty feet above. It's really, really cold. Rows and rows of metal racks are stacked with boxes of fiberglass trays. Everything is labeled by number, probably for the sake of discretion. No one wants to walk through a supermarket of body parts.

On one side of the warehouse is a long table with five computers in a row. "This is where they process orders," says Duncan. "The building is on a mainframe network. Once I hack into one of these computers, I'll disable the alarm system, and we can get out of this icebox."

He points out how to turn on the computer. I flip the red switch, then sit in front of the screen.

"It'd be a lot easier if you would do the typing," I say with annoyance.

"You promised not to hurt my feelings."

"Yes, I did." I type in the words and numbers he dictates. We get in without a hitch.

"They changed all of the security systems once I left," Duncan explains. "What they didn't do was change the software they used, so the override I used to program and test the system still works."

It takes almost no time for Duncan to disable the alarms.

"My fingers are freezing," I say.

"We'll use another computer inside."

The door between the warehouse and offices has a touch pad lock. Duncan tells me to punch in an override password, and it clicks open.

Inside, we head to a small office in the corner. It says

"Human Resources" on the outside. While I boot up the computer, Duncan walks around the cubicles outside, making a quick tour of the place.

It takes us no time to get into their accounting books, which are set up in Great Plains software. "If anyone knew how easy it was to break passwords, they wouldn't even bother."

"What are we looking for?" I ask.

"I worked my way through college as an auditor. It's fun. You never know what you're looking for until you find it. It's kind of intuitive. You look for something that jumps out at you. An unusual payment, a month of high expenses. Then you dive in and tear it apart."

He seems to absorb pages of numbers as fast as I can click to a new screen. I feel the moisture of his breath behind me. He's concentrating so hard that he holds his breath, letting it out in little bursts as his mind jumps from one point to another. Every thirty seconds or so he mumbles, "Uh-huh," mixed with an occasional "Okay," his body stiffening and then relaxing as he resolves a curious number. He's half hunter, half computer.

He has me page through overhead expenses and personnel, then stops me at employee benefits.

"This is interesting," I say. "We're looking at costs charged to their health insurance provider. They have more people insured than they have on their payroll."

"It's probably their families."

"No, they would be listed under the employee."

"Double click to bring up the names."

There are eight Hispanic names. Not unusual. This is Los Angeles. However, among the names is Fernandez Gomez as well as other names from Carol Nims's list.

"How do I bring up those files?" I ask. "They're listed as inactive."

"They're inactive because they're dead. Go to the archives."

"Wait. This one isn't." I bring up the file for José Petén, with an address in Boyle Heights, the heart of East Los Angeles. His records show he's had two MRIs and extensive bloodwork, all done at Abbot Kinney Medical Center. I click on archives and look at the inactive files. All the men had similar tests done at Abbot Kinney, then emergency room expenses. "Show me how to copy these onto disk."

"Sure." With surprising patience, he walks me through it, and I begin to think that maybe these computers aren't such a bad deal after all.

"Where would we look for charitable contributions?" I ask.

"Page down to corporate."

I'm surprised at the extent of their donations, many small community groups, medical schools, and Doctors International. "Look here. The University of Mexico, 5.2 million dollars."

I copy it onto the disk.

Suddenly I stop and listen. The building has that eerie feel you get in cemeteries, of no one being there yet of not being alone. I listen to the low hum of the computer and the air-conditioning.

All I have to do is tense my muscles and Duncan starts scratching again.

From Human Resources, we walk through the center of the building, past rows of drab, gray cubicles—Sales, Administration, Customer Relations, Accounting—departments that never get windows. Then to the other side of the building, where the executive offices face the street. The corner office is Bryant Hillary's. The doors to all of the offices are locked.

Duncan hands me a key. "They change the locks all the time, but they never change the passkey."

"How come?"

"Because if they change the passkey, they have to rekey the whole building. And that's real expensive."

"A few thousand dollars? For a company like this, that's nothing."

"But you see, each department wants to stay within their budget. If they don't, someone might lose his job."

"So building maintenance didn't want to spend the money on rekeying the whole place when you left."

"There you go."

"Didn't they know you had a passkey?"

"I don't know. Doesn't matter, does it?"

I slip the key into the lock. It still works. I open the door and we step inside.

As a child, as soon as spring afternoons melted the snow, I would hike into the White Mountains to explore bear caves. The bears would be awake from their winter naps, gone in search of trout, but their breath, the smell of their sweaty nightmares, hung in the air of the caves. I loved to sit in their abandoned beds, the soft decayed leaves with tufts of bear hair. The danger aroused me. I sensed their power. I felt that if I sat there long enough, I would get some of their strength, that I would know what it was to be a bear.

I have the same feeling standing in Bryant Hillary's office. Something feels oddly familiar, as though I've been here before, as if I know the person who sits behind the desk and throws his L. L. Bean boots on top. He has cartoons from *The New Yorker* taped around the room and plastic action figures, Teletubbies, Power Rangers, Pluto and Mickey, arranged together in lewd positions. A dartboard hangs on the wall, a punching bag in the corner.

On his desk sits a photo of an outdoorsy type of woman, the kind who never wears makeup and always looks stunning. She's laughing. She's pressing to her cheek a two-year-old who doesn't want any part of posing, his yellow curls blowing in the wind, his face earnest, his fingers reaching for her breasts.

On the walls are other photos of Hillary grinning at the camera in exotic locations: in a flat-bottom boat on the Amazon; on an African savanna talking to half a dozen Hutus, giraffes galloping in the background; on a rocky island with thousands of emperor penguins; on top of a high mountain with a mountain bike.

"He looks like a fun guy," I say. "What's he like?"

"Bryant? Oh, the ladies like him. I guess everybody likes him. Friendly, funny, nice, energetic but laid-back. Always encourages people to make the most of themselves."

"But you don't like him."

"He screwed me out of my stock options. Of course I don't like him."

"But there's more to it, isn't there. Jealousy?"

Duncan snorts. "That would make sense. A nerd like me. But no. You know how a computer can have a bad sector and you keep on working, happy as a clam, and suddenly you crash for no good reason?"

It's not within the realm of my experience, but I get the idea. "Hillary has a bad sector?"

"Yeah. I can't describe it, but there's a thing that's wrong. It's like you try to get to know him real well, but he's the same inside as on the outside."

"Sounds like the definition of a saint."

"Hell, no. More like he has some sectors that are empty . . . or not empty, you just can't get to them. Like you click on a file and expect to see a list of documents, but there's another file, so you click on that file and get another file, and it goes on to infinity."

"And you never see what's in the file."

"Right. It's not like he has secrets. You can uncover a secret. This is something no one will ever know."

A cloud passes beneath my eyes, and a shiver descends my spine. The familiarity I felt when I first entered the room becomes clear. I recognize my enemy.

Duncan's incessant scratching spurs me on.

Hillary has two computers: a high-powered Dell on its own table and a laptop on his desk. A few files and papers sit beside the laptop, organized not too neatly, but handy, as if he knows how to get to each one quickly. A black telephone. A bookshelf with books on fly-fishing, biotechnology, immunology, and other highly technical medical books.

I put my hand on the hard drive. It's still warm. I stop and listen. I hear nothing but the susurrus of air-conditioning and Duncan's shallow breathing.

Duncan rocks back and forth like a child who has to pee, his hands scratching at his neck and forearms. He's driving me crazy. Of course, I can't touch him to quiet him. I close my eyes and imagine him as a child, a perfect, bright child, exhausted and napping with a smile on his face. For the moment he stops scratching and sits down.

I look through the papers on Hillary's desk: a study on the swine industry in the United States; a study on rendered animal feed; a study on prions in viral infections; real estate listings for property in Baja.

I don't know what I'm looking for, but I feel it's there. I look through the file that seems strangest. Why would a company that deals in tissue recovery be interested in pig farming? One letter is from Alfred Bates, a pig farmer in North Carolina: "We can make available two hundred swine for your clinical trials. I've discussed the need for industry cooperation with our local association, and they all agree to participate, donating a minimum of fifty swine each."

"Duncan, you're getting dandruff everyplace." He lowers his hand for twenty seconds before scratching his scalp again. I sense he's on the edge of losing it. I take the file on the swine industry. "Let's go."

We creep down the hallway along the office partitions, past the administrative area, and back to the warehouse.

As I squeeze out of the cooling unit, I walk backward smack into a security guard. He's too surprised to reach for his gun. He grabs my arms, his thick fingers squeezing like clamps. I bend my knees, twisting and kicking. I feel a sudden breeze over my head. The clamps release, and the guard falls to the ground.

Duncan stands with a pipe from the cooling unit, looking as if he's just swallowed a dragonfly.

"You're going to have to wash your hands at least a dozen times," I say.

As I screw in the vent, Duncan pours whiskey from a pocket flask over the security guard. The smell will weaken his credibility, whatever he remembers.

Like thieves in the night, we dash down the hill to my car.

I drop Ted Duncan off at his house. I'm too keyed up to go home; I think of going over to Pepper's—she's almost always up this time of night—but decide not to. I don't want to interrupt anything. Instead, I go to Edie's, a diner off Admiralty Way in Marina del Rey that looks out across the docks. I order a slice of apple pie with vanilla ice cream, settle down in a red leather booth, and open the file I stole from Silvanus.

It blows off the top of my head. The next time I notice my apple pie, the ice cream has melted and run over the rim of the dish onto the table.

Inside the file are newspaper clippings. The first is a news release from a company called Biopork. I try to re-member where I've heard that name and realize it was one of the names thrown at me by Minotaur during our lovely tête-à-tête. The news release announces a major advance in pig cloning that could lead to using pigs for human organ transplants. " 'This is a milestone for the 70,000 Americans waiting for organ transplants,' claims Randy Prat of Biopork, 'hearts, pancreatic cells for dia-betic patients, livers, kidneys. Just think of it.' " The tech-nique is called "xenotransplantation." The article goes on to say that previously, the drawback to xenotransplanta-tion was that a certain sugar in the pig organs signaled the human immune system to attack the organ. These cloned pigs didn't have the sugar. "In a few years, organ trans-plantation will be limited only by the number of available operating rooms. Transplants will be as common as flu shots."

The article continues to describe how Biopork introduced a disabled version of the sugar gene into ordinary fetal pig cells, then made copies of the modified cells and injected their DNA into embryos.

Now it makes sense why Minotaur wondered if I was from PETA, the animal rights organization. They must be up in arms about raising pigs for human transplants. I certainly empathize.

A second article is from another company called Porcine Therapeutics, released within days of the Biopork article. Both companies claimed half a dozen piglets with one disabled sugar gene. "Pigs have two sugar-producing genes that have to be disabled to solve the rejection problem. We've only got one under our belts, but it's just a matter of time. We had to get out our findings as fast as we could to bring in potential investors."

One of the potential investors was Silvanus. In the file were letters of intent for Silvanus to buy both companies.

Another article discusses the problems of pig retroviruses that might be transmitted to humans, a problem that is being worked on by Biobreed.

After I get over being appalled, I sense the magnitude of the situation. If pig organs could be used to replace any failed human organ, replacing a body part might become as common as going to the dentist for a new crown. No need to wait for human donors.

What had never made sense to me—the connection between Silvanus, a tissue recovery company, and Biobreed, a drug company that researches pig viruses—is now perfectly clear. Silvanus wants to be the distributor, whether human parts or pig. They want to be the Microsoft of xenotransplantation. It's going to blast open the market by solving the autoimmune system, with either viruses or genetics. I find a quote from Bryant Hillary when interviewed about his purchase of Biobreed: "It's not always the best technology that wins, but the fastest to win market share."

I finish my apple pie, freshen my lipstick, and head toward the Venice canals to Pepper's.

Even before I finish telling Pepper about xenotransplantation, she's on the Internet and printing out pages on the swine industry.

"I think you're up against something bigger than Silvanus."

"You do? What?"

"The U.S. hog industry is worth six hundred billion dollars a year. That doesn't include the economies that support the industry—the feed industry, farm equipment, all the rest. I can't track down a national figure, but Nebraska alone estimates the swine industry is worth seven billion a year to their state economy, and they're only five percent of U.S. production."

"That's a lot of bacon."

"And guess who our number two export country is . . . Mexico."

"Which would make sense why it was so easy to put a price on my head in Mexico."

"The hog industry has one problem. They are so efficient, they've made pork too cheap. They sell at thirty-five dollars per one hundred pounds of hog carcass, and it costs forty dollars to produce."

"How do they survive?"

"They are the major industry in a dozen states. They have a lot of friends in Congress."

"Subsidies?"

"Yup."

"So they need to make pork more expensive."

"Which is difficult because chicken and beef are so cheap. They've been fighting the high-cholesterol rap—'Pork, the other white meat'—and increased exports, but with the strong dollar, competition in Brazil and Argentina, their price is hurting."

"So they need a new market."

"You got it. Now, there's also dozens of biomedical swine producers. If biomedical pigs could be raised for human organ transplant, we're talking billions of dollars for the pork industry as well as the medical community."

"What's the trade association?"

"The Swine Producers of America."

I suddenly get depressed. It's all too huge—not a private tissue recovery company, not a biotech venture capital company, but the swine industry. "It's like taking on automobile manufacturers."

"Not everyone has a car, but almost everyone uses some pork product."

"Isn't North Carolina the largest swine-producing state?"

"No, that's Iowa. North Carolina is second. . . . Dad was stationed there for a few years. But wait . . . you're thinking . . . ?"

"Who would be ruthless enough to murder people, to

send thugs to track me down in Mexico, powerful enough to get favors from Harry Orwell and Vernon Keyes? Who would murder a famous scientist? Not AMPAC. They represent doctors, after all."

"I doubt the Swine Producers of America would go that far. Wait . . . I was reading something. . . ." Pepper digs through the pile of articles. "Here it is. There was a split in the organization over a lawsuit. A group of environmentalists and small pig farmers got together and sued the huge hog farms. They wanted them to pay for environmentally responsible waste disposal and to clean up badly polluted rivers."

"Where was this? North Carolina?"

"Yup. Some of the big hog producers didn't think the trade association was supporting them enough. So they formed a more radical branch."

"What are they called?"

"The Tamworth Husbandry Association, THA. Their number one congressional advocate is Harry Orwell."

"Isn't Tamworth a breed of hog?"

"Yes, a very big, very ornery hog."

CHAPTER

34

"Is your daddy home?" I ask.

The child doesn't answer but drops the receiver. I hear her footsteps run from the phone, then her yelling, "Dad! Some lady's on the phone." I hear his heavy, barefoot steps, a sliding glass door close, then his voice: "Samantha, who is it?" I hear thumping, as though she's jumping up and down in woolly socks. "Go to bed, Sammy. It's past your bedtime." She patters up stairs. He groans as he picks up the receiver from the floor.

"Ortiz here."

"Sounds like you're getting a touch of arthritis in your lower back." I take pleasure in imagining him in boxer shorts with Dalmatians on them, his ample belly jelly-rolling over the elastic.

"This is not a good time."

His voice sounds groggy, as though he just woke from a nap, or maybe he's had a few drinks.

"It's the only time," I say. "Seven Hispanic males have been organ donors at Abbot Kinney Medical Center. They all came in with head trauma of one kind or another. They all have similar antigen maps and came from the same Indian tribe in Mexico. None of them had family in the United States, and all of them were here illegally. Each of their organ donations was approved by the county medical commissioner."

I hear him breathing. Maybe he's writing this down. Maybe he's cutting his toenails. "What else?" he says.

"All seven of those names are listed as covered by a corporate health insurance policy from Silvanus."

"Did they work there?"

"No. They didn't. There are also checks to two landlords in East Los Angeles."

"Silvanus paid their rent?"

"I think so. I copied the company files onto disk."

"How? Wait, don't answer that. I don't want to know."

"There's something else," I say very fast. I'm afraid he'll stop me from finishing. "There was an eighth Hispanic name. His insurance is active. He's not on Carol Nims's organ donor list. I think he may still be alive. His name is José Petén."

Ortiz drops the phone, grunting when he picks it back up. "Come down to the station and give me the information you have. I've talked to Judge Patterson. He says he'll listen to the arguments of the prosecutor, but he doesn't see why he shouldn't set bail."

"I need another day. I need to find José Petén."

"No, you don't. Get your butt in here."

"It's not enough proof, is it?"

"Let me decide about that."

I begin to talk very fast. "You need to interview the doctors. Maybe see if the men had green cards. Maybe we can get Silvanus on immigration violations."

"Frances, don't tell me how to do my job. Where are you now?"

"At home."

"Don't move. I'll be right there."

I hear a car pull up outside my house, the slam of two car doors, heavy footsteps up my redwood stairs, then a slow, determined knock. I open the door. I expect Ortiz, but two police officers, a man and a woman, ask to come in.

It surprises me how young they are, probably in their mid-twenties, their faces innocent, easy to read, wanting to be liked, dreading confrontation. It's hard not to feel sorry for them. "Are you going to put handcuffs on me?"

"That's not necessary," says the female officer. "You're wanted for questioning downtown." She shows me a warrant.

"Did Paul Ortiz send you?"

"I don't know. We were simply told to come pick you up."

"How long will it take?"

"A few hours. They can hold you up to forty-eight hours, but that seldom happens."

It interests me that she said "they can hold you," instead of "we," as if the police machine, its authority, were something outside her job as policewoman. I wonder if all police officers feel so ambiguous about their authority or if it's only the police in Los Angeles.

"Do you think it's going to rain?" I ask.

"Rain was in the forecast," the male officer says. "It's not raining yet, though."

"Thanks," I say. I walk to my closet and pull out my London Fog.

They're so nice, so polite, waiting patiently as I get my purse, put on lipstick, turn off the lights. They do not talk but look around my house, perhaps practicing their observation skills, perhaps thinking about a late dinner.

"I'm ready," I say, and the three of us clomp down my steps to the cruiser as if going for a night on the town.

Detective Lieutenant Rexford Reid, a huge black man, sits across from me, smiling. I have drifted off in my own thoughts, until he says for a second time, grinning with those Good & Plenty teeth of his, "How well did you know Elmer Afner?"

I feel an urge to answer with *How well can we know anyone?* but decide to behave myself. "I visited his shop once."

"Why?"

"I wanted to buy a present for someone."

"Did you buy anything?"

"No. It was much too expensive."

"Where were you on the night of December nineteenth?"

I notice that Lieutenant Reid's shirt has been ironed with too much starch. I wonder if that accounts for his pained smiles. "Was that the night he was murdered?"

"Yes."

"He called me and asked me to come to the store."

"Didn't you find that unusual? To come at night?"

"No. I didn't think about it. He said to drop by that evening, that he'd be in the shop until one o'clock."

"Did you go?"

"Yes."

"What time?"

"Around nine-thirty."

"What happened when you got there?"

"The store seemed closed. But the back door was ajar. I walked in. Then there was a huge explosion. I ran out as fast as I could."

"Did you see Elmer Afner in the store?"

"No."

"What happened after you left the store?"

"I got in my car and drove home."

"Had you visited Elmer Afner at night at any time previously?"

"No."

"We have you on videotape."

I pause as if I have to think about it. "Oh, I know why. My girlfriend and I went to a nightclub near there a few nights before. I don't remember walking past the Golden Bough, but it's certainly possible."

He enjoys watching me lie, and I think I detect a twinkle in his eye. "What's the name of the club?" he asks.

I do not hesitate. "It's called Blue Echo. It's on Melrose."

"That's a lesbian bar."

"True. But there's no cover, and they make fabulous margaritas. You should try it sometime."

He doesn't appear interested in hearing about margaritas. Perhaps he doesn't like them.

"Where have you been for the last month?" he asks.

"I went on a vacation. I needed a break from the harsh L.A. winter."

Those teeth again. I sense I'm not winning him over with my humor.

"We have not ruled you out as a suspect, Miss Oliver. I have to tell you, your story does not convince me. We have credit card reports that you were in Mexico City. Would you want to tell us what you were doing there?"

"I told you. I was on vacation. Mexico City has the finest museums. Have you ever been?"

"Was Elmer Afner blackmailing you?"

"Blackmail? Goodness, no. I live very modestly. He couldn't have hoped to gain much by blackmailing me."

"We can hold you in the women's jail for forty-eight hours."

I suppress all the flip answers that come to mind. In truth, I have no flip answers. The idea of staying overnight here fills me with panic. I press my palms together and look up at him. "I'd like to go home now, if I could."

He snorts at me, then pushes the aluminum chair back and stands. "We may want to question you again, Miss Oliver. You are not planning any more vacations for the near future, are you?"

"No, but I'm open to suggestions."

At ten-thirty A.M., a female detective I've never met tells me that they have conferred with a prosecutor who decided they don't have enough evidence to charge me with a crime. They let me go.

*   *   *

Jurors line the hallways of the County Criminal Courts Building with faces as haggard as those of the defendants. Paralegals scurry. Prosecutors stride by in rumpled suits, looking right to left over the heads of the rest of us, arching their chests with self-importance. The defendants are easy to spot, lagging behind their defense attorneys, tormented by their white shirts and pressed slacks, their hands running through recently trimmed hair. Wives and girlfriends scrunch together on benches along the walls, knees together, hands clasped around their purses; they appear to be the only ones who care.

Then I see him, striding out of a courtroom down the hall, jotting down notes, heading toward the elevator. I feel as though someone's just slugged me in the chest with a baseball bat. I stagger back a step, then find my balance. I follow. It's lunchtime. There's a crowd waiting for the elevator. When the elevator arrives, fifteen people pile in. The elevator doors close. The rest of us wait. I stand behind him, my heart beating rapidly with anger and desire. He scribbles on his pad, glances up at a pretty paralegal, scribbles some more.

The elevator arrives again. He shuffles in toward the back. I step on at the last minute. The elevator doors close. A tense silence fills the elevator, the discomfort of too many strangers in too close a space, holding their breath, trying not to scream or fart. It occurs to me how insane it is to get in an elevator, to violate all your instincts, to trust this machine simply because someone at some time in your life led you to believe that it would transport you safely. I vow at that moment never to ride an elevator again.

There are at least four people between us, but I can feel him. I wonder if the others feel this tension between us. Or is it only me?

The elevator doors open and we all funnel out. I step to the side and let him pass. He doesn't notice me. I follow him outside to Spring Street and down the stairs to the curb, where he waits for a taxi. He is oblivious, carried away by his own thoughts. I stand fifteen feet behind him, watching. I hold on to the railing to steady my dizziness.

Jack turns and sees me. At first I think he doesn't recognize me. Then his body tenses and alarm flashes across his face, as if he's been caught in bed with someone's wife. Just as quickly, he breaks into a warm smile and holds out his long arms for an embrace.

CHAPTER

35

Once a virus such as measles or mumps triggers an initial immune response, a small number of antibody-making cells specific to the invading virus persist while the rest die off in a matter of days. These sentry cells last a lifetime, protecting the body from a subsequent attack. If the same virus dares invade the body again, these cells retarget the virus with swift and vicious force.

Falling in love may feel like a virus, but it doesn't produce the necessary immune stimulation to prevent reinfection.

Jack drives me to a ranch house close to Veteran and National, a flat area of middle-class homes that feels more like suburbia than any other place in Los Angeles, middle-class and supremely prosaic. Jack is house-sitting while his friends vacation in New Zealand.

Lavender lines the walkway up to the front steps. I

enter with the odd sense of violating someone else's privacy. The air is stale. The furniture is from Ikea, simple, modern, cheap, undistinguished. Personal touches are few: a cat calendar, a Snoopy phone. In the living room, one entire wall is bookshelves.

I wonder to myself if I would have fallen in love with him if, when I showed up on his doorstep that first night, it had been here instead of the loft in Santa Monica, or if his accent had been his normal flat midwestern drawl rather than Swedish. "Jack, where do you live?" I ask.

He laughs self-consciously. "Your home is within you. Don't you remember your lessons from Sunday school?"

"They only taught us that because we were poor."

"Those of us who had homes."

His comment resonates with long hours of shared stories: sad childhood memories, university romps, first loves. But I will never hear these stories. It doesn't matter anymore. We are strangers. Even as I kiss his neck and unbutton his shirt, the feeling is overwhelming. We will always be strangers. I want there to be no past, no future, only us, our bodies now, but questions keep squeezing into my consciousness. "Where do you live, Jack?" I whisper.

He hesitates before answering, as if embarrassed. "Denver, I guess. My ex-wife has a guest room that she lets me stay in when I'm there."

I grab his chest hairs between my teeth, pulling lightly, inhaling deeply his bitter, musky smell. I press my cheek to his skin. So close, yet so far. "Isn't it odd how we define people by our past relationships to them," I say. "Ex-husband, ex-roommate, ex-boss, ex-lover? As if who they are is defined by our connection to them."

"I guess I never thought about it."

"We don't talk about ex-friends, do we?"

"Is that what we are?" he asks. "Ex-friends?"

I don't answer. I pull his shirttail out of his pants, unbutton the last button, then slide my palms up his abdomen to his chest.

Everyone talks with great concern about the dangers of suppressed anger. Pepper, in fact, gets angry at me for not getting angry: "Let it out, girl. Don't let it fester. It'll kill you, give you ulcers, cancer, eczema. If you don't let it out, it'll build up and explode like a rotten egg."

I'm not convinced letting out all this anger is particularly good for the world. If you keep it inside, sometimes it fades away. Sometimes it teaches you something you didn't know about yourself. Sometimes it gives you courage and strength. Sometimes it makes you think more clearly, listen more carefully. Sometimes it leads you to philosophize about human frailty, the impossibility of human love, and in listening to the pathetic whimpering of your own ego, you find the strength to forgive.

I sit up in bed wearing a big white T-shirt, courtesy of the very big man who owns this house. I wait for an explanation.

Jack brings me breakfast on a tin tray with a reproduction on it of van Gogh's bedroom at St. Rémy where he went insane. Strawberries, honey, coffee, orange juice, and nine-grain toast with thick slabs of melting butter. Silently, I dip the strawberries in honey and eat them with bites of toast.

I listen to the birds outside, the distant traffic, the crunching in my mouth.

I wait.

Jack pulls up his right foot so it touches the inside of his left thigh, then begins to talk.

"I'm not a photographer. Well, that's not true. I am a photographer, but my job is working as a stringer for *The New York Times*. I do investigative journalism, primarily in Mexico and Central America. You generally don't get a photographer when you do investigative reporting, so you learn to take your own pictures. For me, it's become a hobby, too. Not just a hobby. A passion."

So the photos that seduced me were his. This gives me some comfort.

"I've been covering issues concerning the Maya Indians in Central America for nearly a decade: the revolts in Chiapas, the army massacres in Guatemala, refugee camps across the border in Mexico. I was doing a story on ancient traditions that survive in modern Mayan culture and ran into the Tarascans. I fell in love with them. I spent a month documenting their lives. I discovered that they still bound the heads of their babies, practiced ritual sacrifice and bloodletting, knew the ancient chants of the priests. I also learned that several Tarascan men had come to Los Angeles and disappeared. Their women asked me to find them.

"I thought there might be a good story there, and how could I say no? I pitched it to New York, and they wanted it. The Tarascans gave me the names of the men who had gone to Los Angeles, so I figured I'd give it a try.

"They also gave me the name of Fernandez Gomez, the coyote. His name came up when I did a Nexis research . . . that's a news service database. Turns out I knew the reporter in Arizona who did the story—he writes about the border patrol and the flow of drugs into the United States—so I called him and got the rundown and the names of his contacts. Since the case was closed, a friend of mine in LAPD let me take a look at the file. The DA had frozen Gomez's Bank of America account, and there was a printout of his account activity in the police file. Gomez had nothing like the cash of a drug trafficker, but he received several large checks from Simi Valley Payroll Services."

"Let me guess . . . you found out Silvanus Corporation was their client."

"Right. So I started to investigate Silvanus. Silvanus is the brainchild of Bryant Hillary. He's a real entrepreneur. Out of college he started this business of MRI labs—"

"Yes, I know . . . he got doctors to invest in them, so they ordered unnecessary tests."

"But you're not going to believe how he got his seed money. He bought drug overruns and sold them to third world countries."

"Marketing and distribution. That's how he goes after things."

"Then he started Silvanus, a tissue recovery company. You know the extent of that scam. They basically get the bodies for free, cut them up, sterilize them, package them, and sell them back to the hospitals."

"Did you ever track down any of the Tarascans?"

"No. None had applied for green cards, or driver's licenses, or government assistance. I didn't know where to start. Los Angeles has over three million Mexicans, and a good portion of them are Maya. I couldn't wander East L.A. looking for Mexicans with funny heads."

"What did you do?"

"I discovered that Silvanus sends recovered body tissue all over the world, but they like to harvest bodies locally because flying out doctors to gather tissue from donors is expensive business. Their biggest donors were California medical schools and Abbot Kinney Medical Center. The medical schools made sense to me. They're gigantic and support biomedical research. But why Abbot Kinney?"

"So you investigated their Transplant Department and came across Clyde Faust?"

"He is head of the department. I ran a check on his academic background, and sure enough, he went to Johns Hopkins."

"So you thought Silvanus and Faust might know each other."

"That's what I guessed. I went to interview Dr. Faust the same day Tomás was brought in with head trauma."

"You saw Tomás?"

"Not at first. During our interview, Faust ran out to see him. Well, it struck me as strange that a transplant surgeon should rush out to see a head trauma patient. And he was emotional about it, like he knew the kid."

"So afterward, you looked in on Tomás."

"Yeah. His head was in a viselike apparatus, but I could see the shape of his forehead. I came back every day to see him. I had to talk to him. But he remained comatose. Then, one day I came to see him . . ."

"And they were harvesting his organs."

"And I saw you charging in making a fuss."

"You were there?"

"Yes. I waited and followed you."

"You followed me?"

"Yes."

"You were waiting for me at the Getty, weren't you?" The anger is there again, the sense of violation, of pure hatred. Curiosity swallows my rage in one bite and urges me farther.

"Yes. I could tell you had the scent. Like a bloodhound. Sometimes the smartest thing for an investigative journalist to do is follow someone else's trail."

"Have me do the work for you."

"Following you was work enough." He laughs uncomfortably.

"So you helped get me down to Mexico to find out what you couldn't find out."

"I was at an impasse. New York pulled me off the story. If I went down there, I'd have to pay my own expenses."

"And professional journalists never do that."

"No, they don't." His voice is defensive. He knows I'm questioning his integrity. He also knows my next question is the one he's been dreading, the question that has to be asked, the question that every woman has asked of every man she's been in love with. Even before I speak, I know my voice will come out high and soft like a child's. "Why did you think you had to lie to me?"

He looks at me silently. It's a question no man answers successfully. He pulls me to his chest and holds me tight, partly so I can't look at him, partly so I can sense his vulnerability and the answer he's unable to articulate, partly so I can feel his love.

Do I point out to him that he put his story before us, the very real feelings we had for each other? That he's no better than the doctors who put the science of medicine before the spiritual needs of their patients? Do I want to hear him say he made no promises? Do I whine of betrayal like a girl stood up at her high school prom?

I cannot be angry. Something beyond mortal hurt tugs at me, something vast and unnameable. His nervous sweat smells of honeysuckle and deodorant, his chamois shirt of detergent, and beneath that, the smell of his skin. I feel his mass, his gravity, the pull of his soul. I long to slide my tongue over every part of his body, to consume him. His arms around me fill me with a passion that enters my raw wounds and plunges through me beyond love, beyond death.

I cannot be angry. Nor can I trust.

I kiss him deeply, knowing it may be the last time. I let myself tumble completely, down into the pyramid, down into the waters of Xibalbá, down into the mouth of the Cauac monster.

Then I pull myself back and look into his eyes. "There is someone we must find."

We locate the house in East Los Angeles on the hills of Boyle Heights, a craftsman mansion from the 1920s, now ramshackle, divided into the single bedrooms of a flophouse. The children playing out front tell us he is in the backyard working in his garden.

We find him hoeing around stalks of corn and tomato plants.

He stands about five feet tall. He wears a baseball cap,

but his sloped forehead is clearly visible. He wears baggy jeans that are too long and bunch up around his ankles, a cheap T-shirt, and over that a flannel shirt with specks of white paint. His nose is long and slightly flared at the end, his lips full, his eyes almond shaped, and when I mentally strip him of his clothes, he looks as if he could've stepped out of a seventh-century Mayan stela. His name is José Petén.

He speaks little Spanish and only a few words of English.

Another man, a powerful, stocky Mexican, works beside him. He is oddly protective of him. His name is Ignacio, and he is from Oaxaca. He knows a smattering of several Mayan dialects; some ancient Nahuatl, the language of the Aztecs; Spanish; and English. He acts as José's translator. It's hard for me to follow, but he seems to use Spanish sentence structure, English for the simple words José has learned, then Nahuatl and Mayan for the rest of his vocabulary.

Ignacio tells us that he has lived with José since he came to Los Angeles and that Fernandez Gomez brought him there.

"When he first came, I didn't understand him at all. He knew only Purepecha. But he learned some Spanish, some English, and we manage to talk. I'm a painter, so I've been taking him on jobs. He makes a good living now."

"Ask him when he first came to Los Angeles."

"I can tell you that," says Ignacio. "He uses the long count calendar still. He doesn't get our months and years. He came seven months ago, in June of last year."

"Ask him about Silvanus."

The two men huddle like a coach and his best player,

as if in talking closely they'll understand each other more clearly. Then Ignacio stands up straight and faces us. "He says a car comes to get him once a month and takes him down the back of a snake . . . he means the freeway . . . to a long white building on a hill. He says they perform a blood sacrifice, then bring him home."

Jack looks at me. "He must mean they take his blood."

"Ask him if they use a needle."

Ignacio pantomimes and tries out words for "needle" in three different languages. "He says yes. He also says that sometimes they use the needle in his head."

"Sounds like a biopsy for brain tissue," says Jack.

"Probably taking a sample to test for the Creutzfeldt-Jakob virus," I guess. "Ask him when the last time was."

"He says it was one moon ago."

"Does he know the names of any of the men?"

"He says a Mexican picks him up. And the doctor who talks to him is Bryant Hillary."

"Ask him how he feels."

The question seems to confuse him. "He says without his people, he is dead without being dead. He feels dizzy a lot, off balance, like the air he breathes is not air but water."

"Ask him if he knew a boy named Tomás, son of Florencia."

José catches the names without translation, his eyes lighting up, followed quickly by an impenetrable flatness. He speaks slowly; Ignacio translates. "He says his village sent Tomás here to go to school, but he never saw him here."

"Has he seen any of the other men from his tribe?"

"He says they have come to him in his dreams, and that they have journeyed beyond the Thirteenth Sky."

"Ask him if he wants to go home."

The Tarascan understands that question and shouts, "No!"

"Why not?"

He yanks Ignacio's elbow, his face filled with horror, talking and gesticulating wildly. Ignacio nods his head a lot, begins to translate, then is yanked back for more gestures. "He says that if he goes home, his people will die."

"Would he be willing to make a statement to the police? Tell him if he talks to the police, his people will be safe. No more will die."

They talk. He finally nods.

Jack gives me his cell phone and I call Ortiz, who says he is booked up today but will take José's statement tomorrow if I bring him by. We agree through Ignacio that I'll pick him up tomorrow when the sun is three fingers above the mountains—around eight o'clock.

"Tell him I will take him back to his people. That he will be safe. His people will be safe. I promise."

After Ignacio translates, I see an expression of such longing on José's face that it nearly breaks my heart. He nods his assent, and I am flooded with gratitude.

Perhaps I can save someone.

"After this is over? Then what?"

I know what Jack is asking. Will he and I still be lovers? Will we even be friends?

We lie naked in a borrowed bed in a borrowed house on borrowed time. My thigh is draped over his, my cheek pressed against his chest, my fingers tracing the muscles of his shoulders and neck. I am overwhelmed with an intense longing, an excruciating pain deep inside me, a despair as sharp as the point of a spear. I want to fold myself into him, to dissolve completely into his body, to dissipate into him like vapor.

Yet I know it will never be. I am certain he will never share this feeling I have. Perhaps it's because he lied to me or because I know his desire to love will always be second to his desire to know, believing there is a difference.

Then I feel a snap in my chest, like a wishbone cracked in two. The pain is gone. I realize this is what it's like to have a broken heart, not screaming tantrums and nights of tears, but a sudden relief to numbness.

"Have you ever read the future, Jack?" I ask.

"I don't believe in that kind of thing," he says.

"Sure you do. Haven't you ever said to yourself, 'I knew that was going to happen'?"

"Of course. But that's just good instincts, experience, understanding how things follow one another, not fortune-telling."

"Knowing the truth about something?"

"I guess you could call it that."

"It's exactly the same as fortune-telling." I run my palm down his forehead, over the ridge of bone above his eyes, his lashes, his long, narrow nose, his mouth and chin. "Close your eyes," I say. "Picture yourself in five years, where you get up in the morning, how you spend your day, where you eat lunch. Tell me what your life is like."

After a moment, he answers. "I still write for *The New York Times*, I teach some classes at the University of Denver, I have my own apartment"—he laughs self-consciously—"I win a Pulitzer Prize for a piece I do on Mexico."

"Picture your apartment, where you eat breakfast, the teakettle whistling on the stove."

"There are books all over the place. It's kind of a mess. I'm reading the *International Herald Tribune* and drinking coffee."

"Am I there?"

He's quiet for a moment, then his eyes pop open with a look of alarm. He doesn't answer my question but looks at me blankly. He understands.

He holds me so tight, it hurts. A red passion spreads over him from his toes to the tip of his tongue. He makes love to me urgently, as if his desire alone could change the future, could bring back something that has been lost.

But of course it can't.

Napping, half-awake, half-asleep: Images and conversations spin around in my mind. I think back over the discussion I had with Clyde Faust, the same words over and over again like a broken record; I see his house, his stela, his face rubbery with indignation, his rude and ferocious maid.

I bolt awake. I remember now why her face seemed familiar. I see myself approaching Erlinda at San Clement's, swimming up the church aisle. The woman beside her with a baby. She is Faust's maid.

I call Ortiz, throw on my clothes, and dash out of the house.

CHAPTER

36

I kneel in his garden before the stela of Lady Xoc drawing thorns through her tongue, offering her blood to the war gods, asking them for guidance, for the safe return of her husband.

When I see him, I rise and take a seat on an iron garden bench beneath a pink-blossoming magnolia tree.

"What are you doing here?" Clyde Faust asks. He doesn't seem surprised to find me, only curious.

"I want to talk to you."

"Oh, what about?"

I take a deep breath; the evening air is rich with jasmine. "I want to talk about a little Tarascan boy who lives high up in the mountains in a village that has no name. He spends his days playing with the hairless dogs, helping his mother dig potato roots, gathering corn, fleecing sheep. He's a curious, sensitive boy who likes to whittle wood and hang out with the mask maker in the village.

"Isolated for centuries, the villagers practice many of the ancient customs. They wrap the heads of their babies, a mark of nobility. They perform blood sacrifice and the occasional human sacrifice. Like the aristocracy of the ancient city of Teotihuacán from which they fled, their lives are a continuous spiritual ritual to their gods. Like Tibet, their home is austere, a place of active volcanoes and mysterious underground rivers. They live an intensely spiritual life, a reality more real to them than their lives of shepherding and weaving.

"One day a group of doctors visits the boy's village. Being outsiders, they think they need to yank the rotten teeth from the villagers' mouths, kill the parasites in their stomachs, remove their tumors, and vaccinate them against viruses that, if left alone, they would never encounter. Soon the villagers think they need these doctors. They invite them to come back, which the doctors do, once a year.

"During routine blood tests, the doctors discover that these Indians have a unique immune system, which doesn't aggressively attack foreign antigens. At first the doctors are frightened that the vaccines they gave the Indians will make them sick. Then they become curious. They want to study these Indians, bleed them, probe them, introduce their bodies to foreign antigens. But they need them in a controlled environment.

"The Tarascans have several years of drought. They are desperate, close to starving. One doctor invites a few of the men to America, where he says he will help them get jobs and a place to live. They can make money and send it home so the villagers can buy food.

"A few brave Tarascan men volunteer to go north, to

the land beyond the edge of the world, to the land of the white men.

"The doctors are thrilled by what they discover. They contact a biomedical research company, which hires the top immunologist in the world. With a grant from the University of Mexico, and with the promise of unlimited resources, they lure him to study the Indians' immune system. What the famous immunologist finds is fascinating: a connection between the kuru virus, a virus that attacks the body without causing an antigen response, and the Indians' immune system. While his team of researchers tries to pinpoint the genes responsible for this, the biomedical research company in Los Angeles conducts its own research on the visiting Tarascans.

"The elder Tarascans are very wise. They know their culture must soon interface with the world. They cling fast to their culture, their language, their ceremonies, but not as quaint customs or curiosities of ancient history. No, they believe their ceremonies cause the sun to rise and set, the clouds to rain, the corn to grow. They believe with the end of their culture will come the end of the world. To save their culture . . . the world itself . . . they need an ambassador from their village, someone who speaks Purepecha, Spanish, and English, someone who knows what the outsiders call 'the law,' someone who can ask for help from the rich outsiders.

"So the villagers choose the curious young boy they call Tomás and send him north with a friend of the doctors, a smuggler by the name of Fernandez Gomez, a Tarascan from Michoacán. Apart from smuggling illegal immigrants and occasional drugs, this smuggler makes his living trafficking Mayan and Aztec artifacts. He takes a liking to Tomás and calls him his son. The boy lives with him. He learns English and goes to school. He visits the nice doctor once a month. They take a fun ride into the hills of Simi Valley to a beautiful white building filled with other nice doctors who give him candy and toys. The nice doctors take his blood and give him shots, but he doesn't mind too much. He remembers his mother making blood sacrifices, and he knows he is doing his part to make the sun rise and set, the clouds to rain, and the corn to grow.

"He is a brave boy, a smart boy, but he gets lonely. He carries with him a jade amulet of the jaguar god, an amulet his mother gave him. The amulet reminds him of his love for his people, of his responsibility to his gods.

"Then, one of the Tarascan men gets drunk and has a traffic accident. He's taken to the hospital and pronounced brain-dead. He's a man in his late twenties, healthy and strong. A possible organ donor. The doctors are excited. They want to see if his organs can be transplanted without antigen rejection. They get permission from the county medical commissioner to harvest his organs.

"They take his organs, his bones, cartilage, joints, nearly his entire body. They discover things they never expected. They send results down to their colleague in Mexico. They think they are discovering the key to the elusive and complicated world of immunology. They think they may have the key to curing AIDS, mad cow disease, Alzheimer's, the key to curing the incurable. At night, they work on their acceptance speeches for the Nobel Prize in Medicine.

"With such excitement on the part of the doctors, such

greed on the part of the biomedical company, such hubris on both their parts, they begin to make mistakes, overstep their boundaries. They begin to break laws, not simply immigration laws, but the big laws, God's laws."

Faust, who has listened pensively as if to a patient's long list of maladies, suddenly guffaws. "You have a flair for the dramatic, Miss Oliver." His mocking feels weak, like a left-handed punch from someone who's never had to use his fists. Sweat drips down the side of his neck. I know I'm getting to him.

"One of the Tarascan men tries to commit suicide," I continue. "The hospital staff manages to save his life, but he is seriously brain-damaged and he cannot breathe without a respirator. Again, the doctors get permission from the county medical commissioner to harvest his organs. Their excitement compounds. For the second time, their transplant patients survive without harmful immunosuppressant drugs. There are no rejection episodes. Their survival rate is nearly perfect."

"What we did was no crime," says Faust.

"What about the other Tarascan men?"

"We gave them good, comfortable lives. They had accidents."

"Accidents? You cut them off from one another. Men who had lived in an insular community for hundreds of years. They couldn't survive in such isolation. It killed them."

"Are you saying we caused their accidents?"

"Where they live, the mountains are steep and dangerous, their work difficult. But Tarascan men never have accidents."

"I agree they had a hard time understanding machines. The velocity of cars, for example."

"So you made use of their bodies."

"Well . . . yes." Faust nervously plucks petals off a rose. His eyes darken, become haunted.

"But then things begin to go seriously wrong for you. The coyote you use to bring in the Tarascans, the smuggler Fernandez Gomez, starts giving you problems. He sees the money to be made. He wants in."

"You're guessing."

I can tell I'm guessing right. I taste his fear. My own fear makes me talk faster. "You find a way to take care of him. One day when Gomez is smuggling a truck full of Mayan and Aztec artifacts, he is stopped by police in the middle of the desert. He is shot twice in the head. The police report says he was smuggling drugs, that he resisted arrest, that he brandished a weapon. But there were only two pounds of marijuana in the truck, and Gomez never carried a weapon. The gun and drugs were planted. Ironically, the local doctors keep his body alive long enough to be used as an organ donor. Within three months, the two policemen involved in the case retire to Colorado with full pension.

"Now our little boy Tomás needs a guardian. He lives with the sister of one of the doctor's maids, Erlinda, a Guatemalan who lives in Venice. He's a smart boy, a loving boy. He adapts quickly. He makes friends who teach him how to skateboard on Venice Beach, perhaps much like your grandchildren, Dr. Faust. Then one Saturday when he's doing jumps at Windward Circle, he falls and smacks his head on the cement. He remains comatose at the hospital for many days. The doctors see an opportunity. With the genetic studies going so well, they desperately want another Tarascan for harvesting. But the boy's brain stem is alive. They cannot pronounce him brain-dead.

"Yet the doctors underestimate the little boy. Tomás is not ready to die. He may be comatose, but he understands the doctors' intentions. He's afraid to wake from his coma, afraid for his life, afraid for the lives of his people. He is also afraid of disappointing the doctors. The doctors get impatient. So you get Erlinda to pose as his foster mother, then hire a deathmaiden. But the deathmaiden can't help the child pass on because he isn't ready to go. Tomás wants to live."

"You don't understand," says Faust. "There was another child his age who desperately needed a heart. There was a huge probability that even if Tomás did come out of his coma, he would have brain damage. And here was another child with a chance at a full life."

"A child whose successful transplant would be the subject of television talk shows and scientific papers."

"We made a choice."

"Yes, you made a choice. Erlinda gives him a needle prepared by one of the doctors."

"You're reaching again."

"I don't think so. She had some training as a nurse. She injects him at his intravenous feed. The needle is filled with a narcotic that's extremely difficult to detect called alpha-methylfentanyl."

"It wasn't my idea. Bryant Hillary made the drug."

"Of course he did. His undergraduate work was in chemistry. He made LSD in medical school to help pay his tuition."

"I swear, I didn't know about it. I didn't know about the alpha-methylfentanyl until Bryant told me that the coroner's office had found it."

"How did he find out about that?"

"You don't run a business in tissue recovery without having a very close relationship with the coroners' offices in all the major cities. When Matty Webster sent the sample up to UC Davis, one of the forensic toxicologists from the Alameda County Coroner's Office was using the university facilities. He called Bryant."

"Then Bryant got Matty Webster a job offer he couldn't refuse."

"We couldn't have someone questioning the process we've set up for organ recovery."

"Then you had another complication. One of Fernandez Gomez's clients, someone from whom you bought artifacts, tried to blackmail you. His ex-wife worked for Kira Katsumi in Mexico City. She told him about her research, and he put it together. He confronted you and demanded money. So you killed him."

"I didn't kill anyone. Things were spinning out of my control. Bryant was talking up his findings in the industry, raising capital; he started buying up his competitors. He sees this as the biggest change in medicine since penicillin."

"Then I came along."

"We realized we had a problem with you. You were clamping down like a pit bull, and you weren't going to let up."

"So you got the Tamworth Husbandry Association involved, which is known for its persuasive tactics."

"It wasn't me." Faust's white shirt grays as it absorbs

his sweat. He prowls his patio, sweating, itching. "Bryant was working with the trade association to keep anti-xenotransplantation legislation out of Congress. We couldn't make this kind of investment, then have Congress pass legislation banning cross-species transplants. THA saw the potential for their biomedical swine producers. Bryant told them he had a problem with you. The THA doesn't fool around."

"So they killed Afner and set me up for his murder."

"I swear it wasn't my decision. I'm sorry we had to get you involved, but at the time, it seemed like a good way to take care of two problems at once."

"Then you had AMPAC put pressure on the Society of Deathmaidens, threatening to block passage of a Medicare bill that would pay for our services; you got Vernon Keyes and Harry Orwell to rally the conservative coalition against us."

"But you didn't stop. We had to do something."

"The cover-up started in earnest. Bodies began to pile up: Tomás, Elmer Afner, Manuel Guerrero. Then Kira Katsumi . . ."

"We were on the edge of announcing our break-through. Silvanus was making a public offering. We couldn't have any kind of scandal. What happened to Katsumi . . . it didn't have to be that way . . . they took things into their own hands."

"How do you justify his murder, a brilliant colleague, a man you admired and respected?"

"I wasn't responsible for his death. It was all Bryant. You don't understand. We're developing a therapy that will save millions of lives." He draws back his shoulders in self-righteousness: He is a good man, a man who loves his patients, a man who's done his best.

"And make billions of dollars."

"I renounced it. I sold my stock before the public offering."

"There is one death you are responsible for . . . the death of a little boy."

"That was sad, but necessary. A therapeutic misadventure."

"It was murder. A little boy, innocent, bright, full of joy, a boy who played with sheep in the mountains high above the clouds, was murdered because a wealthy couple wanted a new heart for their own child."

"You misrepresent things. They were an ordinary couple."

"A white couple?"

"That's immaterial. You wouldn't want his body to go to waste, would you?"

"Tomás wasn't going to die. Tomás was a little boy who in his own time, reassured and loved, would have awakened to skateboard again on Venice Beach."

"You presume, Miss Oliver. You don't know."

"I do know." I hear the anger shaking my voice, the granite of my soul trembling in an earthquake. "You sacrificed a little boy."

"Jesus Christ! Okay, then. We sacrificed one boy to save millions."

The hot, dry air pulses with his confession. I let it sit there; it settles on the white roses, loosening their petals. In the next breeze, they fall to the ground. My voice is even and dispassionate; my vengeance sated, I feel nothing for him. "And the others?"

Faust's angry red face slowly fades to the color of ash. In the uncomfortable silence, his shoulders slump and remain motionless; I see anguish in his eyes.

"Do you think you're safe?" I ask. "Elmer Afner left an insurance policy."

Faust stumbles, distraught; he reaches out to support himself against the stela of Lady Xoc, his nose nearly touching her upturned ecstatic face.

"In a security box in a West Hollywood branch of Bank of America, Elmer Afner left a list of his clients who knowingly bought stolen art from him. You're on that list. He documented what Fernandez Gomez told him, the smuggling of Tarascans, their untimely deaths. He bribed Erlinda and knew about Tomás's murder. He documented it all."

Faust's shirt is soaked; he wipes his hands on his trousers. "I didn't mean for it to happen like this."

"Why did you do it?"

"We will save lives," Faust whispers pathetically.

"The district attorney is on the case. Bryant Hillary, THA, AMPAC, the stockholders of Silvanus . . . they're not the ones who will take the fall. They will find someone appropriate."

At first Faust's eyes open very wide, mouth squeezed shut, looking at me as if he's seen an avenging angel; then he trembles and sinks to his knees, sobbing.

I pick up my purse and, as the cool wind blows over the magnolia tree, casting pink petals over his head, walk to my Jag.

CHAPTER

37

I unwrap the wire I wore under my blouse and lay it beside the tape on the dining room table; I will return both to Ortiz in the morning.

I lie down, exhausted. Faust's confession gave me no pleasure. I suspect it will do little good. I allow myself only three hours of sleep, not that I imagine those hours will bring me any rest. I set the alarm and pull the quilt over my head.

I fall into a deep, ugly sleep. I dream I am lying naked in a damp cave in absolute darkness. Black straps pin me to a table. Electrodes are attached to my lips, fingers, and genitals.

I struggle to get away, but the straps dig into my skin. Rocks begin to fall from the roof of the cave. The ground shakes violently, and the table jumps beneath me. Stalactites snap from the cave ceiling and crash into the ground around me like missiles. A boulder breaks from the wall and tips over the table. There's a loud crack. A deep fissure breaks in the earth, and suddenly I am falling into a black tunnel miles into the center of the earth.

My clock radio screams in my ears, voices of frightened Spanish-speaking children, sirens, cement crumbling, men yelling, and over these sounds the clipped tones of a reporter from NPR. My heart is racing, and I don't know why. It takes me several minutes to be awake enough to understand what is happening.

An earthquake has hit north of Mexico City. The epicenter is ten miles from San Miguel de Allende.

When I arrive at the appointed time to pick up José in Boyle Heights, Ignacio says José is gone.

"What?" I cry desperately.

Ignacio hops from foot to foot, embarrassed at letting me down. "He told me he had a vision. He said that he had to go make a sacrifice."

"Is he coming back?"

"I don't know. I don't think he meant to disappoint you," Ignacio says apologetically. "He just can't get our sense of time."

"That's not important. Do you know where he is?"

"Not exactly. He could be with some people in the neighborhood who practice Santeria, a religion based around sacrifice."

"Where would I find them?"

"I don't know. They're real secretive. He never would talk to me about it."

"Did you ever meet these people?"

"No."

I hand him a card. "Call me as soon as he shows up. Please."

I leave Boyle Heights completely floored. What spooked José? My talk with Faust may have put him in danger. I'm furious with myself for not recognizing that. How could I be so stupid? I figured he was too valuable to Silvanus to be in any real danger. If José's vision was right, I figured wrong.

As soon as I get to Pepper's, I call Ortiz.

"Santeria? Why in hell do you want to know about Santeria?" Ortiz is shouting into the telephone. I must've caught him on a bad day.

"I'm going through a spiritual phase. I want to explore alternatives to my New England Puritan upbringing."

I hear him shout in Spanish to someone in the station. "This has to do with the Tarascans, doesn't it?"

"I remember something from the *Los Angeles Times* a while back about homicide detectives thinking they had a serial murderer on their hands and it turned out to be animal bones from a Santeria sacrifice."

"Yeah . . . I don't know much about it . . . some kind of Afro-Cuban religion like voodoo or something. The sheriff's department has problems with them in Angeles National Forest. Why don't you call Bob McNally. He's the county sheriff's deputy for Crescenta Valley who's been handling that."

I leave a message for Bob McNally. He calls me back in ten minutes.

McNally sounds like a young man who likes being the expert. "Sure . . . we get calls all the time. Hikers, bikers, families on picnics—they find bones all over the place. You go up to Angeles National Forest on a good day and you'll see dead goats and chickens everywhere. It's fucking unbelievable. Hikers run into a thighbone from a goat and they think there's been a homicide, so they call the police. Can't blame them . . . how would they know? The animal rights folks call us all the time, too, but we tell 'em it's a freedom of religion thing."

"Sacrificing animals is legal?"

"Amazing, isn't it. California law says it's only illegal if the animals belong to someone else or if someone witnesses the animals' killing and reports it. These guys only sacrifice animals raised to be eaten—that's how they get around animal abuse laws."

"Is this a big problem?"

"I don't know if you'd call it a problem. There's a chance of fire from the votive candles they use. And all those dead carcasses . . . that could get to be a health issue. But mostly it freaks out the other people who use the park. It's pretty nasty to go there for a picnic with your kids and see a bunch of dead chickens all over the place."

"Are there a lot of Santeria practitioners?"

"We estimate there's between fifty thousand and eighty thousand people who regularly practice Santeria in Southern California. The religion came from central Africa, but it's gotten real popular among Latinos. It's real hip right now. They don't have churches, so they practice their rituals in botanicas or in the forests. They think the woods are sacred places where their gods live. They call them *orishas*. Anyhow, during their rituals, they sacrifice animals—mostly chickens and goats— then they rip off their clothes and bathe in the mountain streams and bury their clothes—it's like a cleansing ceremony."

I think about the size of the park—sixty-six miles along the ridge of the San Gabriel Mountains. "Do they gather at any specific places?"

"They have a couple of spots they like near caves and streams—they think the caves are sacred—but around the twenty-eight-mile marker is their favorite spot. Near Skull Rock."

"Is that the main spot?"

"Pretty much. They go early on Sunday morning."

Something tells me this is where I will find José Petén.

I drive toward Pasadena, then north up Angeles Crest Highway into the San Gabriel Mountains. As the Jag glides up the tortuous road, a dense fog creeps out of the deep ravines, sweeping over the road, drifting up the rocky cliffs. I climb a landscape of manzanita trees, sage, and jimsonweed to a forest of Jeffrey pine, white alder, and scrub oak.

After a half hour up the side of the mountains, I pull off and hide my car near the twenty-eight-mile marker behind a thicket of oak trees. Low clouds reflect enough light for me to see. The air is heavy with the smell of cliff asters and Oriental mustard. I climb the steep dirt path that zigzags up the jagged cliffs to a small cave called Skull Rock by the locals.

Gravel trickles down the sheer precipice above me and rolls onto the path. A stray coyote scampers away, his blue eyes glowing in the dark.

Within fifty yards my breathing becomes labored, my calves ache, my blouse is wet with sweat. My foot slides into a crack in the dirt eroded by the last rains. My ankle twists, sending lightning bolts up my calf. The pain is oddly reassuring.

Along the path, among the miner's lettuce, lupine, and deer weed, I see a dead chicken. A doll fashioned out of burlap and purple ribbon lies beside it. Farther up, red, black, and white squares of fabric lie scattered on the ground. A cluster of white votive candles, the leg bone of a goat, a grocery bag filled with clothing. On the side of Skull Rock is a crude painting of an *orisha,* almond eyes with a red-and-yellow flaming headdress.

A fog rolls in over the lights of Pasadena, and the dark sky pulses with an eerie gray glow as if a candle were sputtering behind the clouds.

In a clearing, a dozen Mexican men and women sit around a circle of white votive candles. As I approach, they scramble into the forest except for one man with a high sloping forehead. José Petén recognizes the blouse I am wearing, the *huipil* Florencia gave me. His face is inscrutable, his eyes dark as a bottomless cenote. A headless chicken lies at his feet, its white-and-brown feathers smeared in blood; in his hand, a knife drips with blood.

With gestures and broken Spanish, I try to tell him I will take him back to his people, that his people need him, that they need his knowledge of the outside world and his language skills, that he is in terrible danger here. His eyes soften with longing, and I think he believes me.

Suddenly I hear footsteps behind me. José's eyes widen with fear, but he doesn't run. That tells me there's a gun pointed at my back.

I turn and see a short, athletic-looking man bounding up the path dressed in khaki pants, boots, and a red Patagonia jacket. Bryant Hillary is not at all what I expected from his office photo: He is short and muscular, a mop of blond hair, an elfin smile, and twinkling, mischievous eyes; he looks like a five-year-old who's just put a frog in your shoes and can't wait for you to find it. He reminds me of Mickey Rooney, the same jack-in-the-box kind of energy; I half expect him to break into a tap-dance routine.

He is not alone. Two stocky men in black leather jackets walk on either side of him. Both have guns drawn. One of them screws on a silencer. Their intentions are clear.

All three men are grinning from the exertion—not pleasant smiles, to be sure.

Bryant Hillary's charisma emanates from him like the heat from a coal, then pulls you in like a magnet. He sets off a feeling something like desire above my pelvis; I recognize it for what it is—pure hate.

"You've led me right to him, Miss Oliver. You couldn't have done a better job. Congratulations."

Fog engulfs us completely now. Beyond the circle of candles, the trees and rocks are mere shadows.

"Leave him alone," I beg. "Let him return to his mountains. You have what you want. Your IPO, your fame. You have money, power, a beautiful wife and child. What more do you want?"

"You can't stand in the way of medical progress, Miss Oliver. As doctors, we pledge to save lives any way we can."

"Was that in your heart when you killed Tomás? When you instructed Erlinda to inject him with a needle you prepared? When you took Tarascans from the only world they'd ever known and sacrificed them to the god of biotechnology? Did you do it for the money? For the Nobel Prize?"

"No. The Nobel Prize will go to Katsumi's colleagues, who deserve it. I did what I did because it was a challenge. I was uniquely positioned to do something no one else could do. I have to say it was rather fun."

I expect to see relief on Hillary's face when he tells me the truth. Then I realize Hillary never lied. He never had to. He had others lie for him. Lying is for the compromised, not the truly evil. The truly evil feel no remorse. In them, there is a kind of innocence.

He is motivated not by anything so human as greed or ego, but by what he sees as a virtuous desire to know, to help his fellow man. Nothing makes an enemy more formidable than a sincere belief in the rightness of his own actions. Righteousness claims the greatest crimes against humanity: the Crusades, the Inquisition, the Holocaust. If doubt gives most of us sleepless nights, it also saves us from committing such crimes.

He motions to the two other men, who raise their guns. "It occurs to me that the *orishas* are probably getting sick of chicken. If the police ever find your bodies, Santeria worshipers will get the blame." One of the bodyguards yanks my hands behind my back to bind them.

Suddenly José Petén howls, charging at Hillary, slashing at his neck with his knife, cutting clear through; Hillary's head thuds to the ground. Two guns go off simultaneously; José staggers backward, multiple gunshots to his chest, his head slamming against Skull Rock beneath the *orisha*.

Down by the highway, patrol cars screech to a halt: sirens, lights flashing red and yellow, heavy footsteps pounding up the path. Nine officers, led by Ortiz and McNally, charge up the hill to Skull Rock.

Hillary's head rolls down the hill, almost kicked by one of the officers as he runs up. Hillary's bodyguards drop their weapons. They're professionals; in a nanosecond, they calculate their probable prison sentences and the years they might bargain away for cooperation. They stand legs apart, arms away from their sides; polite and docile as two debutantes escorted to the ballroom floor, they offer their wrists to be handcuffed.

I run to José and fold him into my arms; blood gushes out of his chest and back. *No, please no, don't let him die.* I rock him, tears streaming down my face, grieving for his people, for Tomás, for my stupid, hopeless failures, for my godless and misguided culture. His warm blood soaks through my clothes. I hold him gently as his face turns the color of ash, as his visible heart muscles stop, as his body relaxes. I would give anything to save him, but it's not my sacrifice to make.

The fog dissipates; the lights of the Los Angeles basin stretch out before us, a galaxy of stars. The sky opens above us. I take José's hand and we drift above the forest, above the California oak and the cactus, above the twinkling city to First Sky. Clouds drift under our feet, and we walk above the seas stretched out across the world to Second Sky. Darkness engulfs us as we shoot into the void, through the Third and Fourth Skies, the earth a blue button in the distance, the Milky Way at our feet, until we reach the Thirteenth Sky, our souls stretched from one side of the universe to the other.

I let go of his hand and see his spirit ascend beyond the Thirteenth Sky, where Mayan gods are born and reborn.

I kiss his forehead. His blood soaks into the ground and runs down the face of Skull Rock. As he dies in my arms, part of me dies, too, part of the world dies, part of whatever we call God dies, and part of Tomás dies again.

I lay his body beside the headless Hillary.

Suddenly lightning strikes a mountain mahogany. Rain slams against the rocks, drumming frenetically.

Ortiz and McNally stop, mesmerized, five feet behind me. A dozen others wait at the base of the crest.

Jack is there; he takes me by the elbow and tries to lead me away, but my feet are rooted to the earth. At the base of Skull Rock, two bodies lie beside each other like exhausted lovers, their blood flowing like bolts of red silk, mixing with the rain, cascading down the rocky slope into the earth.

The police autopsy report will describe the number of bullet wounds and knife entries, what arteries were cut at what angle, the precise time their hearts stopped, the amount of blood lost, the weights of their brains, hearts, and livers, the contents of their stomachs. But nothing in the autopsy will show what really happened, their descent into the waters of Xibalbá and their release beyond the Thirteenth Sky.

Epilogue

On my west-facing balcony, I sit and look out over Santa Monica Bay. On the cedar deck, I set a shallow dish filled with copal and a shredded photo of the dead Tarascan men. On the back of the photo, I wrote their names and everything I know about them. I place Tomás's jade of the jaguar god on the fragmented images. I prick the tips of my fingers and drip blood onto the scraps of paper. Then I light it. Incense ascends from the flames, dancing like a cobra, the pungent smell penetrating my hair and skin. Ashes float up into the air, carried away by the sea breeze.

I borrow the religion of another culture because I have none of my own. I know no rituals for grieving. I am an impostor, but my sorrow is real. I do this for Florencia. For eight brave Tarascan men.

And for Tomás.

When talk show hosts ask august celebrities if they would change anything in their lives, they always say no. I don't believe them. If I could change my choices, I don't know where I'd begin. I might start by doing the exact opposite of everything I've ever done.

Several months have passed since José Petén died in my arms. That night, my fever came back with a vengeance. Pepper stayed at my house for a week to nurse me, glowering at me every time I tried to get out of bed. As soon as I was well enough, I was down at the station repeating my story.

When confronted by Detective Lieutenant Ortiz with my tape, Clyde Faust confessed his part in the deaths of Tomás and Elmer Afner. There was a flurry of newspaper coverage; then the case was dismissed for lack of evidence. For a time, I had hope of a complete investigation, but now when I call Ortiz, he has less and less to tell me. I guess I'm not surprised things have gone no farther.

I have no illusion that medicine will ever question the ethics of organ transplantation or that indigenous Indian cultures have a chance of surviving in this world. I only hope that the day we all walk around with pig hearts beating in our chests is yet a few years away.

Several weeks ago, Biobreed released a news brief stating they haven't been able to eliminate pig retroviruses that tag along with their cloned pig organs. They also are having problems with long-term organ rejection. Silvanus has been slowed down by accounting scandals. Their initial public offering of $16 a share spiked up to $120 in a week but after a month fell to thirty cents a share.

After the earthquake, Vernon Keyes was caught by the West Hollywood police getting a blow job from a black transvestite in the back of a Lincoln Town Car. The tide has changed once again, our enemies drawn out by the undertow.

I have little doubt that Marion Godlove is strong enough to pull the society together, to rebuild the organization. I heard she is considering Cuba as the site for a new school. I will never know whether or not she betrayed me intentionally. She got her Medicare bill passed. I know the Society of Deathmaidens will survive. As long as people face death with fear, there will be deathmaidens. As long as medicine insists on treating the body rather than the spirit, people will seek us out.

But the society will have to survive without me. I cannot be part of it. I find it too easy to slip into other realities. If I want to live, if I want to do good, I must stay centered in this reality. I dare not daydream or let my mind wander.

It is a struggle to stay here and now. Every day I fight for my sanity. I pinch myself until my thighs are black and blue. I wonder why I try so hard, why I don't let go. When you have lost everything you care about, it's hard to find a reason to go on.

But then I think of Tomás, and it helps.

I tell myself that the future sits before me like a paint-by-numbers canvas, that all I have to do is dab in the colors. With palette in hand, I wait for direction before an empty easel. Meanwhile, I live my life.

I try to stay busy with people around me all the time. I am studying to become a doctor of Chinese herbal medicine. I will heal with herbs and acupuncture, not because I need these props to heal, but because they ground me. On the weekends, I volunteer at animal shelters, giving vaccinations, cleaning cages. I stay far away if any animal needs to be put to sleep.

Pepper has been commissioned by the Getty to produce a gigantic garden sculpture, a Gordian knot of twisted ceramic tubes. It's a huge project, and she enlists me to knead grog into massive piles of red earth, a task I find pleasurable.

Jack went off on an assignment to Australia. I don't expect to hear from him again, although I wouldn't be surprised.

I spend little time at home now. It is a quiet place that seduces me with dreams. When I am here, Cat demands my attention, as if she knows not to let me slip into a contemplative mood. And if I sit for a moment on my balcony to gaze at the lights of Santa Monica, the tangerine sunsets, the dusty blue sunrises, the purple ring of snow-covered mountains in the distance, she scratches my leg. *I am here. Look at me. Feed me. Pet me. Love me.*

She does not let me forget her mortal needs.

AUTHOR'S NOTE

The hospice movement presents a compassionate and holistic alternative to dying in a hospital. Today in the United States there are more than three thousand hospice programs caring for more than half a million people each year.

However, the Society of Deathmaidens and the Institute for Eternal Living are entirely fabrications of the author's imagination.

Those who would like to know more about hospice options may want to contact:

Hospice Foundation of America
2001 S Street NW #300
Washington, DC 20009
Phone: 1-800-854-3402
Web site: www.hospicefoundation.org

The Tarascans are an Indian tribe located in the Michoacán Mountains of Mexico. As far as the author knows, they do not practice animal or human sacrifice.

The author would like to acknowledge the help and support of the following people: Michael Connelly, Sandy Eiges, Sara Ann Freed, John Houghton, Julie Lu, and Philip Spitzer.

ABOUT THE AUTHOR

RUTH FRANCISCO, a graduate of Swarthmore College, studied voice and drama in New York City and then moved to Los Angeles to work in the film industry. She currently lives in Los Angeles. *Confessions of a Deathmaiden* was her first novel.

More
Ruth Francisco!

Please turn this page
for a preview of

GOOD MORNING, DARKNESS

available where
books are sold.

PART ONE

Vigils

I found the first arm. The second one washed up on Malibu Beach, seven miles north of here. The rest of the body must've gotten eaten by sharks.

The newspapers gave credit to a jogger who came by later, and that's okay by me. I'm legal and everything. I was born here. But that doesn't mean I want to talk to cops.

Two or three times a week, I get up at four-thirty and take my beat-up Toyota truck down Washington Boulevard to the beach. I go to fish. They say the fish are too polluted to eat, but it tastes better than what you can buy at the store, and it's free. In the two hours before work, I catch enough bonito, bass, or barracuda to feed my family and my neighbors for a few days. When I snag a halibut, I give some to Consuello Rosa, my landlady, and she lets the rent slide awhile.

Usually I fish off the jetty in Marina del Rey, at the end of the channel, because it's quiet and beautiful. That's the real reason I fish. My younger kids prefer to eat hot dogs, and the fourteen-year-old won't eat nothing her mother cooks, period. So I fish for myself.

The marina fills me with a peace that I used to feel at church before I found out you can't live your life by their rules and survive in this world. I guess you could call the feeling I get joy. Every time I go fish, I'm amazed that a Mexican like me can wake up in a stucco dump in Culver City and after a five-minute drive be walking past the most beautiful million-dollar mansions in the world. They're not hidden behind high walls covered in concertina, like in Mexico. You can see into their living rooms. Not that I'd want that life. I feel lucky. The people who own those mansions have to take care of them. They have to hire maids and gardeners, make mortgage payments, buy insurance, worry about earthquakes and property taxes. I get to enjoy their gardens and their beautiful views and don't have to worry about nothing. Late at night, when I fall to sleep on the sofa so I won't wake the little ones who've crawled in bed with the wife, I close my eyes and I imagine I'm looking out a picture window at the marina, the moonlight reflecting on the sailboats and the rippling water. I fall asleep with a smile on my face.

On the morning I found the arm, I'd decided to go fishing on Venice Pier for a change. That's about a mile north of the marina. I woke around four on the sofa with a toy truck in the middle of my back. When I got down to the beach, it was still dark. The moon was setting over the ocean, cutting a white path to the horizon. I threaded left-over chorizo on my fishing lines for bait. I like to think that it's like home cooking for the fish who got spawned down in Baja. I don't want them to forget where they come from. I threw in three lines, then unscrewed my thermos and poured myself some coffee. I was leaning on my elbows, not thinking about much, watching the black night fade to gray and the low mist pulling back from the shore like a puddle drying up on hot asphalt.

Then I saw the arm.

It lay on the sand about twenty feet from the water, where the beach is hard and smooth. The tide must've brought it in and left it.

At first I thought it was a piece of rain gutter like I bought from Home Depot the other day for a job. Then I saw it was an arm. I climbed down from the pier to take a closer look, hoping it was from a mannequin but knowing deep inside it wasn't. I didn't have to get close to know it was too bloated to be plastic. It was a left arm. It didn't smell like the seals I've found on the beach or the whale from a few years back. That you could smell for a mile. But then the morning was still cool. I could tell it was a woman's arm, white with fine hair. The fingernails had chipped pearl and clear nail polish, which, 'cause I have a fourteen-year-old daughter, I knew was called a French manicure. There was a pretty ring on her third finger.

I probably would've taken the ring if her fingers hadn't been so swollen. I looked to make sure no one else was around, then squatted by the arm. There was a small scar on her elbow and bites on the inside of her triceps, where fish had nibbled. I touched the skin; it didn't bounce back. It felt like a mushroom—fragile and a little slippery. I wasn't repulsed, but maybe a little sad, like when you stop to move roadkill to the side of the highway and realize it's an animal you don't see much anymore, like a silver fox or a bobcat.

As I stood up, the waves pushed a white rose onto the beach. Most of its petals were gone, and it had a long stem, like the expensive kind people buy to throw off their sailboats along with someone's ashes.

The sun was beginning to come up, and it was going to be one of those hot spring mornings that acts like summer's in a hurry. I knew someone else would come by, so I went back to my fishing poles and kept an eye on the arm. In a half hour a jogger found it, a white man in his forties running on the beach. He was working at it like his lower back hurt, and I bet he was glad when he saw the arm and had an excuse to stop. He touched the arm with the toe of his sneaker like he thought it might still be alive. That made me laugh. He reached into his pocket and whipped out a cell phone.

From then on, it was his arm.

A lady with a couple of dogs walked toward him, and he yelled at her to put them on a leash. She looked pissed until she saw what he was fussing about. By the time the cops showed up, there was a ring of people and dogs around the arm. For some reason, the dog people weren't afraid of getting tickets for having their dogs on the beach. Maybe they were too excited to care. They all stood there, dogs barking away, until the police told everyone to go home.

Plainclothes detectives and the coroner showed up twenty minutes later. They spent an hour poking at it, taking its temperature, snapping photos. I even saw one of the detectives bend down and sniff it. Finally, they put the arm in a blue plastic bag and drove off with it.

It wasn't until that evening, after I told the kids and the wife about it, and the neighbors on both sides, and my cousin Paco who dropped by just in time for dinner, after the house finally got quiet and I was drinking a glass of tequila behind the garage on the brick patio I'll finish one of these days, that I thought about the woman the arm belonged to, of what she must've looked like.

That was when I realized I knew who she was.